He's standing with his back to me near my locker. A surge of electricity zings through me as I recognize him. In a flash I'm in the vision, seeing him both in the black fleece jacket among the trees and for real, just down the hall simultaneously.

I take a step toward him, my mouth opening to call his name. Then I remember that I don't know it. Like always, it's as if he hears me anyway and starts to turn, and my heart skips a beat when I don't wake up but see his face now, his mouth curling up in a half smile as he jokes with the guy next to him.

He glances up and his eyes meet mine.

I have to save him, I think.

That's when I faint.

UNEARTHLY

CYNTHIA HAND

HARPER TEEN
An Imprint of HarperCollinsPublishers

HarperTeen is an imprint of HarperCollins Publishers.

Unearthly
Copyright © 2011 by Cynthia Hand

Library of Congress Cataloging-in-Publication Data
Unearthly / Cynthia Hand. — 1st ed.
  p. cm.
Summary: Sixteen-year-old Clara Gardner's purpose as an angel-blood
begins to manifest itself, forcing her family to pull up stakes and move
to Jackson, Wyoming, where she learns that danger and heartbreak
come with her powers.
ISBN 978-0-06-199617-7
[1. Angels—Fiction. 2. Supernatural—Fiction. 3. High schools—
Fiction. 4. Schools—Fiction. 5. Moving, Household—Fiction. 6. Family
life—Wyoming—Fiction. 7. Jackson (Wyo.)—Fiction.] I. Title.
PZ7.N35Une 2011   2010017849
[Fic]—dc22   CIP
                                                                AC

Typography by Andrea Vandergrift
11 12 13 14 15 LP/BV 10 9 8 7 6 5 4 3 2

First paperback edition, 2011

For John

The Nephilim were on the earth in those days—
and also afterward—when the angels went
to the daughters of men and had children by them.
They were the heroes of old, men of renown.

—Genesis 6:4

PROLOGUE

In the beginning, there's a boy standing in the trees. He's around my age, in that space between child and man, maybe all of seventeen years old. I'm not sure how I know this. I can only see the back of his head, his dark hair curling damply against his neck. I feel the dry heat of the sun, so intense, drawing the life from everything. There's a strange orange light filling the eastern sky. There's the heavy smell of smoke. For a moment I'm filled with such a smothering grief that it's hard to breathe. I don't know why. I take a step toward the boy, open my mouth to call his name, only I don't know it. The ground crunches under my feet. He hears me. He starts to turn. One more second and I will see his face.

That's when the vision leaves me. I blink, and it's gone.

1

ON PURPOSE

The first time, November 6 to be exact, I wake up at two
a.m. with a tingling in my head like tiny fireflies dancing
behind my eyes. I smell smoke. I get up and wander from
room to room to make sure no part of the house is on fire.
Everything's fine, everybody sleeping, tranquil. It's more
of a campfire smoke, anyway, sharp and woodsy. I chalk it
up to the usual weirdness that is my life. I try, but can't get
back to sleep. So I go downstairs. And I'm drinking a glass
of water at the kitchen sink, when, with no other warning, I'm in the middle of the burning forest. It's not like a
dream. It's like I'm *physically* there. I don't stay long, maybe
all of thirty seconds, and then I'm back in the kitchen,

standing in a puddle of water because the glass has fallen from my hand.

Right away I run to wake Mom. I sit at the foot of her bed and try not to hyperventilate as I go over every detail of the vision I can remember. It's so little, really, just the fire, the boy.

"Too much at once would be overwhelming," she says. "That's why it will come to you this way, in pieces."

"Is that how it was when you received your purpose?"

"That's how it is for most of us," she says, neatly dodging my question.

She won't tell me about her purpose. It's one of those off-limits topics. This bugs me because we're close, we've always been close, but there's this big part of her that she refuses to share.

"Tell me about the trees in your vision," she says. "What did they look like?"

"Pine, I think. Needles, not leaves."

She nods thoughtfully, like this is an important clue. But me, I'm not thinking about the trees. I'm thinking about the boy.

"I wish I could have seen his face."

"You will."

"I wonder if I'm supposed to protect him."

I like the idea of being his rescuer. All angel-bloods have purposes of different types—some are messengers, some witnesses, some meant to comfort, some just doing things that cause other things to happen—but *guardian* has a nice ring to it. It feels particularly angelic.

"I can't believe you're old enough to have your purpose," Mom says with a sigh. "Makes me feel old."

"You *are* old."

She can't argue with that, being that she's over a hundred and all, even though she doesn't look a day over forty. I, on the other hand, feel exactly like what I am: a clueless (if not exactly ordinary) sixteen-year-old who still has school in the morning. At the moment I don't feel like there's any angel blood in me. I look at my beautiful, vibrant mother, and I know that whatever her purpose was, she must have faced it with courage and humor and skill.

"Do you think . . . ," I say after a minute, and it's tough to get the question out because I don't want her to think I'm a total coward. "Do you think it's possible for me to be killed by fire?"

"Clara."

"Seriously."

"Why would you say that?"

"It's just that when I was standing there behind him, I felt so sad. I don't know why."

Mom's arms come around me, pull me close so I can hear the strong, steady beating of her heart.

"Maybe the reason I'm so sad is that I'm going to die," I whisper.

Her arms tighten.

"It's rare," she says quietly.

"But it does happen."

"We'll figure it out together." She hugs me closer and smoothes the hair away from my face the way she used to when I had nightmares as a kid. "Right now you should rest."

I've never felt more awake in my life, but I stretch out on her bed and let her pull the covers over us. She puts her arm around me. She's warm, radiating heat like she's been standing in sunshine, even in the middle of the night. I inhale her smell: rosewater and vanilla, an old lady's perfume. It always makes me feel safe.

When I close my eyes, I can still see the boy. Standing there waiting. For me. Which seems more important than the sadness or the possibility of dying some gruesome fiery death. He's waiting for me.

I wake to the sound of rain and a soft gray light seeping through the blinds. I find Mom standing at the kitchen stove scraping scrambled eggs into a serving bowl, already dressed and ready for work like any other day, her long, auburn hair still wet from the shower. She's humming to herself. She seems happy.

"Morning," I announce.

She turns, puts down the spatula, and crosses the linoleum to give me a quick hug. Her smile is proud, like that time I won the district spelling bee in third grade: proud, but like she never expected anything less.

"How are you doing this morning? Hanging in there?"

"Yeah, I'm fine."

"What's going on?" my brother, Jeffrey, says from the doorway.

We turn to look at him. He's leaning against the doorjamb, still rumpled with sleep and smelly and grumpy as usual. He's never been what you might call a morning person. He stares at us. A flicker of fear crosses his face, like he's bracing for horrible news, like someone we know has died.

"Your sister has received her purpose." Mom smiles again, but it's less jubilant than before. A cautious smile.

He looks me up and down like he'll be able to find evidence of the divine somewhere on my body. "You had a vision?"

"Yeah. About a forest fire." I shut my eyes and see it all again: the hillside crowded with pine trees, the orange sky, the smoke rolling past. "And a boy."

"How do you know it wasn't just a dream?"

"Because I wasn't asleep."

"So what does it mean?" he asks. All this angel-related information is new to him. He's still in that time when the supernatural stuff can be exciting and cool. I envy him that.

"I don't know," I tell him. "That's what I've got to find out."

I have the vision again two days later. I'm in the middle of jogging laps around the outside edge of the Mountain View High School gymnasium, and suddenly it hits me, just like that. The world as I know it—California, Mountain View, the gym—promptly vanishes. I'm in the forest. I can actually *taste* the fire. This time I see the flames cresting the ridge.

And then I almost crash into a cheerleader.

"Watch it, dorkina!" she says.

I stagger to one side to let her pass. Breathing hard, I lean against the folded-up bleachers and try to get the vision back. But it's like trying to return to a dream after you're fully awake. It's gone.

Crap. No one's ever called me a dorkina before. Derivative of dork. Not good.

"No stopping," calls Mrs. Schwartz, the PE teacher. "We want to get an accurate record of how fast you can run a mile. That means you, Clara."

She must have been a drill sergeant in another life.

"If you don't make it in less than ten minutes you'll have to run it again next week," she hollers.

I start running. I try to focus on the task at hand as I swoop around the next corner, keeping my pace quick to make up some of the time I've lost. But my mind wanders back to the vision. The shapes of the trees. The forest floor under my feet strewn with rocks and pine needles. The boy standing there with his back to me as he watches the fire approach. My suddenly so-very-rapidly-beating heart.

"Last lap, Clara," says Mrs. Schwartz.

I speed up.

Why is he there? I wonder, not closing my eyes but still

seeing his image like it's burned onto my retinas. Will he be surprised to see me? My mind races with questions, but underneath them all there is only one:

Who is he?

At that point I blow past Mrs. Schwartz, sprinting hard.

"Good, Clara!" she calls. And then, a minute later, "That can't be right."

Slowing to a walk, I circle back to find out my time.

"Did I get it under ten minutes?"

"I clocked you at five forty-eight." She sounds truly shocked. She looks at me like she's having visions too, of me on the track team.

Whoops. I wasn't paying attention, wasn't holding back. I'm going to catch some major flack if Mom finds out.

I shrug.

"The watch must have been messed up," I explain, trying for laid-back, hoping she'll buy it even though it means I'll have to run the stupid thing again next week.

"Yes," she says, nodding distractedly. "I must have started it wrong."

That night when Mom gets home she finds me slouched on the couch watching reruns of *I Love Lucy*.

"That bad, huh?"

"It's my fallback when I can't find *Touched by an Angel*," I reply sarcastically.

She pulls a pint of Ben and Jerry's Chubby Hubby out of a

paper sack. Like she read my mind.

"You're a goddess," I say.

"Not quite."

She holds up a book: *Trees of North America, A Guide to Field Identification*.

"Maybe my tree's not in North America."

"Let's just start with this."

We take the book to the kitchen table and bend over it together, searching for the exact type of pine tree from my vision. To someone on the outside we'd look like nothing more than a mother helping her daughter with her homework, not a pair of part-angels researching a mission from heaven.

"That's it," I say at last, pointing to a picture in the book and then rocking back in my chair, feeling pretty pleased with myself. "The lodgepole pine."

"Twisted yellowish needles found in pairs," Mom reads from the book. "Brown, egg-shaped cone?"

"I didn't get a close look at the pinecones, Mom. It's just the right shape, with the branches starting partway up the trunk like that, and it feels right," I answer around a spoonful of ice cream.

"Okay." She consults the book again. "It looks like the lodgepole pine is found exclusively in the Rocky Mountains and the northwestern coast of the U.S. and Canada. The Native Americans liked to use the trunks for the main supports in their wigwams. Hence the name *lodgepole*. And," she continues, "it says here that the cones require extreme heat—like, say, from a forest fire—to open and release their seeds."

"This is *so* educational," I quip. Still, the idea of a tree that only grows in burned places sends a quiver of excitement through me. Even the tree has a kind of predestined meaning.

"Good. So we know roughly where this will happen," says Mom. "Now all we have to do is narrow it down."

"And then what?" I examine the picture of the pine tree, suddenly imagining the branches in flames.

"Then we'll move."

"Move? As in leave California?"

"Yes," she says. Apparently she's serious.

"But—" I sputter. "What about school? What about my friends? What about your job?"

"You'll go to a new school, I imagine, and make new friends. I'll get a new job, or find a way to do my job from home."

"What about Jeffrey?"

She gives a little laugh and pats my hand like it's a silly question. "Jeffrey will come, too."

"Oh yeah, he'll love that," I say, thinking about Jeffrey with his army of friends and his never-ending parade of baseball games, wrestling matches, football practices, and everything else. We have lives, Jeffrey and I. For the first time it occurs to me that I'm in for so much more than I've anticipated. My purpose is going to change everything.

Mom closes the book about trees and meets my eyes solemnly across the kitchen table.

"This is the big stuff, Clara," she says. "This vision, this purpose—it's why you're here."

"I know. I just didn't think we'd have to move."

I look out the window into the yard I've grown up playing in, my old swing set that Mom has never gotten around to taking down, the row of rosebushes against the back fence that have been there for as long as I can remember. Behind the fence I can barely make out the hazy outline of the distant mountains that have always been the edges of my world. I can hear the Caltrain rumble as it crosses Shoreline Boulevard, and, if I concentrate hard enough, the faint music from Great America two miles away. It seems impossible that we would ever leave this place.

A corner of Mom's mouth quirks up into a sympathetic smile.

"You thought you could just fly in somewhere for the weekend, complete your purpose, and fly back?"

"Yeah, maybe." I glance away sheepishly. "When are you going to tell Jeffrey?"

"I think that should wait until we know where we're going."

"Can I be there when you tell him? I'll bring popcorn."

"Jeffrey's turn will come," she says, a muted sadness coming up in her eyes, that look she gets when she thinks we're growing up too fast. "When he receives his purpose you'll have to deal with that too."

"And then we'll move again?"

"We'll go where his purpose leads us."

"That's crazy," I say, shaking my head. "This all seems crazy. You know that, right?"

"Mysterious ways, Clara." She grabs my spoon and digs a big chunk of Chubby Hubby out of the carton. She grins, shifting back into mischievous, playful Mom right before my eyes. "Mysterious ways."

Over the next couple weeks the vision repeats every two or three days. I'll be minding my own business and then bang—I'm in a service announcement for Smokey the Bear. I come to expect it at odd times, on the ride to school, in the shower, eating lunch. Other times I get the sensation without the vision itself. I feel the heat. I smell smoke.

My friends notice. They stick me with an unfortunate new nickname: Cadet, as in Space Cadet. I guess it could be worse. And my teachers notice. But I get the work done, so they don't give me too much grief when I spend the class period scribbling away in my journal on what can't possibly be class notes.

If you looked at my journal a few years ago, that fuzzy pink diary I had when I was twelve with Hello Kitty on the cover, locked with a flimsy gold key I kept on a chain around my neck to keep it safe from Jeffrey's prying eyes, you'd see the ramblings of a perfectly normal girl. There are doodles of flowers and princesses, entries about school and the weather, movies I liked, music I danced around to, my dreams of playing the Sugar Plum Fairy in *The Nutcracker*, or how Jeremy Morris sent one of his friends to ask me to be his girlfriend and of course I said no because why would I want to go out with someone too cowardly to ask me out himself?

Then comes the angel diary, which I started when I was fourteen. This one's a midnight blue spiral-bound notebook with a picture of an angel on it, a serene, feminine angel who looks eerily like Mom, with red hair and golden wings, standing on the sliver of the crescent moon surrounded by stars, beams of light radiating from her head. In it I jotted down everything Mom ever told me about angels and angel-bloods, every fact or piece of speculation I could coax out of her. I also recorded my experiments, like the time I cut my forearm with a knife just to see if I would bleed (which I did, *a lot*) and carefully noted how long it took to heal (about twenty-four hours, from when I made the cut to when the little pink line completely disappeared), the time I spoke Swahili to a man in the San Francisco airport (imagine the surprise for both of us), or how I could do twenty-five *grands jetés* back and forth across the floor of the ballet studio without getting winded. That was when my mom started seriously lecturing me about keeping it cool, at least in public. That's when I started to find myself, not just Clara the girl, but Clara the angel-blood, Clara the supernatural.

Now my journal (simple, black, moleskin) focuses entirely on my purpose: sketches, notes, and the details of the vision, especially when they involve the mysterious boy. He constantly lingers at the edges of my mind—except for those disorienting moments when he moves blindingly to center stage.

I grow to know him through his shape in my mind's eye. I know the sweep of his broad shoulders, his carefully disheveled hair, which is a dark, warm brown, long enough to cover his ears and brush against his collar in the back. He keeps his hands tucked into the pockets of his black jacket, which is kind of fuzzy, I notice, maybe fleece. His weight is always shifted slightly to one side, as if he's getting ready to walk away. He looks lean, but strong. When he begins to turn I can see the faintest outline of his cheek, and it never fails to make my heart beat faster and my breath hitch in my throat.

What will he think of me? I wonder.

I want to be awe-inspiring. When I appear to him in the forest, when he finally turns and sees me standing there, I want to at least *look* the part of an angel. I want to be all glowy and floaty like my mom. I'm not bad looking, I know. Angel-bloods are a fairly attractive bunch. I have good skin and my lips are naturally rosy so I never wear anything but gloss. I have very nice knees, or so I'm told. But I'm too tall and too skinny, and not in the willowy supermodel sort of way but in a storklike, all-arms-and-legs sort of way. And my eyes, which come across as storm-cloud gray in some lights and gunmetal blue in others, seem a bit too big for my face.

My hair is my best feature, long and wavy, bright gold with a hint of red, trailing behind me wherever I go like an afterthought. The problem with my hair is that it's also completely unruly. It tangles. It catches in things: zippers, car doors, food. Tying it back or braiding it never works. It's like a living thing trying to break free. Within moments of wrestling it down, there are strands in my face, and within the span of an hour it usually slides out of its confines completely. It takes the word *unmanageable* to a whole new level.

So with my luck, I'll never make it in time to save the boy in the forest because my hair will have snagged on a tree branch a mile back.

"Clara, your phone's ringing!" Mom hollers from the kitchen. I jump, startled. My journal lays open on my desk in front of me. On the page is a careful sketch of the back of the boy's head, his neck, his tousled hair, the hint of cheek and eyelashes. I don't remember drawing it.

"Okay!" I yell back. I close the journal and slide it under my algebra textbook. Then I run downstairs. It smells like a bakery. Tomorrow's Thanksgiving, and Mom's been making pies. She's wearing her fifties housewife apron (which she's had since the fifties, although she wasn't a housewife back then, she assures us) and it's dusted with flour. She holds the phone out to me.

"It's your dad."

I raise an eyebrow at her in a silent question.

"I don't know," she says. She hands me the phone, then turns and discreetly exits the room.

"Hi, Dad," I say into the phone.

"Hi."

There's a pause. Three words into our conversation and he's already out of things to say.

"So what's the occasion?"

For a moment he doesn't say anything. I sigh. For years I used to practice this speech about how mad I was at him for leaving Mom. I was three years old when they split. I don't remember them fighting. All I retained from the time they were together are a few brief flashes. A birthday party. An afternoon at a beach. Him standing at the sink shaving. And then there's the brutal memory of the day he left, me standing with Mom in the driveway, her holding Jeffrey on her hip and crying brokenheartedly as he drove away. I can't forgive him for that. I can't forgive him for a lot of things. For moving clear across the country to get away from us. For not calling enough. For never knowing what to say when he does call. But most of all I can't get past the way Mom's face pinches up whenever she hears his name.

Mom won't discuss what happened between them any more than she'll dish about her purpose. But here's what I do know: My mother is as close to being the perfect woman as this world is likely to see. She's half *angel*, after all, even though my dad doesn't know that. She's beautiful. She's smart and funny. She is magic. And he gave her up. He gave us all up.

And that, in my book, makes him a fool.

"I just wanted to know if you're okay," he says finally.

"Why wouldn't I be okay?"

He coughs.

"I mean, it's rough being a teenager, right? High school. Boys."

Now this conversation has gone from unusual to downright strange.

"Right," I say. "Yeah, it's rough."

"Your mom says your grades are good."

"You talked to Mom?"

Another silence.

"How's life in the Big Apple?" I ask, to steer the conversation away from myself.

"The usual. Bright lights. Big city. I saw Derek Jeter in Central Park yesterday. It's a terrible life."

He can be charming, too. I always want to be mad at him, to tell him that he shouldn't bother trying to bond with me, but I can never keep it up. The last time I saw him was two years ago, the summer I turned fourteen. I'd been practicing my "I-hate-you" speech big-time in the airport, on the plane, out of the gate, in the terminal. And then I saw him waiting for me by the baggage claim, and I filled up with this bizarre happiness. I launched myself into his arms and told him I'd missed him.

"I was thinking," he says now. "Maybe you and Jeffrey could come to New York for the holidays."

I almost laugh at his timing.

"I'd like to," I say, "but I kind of have something important going on right now."

Like locating a forest fire. Which is my one reason for being on this Earth. Which I will never be able to explain to him in a thousand years.

He doesn't say anything.

"Sorry," I say, and I shock myself by actually meaning it. "I'll let you know if things change."

"Your mom also told me you passed Driver's Ed." He's clearly trying to change the subject.

"Yes, I took the test and parallel parked and everything. I'm sixteen. I'm legal now. Only Mom won't let me take the car."

"Maybe it's time we see about getting you a car of your own."

My mouth drops open. He's just full of surprises.

And then I smell smoke.

17

The fire must be farther away this time. I don't see it. I don't see the boy. A hot gust of gritty wind sends my hair flying out of its ponytail. I cough and turn away from the blast, swiping hair out of my face.

That's when I see the silver truck. I'm standing a few steps away from where it's parked on the edge of a dirt road. AVALANCHE, it says in silver letters on the back. It's a huge truck with a short, covered bed. It's the boy's truck. Somehow I just know.

Look at the license plate, I tell myself. *Focus on that.*

The plate is a pretty one. It's mostly blue: the sky, with clouds. The right side is dominated by a rocky, flat-topped mountain that looks vaguely familiar. On the left is the black silhouette of a cowboy astride a bucking horse, waving his hat in the air. I've seen it before, but I don't automatically know it. I try to read the numbers on the plate. At first all I can make out is the large number stacked on the left side: 22. And then the four digits on the other side of the cowboy: 99CX.

I expect to feel crazy happy then, excited to have such an enormously helpful piece of information handed to me as easily as that. But I'm still in the vision, and the vision is moving on. I turn away from the truck and walk quickly into the trees. Smoke drifts across the forest floor. Somewhere close by I hear a crack, like a branch falling. Then I see the boy, exactly the same as he's always been.

His back turned. The fire suddenly licking the top of the ridge. The danger so obvious, so close.

The crushing sadness descends on me like a curtain dropping. My throat closes. I want to say his name. I step toward him.

"Clara? You okay?"

My dad's voice. I float back to myself. I'm leaning against the refrigerator, staring out the kitchen window where a hummingbird hovers near my mom's feeder, a blur of wings. It darts in, takes a sip, then flits away.

"Clara?"

He sounds alarmed. Still dazed, I lift the phone to my ear.

"Dad, I think I'm going to have to call you back."

2

YONDER IS JACKSON HOLE

On the road to Wyoming, there are lots of signs. Most of them warn of some kind of danger: WATCH FOR DEER. WATCH FOR FALLING ROCK. TRUCKS, CHECK YOUR BRAKES. TUNE IN FOR ROAD CLOSURES. ELK CROSSING NEXT 2 MILES. SNOW SLIDE AREA, NO PARKING OR STOPPING. I drive my car behind Mom's the whole way from California with Jeffrey in the passenger seat, trying not to freak out about how all the signs point to the fact that we're headed someplace wild and dangerous.

At the moment I'm driving through a forest made up entirely of lodgepole pines. Talk about surreal. I can't get over the sight of all the Wyoming license plates on the cars speeding past, many with the fateful number 22 on the left side. That number has brought us a long way, through six short weeks of crazy preparation, selling our house, saying good-bye to the friends and neighbors I've known my entire life, and packing up and moving to a place where none of us knows a single solitary soul: Teton County, Wyoming, which according to Google is county number 22, population just over 20,000. That's roughly five people per every square mile.

We're moving to the boonies. All because of me.

I've never seen so much snow. It's terrifying. My new Prius (courtesy of dear old Dad) is getting a real workout on the snowy mountain road. But there's no turning back now. The guy at the gas station assured us that the pass through the mountains is perfectly safe, so long as a storm doesn't come up. All I can do is clutch the steering wheel and try not to pay attention to the way the mountainside plunges off a few feet from the edge of the road.

I spot the WELCOME TO WYOMING sign.

"Hey," I say to Jeffrey. "This is it."

He doesn't answer. He slumps in the passenger seat, angry music pounding from his iPod. The farther we get from California and his sports teams and his friends, the more sullen he becomes. After two days on the road, it's getting old. I grab the wire and yank one of his earbuds out.

"What?" he says, glaring at me.

"We're in Wyoming, doofus. We're almost there."

"Woo freaking hoo," he says, and stuffs the earbud back in.

He's going to hate me for a while.

Jeffrey was a pretty easygoing kid before he found out about the angel stuff. But I know how that goes. One minute you're a happy fourteen-year-old—good at everything you try, popular, fun—the next you're a freak with wings. It takes some adjustment. And it was only like a month after he got the news that I received my little mission from heaven. Now we're dragging him off to Nowheresville, Wyoming, in January, no less, right smack in the middle of the school year.

When Mom announced the move, he yelled, "I'm not going!" with his fists clenched at his sides like he wanted to hit something.

"You are going," Mom replied, looking up at him coolly. "And I wouldn't be surprised if you find your purpose in Wyoming, too."

"I don't care," he said. Then he turned and glared at me in a way that makes me cringe every time I remember it.

Mom, for her part, obviously digs Wyoming. She's been back and forth a few times scouting for a house, enrolling Jeffrey and me in our new school, smoothing out the transition between her job at Apple in California and the work she'll be doing for them from home after we move. She has chattered for hours about the beautiful scenery that will now be a part of our everyday lives, the fresh air, the wildlife, the weather, and how much we'll love the winter snow.

That's why Jeffrey is riding with me. He can't stand to listen to Mom blather on about how great it's all going to be. The first time we stopped for gas on the trip he got out of her car, grabbed his backpack, walked over to mine, and got in. No explanation. I guess he decided that he currently hates her more than he does me.

I grab the earbud again.

"It's not like I wanted this, you know," I tell him. "For what it's worth, I'm sorry."

"Whatever."

My cell rings. I dig around in my pocket and toss the phone to Jeffrey. He catches it, startled.

"Could you get that?" I ask sweetly. "I'm driving."

He sighs, opens the phone, and puts it to his ear.

"Yeah," he says. "Okay. Yeah."

He flips the phone closed.

"She says we're about to come up on Teton Pass. She wants us to pull over at the lookout."

Right on cue we come around a corner and the valley where we'll be living opens up below a range of low hills and jagged blue-and-white mountains. It's an amazing view, like a scene from a calendar or a postcard. Mom pulls into a turnoff for the "scenic overlook" and I come to a careful stop next to her. She practically bounds out of the car.

"I think she wants us to get out," I say to Jeffrey.

He just stares at the dashboard.

I open the door and swing out into the mountainy air. It's like stepping into a freezer. I tug my suddenly-much-too-thin Stanford hoodie over my head and jam my hands deep into the pockets. I can literally see my breath floating away from me every time I exhale.

Mom walks up to Jeffrey's door and taps on the window.

"Get out of the car," she commands in a voice that says she means business.

She waves me toward the ridge, where a large wooden sign shows a cartoon cowboy pointing into the valley below. HOWDY STRANGER, it reads. YONDER IS JACKSON HOLE. THE LAST OF THE OLD WEST. There's a scattering of buildings on either side of a gleaming silver river. That's Jackson, our new hometown.

"Over there is Teton National Park and Yellowstone." Mom points toward the horizon. "We'll have to go there in the spring, check it out."

Jeffrey joins us on the ridge. He isn't wearing a jacket, just jeans and a T-shirt, but he doesn't look cold. He's too mad to shiver. His expression as he surveys our new environment is carefully blank. A cloud moves over the sun, casting the valley in shadow. The air instantly feels about ten degrees colder. I'm suddenly anxious, like now that I've officially arrived in Wyoming the trees will burst into flame and I'll have to fulfill my purpose on the spot. So much is expected of me in this place.

"Don't worry." Mom puts her hands on my shoulders and squeezes briefly. "This is where you belong, Clara."

"I know." I try to muster a brave smile.

"You," she says, moving to Jeffrey, "are going to love the sports here. Snow skiing and waterskiing and rock climbing and all kinds of extreme sports. I give you full permission to hurl yourself off stuff."

"I guess," he mutters.

"Great," she says, seemingly satisfied. She snaps a quick picture of us. Then she moves briskly back to the car. "Now let's go."

I follow her as the road twists down the mountain. Another sign catches my eye. WARNING, it says, SHARP CURVES AHEAD.

Right before we reach Jackson we turn onto Spring Gulch Road, which takes us to another long, winding road, this one with a big iron gate we need a pass code to get through. That's my first inkling that our humble abode is going to be fairly posh. My second clue is all the enormous log houses I see tucked away in the trees. I follow Mom's car as she turns down a freshly plowed driveway and makes her way slowly through a forest of lodgepole pine, birch, and aspen trees, until we reach a clearing where our new house poses on a small rise.

"Whoa," I breathe, gazing up at the house through the windshield. "Jeffrey, look."

The house is made of solid logs and river rock, the roof

covered with a blanket of pure white snow like what you see on a gingerbread house, complete with a set of perfect silver icicles dangling along the edges. It's bigger than our house in California, but cozier somehow, with a long, covered porch and huge windows that look out on a mind-bogglingly spectacular view of the snow-covered mountain range.

"Welcome home," Mom says. She's leaning against her car, taking in our stunned reactions as we step out into the circular drive. She is so pleased with herself for finding this house she's practically bursting into song. "Our nearest neighbor is almost a mile away. This little wood is all ours."

A breeze stirs the trees so that wisps of snow drift down through the branches, like our house is in a snow globe resting on a mantelpiece. The air feels warmer here. It's absolutely quiet. A sense of well-being washes over me.

This is home, I think. We're safe here, which comes as a huge relief because, after weeks of nothing but visions and danger and sorrow, the uncertainty of moving and leaving everything behind, the insanity of it all, I can finally picture us having a life in Wyoming. Instead of only seeing myself walking into a fire.

I glance over at Mom. She's literally glowing, getting brighter and brighter by the second, a low vibrating hum of angelic pleasure rolling off her. Any second now and we'll be able to see her wings.

Jeffrey coughs. The sight is still new enough to weird him out.

"Mom," he says. "You're doing the glory thing."

She dims.

"Who cares?" I say. "There's no one around to see it. We can be ourselves here."

"Yes," says Mom quietly. "In fact, the backyard would be perfect for practicing some flying."

I stare at her in dismay. Mom has tried to teach me to fly exactly two times, and both were complete disasters. In fact, I've essentially given up on the idea of flight altogether and accepted that I'm going to be an angel-blood who stays earthbound, a flightless bird, like an ostrich maybe, or, in this weather, a penguin.

"You might need to fly here," Mom says a bit stiffly. "And you might want to try it out," she adds to Jeffrey. "I bet you'd be a natural."

I can feel my face getting hot. Sure, Jeffrey will be a natural when I can't even make it off the ground.

"I want to see my room," I say, and escape to the safety of the house.

That afternoon we stand for the first time on the board-walk of Broadway Avenue in Jackson, Wyoming. Even in January, there are plenty of tourists. Stagecoaches and horse-drawn carriages pass by every few minutes, along with a never-ending string of cars. I can't help but scan for one particular silver truck: the mysterious Avalanche with the license plate 99CX.

"Who knew there'd be so much traffic?" I remark as I watch the cars go by.

"What would you do if you saw him right now?" Mom asks. She's wearing a new straw cowboy hat that she was unable to resist in the first gift shop we went into. A cowboy hat. Personally I think she's taking this Old West thing a bit too far.

"She'd probably pass out," says Jeffrey. He bats his eyelashes wildly and fans himself, then pretends to collapse against Mom. They both laugh.

Jeffrey has already bought himself a T-shirt with a snowboarder on it and is deliberating on a real, honest-to-goodness snowboard he liked in a shopwindow. He's been in a much better mood since we arrived at the house and he saw that all is not completely lost. He's acting a lot like the old Jeffrey, the one who smiles and teases and occasionally speaks in full sentences.

"You two are hilarious," I say, rolling my eyes. I jog ahead toward a small park I notice on the other side of the street. The entrance is a huge arch made of elk antlers.

"Let's go this way," I call back to Mom and Jeffrey. We hurry across the crosswalk right as the little orange hand starts to flash. Then we linger for a minute under the arch, gazing up at the latticework of antlers, which vaguely resemble bones. Overhead the sky darkens with clouds, and a cold wind picks up.

"I smell barbecue," says Jeffrey.

"You're just a giant stomach."

"Hey, can I help it if I have a faster metabolism than normal people? How about we eat there." He points up the street where a line of people stand waiting to get into the Million Dollar Cowboy Bar.

"Sure, and I'll buy you a beer, too," Mom says.

"Really?"

"No."

As they bicker about it, I'm struck with the sudden urge to document this moment, so I'll be able to look back and say, this was the beginning. Part one of Clara's purpose. My chest swells with emotion at the thought. A new beginning, for us all.

"Excuse me, ma'am, would you mind taking our picture?" I ask a lady walking past. She nods and takes the camera from Mom. We strike a pose under the arch, Mom in the middle, Jeffrey and me on either side. We smile. The woman tries to snap a picture, but nothing happens. Mom steps over to show her how to work the flash.

That's when the sun comes out again. I suddenly become super aware of what's going on around me, like it's all slowing down for me to encounter piece by piece: the voices of the other people on the boardwalk, the flash of teeth when they speak, the rumble of engines and the tiny squeal of brakes as cars stop at the red light. My heart is beating like a slow, loud drum. My breath drags in and out of my lungs. I smell horse manure and rock salt, my own lavender shampoo, Mom's splash of vanilla, Jeffrey's manly deodorant, even the faint aroma of decay that still clings to the antlers above us. Classical music pours from underneath the glass doors of one of the art galleries. A dog barks in the distance. Somewhere a baby is crying. It feels like too much, like I'll explode trying to take it all in. Everything's too bright. There's a small, dark bird perched in a tree in the park behind us, singing, fluffing its feathers against the cold. How can I see it, if it's behind me? But I feel its sharp black eyes on me; I see it angle its head this way and that, watching me, watching, until suddenly it takes off from the tree and swirls up into the wide-open sky like a bit of smoke, disappearing into the sun.

"Clara," Jeffrey whispers urgently close to my ear. "Hey!"

I jerk back to earth. Jackson Hole. Jeffrey. Mom. The lady with the camera. They're all staring at me.

"What's going on?" I'm dazed, disconnected, like some part of me is still up in the sky with the bird.

"Your hair's, like, shining," murmurs Jeffrey. He glances away like he's embarrassed.

I look down. Gasp. Shining is not the word. My hair is an iridescent silvery-gold riot of light and color. It blazes.

It catches the light like a mirror reflecting the sun. I slide my hand down the warm, luminous strands, and my heart, which seemed to beat so slowly a few moments before, begins to thump painfully fast. What's happening to me?

"Mom?" I call weakly. I look up into her wide blue eyes. Then she turns toward the lady, all perfectly composed.

"Isn't it a beautiful day?" Mom says. "You know what they say: You don't like the weather in Wyoming, wait ten minutes."

The lady nods distractedly, still staring at my supernaturally radiant hair like she's trying to figure out a magician's trick. Mom crosses to me and briskly gathers the length of my hair into her hand like a piece of rope. She shoves it into the collar of my hoodie and pulls the hood up over my head.

"Just stay calm," she whispers as she moves into place between Jeffrey and me. "All right. We're ready now."

The lady blinks a few times, shakes her head like she's trying to clear it. Now that my hair is covered, it's like everything returns to normal, like nothing unusual has happened. Like we imagined it all. The lady lifts the camera.

"Say cheese," she instructs us.

I do my best to smile.

We end up at Mountain High Pizza Pie for dinner, because it's the easiest, closest place. Jeffrey scarfs his pizza while Mom and I pick at ours. We don't talk. I feel like I've been caught

31

doing something terrible. Something shameful. I wear my hood over my hair the entire time, even in the car as we make our way slowly back to the house.

When we get home Mom goes straight into her office and closes the door. Jeffrey and I, for lack of anything better to do, start to hook up the TV. He keeps looking over at me like I'm about to burst into flames.

"Would you stop gawking?" I exclaim finally. "You're freaking me out."

"That was weird, back there. What did you do?"

"I didn't *do* anything. It just happened."

Mom appears in the doorway with her coat on.

"I have to go out," she says. "Please don't leave the house until I get back." Then, before we can question her, she's gone.

"Perfect," mutters Jeffrey.

I toss him the remote and retreat upstairs to my room. I still have a lot of unpacking to do, but my mind keeps flashing back to that moment under the archway when it felt like the whole world was trying to crawl inside my head. And my hair! Unearthly. The look on the lady's face when she saw me that way: puzzled at first, confused, then a little frightened, like I was some kind of alien creature who belonged in a lab with scientists looking at my dazzling hair under a microscope. Like I was a freak.

I must have fallen asleep. The next thing I know Mom's standing in the doorway to my bedroom. She tosses a box of Clairol hair dye on my bed. I pick it up.

"Sedona Sunset?" I read. "You're kidding me, right? Red?"

"Auburn. Like mine."

"But why?" I ask.

"Let's fix your hair," she says. "Then we'll talk."

"It's going to be this color for school!" I whine as she works the dye into my hair in the bathroom, me sitting on the closed toilet with an old towel around my shoulders.

"I love your hair. I wouldn't ask you if I didn't think it was important." She steps back and examines my head for spots she might have missed. "There. All done. Now we have to wait for the color to set."

"Okay, so you're going to explain this to me now, right?"

For all of five seconds she looks nervous. Then she sits down on the edge of the bathtub and folds her hands into her lap.

"What happened today is normal," she says. It reminds me of when she told me about my period, or how she approached the topic of sex, all clinical and rational and perfectly spelled out for me, like she'd been rehearsing the speech for years.

"Um, hello, how was today normal?"

"Okay, not *normal*," she says quickly. "Normal for us. As your abilities begin to grow, your angelic side will start to manifest itself in more noticeable ways."

"My angelic side. Great. Like I don't have enough to deal with."

"It's not so bad," Mom says. "You'll learn to control it."

"I'll learn to control my hair?"

She laughs.

"Yes, eventually, you'll learn how to hide it, to tone it down so that it can't be perceived by the human eye. But for now, dyeing seems the easiest way."

She always wears hats, I realize. At the beach. At the park. Almost any time we go out in public, she wears a hat. She owns dozens of hats and bandanas and scarves. I'd always assumed it was because she was old school.

"So it happens to you?" I ask.

She turns toward the door, smiling faintly.

"Come in, Jeffrey."

Jeffrey slinks in from my room, where he's been eavesdropping. The guilt on his face doesn't last long. He shifts straight to rampant curiosity.

"Will I get it, too?" he asks. "The hair thing?"

"Yes," she answers. "It happens to most of us. For me the first time was 1908, July, I believe. I was reading a book on a park bench. Then——" She lifts her fist up to the top of her head and opens her hand like a kind of explosion.

I lean toward her eagerly. "And was it like everything slowed down, like you could hear and see things that you shouldn't have been able to?"

She turns to look at me. Her eyes are the deep indigo of the sky just after darkness falls, punctuated with tiny points of light as if she's literally being lit up from within. I can see myself in them. I look worried.

"Was that what it was like for you?" she asks. "Time slowed down?"

I nod.

She makes a thoughtful little *hmm* noise and lays her warm hand over mine. "Poor kid. No wonder you're so shaken up."

"What did you do, when it happened with you?" Jeffrey asks.

"I put on my hat. In those days, proper young ladies wore hats out of doors. And luckily, by the time that wasn't true anymore, hair dye had been invented. I was a brunette for almost twenty years." She wrinkles up her nose. "It didn't suit me."

"But what *is* it?" I ask. "Why does it happen?"

She pauses like she's considering her words carefully. "It's a part of glory breaking through." She looks slightly uncomfortable, as if we can't quite be trusted with this information. "Now, that's enough class for today. If this kind of thing happens again, in public I mean, I find it works best to just act normally. Most of the time, people will convince themselves that they didn't really see anything, that it was a trick of the light, an illusion. But it wouldn't be a bad idea for you to wear a hat more often now, Jeffrey, to be safe."

"Okay," he says with a smirk. He practically sleeps in his Giants cap.

"And let's try not to call attention to ourselves," she continues, looking at him pointedly, clearly referring to the way he feels the need to be the best at everything: quarterback, pitcher, the all-star varsity kind of guy. "No showing off."

His jaw tightens.

"Shouldn't be a problem," he says. "There's nothing to go out for in January, is there? Wrestling tryouts were in November. Baseball's not until spring."

"Maybe that's for the best. It gives you some time to adjust before you pick up anything extracurricular."

"Right. For the best." His face is a mask of sullenness again. Then he retreats to his room, slamming the door behind him.

"Okay, so that's settled," Mom says, turning to me with a smile. "Let's rinse."

My hair turns out orange. Like a peeled carrot. The moment I see it I seriously consider shaving my head.

"We'll fix it," Mom promises, trying hard not to laugh. "First thing tomorrow. I swear."

"Good night." I close the door in her face. Then I throw myself down on the bed and have a good long cry. So much for my shot at impressing Mystery Boy with his gorgeous wavy brown hair.

After I calm down I lie in bed listening to the wind knock at my window. The woods outside seem huge and full of darkness. I can feel the mountains, their massive presence looming behind the house. There are things happening now that I can't control—I'm changing, and I can't go back to the way things were before.

The vision comes to me then like a familiar friend, sweeping my bedroom away and depositing me in the middle of the smoky forest. The air is so hot, so dry and heavy, difficult to breathe. I see the silver Avalanche parked along the edge of the road. Automatically I turn toward the hills, orienting myself to where I know I will find the boy. I walk. I feel the sadness then, a grief like my heart's being cut out, growing with every step I take. My eyes fill with useless tears. I blink them away and keep walking, determined to reach the boy, and when I see him, I stop for a minute and simply take him in. The sight of him standing there so unaware fills me with a mix of pain and yearning.

I think, I'm here.

3

I SURVIVED THE BLACK PLAGUE

The first thing that catches my eye as I drive into the parking lot of Jackson Hole High School is a large silver truck parked in the back of the lot. I squint to see the license plate.

"Whoa!" yells Jeffrey as I nearly rear-end another much-older, much-rustier blue truck in front of me. "Learn to drive already!"

"Sorry." I try to wave apologetically to the guy driving the blue truck, but he yells something out his window that I'm pretty sure I don't want to understand and screeches away across the parking lot. I park the Prius carefully in an empty space and sit for a minute, trying to get myself together.

Jackson Hole High doesn't resemble a school so much as

a resort, a large brick building framed by a series of huge log beams along the front, kind of like pillars but with a more rustic feel. Like everything else in our new hometown, it's postcard perfect, all shining windows and evenly spaced, white-trunked trees that are beautiful even without leaves, not to mention the gorgeous towering mountains in the background on three sides. Even the fluffy white clouds in the sky look deliberately placed.

"Later," says Jeffrey, jumping out of the car. He grabs his backpack and swaggers toward the front door of the school like he owns the place. A few girls in the parking lot turn to check him out. He flashes them an easy smile, which immediately starts up the whisper/giggle thing that always trailed him at our old school.

"So much for not calling attention to ourselves," I mutter. I apply another coat of lip gloss and inspect my reflection in the rearview mirror, cringing at my humiliating hair color. In spite of my mom's and my best efforts over the past week, it's still orange. We've tried everything, re-dyed it like five times, even tried to dye it jet-black, but the color always washes out to the same horrendous, eye-stabbing orange. It's like some kind of cruel cosmic joke.

"You can't always rely on your looks, Clara," Mom said after failed-attempt number five. Like she's one to talk. Like she's ever looked less than gorgeous a day in her life.

"I've *never* relied on my looks, Mom."

"Sure you have," she said a bit too cheerfully. "You aren't vain about it, but still. You knew that when the other students at Mountain View High looked at you, they saw this pretty strawberry blonde."

"Yeah, so now I'm not strawberry blonde *or* pretty," I said miserably. Yes, I was wallowing. But the hair is just so horrifically orange.

Mom put a finger under my chin and forced my head up to look at her.

"You could have neon green hair, and it wouldn't take away how beautiful you are," she said.

"You're my mother. You're legally required to say that."

"Let's try to remember that you're not here to win a beauty pageant. You're here for your purpose. Maybe this hair problem means that things aren't going to be as easy for you here as they were in California. And maybe there's a reason for that."

"Right. A very good reason, I'm sure."

"At least the dye will cover the bright stuff. So you won't have to worry about keeping your hair covered."

"Yay for me."

"You'll just have to make the best of it, Clara," she said.

So here I am, making the best of it, like I really have a choice. I get out of the car and sneak to the back of the parking lot to inspect the silver truck. AVALANCHE, it reads in silver letters across the back fender. License plate 99CX.

He's here. I force myself to breathe. He's really here.

Now there's nothing left to do but walk into the school with my crazy, unruly, insanely bright-orange hair. I watch the other students stream into the building in their little groups, laughing and talking and goofing around. All total strangers, every single one of them. Except one. Although I'm a stranger to him. My hands are simultaneously sweaty and clammy. A flock of butterflies flaps around in my stomach. I've never been more nervous in my life.

You've got this, Clara, I think. Next to your purpose, this school thing should be a snap.

So I straighten my shoulders, trying for Jeffrey's confidence, and head for the door.

My first mistake, I realize almost immediately, was assuming that even with the designer exterior, this high school would be essentially like any other. Boy, was I ever wrong. The school is as high-end on the inside as it appears on the outside. Almost all of the classrooms have tall ceilings and floor-to-ceiling windows with mountain views. The cafeteria is a cross between the inside of a ski lodge and an art museum. There are paintings, murals, and collages in practically every nook and cranny of the place. It even smells better than regular schools: pine and chalk and a fragrant mix of expensive perfumes. My old cinder-block school in California seems like a prison in comparison.

I've stumbled into the land of pretty people. And here I thought I'd come from the land of pretty people. You know how sometimes on TV they'll show you a picture of a celebrity from high school, and that person looks perfectly normal, not really any more attractive than anyone else? And you think, what happened? Why is Jennifer Garner so hot now? I'll tell you: money happened. Facials, fancy haircuts, designer clothes, and personal trainers happened. And the kids at Jackson Hole High had that celebrity polish, except for the few here and there who looked like genuine cowboys, complete with Stetsons, pearl buttons on their western-style plaid shirts, too-tight Wranglers, and scuffed cowboy boots.

Plus, the curriculum is fancy. Sure, you can take an art class, if you feel like learning to draw, but you can also take AP Studio Art, which prepares you to enter Jackson Hole's lively art scene. There's a class called Power Sports, which teaches you how to tune up your motorcycle, ATV, or snowmobile. You can learn how to start your own business, draft your dream house, develop your passion for French cuisine, or take your first steps toward becoming an engineer. Just in case you want to get your pilot's license, the school offers a couple courses in aerodynamics. The world is your oyster at Jackson Hole High.

It's definitely going to take some getting used to.

I thought the other students would be excited to see me, or curious at the very least. I'm fresh meat, after all, and from California, and maybe I have some big-city wisdom to offer the natives. Wrong again. For the most part, they completely ignore me. After I make it through three periods (trigonometry, French III, College Prep Chemistry) where nobody even bothers with a simple howdy, I'm ready to dash for my car and drive straight back to California, where I've known everybody for forever and they've known me, where right this minute my friends and I would be dishing about our holidays and comparing schedules, and I'd be pretty and popular. Where life is ordinary.

But then I see him.

He's standing with his back to me near my locker. A surge of electricity zings through me as I recognize his shoulders, his hair, the shape of his head. In a flash I'm in the vision, seeing him both in the black fleece jacket among the trees and for real, just down the hall simultaneously, like the vision is a thin veil laid on top of reality.

I take a step toward him, my mouth opening to call his name. Then I remember that I don't know it. Like always, it's as if he hears me anyway and starts to turn, and my heart skips a beat when I don't wake up but see his face now, his mouth curling up in a half smile as he jokes with the guy next to him.

He glances up and his eyes meet mine. The hallway melts away. It's only him and me now, in the forest. The vision comes from behind him, the fire on the hillside roaring toward us, faster than it could ever possibly happen.

I have to save him, I think.

That's when I faint.

I wake to a girl with long, golden brown hair sitting on the floor next to me, her hand on my forehead, talking in a low voice like she's trying to calm an animal.

"What happened?" I look around for the boy, but he's gone. Something hard pokes into my back, and I realize I'm lying on my chemistry book.

"You fell," says the girl, as if that isn't obvious. "Do you have epilepsy or something? It looked like you were having some kind of seizure."

People are staring. I feel the heat rising in my cheeks.

"I'm okay," I say, sitting up.

"Easy." The girl jumps up and reaches down to help me. I take her hand and let her haul me to my feet.

"I'm kind of a klutz," I say, like that explains it.

"She's okay. Go to class," the girl says to the kids who are still gawking. "Did you eat this morning?" she asks me.

"What?"

"Could be a blood sugar thing." She puts her arm around me and steers me down the hallway. "What's your name?"

"Clara."

"Wendy," she says in response.

"Where are we going?"

"The nurse."

"No," I object, breaking free of her arm. I straighten and

attempt to smile. "I'm fine, really."

The bell rings. Suddenly the hallway's deserted. Then from around the corner bustles a plump, yellow-haired woman wearing blue nursing scrubs, walking fast. Behind her is the boy. *My* boy.

"There she goes again," Wendy says as I wobble into her.

"Christian," orders the nurse quickly as they rush toward me.

Christian. His name.

His arm comes under my knees, and he lifts me. My arm is around his shoulder, my fingers inches away from the spot where his neck meets his hair. His smell, a mixture of Ivory soap and some wonderful, spicy cologne, washes over me. I look up into his green eyes, so close that I can see flecks of gold in them.

"Hi," he says.

Heaven help me, I think as he smiles. It's just too much.

"Hi," I murmur, looking away, flushing to the roots of my loose, very-orange hair.

"Hold on to me," he says, and then he's carrying me down the hall. Over his shoulder I see Wendy watching me, before she turns and walks the other way.

When we reach the nurse's office he puts me down gently onto a cot. I do my best not to gape at him.

"Thank you," I stammer.

"No problem." He smiles again in a way that makes me glad I'm sitting down. "You're pretty light."

My jumbled brain tries to make sense of these three words and put them in order, with little success.

"Thank you," I say again, lamely.

"Yes, thank you, Mr. Prescott," says the nurse. "Now get to class."

Christian Prescott. His name is Christian Prescott.

"See ya," he says, and just like that, he's walking away.

I wave as he rounds the corner, then feel like an idiot.

"Now," says the nurse, turning to me.

"Really," I say. "I'm fine."

She looks unconvinced.

"I could do jumping jacks—that's how fine I am," I say, and I can't wipe the stupid smile off my face.

Thus I arrive at Honors English late. The students have pulled their chairs into a circle. The teacher, an older man with a short, white beard, motions for me to come in.

"Pull up a chair. Miss Gardner, I presume?"

"Yes." I feel the whole class staring directly at me as I grab a desk from the back of the room and drag it toward the circle. I recognize Wendy, the girl who helped me in the hall. She scoots her desk over to make room for me.

"I'm Mr. Phibbs," says the teacher. "We're in the middle of an exercise that's largely for your benefit, so I'm glad

46

you could join us. Everyone must give three unique facts about themselves. If anyone else in the circle has one in common, they raise their hand, and the person whose turn it is has to choose something else. We're currently on Shawn, who was finishing up by claiming that he has the most . . . rocking snowboard in Teton County. . . ." Mr. Phibbs raises his bushy eyebrows. "Which Jason here contested."

"I ride the beautiful pink lady," brags the boy who I assume is Shawn.

"No one can argue that's unique," says Mr. Phibbs with a cough. "So now we're on to Kay. And say your name, please, for the new girl."

Everyone looks to a petite brunette with large brown eyes. She smiles as if it's the most natural thing in the world for her to be the center of attention.

"I'm Kay Patterson," she says. "My parents own the oldest fudge shop in Jackson. I've met Harrison Ford lots of times," she adds as her second thing, "because our fudge is his favorite. He said that I look like Carrie Fisher from *Star Wars*."

So she's vain, I think. Although if you dressed her up in a white gown and put the cinnamon-roll buns on either side of her head, she really could pass for Princess Leia. She's very attractive, definitely one of the pretty people, with a peaches-and-cream complexion and brown hair that falls past her shoulders in perfect curls, so shiny that it almost doesn't look like hair.

"And," Kay adds as her final touch, "Christian Prescott is my boyfriend."

I dislike her already.

"Very good, Kay," says Mr. Phibbs.

Next is Wendy. She's blushing, obviously mortified to be speaking in front of the entire class about herself.

"I'm Wendy Avery," she says with a shrug. "My family manages a ranch outside Wilson. I don't know what else is that unique about me. I want to be a veterinarian, not a big surprise because I love horses. And I've made my own clothes since I was six years old."

"Thank you, Wendy," says Mr. Phibbs. She rocks back with a small sigh of relief. From the desk next to hers, Kay stifles a yawn. It's a small, ladylike gesture, but it makes me dislike her even more.

Silence.

Oh crap, I realize, they're waiting for me.

All the things I've been considering fly out of my brain. Instead I think of all the things I can't tell them, like *I can speak any language on Earth fluently. I have wings that appear when I ask them to, and I'm supposed to be able to fly, but I suck at it. I'm a natural blonde. I have an impeccable sense of direction, which I think is supposed to help with the flying thing, but it doesn't. Oh, and I'm here on a mission to save Kay's boyfriend.*

I clear my throat. "So I'm Clara Gardner, and I moved

here from California."

The other students snicker as a guy across the circle raises his hand.

"That's one of Mr. Lovett's unique facts," says Mr. Phibbs, "only you weren't here when he said it. You'll find that there are quite a few students here who have migrated from the Golden State."

"Okay, well, let me try again." Specificity is obviously the key here. "I moved here from California about a week ago, because I heard such great things about the fudge."

The class laughs, even Kay, who seems pleased. I suddenly feel like a stand-up comedian who's just told the opening bit. But anything's better than being known as the redheaded dork ina who passed out in the middle of the hall after third period. So jokes it will be.

"Birds are weirdly attracted to me," I continue. "They kind of stalk me wherever I go." This is true. My current theory about this is because they smell my feathers, although it's impossible to know for sure.

"Are you raising your hand, Angela?" asks Mr. Phibbs.

Startled, I glance to my right, where a raven-haired girl in a violet-colored tunic dress over black leggings is quickly lowering her hand.

"No, just stretching," she says casually, looking at me with grave amber eyes. "I like the bird thing, though. That's funny."

But nobody's laughing this time. They're staring at me. I swallow.

"Okay, one more, right?" I say a little desperately. "My mom is a computer programmer, and my dad is a physics professor at NYU, which probably means that I should be good at math." I make a pained face. The idea that I can't do math is bogus of course. I'm good at math. It's a language after all, which is why Mom understands the way computers talk to one another without having to work at it. And probably why she was attracted to Dad to begin with, who's like a human calculator even without a drop of angel blood running through his veins. Jeffrey and I both find it ridiculously easy.

This doesn't get a laugh, either, just a pity chuckle from Wendy. I'm apparently not cut out to be a stand-up comedian.

"Thank you, Clara," says Mr. Phibbs.

The last student to name her three things is the black-haired girl who looked at me so attentively when I mentioned the weird thing with the birds. Her name, she says, is Angela Zerbino. She tucks her side-swept bangs behind her ear and lists her three unique things quickly.

"My mother owns the Pink Garter. I've never met my father. And I'm a poet."

Another awkward silence. She looks around the circle like she's daring someone to challenge her. Nobody meets her eyes.

"Good," says Mr. Phibbs, clearing his throat. He peruses his notes. "Now we know each other better. But how do people really get to know each other? Is it with facts, the specifics about ourselves that distinguish us from the other six and a half billion people on this planet? Is it our brains that make us different, the way each person is like a computer programmed with a different mix of software, memories, habits, and genetic makeup? Is it what we do, the actions we take? What would your three things have been, I wonder, if I'd told you to name the most defining actions you have taken in your life?"

I see a flash of the fire in my mind's eye.

"This spring we'll be spending a lot of time discussing what it is to be unique," continues Mr. Phibbs. He stands and hobbles over to the small table at the back of the room, where he picks up a stack of books and begins to pass them out.

"Our first book of the semester," he says.

Frankenstein.

"It's alive!" yells the guy with the pink lady on his snowboard, holding up his book as if he expects it to be struck by lightning. Kay Patterson rolls her eyes.

"Ah, you're channeling Dr. Frankenstein already." Mr. Phibbs turns to the whiteboard and writes the name *Mary Shelley* in black marker, along with the year *1817*. "This book was written by a woman not much older than you are now, who was reflecting on the battle between science and the natural world."

He launches into a lecture about Jean-Jacques Rousseau

and the impact his ideas had on art and literature at the time that Mary Shelley was writing. I try not to stare at Kay Patterson. I wonder what kind of girl she is, to snag a guy like Christian. And then, since I don't know anything about him other than what the back of his head looks like, and that he likes to rescue girls who pass out in the hall, I wonder what kind of guy Christian is.

I realize that I'm chewing on my pencil eraser. I put my pencil down.

"Mary Shelley wanted to explore what it is that makes us human," Mr. Phibbs concludes. He glances over at me, meets my eyes like he knows I haven't been listening to a thing he's said for the past ten minutes, then looks away.

"I guess we'll find out," he says as he holds up the book, and then the bell rings.

"You can sit at my table for lunch, if you want," Wendy offers as we're leaving the classroom. "Did you pack your lunch? Or were you planning to go off campus?"

"No, I thought I'd get something here."

"Well, I think today it's chicken-fried steak." I make a face. "But you can always get pizza, or a peanut butter sandwich. Those are the JHHS staples."

"Healthy."

I shuffle through the line to get my food and follow Wendy over to her table, where a bunch of nearly identical-looking girls peer up at me expectantly. Wendy rattles off their names: Lindsey, Emma, and Audrey. They seem friendly enough. Definitely not pretty people, all wearing T-shirts and jeans, braids and ponytails, not a lot of makeup. But nice. Normal.

"So, you're like a group?" I ask as I sit down.

Wendy laughs.

"We call ourselves the Invisibles."

"Oh . . . ," I say, unsure of whether she's joking or how to respond.

"We're not freaks or geeks," says Lindsey, Emma, or Audrey, I can't tell which. "We're just, well, you know, *invisible*."

"Invisible to—"

"The popular people," says Wendy. "They don't see us."

Great. I fit right in with the Invisibles.

Across the cafeteria I catch a glimpse of Jeffrey sitting with a bunch of guys in letterman jackets. A little blond girl is gazing up at him adoringly. He says something. Everybody at his table laughs.

Unbelievable. In less than one day, he's Mr. Popular.

Someone pulls a chair up next to me. I turn. There is Christian, straddling the chair. For a moment all I can focus on is his green eyes. Maybe I'm not so invisible after all.

"So I hear you're from California," he says.

"Yes," I murmur, hurrying to chew and swallow a bite of

53

peanut butter sandwich. The room is quieter now. The girls at the Invisibles table are gazing at him with wide eyes, as if he's never crossed into their territory before. As a matter of fact, pretty much everyone in the cafeteria is looking at us, a curious and almost predatory stare.

I take a quick sip of milk and give him what I hope is a food-free smile.

"We moved here from Mountain View. That's south of San Francisco," I manage.

"I was born in L.A. We lived there until I was five, although I don't really remember much."

"Nice." My mind races for the right response to this information, some way to acknowledge this amazing thing we have in common. But I've got nothing. The most I can come up with is a nervous giggle. A *giggle*, for crying out loud.

"I'm Christian," he says suavely. "I didn't get the chance to introduce myself before."

"Clara." I put my hand out to shake, a gesture he seems to find charming. He takes my hand, and it's like my vision and the real world clap together at this moment. He smiles this stunning, lopsided smile. He's real. His hand around mine is warm and confident, just the right amount of pressure. I'm instantly dizzy.

"Nice to meet you, Clara," he says, shaking my hand.

"Totally."

He smiles again. *Hot* is really not an adequate enough word for this guy. He is crazy beautiful. And it's more than his looks—the intentionally messy waves of his dark hair; the strong eyebrows that make his expression a bit serious, even when he smiles; his eyes, which I notice can look emerald in one light and hazel in another; the sweetly sculpted angles of his face; the curve of his full lips. I've been seeing him from the front for all of ten minutes total and already I'm obsessing about his lips.

"Thank you for before," I say.

"You're very welcome."

"Hey, ready to go?" Kay walks up and puts her hand on the back of his neck in a decidedly possessive gesture, spearing her fingers through his hair. Her expression is so carefully neutral it could have been sprayed on, like she couldn't care less who her boyfriend's talking to. Christian turns to look up at her, his face practically even with her breasts. Around her neck dangles a shiny silver half heart with the initials C.P. stamped into it. He smiles.

Spell effectively broken.

"Yeah, just a sec," he says. "Kay, this is—"

"Clara Gardner," she says, nodding. "She's in my English class. Moved here from California. Doesn't like birds. No good at math."

"Yeah, that's me in a nutshell," I say.

"What? Did I miss something?" asks Christian, confused.

"Nothing. Just a stupid exercise we did in Phibbs's class. We better go if we want to get back before next period," she says, then turns to me and smiles, a flash of perfect white teeth. I'd bet money that she wore braces at some point. "There's this great Chinese place we like to hit for lunch about a mile from here. You'll have to try it sometime with your friends." Translation: *You and I will never be friends.*

"I like Chinese," I say.

Christian hops up from the chair. Kay tucks her arm in his and smiles at him from under her lashes and starts to lead him out of the cafeteria.

"Nice to meet you," he calls back to me. "Again."

And then he's gone.

"Wow," remarks Wendy, who's been sitting right next to me the entire time without making a sound. "Impressive attempt at flirtation."

"I guess I was inspired," I say a bit dazedly.

"Well, I don't think there are many girls here who aren't inspired by Christian Prescott," she says, which makes the other girls titter.

"Freshman year I had this fantasy that he'd ask me to the prom and I'd be crowned queen," sighs the one I think is Emma, who then flushes bright red. "I'm over it now."

"I'd put money on Christian being prom king this year." Wendy scrunches up her nose. "But Kay's the queen. You'd better watch your back."

"Is she that bad?"

Wendy laughs, then shrugs.

"She and I were good friends in grade school, had

56

sleepovers and tea parties with our dolls and all of that, but when we hit junior high, it was like . . ." Wendy shakes her head sadly. "She's spoiled. But she's nice enough when you get to know her, I guess. She can be really sweet. But don't get on her bad side."

I'm pretty sure I'm already on Kay Patterson's bad side. I could tell by the way she'd kept her voice light, friendly, but beneath it was an undercurrent of contempt.

I glance around the cafeteria. I notice the black-haired girl from English, Angela Zerbino. She's sitting by herself, her lunch untouched in front of her, reading a thick black book. She looks up. She nods, just the tiniest bob of her head, like she wants to acknowledge me. I hold her gaze for a moment, then look away. She goes back to reading her book.

"What about her?" I ask Wendy, tilting my head to indicate Angela.

"Angela? She's not a social reject or anything. It's like she prefers to be alone. She's sort of intense. Focused. She's always been that way."

"What's the Pink Garter? It sounds like a . . . you know, a place where . . . you know . . ."

Wendy laughs. "A whorehouse?"

"Yeah," I say, embarrassed.

"It's a dinner theater in town," says Wendy, still laughing. "Cowboy melodramas, a few musicals."

"Oh," I say, finally getting it. "I thought it was strange

when she said in class that her mother owned a whorehouse and she didn't know her father. A little TMI, if you know what I mean."

Now everyone at the table is laughing. I look again at Angela, who has turned a bit so I can't see her face.

"She seems nice," I backpedal.

Wendy nods.

"She is. My brother had a crush on her for a while."

"You have a brother?"

She snorts like she wishes she could give a different answer.

"Yes. He's my twin, actually. He's also a pain."

"I know the feeling." I gaze over at Jeffrey in his circle of new friends.

"And speak of the devil," says Wendy, grabbing the sleeve of a boy who's passing by our table.

"Hey," he protests. "What?"

"Nothing. I was just telling the new girl about my awesome brother and now here you are." She flashes a huge smile at him, the kind that says she might not be telling the whole truth.

"Behold, Tucker Avery," she says to me, gesturing up at him.

Her brother resembles her in nearly every way: same hazy blue eyes, same tan, same golden brown hair, except his hair is short and spiky and he's about a foot taller. He is definitely part of the cowboy group, although toned down from some of the others, wearing a simple gray tee, jeans, and cowboy boots. Also hot, but in a completely different way than Christian, less refined, more tan and muscle and a hint of stubble along his jaw. He looks like he's been working under the sun his whole life.

"This is Clara," says Wendy.

"You're the girl with the Prius who almost rear-ended my truck this morning," he says.

"Oh, sorry about that."

He looks me up and down. I feel myself blush for probably the hundredth time that day.

"From California, right?" The word *California* seems like an insult coming from him.

"Tucker," Wendy warns, pulling at his arm.

"Well, I doubt that I would have done any damage to your truck if I'd hit you," I retort. "It looks like the back end is about to rust off."

Wendy's eyes widen. She seems genuinely alarmed.

Tucker scoffs. "That rusty truck will probably be towing you out of a snowbank next time there's a storm."

"Tucker!" exclaims Wendy. "Don't you have a rodeo team meeting or something?"

I'm busy trying to think of a comeback involving the incredible amount of money I will save this year driving my Prius as opposed to his gas-guzzling truck, but the right words aren't forming.

"You're the one who wanted to chat," he says to Wendy.

"I didn't know you were going to act like a pig."

"Fine." He smirks at me. "Nice to meet you, Carrots," he says, looking directly at my hair. "Oh, I mean Clara."

My face flames.

"Same to you, Rusty," I shoot back, but he's already striding away.

Great. I've been at this school for less than five hours and I've already made two enemies simply by existing.

"Told you he was a pain," says Wendy.

"I think that might have been an understatement," I say, and we both laugh.

The first person I see when I come into my next class is Angela Zerbino. She's sitting in the front row, already bent over her notebook. I take a seat a few rows back, looking around the classroom at all the portraits of the British monarchy that are stapled to the top of the walls. A large table at the front of the room displays a Popsicle-stick model of the Tower of London and a papier mâché replica of Stonehenge. In one corner is a mannequin wearing a suit of chain mail, in another, a large wooden board with three holes in it: real stockades.

This looks like it could be interesting.

The other students trickle in. When the bell rings, the teacher ambles out from a back room. He's a scrawny guy with long hair pulled back in a ponytail and thick glasses, but he somehow comes off as cool, wearing his dress shirt and tie over black jeans and cowboy boots.

"Hi, I'm Mr. Erikson. Welcome to spring semester of British History," he says. He grabs a jar off the table and shakes the papers inside. "First I thought we'd start by dividing up into British citizens. In this canister are ten pieces of paper with the word *serf* on it. If you draw one of those, you're basically a slave. Deal with it. There are three pieces of paper with the word *cleric*; if you draw those, you're part of the church, a nun or a priest, whichever is appropriate."

He glances toward the back of the room where a student has just slipped in the door. "Christian, nice of you to join us."

It takes all of my willpower not to turn around.

"Sorry," I hear Christian say. "Won't happen again."

"If it does you'll spend five minutes in the stocks."

"Definitely won't happen again."

"Excellent," says Mr. Erikson. "Now where was I? Oh yes. Five pieces of paper have the words *lord/lady*. If you draw one of these, congratulations, you own land, maybe even a serf or two. Three say *knight*—you get the idea. And there is one, and only one, paper with the word *king*, and if you draw that one, you rule us all."

He holds the jar out to Angela.

"I'm going to be queen," she says.

"We shall see," says Mr. Erikson.

Angela draws a paper from the jar and reads it. Her smile fades. "Lady."

"I wouldn't whine about it," Mr. Erikson tells her. "It's a good life, relatively speaking."

"Of course, if I want to be sold off to the richest man who offers to marry me."

"Touché," says Mr. Erikson. "Lady Angela, everybody."

He makes his way around the room. He already knows the students and calls them by name.

"Hmmm, red hair," he says when he gets to me. "Could be a witch."

Someone snickers behind me. I steal a quick look over my shoulder to see Wendy's obnoxious brother, Tucker, sitting in the seat behind mine. He flashes me a devilish grin.

I draw a paper. Cleric.

"Very good, Sister Clara. Now you, Mr. Avery."

I turn to watch Tucker draw from the jar.

"A knight," he reads, looking pleased with himself.

"Sir Tucker."

The role of king goes to a guy I don't know, Brady, who is, judging by the muscles and the way he accepts his rule like he deserves it instead of drawing it by chance, a football player.

Christian goes last.

"Ah," he says faux mournfully, reading his paper. "I'm a serf."

Mr. Erikson follows this up by going around the room

with a set of dice and making us roll to see if we survive the Black Plague. The odds of surviving are not good for serfs, or clerics, since they tended the sick, but miraculously I survive. Mr. Erikson rewards me with a laminated badge that reads, I SURVIVED THE BLACK PLAGUE.

Mom will be so proud.

Christian doesn't make it. He receives a badge decorated with a skull and crossbones, which reads, I PERISHED IN THE BLACK PLAGUE. Mr. Erikson marks his death down in a notebook he has to keep track of our new lives. He assures us that the usual rules of life and death don't apply as far as this exercise is concerned.

Still, I can't help but take Christian's immediate demise as a bad sign.

Mom is waiting for us at the front door when we get home.

"Tell me everything," she commands as soon as I cross the threshold. "I want to know all the details. Does he go to your school? Did you see him?"

"Oh, she saw him," Jeffrey says before I can answer. "She saw him and she passed out in the middle of the hallway. The whole school was talking about it."

Her eyes widen. She turns to me. I shrug.

"I told you she'd pass out," says Jeffrey.

"You're a genius." Mom moves to ruffle his hair but he dodges her and says, "Too fast for you," before her hand lands. "I put some chips and salsa out for you in the kitchen," she says.

"What happened?" she asks after Jeffrey goes to stuff his face.

"Pretty much what Jeffrey said. Just keeled over in front of everybody."

"Oh, honey." She offers me a sympathetic pout.

"When I woke up, there was this girl who helped me. I think she could be a friend. And then . . ." I swallow. "He came back with the nurse and carried me to the nurse's office."

Her mouth drops open. I've never seen her look so astonished. "He carried you?"

"Yes, like some lame damsel in distress."

She laughs. I sigh.

"Did you tell her his name yet?" comes Jeffrey's voice from the kitchen.

"Shut up," I call.

"His name is Christian," he calls back. "Can you believe that? We came all this way so Clara could save a guy named Christian."

"I'm aware of the irony."

"But you know his name now," Mom says softly.

"Yes." I'm unable to hold back a smile. "I know his name."

"And it's all happening. The pieces are coming together." She looks more serious now. "Are you ready for this, kiddo?"

It's all I've thought about for weeks, and I've known for the past two years that my time would come. But still, am I ready?

"I think so?" I say.

I hope.

4

WINGSPAN

I was fourteen when Mom told me about the angels. One morning at breakfast she announced that she was keeping me out of school for the day and we were going on a mother-daughter outing, just she and I. We dropped Jeffrey off at school and drove about thirty miles from our house in Mountain View to Big Basin Redwoods State Park, in the mountains near the ocean. My mom parked in the main lot, slung a backpack over her shoulder, said, "Last one up is a slowpoke," and headed straight off along a paved trail. I had to practically jog to keep up with her.

"Some mothers take their daughters to get their ears pierced," I called after her. There was no one else on the trail.

Fog shifted through the redwoods. The trees were as much as twenty feet in diameter, and so tall you couldn't see where they stopped, only the small gaps between the branches, where beams of light slanted onto the forest floor.

"Where are we going?" I asked breathlessly.

"Buzzards Roost," Mom said over her shoulder. Like that helped.

We hiked past deserted campgrounds, splashed across creeks, ducked under gigantic mossy beams where trees had fallen across the path. Mom was quiet. This wasn't one of those mother-daughter bonding times like when she took me to Fisherman's Wharf or the Winchester Mystery House or IKEA. The stillness of the forest was punctuated only by our breathing and the scuff of our feet on the trail, a silence so heavy and suffocating that I wanted to yell something just to shatter it.

She didn't speak again until we reached a huge outcropping of rock jutting out of the mountainside like a stone finger pointing to the sky. To get to the top we had to climb about twenty feet of sheer rock face, which Mom did quickly, easily, without looking back.

"Mom, wait!" I called, and scrambled after her. I'd never climbed so much as the rock wall in a gym. Her shoes flicked a spray of rubble down the slope. She disappeared over the top.

"Mom!" I yelled.

She peered down at me.

"You can do this, Clara," she said. "Trust me. It will be worth it."

I didn't really have a choice. I reached up and grabbed at the cliff face and started to climb, telling myself not to look down where the mountain dropped off beneath me. Then I was at the top. I stood next to Mom, panting.

"Wow," I said, looking out.

"Pretty amazing, right?"

Below us stretched the valley of redwoods rimmed by the distant mountains. This was one of those top-of-the-world places, where you could see for miles in every direction. I closed my eyes and spread my arms, letting the wind move past me, smelling the air—a heady combination of trees and moss and growing things, a hint of dirt and creek water and pure, clean oxygen. An eagle turned in a slow circle over the forest. I could easily imagine what that would feel like, to glide through the air, nothing between you and endless blue heaven but little tufts of cloud.

"Have a seat," Mom said. I opened my eyes and turned to see her sitting on a boulder. She patted the space beside her. I sat down next to her. She rummaged in her pack for a bottle of water, opened it, and drank deeply, then offered the bottle to me. I took it and drank, watching her. She was distracted, her eyes distant, lost in thought.

"Am I in trouble?" I asked.

She started, then laughed nervously.

"No, honey," she said. "I just have something important to tell you."

My head spun with all of the things that she might be about to spring on me.

"I've been coming to this spot for a really long time," she said.

"You've met a guy," I guessed. It seemed like a distinct possibility.

"What are you talking about?" Mom asked.

Mom had never dated much, even though everyone who met her liked her immediately, and men followed her around the room with their eyes. She liked to say that she was too busy for a steady relationship, too wrapped up with her job at Apple as a computer programmer, too occupied with being a single mom the rest of the time. I thought she was still hung up on Dad. But maybe she had some secret passionate affair she was about to confess to me. Maybe within a couple of months I'd be standing in a pink dress with flowers in my hair, watching her marry some guy I was supposed to call Dad. It'd happened to a couple of my friends.

"You brought me out here to tell me about this guy you met, and you love him, and you want to marry him or something," I said quickly, not looking at her because I didn't want her to see how much I hated the idea.

"Clara Gardner."

"Really, I'd be okay with it."

"That's very sweet, Clara, but wrong," she said. "I brought you out here because I think you're old enough to know the truth."

"Okay," I said anxiously. That sounded big. "What truth?"

She took a deep breath and let it out, then leaned toward me.

"When I was about your age I lived in San Francisco with my grandmother," she began.

I knew a little about this. Her father was out of the picture before she was born, and her mother died giving birth to her. I always thought it sounded like a fairy tale, like my mom was the orphaned, tragic heroine in one of my books.

"We lived in a big white house on Mason Street," she said.

"Why haven't you taken me there?" We'd been to San Francisco many times, at least two or three times a year, and she'd never said anything about a house on Mason Street.

"It burned down years ago," she said. "There's a souvenir shop there now, I think. Anyway, early one morning I woke up to the house violently shaking. I had to grab on to the bedpost so I wouldn't be tossed right out of bed."

"Earthquake," I assumed. Growing up in California, I'd been through a few earthquakes, none that lasted more than a few seconds or done any real damage, but still pretty scary.

Mom nodded. "I could hear the dishes falling out of the china cabinet and windows breaking all over the house. Then there was a loud groaning sound. The wall of my bedroom

70

gave way, and the bricks from the chimney crashed down on top of me in bed."

I stared at her in horror.

"I don't know how long I lay there," Mom said after a minute. "When I opened my eyes again I saw the figure of a man standing over me. He leaned down and said, 'Be still, child.' Then he lifted me in his arms, and the bricks slid off my body like they weighed nothing. He carried me to the window. All the glass was broken out, and I could see people running out of their houses into the street. And then a strange thing happened, and we were someplace else. It still resembled my room, only different somehow, like someone else was living there, undamaged as if the quake had never happened. Outside the window there was so much light, so bright it hurt to look."

"Then what happened?"

"The man set me on my feet. I was amazed that I could stand. My nightgown was a mess, and I was a bit dizzy, but aside from that I was fine.

"'Thank you,' I said to him. I didn't know what else to say. He had golden hair that gleamed in the light like nothing I'd ever seen before. And he was tall, the tallest man I'd ever seen, and very handsome."

She smiled at the memory. I rubbed at the goose bumps that had jumped up along my arms. I tried to picture this tall, fine-looking guy with shiny blond hair, like some kind of Brad Pitt sweeping in to rescue my mom. I frowned. The image made me uneasy, and I couldn't put my finger on why.

"He said, 'You're welcome, Margaret,'" Mom said.

"How did he know your name?"

"I wondered that myself. I asked him. He told me that he was a friend of my father's. They served together, he said. And he said that he'd been watching me from the day that I was born."

"Whoa. Like your own personal guardian angel."

"Exactly. Like my guardian angel," Mom said, nodding. "Although he wouldn't call himself that, of course."

I waited for her to go on.

"That's what he was, Clara. I want you to understand. He was an angel."

"Right," I said. "An angel. Like with wings and everything, I'm sure."

"I didn't see his wings until later, but yes."

She looked dead serious.

"Uh-huh," I said. I pictured the angel in the stained-glass window at church, wearing a halo and purple robes, huge golden wings fanned out behind him. "Then what happened?"

This really can't get any weirder, I thought.

And then it did.

"He told me that I was special," she said.

"Special how?"

"He said that my father was an angel and my mother human, and I was Dimidius, which means half."

I laughed. I couldn't help it. "Come on. You're kidding, right?"

"No." She looked at me steadily. "It's not a joke, Clara. It's the truth."

I stared at her. The thing was, I trusted her. More than anybody. As far as I knew, she'd never lied to me before, not even those little white lies that so many parents tell their kids to get them to behave or believe in the tooth fairy or whatever. She was my mom, sure, but she was also my best friend. Cheesy but true. And now she was telling me something crazy, something impossible, and she was looking at me like everything depended on my reaction.

"So you're saying . . . you're saying that you're half angel," I said slowly.

"Yes."

"Mom, really, come on." I wanted her to laugh and tell me that the angel stuff was some kind of dream she had, like in *The Wizard of Oz* where Dorothy wakes up and finds out the whole Oz thing was a big, colorful hallucination from getting conked on the head. "So then what happened?"

"He brought me back to Earth. He helped me find my grandmother, who was by that point hysterical, convinced I'd been crushed. And when the fires burned through our neighborhood, he helped us evacuate to Golden Gate Park. He stayed with us for three days, and then I didn't see him again for years."

I was quiet, bothered by the details of her story. About

a year before, my class had gone on a field trip to a San Francisco museum because they opened up a new exhibit about the great San Francisco earthquake. We'd looked at all the pictures of the broken buildings, the cable cars thrown off their tracks, the blackened skeletons of the burned up houses. We'd listened to old recordings of people who'd been there, their voices sharp and quivery as they described the terrible disaster.

Everybody had been making such a huge deal out of it that year because it was the hundred-year anniversary of when the quake had happened.

"You said there were fires?" I asked.

"Terrible fires. My grandmother's house burned to the ground."

"And *when* was this?"

"It was April," she said. "1906."

I felt like I was going to throw up. "That would make you what, a hundred and ten?"

"A hundred and sixteen, this year."

"I don't believe you," I stammered.

"I know it's hard."

I stood up. Mom reached for my hand, but I jerked it away. Hurt flashed in her eyes. She stood up too and took a step back, giving me some space, nodding slightly as if she completely understood what I was going through. Like she knew that she was unraveling everything.

I couldn't get enough air in my lungs.

She was crazy. That was the only explanation that made sense. My mom, who up to that point seemed like the best mother ever, my own personal version of the *Gilmore Girls*, the envy of all my friends with her beautiful auburn hair and fabulous dewy skin and quirky sense of humor, was actually a raving lunatic.

"What are you doing? Why are you telling me this?" I asked, blinking back furious tears.

"Because you need to know that you're special, too."

I stared at her incredulously.

"I'm special," I repeated. "Because if you're a half angel then that would make me what, a quarter angel?"

"Quarter angels are called Quartarius."

"I want to go home now," I said dully. I needed to call Dad. He might know what to do. I needed to find my mom some help.

"I wouldn't have believed it either," she said. "Not without proof."

At first I thought that the sun must have come out from behind the clouds, suddenly brightening the ledge where we stood looking out, but then I understood, slowly, that this light was stronger than that. I turned and shielded my eyes from the sight of my mom with light beaming off her. It was like looking at the sun, so intense my eyes watered. Then she dimmed slightly and I saw that she had wings—enormous snowy wings unfurling behind her.

"This is glory," she said, and I understood the words she

said even though she wasn't speaking English, but a strange language like two notes of music played on every syllable, so eerie and alien it made the hairs stand up on the back of my neck.

"Mom," I breathed helplessly.

Her wings extended like they were literally catching the air and pushed down once. The sound they made was like a single heartbeat low in the earth. My hair blew back with the force. She lifted off the ground slowly, impossibly graceful and light, still glowing all over. Then she suddenly shot out over the tree line, tucking her body up and moving fast across the entire length of the valley until she was only a bright speck on the horizon. I was left stunned and alone, the rock ledge empty and silent, darker now that she wasn't there to light it.

"Mom!" I called.

I watched her circle around and glide her way back to me, more slowly this time. She swept right up where the mountain dropped off and hovered, treading the air gently.

"I think I believe you," I said.

Her eyes sparkled.

For some reason I couldn't stop crying.

"Honey," she said, "it's going to be all right."

"You're an angel," I gasped through the tears. "And that means that I—"

I couldn't get the words out.

"That means you're part angel, too," she said.

That night I stood in the middle of my bedroom with the door locked and willed my wings to appear. Mom had assured me that I'd be able to summon them, in time, and even use them to fly. I couldn't imagine. It was too wild. I stood in front of the full-length mirror in my cami and underwear and thought of the Victoria's Secret models in the Angel commercials, their wings curled sexily around them. No wings appeared. I wanted to laugh at the ridiculousness of the whole idea. Me, with wings sprouting from my shoulder blades. Me, part angel.

The thing about my mother being a half angel made total sense—as much as my mother being some kind of supernatural being made sense, anyway. She'd always seemed suspiciously beautiful to me. Unlike me with my brooding stubbornness, my flares of temper, my sarcasm, she was so graceful and even-tempered. Perfect to the point of being irritating. I couldn't name one flaw.

Unless you count lying to me for my entire life, I thought, allowing myself a flash of bitterness. Shouldn't there be some kind of rule, anyway, that angels can't lie?

Only she hadn't actually lied. Not once had she ever said to me, "You know what? You're *not* different from other people." She'd always told me exactly the opposite, in fact. She'd always said I was special. I'd just never believed her until now.

"You're better at things," she'd told me as we stood at the

top of Buzzards Roost. "Stronger, faster, smarter. Haven't you noticed?"

"Um, no," I said quickly.

But that wasn't true. I'd always had a sense that I was different from other people. Mom has a video of me walking when I was only seven months old. I learned to read by the age of three. I was always the first in my class to master the multiplication tables and memorize the fifty states, that kind of thing. Plus I was good at the physical stuff. I was fast and quick on my feet. I could jump high and throw hard. Everybody always wanted me on their team when we played games in PE.

Still, I wasn't like a child prodigy or anything. I wasn't exceptional at any one thing. As a toddler I didn't golf like Tiger Woods, or write my own symphonies by age five, or play competitive chess. Generally, things just came a little easier for me than they did for other kids. I noticed, sure, but I never really gave it much thought. If anything, I'd assumed I was better at stuff because I didn't spend too much time sitting around watching crap on TV. Or because my mom is one those parents who made me practice, and study, and read books.

Now I didn't know what to think. Everything was falling into place. And out of place, at the same time.

Mom smiled. "So often we only do what we think is expected of us," she said. "When we are capable of so much more."

At that point, I got so dizzy that I had to sit down. And

Mom had started talking again, telling me the basics. Wings: check. Stronger, faster, smarter: check. Capable of so much more. Something about languages. And there were a couple rules: *Don't tell Jeffrey—he's not old enough. Don't tell humans— they won't believe you and even if they did, they couldn't handle it.* My neck still tingled when I remembered the way she'd said "humans," like the word suddenly didn't apply to us. Then she had spoken about purpose and how, soon enough, I'd receive mine. It was important, she'd said, but it wasn't something she could easily explain. After that she'd basically shut up and stopped answering my questions. There were some things, she'd told me, that I had to learn over time. By experience. And then there were other things I didn't need to know quite yet.

"Why didn't you tell me all this before?" I'd asked her.

"Because I wanted you to live a normal life for as long as you could," she'd answered. "I wanted you to be a normal girl."

Now I would never be normal again. That much was clear.

I looked at my reflection in the bedroom mirror. "Okay," I said. "Show me . . . *the wings!*"

Nothing.

"Faster than a speeding bullet!" I announced to the reflection, striking my best Superman pose. Then my smile in the mirror faded and the girl on the other side stared back at me skeptically.

"Come on," I said, spreading my arms. I rotated my shoulders forward so that my shoulder blades stuck out and squeezed my eyes shut and thought hard about wings. I imagined them erupting out of me, piercing the skin, unfolding themselves behind me the way that Mom's had on the mountaintop. I opened my eyes.

Still no wings.

I sighed and flopped down on my bed. I switched off the lamp. There were glow-in-the-dark stars on my ceiling, which seemed so silly now, so juvenile. I glanced over at my alarm clock. It was after midnight. School tomorrow. I had to make up a spelling test I'd missed in third period, which seemed even more ridiculous.

"Quartarius," I said, my mom's name for a quarter angel.

Q-U-A-R-T-A-R-I-U-S. Clara is a Quartarius.

I thought about my mom's strange language. Angelic, she'd called it. So uncanny and beautiful, like notes of a song.

"Show me my wings," I said.

My voice sounded strange that time, like there were other higher and lower echoes around my words. I gasped.

I could speak it.

And then I felt my wings under me, lifting me upward slightly, one folded beneath the other. They stretched nearly to my heels, glowing white even in the darkness.

"Holy crap!" I exclaimed, then clapped both of my hands over my mouth.

Very slowly, afraid that I'd make the wings go away again,

I got up and turned on the light. Then I stood in front of the bedroom mirror and looked at my wings for the first time. They were real—real wings with real feathers, weighty and tingling and absolute proof that what happened earlier with my mom was no joke. They were so beautiful it made my chest tight to look at them.

Gently, I touched them. They were warm, alive. I could move them, I found, the same way I could move my arms. Like they were truly a part of me, an extra set of limbs that I'd been oblivious to my whole life up to now. I would have guessed that I had a good ten- to twelve-foot wingspan, but it was hard to be sure. All that wing simply didn't fit in the mirror.

Wingspan, I thought, shaking my head. I have a wingspan. This is insane.

I examined the feathers. Some were very long, smooth and sharp, others softer, more rounded. The shortest feathers, the ones closest to my body where my wings connected at the shoulder, were small and downy, about the size of my thumb. I grabbed one of them and pulled until it came free, which stung so fiercely my eyes teared up. I gazed intently at that feather in my hand, trying to get my head around the fact that it came from me. For a moment it just lay there in my palm, and then, slowly, it started to dissolve, like it was evaporating into the air, until there was nothing left.

I had wings. I had feathers. I had angel blood in me.

What happens now? I wondered. I learn to fly? I dangle from a cloud strumming a harp? I'll receive messages from God? Dread uncurled itself in my gut. Our family was hardly what you'd call religious, but I'd always believed in God. But I was finding out then that there was a big difference between believing in God and knowing that he exists and apparently has some great master plan for my life. It was pretty freaky, to say the least. My understanding of the universe and my place in it had been turned completely upside down in less than twenty-four hours.

I didn't know how to make the wings go away again, so I folded them against my back as tightly as I could and lay down on my bed, angling my arms so I could feel the wings underneath me. The house was quiet. It felt like everyone else on the Earth was asleep. Everyone else was the same, and I had changed. All I could do that night was lie there with this knowledge, amazed and frightened, stroking the feathers under me gently, until I fell asleep.

5

HOT BOZO

Christian and I only have one class together, so catching his attention is no easy task. Every day I try to pick my seat in British History so there's a chance that he'll sit next to me. And so far in the span of two weeks, the stars align exactly three times and he ends up in the desk next to mine. I smile and say hello. He smiles back and says hi. For a moment, an undeniable force seems to draw us together like magnets. But then he opens his notebook or checks his cell phone under his desk, signifying that our *Nice weather we're having* chit-chat is over. It's like, in those few crucial seconds, one of the magnets gets flipped around and pulls him away from me. He's not rude or anything; he just isn't all that interested in getting to know me. And why should he be? He has no idea the future that awaits us.

So for an hour each day I secretly watch him, trying to memorize everything I can, unsure of what might be useful to me someday. He likes to wear button-down dress shirts with the sleeves rolled casually to his elbow and the same version of Seven jeans in slightly different shades of black or blue. He uses notebooks made from recycled paper and writes with a green ballpoint pen. He almost always knows the right answer when Mr. Erikson calls on him, and if he doesn't he makes a joke about it, which means that he's smart plus humble plus funny. He likes Altoids. Every so often he reaches into his back pocket for the little silver tin and pops a mint into his mouth. To me that says he expects to be kissed.

On that note, Kay meets him right outside class every day. Like she saw the way the new girl looked at her man that first day in the cafeteria, and she never wants him vulnerable to that again. So all I have are the precious pre-class minutes, and so far nothing I've done or said has elicited a significant response from Christian.

But tomorrow is T-Shirt Day. I need a shirt that will start a conversation.

"Don't stress about it," says Wendy after school as I parade a line of T-shirts in front of her. She's sitting on the floor of my room by the window, legs curled under her, the very picture of the BFF helping to make a huge fashion decision.

"Should it be a band?" I ask. I hold out a black tee from a Dixie Chicks tour.

"Not that one."

"Why?"

"Trust me."

I pick up one of my favorites, forest green with a print of Elvis on it that I got on a trip to Graceland a few years before. Young Elvis, dreamy Elvis, bending over his guitar.

Wendy makes a noncommittal noise.

I hold up a hot-pink shirt that reads, EVERYONE LOVES A CALIFORNIA GIRL. This could be the winner, a chance to play up what Christian and I have in common. But it will also clash with my orange hair.

Wendy scoffs. "I think my brother is planning on wearing a shirt that says, 'Go back to California.'"

"Shocker. What's his deal with Californians, anyway?"

She shrugs. "It's a long story. Basically my grandpa owned the Lazy Dog Ranch, and now some rich Californian owns it. My parents only manage it for him, and Tucker has rage issues. Plus, you insulted Bluebell."

"Bluebell?"

"Around these parts, you can't disrespect a man's truck without dire consequences."

I laugh. "Well, he should get over himself. He tried to get me burned at the stake in Brit History yesterday. Here I am minding my own business, taking notes like a good little girl, and out of the blue Tucker raises his hand and accuses me of being a witch."

"Sounds like something Tucker would do," admits Wendy.

"Everybody had to vote on it. I barely escaped with my nun's life. Obviously I'll have to return the favor."

Christian, I remember happily, voted against burning me. Of course his vote doesn't count much because he's a serf. But still, he didn't want to see me dead, even in theory. That has to count for something.

"You know that'll just encourage him, right?" Wendy says.

"Eh, I can handle your brother. Besides, there's some kind of prize for the students who can last the whole semester. And I'm a survivor."

Now it's Wendy's turn to laugh. "Yeah, well, so is Tucker."

"I can't believe you shared a womb with him."

She smiles. "There are definitely moments I can't believe it either," she says. "But he's a good guy. He just hides it well sometimes."

She gazes out the window, her cheeks pink. Have I offended her? For all her playful talk about how much of a pain Tucker is, is she sensitive about him? I guess I can understand why. I can make fun of Jeffrey all I want, but if somebody else messes with my little brother, they better watch out.

"So, Elvis then? I'm running out of options here."

"Sure." She leans back against the wall and stretches her arms over her head, as if the conversation has exhausted her. "Nobody really cares."

"Yeah, well, you've been here forever," I remind her. "You're accepted. I feel like if I make one wrong move, I might get chased off school property by an angry mob."

"Oh please. You'll be accepted. I accepted you, didn't I?"

That she had. After two weeks I'm still eating lunch at the Invisibles lunch table.

So far I've identified two basic groups at Jackson Hole High School: the Haves—the pretty people, comprised of the wealthy Jackson Holers, whose parents own restaurants and art galleries and hotels; and the much smaller and less conspicuous Have-Nots—the kids whose parents work for the rich Jackson Holers. To see the great divide between these groups, you only have to look from Kay, in all her coiffed perfection and French-tipped manicured fingernails, to Wendy, who, though undeniably pretty, usually wears her sun-streaked hair in a simple braid down her back, and her fingernails are polish free and sports clipped.

So where do I fit in?

I'm quickly starting to figure out that our large house with a mountain view means that we have the big bucks, money Mom never mentioned back in California. Apparently we're loaded. Still, Mom raised us without any idea of wealth. She lived through the Great Depression, after all, insists that Jeffrey and I save a portion of our allowance each week, makes us eat every morsel of food on our plates, darns our socks and mends our clothes, and sets the thermostat to low because we can always put on another sweater.

"Yes, you accepted me, but I'm still trying to figure out why," I say to Wendy. "I think you must be some kind of a freak. Either that or you're trying to convert me to your secret horse religion."

"Darn, you got me," she says theatrically. "You thwarted my evil plan."

"I knew it!"

I like Wendy. She's quirky and kind, and just solidly good people. And she's saved me from being labeled as a freak or a loner, as well as from the sting of missing my friends back in Cali. When I call them, already it feels like we don't have much to talk about now that I'm out of the loop. It's obvious that they're moving on with their lives without me.

But I can't think about that or whether I'm a Have or Have-Not. My real problem has nothing to do with being rich or poor but instead with the fact that most of the students at Jackson Hole High have known each other since kindergarten. They formed all their cliques years ago. Even though my natural inclination is to stick with the more modest crowd, Christian is one of the pretty people, so that's where I need to be. But there are obstacles. Huge, glaring obstacles. The first being lunch. The popular crowd usually goes off campus. Of course. If you have money, and a car, would you stay on campus and dine on chicken-fried steak? I think not. I have money, and a car, but the first week of class I did a 180 on the icy roads on the way to school. Jeffrey said it was better than Six Flags, that little spin we took in the middle of the highway. Now we ride the bus, which means I can't go off campus for lunch unless someone gives me a ride, and people aren't exactly lining up with offers. Which leads me to obstacle number two: Apparently I'm shy, at least around people who don't pay much attention to me. I never noticed this in California. I never needed to be outgoing at my old school; my friends there kind of naturally gravitated to me. Here it's a whole different story, though, largely because of obstacle number three: Kay Patterson. It's hard to make a lot of friends when the most popular girl in school is giving you the stink-eye.

The next morning Jeffrey wanders into the kitchen wearing his IF IDIOTS COULD FLY, THIS PLACE WOULD LOOK LIKE AN AIRPORT shirt. I know that everyone at school will think it's funny and not be at all offended, because they like him. Things are so easy for him.

"Hey, you feel like driving today?" he asks. "I don't want to walk to the bus stop. It's too cold."

"You feel like dying today?"

"Sure. I like risking my life. Keeps things in perspective."

I chuck my bagel at him and he catches it in midair. I look at the closed door to Mom's office. He smiles hopefully.

"Fine," I tell him. "I'll go warm up the car."

"See," he says as we slowly make our way down the long road to school. "You can handle this driving-on-snow thing. Pretty soon you'll be like a pro."

He's being suspiciously nice.

"Okay, what's up with you?" I ask. "What do you want?"

"I got on the wrestling team."

"How'd you pull that off if tryouts were back in November?"

He shrugs like it's no big deal. "I challenged the best wrestler on the team to a match. I won. It's a small school. They need contenders."

"Does Mom know?"

"I told her I'm on the team. She wasn't thrilled. But she can't forbid us from all school activities, right? I'm tired of this 'we better lay low, or someone will figure out we're different' crap. I mean, it's not like if I win a match people are going to say, who's that kid, he's a really good wrestler, he must be an *angel*."

"Right," I agree uneasily. But then Mom isn't the type to make rules simply because she can. There has to be an explanation for her cautiousness.

"The thing is, I need a ride to some of the practices," he says, shifting in his seat uncomfortably. "Like, all of them."

For a minute it's quiet, the only sound the heater blowing across our legs.

"When?" I ask finally. I brace myself for bad news.

"Five thirty a.m."

"Ha."

"Oh, come on."

"Get Mom to drive you."

"She said that if I was going to insist on being on the wrestling team, I'd have to find my own ride. Take responsibility for myself."

"Well, good luck with that," I laugh.

"Please. It'll just be for a few weeks. Then my buddy Darrin will turn sixteen and he can pick me up."

"I'm sure Mom will love that."

"Come on, Clara. You owe me," he says quietly.

I do owe him. It's because of me that his life is upside down. Not that he seems to be suffering much.

"I don't owe you squat," I say. "But . . . okay. For like six weeks, tops, and then you'll have to get someone else to be your chauffeur."

He looks genuinely happy. We might be on some kind of road to recovery, he and I, like it used to be. Redemption, isn't that what they call it? Six weeks of early mornings doesn't seem like too big a price to pay for him not hating me anymore.

"There's one condition though," I tell him.

"What?"

I put in my Kelly Clarkson CD. "We get to listen to my tunes."

Wendy's wearing a shirt that reads, HORSES ATE MY HOMEWORK.

"You're adorkable," I whisper as we slip into our seats for

91

Honors English. Her current crush, Jason Lovett, is staring in our direction from across the room. "Don't look now, but Prince Charming is totally checking you out."

"Shut up."

"I hope he can ride a horse, since you're supposed to ride off into the sunset together."

The bell rings and Mr. Phibbs hurries to the front of the classroom.

"Ten extra credit points to the first student who can correctly identify the quotation on my shirt," he announces. He stands up straight and rolls his shoulders back so we can read the words written across his chest. We all lean forward to squint at the tiny print: IF SCIENCE TEACHES ANYTHING, IT TEACHES US TO ACCEPT OUR FAILURES, AS WELL AS OUR SUCCESSES, WITH QUIET DIGNITY AND GRACE.

Easy. We only finished the book last week. I look around, but there are no raised hands. Wendy's trying not to make eye contact with Mr. Phibbs so he won't call on her. Jason Lovett is trying to make eye contact with Wendy. Angela Zerbino, who can usually be counted on to chime in with the right answer, is scribbling away in her notebook, probably composing some twisted epic poem about the injustice of her life. Someone in the back of the room blows his nose, and another girl starts to click her fingernails on the top of her desk, but nobody says anything.

"Anyone?" asks Mr. Phibbs, crestfallen. Here he's gone

through all the trouble to have the shirt made, and none of his fine Honors English students can identify a passage from a book they just studied.

Screw it. I raise my hand.

"Miss Gardner," says Mr. Phibbs, brightening.

"Yeah, it's *Frankenstein*, right? The irony in the quote is that Dr. Frankenstein says it moments before he tries to strangle the monster he created. So much for dignity, I guess."

"Yes, it is quite ironic," chuckles Mr. Phibbs. He marks down my ten extra points. I try to look excited by this.

Wendy slips a piece of paper onto my desk. I take a moment to unfold it discreetly.

Smarty-pants, it reads. *Guess who's not here today?* She's drawn a smiley face in the margins. I survey the classroom again. Then I realize that nobody's trying to glare a hole in the back of my head.

Kay isn't here.

I smile. It's going to be a beautiful day.

"I brought the brochure for the veterinary internship that I was telling you about," Wendy tells me as the bell rings for lunch. She follows me as I dart into the hallway, hurry down the stairs, and book it for my locker. She has to jog to keep up.

"Whoa, are you starving, or what?" she laughs as I fumble with my locker combination. "They're serving the meatball sub today. That and the baked potato bar are the best things on the menu all year."

"What?" I'm distracted, scanning the sea of passing faces for a set of familiar green eyes.

"Anyway, the internship is in Montana. It's amazing, really."

There. There's Christian, standing at his locker. No Kay anywhere in sight. He puts on his jacket—black fleece!— and picks up his keys. A jolt of quivery excitement shoots straight to my stomach.

"I'm going out for lunch today," I say quickly, grabbing my parka.

Wendy's mouth shapes into a little O of surprise. "You drove?"

"Yeah. Jeffrey roped me into driving him for the next few weeks."

"Cool," she says. "We could go to Bubba's. Tucker used to work there, so they always give me a discount. That's good eating, trust me. Let me get my coat."

Christian's leaving. I don't have a lot of time.

"Actually, Wen, I have a doctor's appointment," I say unsteadily, hoping she won't ask me which doctor.

"Oh," she says. I can tell that she's not sure if she believes me.

"Yeah, and I don't want to be late." He's almost to the door. I shut my locker and turn toward Wendy, trying not to gaze directly into her eyes. I'm a terrible liar. But there's no time for guilt now. This has to do with my purpose, after all. "I'll see you after school, okay? I've got to go."

Then I practically sprint for the exit.

I follow Christian's silver Avalanche out of the parking lot, keeping a couple of cars between us so I don't appear to be tailing him. He drives to a Pizza Hut a few blocks from school. He climbs down from the cab with a guy I faintly recognize from my English class.

I plan my approach. I'll pretend like I just stumbled into them.

"Oh hey," I murmur to myself in the rearview mirror, feigning surprise. "You guys come here, too? Mind if I sit with you?"

And then he'll look up at me with those swimmable green eyes and say "yeah" in that slightly husky voice, and he'll scoot to make room for me at the table, and the chair will still be warm from the heat of his body. And I'll somehow untie my tongue and say something amazingly witty. And he'll finally see who I really am.

It's not a foolproof plan, but it's the best I can do on such short notice.

The place is packed. I locate Christian at the back, squeezed into a round booth with five other people. There's definitely no room for me, and no way I can casually wander by without making my intentions pathetically obvious. Foiled again.

I find a tiny table in the front corner across from the arcade. I choose the chair facing away from Christian and his pals so they can't see my face, although I'm sure they'll recognize my wild orange hair if they give me more than a cursory glance. I need to come up with a new plan.

As I wait for someone to come take my order, Christian and the other two guys at his table jump up and run to the arcade like little boys out for recess. I suddenly have a clear view of them as they gather around a pinball machine, Christian in the center putting his quarters in. I watch him lean into the machine as he plays, his strong eyebrows pushed together in concentration, his hands flicking rapidly against the sides. He's wearing a long-sleeved navy tee that says, WHAT'S YOUR SIGN? in white letters; then there's a white stripe across the chest with a black diamond symbol, a blue square, and a green circle. I have no idea what it means.

"Oh, man." The other guys grunt like a bunch of sympathetic cavemen as Christian apparently lets the ball slip past the paddles, not just once, but twice, three times. Pinball is clearly not his forte.

"Dude, what's with you today?" says the guy from my English class, Shawn, I think his name is, the one with the unhealthy obsession with his snowboard. "You're off your game, man. Where are the lightning-fast reflexes?"

Christian doesn't answer for a minute—he's still playing. Then he groans and turns away from the machine.

"Hey, I've got a lot on my plate right now," he says.

"Yeah, like making chicken soup for poor widdle Kay," teases the other guy.

Christian shakes his head. "You mock, but women love soup. More than flowers. Trust me."

I try to summon the courage to go talk to him. In California it was a well-known fact that I could play a mean game of pinball. I'll be that cool chick who rocks at video games. That's loads better than showing up at his table like a lost puppy. It's my chance.

"Hey," says Shawn as I'm standing up to go over there. "Isn't that Bozo?"

Who?

"What?" says Christian. "Who's Bozo?"

"You know, the new girl. The one from Cali."

What's sad is that it actually takes a minute for me to understand that he's talking about me. Sometimes it sucks to have supernaturally good hearing.

"She's totally staring at you, dude," says Shawn.

Quickly I look away, the name settling into the pit of my stomach like wet cement. Bozo. As in, the clown. As in, I may never show my face (or my hair) in public again for the rest of my life.

And the hits just keep on coming.

"She's got big eyes, doesn't she? Like an owl," the other guy says. "Hey, maybe she's stalking you, Prescott. I mean, she's hot, but she kind of gives off that crazy chick vibe, don't you think?"

Shawn laughs. "Dude. Hot Bozo. Best nickname ever."

I know he's not trying to be mean to my face; he reasonably assumes that I can't hear him from the other side of the noisy restaurant. But I hear his words like he's speaking into a microphone. A flash of intense heat darts from my head to my toes. My stomach churns. I have to get out of there fast, because the longer I stand there, the more certain I become that one of two things is going to happen: I'm going to puke or I'm going to cry. And I'd rather die than do either in front of Christian Prescott.

"Cut it out, guys," mutters Christian. "I'm sure she's just here getting lunch."

Yes, yes I am. And now I'm leaving. Right now.

British History, thirty minutes later. I've parked myself at the desk farthest away from the door. I try not to think the word *Bozo*. I wish I had a hoodie to pull up over my clown hair.

Mr. Erikson sits on the edge of the table, wearing an oversize black tee that reads, CHICKS DIG HISTORIANS.

"Before we start today, I want to assign you to your partners for the special projects you'll be doing," he announces, opening his grade book. "Together you'll need to choose a topic—anything goes as long as it's related in some way to the history of England, Wales, Ireland, or Scotland—research it thoroughly over the next few months, then you'll present what you've learned to the class."

Someone kicks the back of my chair.

I dare a glance over my shoulder. Tucker. How does this guy always end up behind me?

I ignore him.

He kicks my chair again. Hard.

"What is your problem?" I whisper over my shoulder.

"You."

"Could you please be more specific?"

He grins. I resist the urge to turn around and bash my hefty *Oxford Illustrated History of Britain* textbook across his skull. Instead I go with a classic: "Stop it."

"Is there a problem, Sister Clara?" asks Mr. Erikson.

I contemplate telling him that Tucker's having a hard time keeping his feet to himself. I can feel all the eyes turning toward me, which is the last thing I want to happen. Not today.

"No, just excited about the project," I say.

"Good to be excited about history," says Mr. Erikson. "But try to contain yourself until I've assigned you a partner, okay?"

Just don't pair me with Tucker, I pray, as serious a prayer as I've ever had. I wonder if the prayers of angel-bloods count more than regular people's. Maybe if I close my eyes and wish with all my heart to get paired with Christian, it will miraculously happen. Then we'll have to spend time together after school working on our project, time when Kay can't interfere, time when I can prove to him that I'm no owl-eyed crazy Bozo chick, and I will finally get something right.

Christian, I request to the heavens. *Please,* I add, just to be polite.

Christian gets paired with King Brady.

"Don't forget that you're a serf," says Brady.

"No, sire," replies Christian humbly.

"And last, but certainly not least, I thought Sister Clara and Lady Angela might make a dynamic duo," says Mr. Erikson. "Now please take a few minutes with your partner to plan some time to work on your project."

I try to smile to mask my disappointment.

As usual, Angela is sitting at the front of the class. I drop into the seat next to hers and pull my desk closer.

"Elvis," she says, looking at my tee. "Nice."

"Oh. Thanks. I like yours, too."

Her shirt's a copy of that famous Bouguereau painting of the two little naked angels, the boy angel leaning in to kiss the girl angel on the cheek.

"That's like, *Il Primo Bacio,* right? *The First Kiss*?"

"Yes. My mom drags me off to see her family in Italy every summer. I got this shirt in Rome for two Euros."

"Cool." I don't know what else to say. I examine her shirt more closely. In the painting, the boy angel's wings are tiny and white. Highly unlikely that they'd be able to lift his chubby body off the ground. The girl angel is looking down, like she's not even into the whole kissing thing. She's taller than the boy, leaner, more mature. Her wings are dark gray.

"So, I thought we could meet Monday at my mom's theater, the Pink Garter. There's no show being rehearsed right now so we have a lot of space to work," says Angela.

"Sounds terrific," I say with about a teaspoonful of enthusiasm. "So, after school on Monday?"

"I have orchestra. It gets out around seven. Maybe I could meet you at the Garter at seven thirty?"

"Great," I say. "I'll be there."

She's staring at me. I wonder if she calls me Bozo, too, with her friends, whoever they are.

"You okay?" she asks.

"Yeah, sorry." My face feels hot and tight as a sunburn. I manage another wooden smile. "It's just been one of those days."

That night I dream of the forest fire. It's the same as always: the pines and aspens, the heat, the approaching flames, Christian standing with his back turned watching it. Smoke curls through the air. I walk to him.

"Christian," I call out.

He turns toward me. His eyes capture mine. He opens his mouth to say something. I know what he says will be important, another clue, something crucial to understanding my purpose.

"Do I know you?" he asks.

"We go to school together," I say to remind him.

Nothing.

"I'm in your British History class."

Still not ringing any bells.

"You carried me to the nurse's office on my first day of school. I passed out in the hall, remember?"

"Oh, right, I remember you," he says. "What was your name again?"

"Clara." I don't have time to remind him of my existence. The fire's coming. "I have to get you out of here," I say, grabbing his arm. I don't know what I'm supposed to do. I just know we have to go.

"What?"

"I'm here to save you."

"Save me?" he says incredulously.

"Yes."

He smiles, then puts his fist up to his mouth and laughs into it.

"I'm sorry," he says. "But how could *you* save *me*?"

"It was just a dream," says Mom.

She pours me a cup of raspberry tea and sits down at the kitchen counter, looking serene as ever, if not a bit tired and rumpled, which is only fair since it's four in the morning and her daughter just woke her up freaking out.

"Sugar?" she offers.

I shake my head.

"How do you know it was a dream?" I ask.

"Because it seems like your vision always happens while you're awake. Some of us dream our visions, but not you. And because I have a very hard time believing that Christian wouldn't remember your name."

I shrug. Then, because that's what I always do, I tell her everything. I tell her about the way I feel drawn to Christian and the few times in class when we talked and how I never know what to say. I tell her about Kay, and my brilliant idea to invite myself to lunch at Christian's table, and how it had backfired big-time. And I tell her about Bozo.

"Bozo?" she says with her quiet smile when I'm finally done talking.

"Yeah. Although one guy decided to go with Hot Bozo." I sigh and drink a swallow of tea. It burns my tongue. "I'm a freak."

Mom playfully shoves me. "Clara! They called you hot."

"Um, not exactly," I say.

"Don't go feeling too sorry for yourself. We should think of some other ones."

"Other ones?"

"Other names they could call you. So if you ever hear

them again you'll be prepared with a comeback."

"What?"

"Pumpkinhead."

"Pumpkinhead," I repeat slowly.

"That was a major insult, when I was a kid."

"Back in what, 1900?"

She pours herself some more tea. "I got Pumpkinhead many times. They also called me Little Orphan Annie, which was a popular poem back then. And Maggot. I *hated* Maggot."

It's hard for me to imagine her as a child, let alone one that other kids picked on. It makes me feel slightly (but only slightly) better about being called Bozo.

"Okay, what else you got?"

"Let's see. Carrots. That's another common one."

"Somebody already called me that," I admit.

"Oh, oh—Pippi Longstocking."

"Oh, snap," I laugh. "Bring it on, Matchstick!"

And so on it goes, back and forth until we're both laughing hysterically and Jeffrey appears in the doorway, glaring.

"I'm sorry," Mom says, still giggling wildly. "Did we wake you?"

"No. I have wrestling." He brushes past us to the refrigerator, gets out a carton of orange juice, pours himself a glass, drinks it in about three gulps, and sets it on the counter while we try to simmer down.

I can't help it. I turn to Mom.

"Are you a member of the Weasley family?" I ask.

"Nice one. Ginger Nut," she shoots back.

"What does that even mean? But you, you definitely have gingervitis."

And off we go again like a couple of hyenas.

"You two need to seriously consider cutting back on the caffeine. Don't forget, Clara, you're driving me to practice in like twenty minutes," says Jeffrey.

"You got it, bro."

He goes upstairs. Our laughter finally dies down. I wipe my eyes. My sides hurt.

"You kind of rock, you know that?" I say to Mom.

"This was fun," she says. "It's been too long since I've laughed that hard."

It gets quiet.

"What's Christian like?" she asks then, offhandedly like she's just making small talk. "I know he's gorgeous, and apparently he has a bit of hero complex, but what's he like? You've never told me."

I blush.

"I don't know." I shrug awkwardly. "He's a big mystery, and it feels like it's my job to unlock it. Even his T-shirt today was like a code. It said, 'What's your sign?' and underneath there was a black diamond, a blue square, and a green circle. I have no idea what that's supposed to mean."

"Hmm," says Mom. "That *is* mysterious."

She darts into her office for a few minutes, then emerges smiling with a page she's printed off the internet. My hundred-year-old mother can Google with the best of them.

"Skiing," she announces triumphantly. "The symbols are posted on signs at the top of ski runs to indicate the difficulty of the slope. Black diamond is difficult, blue square's intermediate, and green circle is, supposedly, easy. He's a skier."

"A skier," I say. "See? I didn't even know that. I mean, I know he's left-handed and he wears Obsession and he doodles in the margins of his notebook when he's bored in class. But I don't know him. And he *really* doesn't know me."

"That will change," she says.

"Will it? Am I even supposed to get to know him? Or just save him? I keep asking myself, why? Why him? I mean, people die in forest fires. Maybe not a lot of people, but some do every year, I'm sure. So why am I being sent here to save him? And what if I can't? What happens then?"

"Clara, listen to me." Mom leans forward and takes my hands in hers. Her eyes aren't sparkling anymore. The irises are so dark they are nearly purple. "You aren't being sent on a mission that you don't have the power to accomplish. You have to find that power inside you somewhere, and you have to refine it. You were made for this purpose. And Christian isn't some random boy that you're supposed to encounter for no reason. There is a reason, for all of this."

106

"You think Christian might be important, like he'll be president someday or find the cure for cancer?"

She smiles.

"He's terribly important," she says. "And so are you."

I really want to believe her.

6

A-SKIING I WILL GO

Sunday morning we drive to Teton Village, a big, famous ski resort area a few miles outside Jackson. Jeffrey dozes in the backseat. Mom looks tired, probably from too many late nights working and too many serious discussions with her daughter in the wee hours of the morning.

"We turn before we hit Wilson, right?" she asks, clutching the wheel at the ten and two positions and squinting through the windshield like the sun is hurting her eyes.

"Yeah, it's like Highway 380, on the right."

"It's 390," says Jeffrey, his eyes still closed.

Mom pinches the bridge of her nose, blinks a few times, then adjusts her hands on the steering wheel.

"What's with you today?" I ask.

"Headache. There's a project for work not coming together as I'd planned."

"You're sure working a lot. What kind of project?"

She turns carefully onto Highway 390.

"Now what?" she asks.

I consult the MapQuest directions I printed.

"Just keep going for about five miles until we hit the resort somewhere on the left. We shouldn't be able to miss it."

We drive for a few minutes, past restaurants and business areas, a few dude ranches. Suddenly the ski area opens up on one side of us, the mountain rising behind it cut into big white lanes through the trees, the tram running all the way to the top. It looks crazy steep, all of it. Mount Everest kind of steep.

Jeffrey sits up to get a better look.

"That is one wicked mountain," he says like he can't wait another minute to toss his body down it. He checks his watch.

"Come on, Mom," he says. "Do you have to drive like a grandma?"

"Do you need some money?" asks Mom, ignoring his comment. "I gave Clara some money for lessons."

"I don't need lessons. I just need to get there sometime in the next millennium."

"Lay off, doofus," I say. "We'll get there when we get there. We're like less than a mile now."

"Maybe you should let me out and I could walk. It'd be faster."

"Both of you, be qu—" Mom starts to say, but then we slide on the ice. She hits the brakes and we drift sideways, picking up speed. Mom and I both scream as the car careens off the road and crashes through a snowbank. We come to a stop at the edge of a small field. She takes a deep, shaky breath.

"Hey, you're the one who said we'd love the winters here," I remind her.

"Perfect," says Jeffrey sarcastically. He unbuckles his seat belt and opens the door. The car is resting in about two feet of snow. He glances at his watch again. "That's just perfect."

"What, you have an important meeting you have to get to?" I ask.

He shoots me a disgusted look.

"Oh, I get it," I say. "You're meeting up with someone. What's her name?"

"None of your business."

Mom sighs and puts the car in reverse. The car moves back about a foot and then the tires spin. She pulls forward and tries again. No luck. We're stuck. In a snowbank. In plain sight of the ski hill. It really can't get more humiliating.

"I could get out and push," says Jeffrey.

"Just wait," Mom says. "Someone will come."

Right on cue, a truck pulls off to the side of the road. A guy gets out and tromps through the snow toward us. Mom rolls down the window.

"Well, well, well, what have we here?" he asks.

My mouth falls open. Tucker leans in the window, grinning from ear to ear.

Oh yes, it can get more humiliating.

"Hey, Carrots," he says. "Jeff."

He nods to my brother like the two are best buds. Jeffrey nods back. Mom smiles up at him.

"I don't think we've met," she says. "I'm Maggie Gardner."

"Tucker Avery," he says.

"You're Wendy's brother."

"Yes, ma'am."

"We could really use some help," she says sweetly as I slump down in the seat and wish I was dead.

"Sure thing. Just sit tight."

He jogs back to his truck and returns with tow cables, which he hooks to the underside of the car quickly, like he's done this kind of thing a million times before. He gets back in his truck, pulls up behind us, and attaches the cables to his truck. Then he tows us smoothly onto the road. The whole thing takes all of five minutes.

Mom gets out of the car. She gestures for me to do the same. I look at her like she's crazy, but she persists.

"You need to say thank you," she says under her breath.

"Mom."

"Now."

"All right." I get out. Tucker is kneeling in the snow unhooking the cable from his truck. He looks up at me and smiles again, revealing a dimple in his left cheek.

"In case you couldn't tell, that was my rusty truck towing you out of a snowbank," he says.

"Thank you so much," says my mom. She looks pointedly at me.

"Yes, thank you," I say through gritted teeth.

"Don't mention it," he says cordially, and in that moment I see that Tucker can be charming when he wants to be.

"And tell Wendy we said hello," Mom says.

"Will do. Nice to meet you, ma'am." If he'd been wearing his cowboy hat, he would have tipped it at her. Then he gets back in his truck and drives off without another word.

I look toward the ski hill, the same direction Tucker went, rethinking the whole skiing thing entirely.

But Christian's a skier, I remind myself. So a-skiing I will go.

"That Tucker seems like a nice young man," says Mom as we walk back to the car. "How come you've never told me about him before?"

Fifteen minutes later I'm standing in the area where students are supposed to meet their instructors, which is teeming with little, screaming kids wearing helmets and goggles. I feel completely out of my element, like an astronaut about to take his first steps on an alien planet. I'm wearing rented skis, rented ski boots that feel weird and tight and make me walk funny, plus every other kind of snow gear my mom was able to convince me to put on. I drew the line at goggles, and I stuck the unflattering wool hat into my jacket pocket, but from the neck down every inch of me is covered and padded. I don't know if I can move, let alone ski. My instructor, who's supposed to meet me at nine a.m. sharp, is already five minutes late. I just watched my pain-in-the-butt brother jump on the ski lift like it's no big deal and carve his way down a few minutes later like he was born on a snowboard, a blond girl by his side. Life sucks. That and my feet are cold.

"Sorry I'm late," says a rumbly voice from behind me. "I had to drag some Californians out of a snowbank."

It can't be true. Fate is not so cruel. I pivot to meet Tucker's blue eyes.

"Lucky for them," I say.

His lips twitch like he's trying not to laugh. He seems like he's in a good mood.

"So you go around pulling idiots out of the snow and teaching them how to ski," I say.

He shrugs. "It pays for the season pass."

"Are you any good at it?"

"Pulling idiots out of the snow? I'm the best."

"Ha-ha. You're hilarious. No—teaching them to ski."

"I guess you'll find out."

He starts right into a lesson on how to balance, position my skis, and turn and stop. He treats me like I'm any other student, which is great. I even relax a little. It all seems fairly simple when you break it down.

But then he tells me to get on the rope tow.

"It's easy. Just hold on to it and let it tug you up the hill. When you get to the top, let go."

He apparently thinks I'm a moron. I make my way awkwardly over to the line, then struggle up to the edge, where the greasy black cable drags through the snow. I reach down and grab it. It jerks at my arms, and I lurch forward and almost fall, but somehow I manage to get my skis in line and straighten up and let it tug me up the hill. I dart a quick look over my shoulder to see if Tucker is laughing. He's not. He looks like some Olympic judge getting ready to mark a scorecard. Or some guy about to witness a horrific accident.

At the top of the hill I drop the cable and struggle to get away before the next kid plows into me. Then I stand for a moment looking down. Tucker waits at the bottom. It's not a steep slope, and there are no trees to crash into, which is comforting. But behind Tucker the slope keeps dropping, past the ski lift, the lodge, the small shops lined up in a path to the parking lot. I have a sudden picture of myself lying halfway underneath a car.

"Come on!" Tucker shouts. "The snow won't bite."

He thinks I'm scared. Okay, I *am* scared, but the idea of Tucker thinking I'm chicken makes my jaw tighten in determination. I position my skis in a careful V, the way he showed me. Then I push off.

The cold air rushes my face, catches my hair and flutters it behind me like a banner. I put a bit of pressure on one foot and glide slowly to the left. I try again, this time arcing to the right. Back and forth, I make my way down the hill. I go straight for a while, picking up some speed, then try again. Easy. When I get closer to Tucker, I put my weight evenly on both feet and push the V wider, the way he taught me. I stop. Piece of cake.

"Maybe I could try it the other way," I say. "With my skis straight."

He stares at me, frowning, good mood apparently gone.

"I guess you want me to believe that this is your first time skiing," he says.

I look into his frowning face, startled. Surely he didn't expect me to crash on that little hill? I glance back at the other beginners. They resemble a flock of confused ducklings, just trying not to bump into each other. They don't crash so much as flop over.

I should lie to Tucker now, tell him I've done this before. That'd be the low-profile thing to do. But I don't want to lie to another Avery this week.

"Should I try it again?"

"Yeah," he says. "I think you should try it again."

This time he rides up behind me, and when I ski down, he's right beside me. He makes me so nervous that I almost fall a couple of times, but I keep thinking about how humiliating it would be to crash and burn in front of Tucker, and manage to stay upright. When we get to the bottom he demands that we go again, this time skiing parallel style, which I like much better. It's more graceful. It's fun.

"I've been teaching this class for two years," he says when we get to the bottom around the fifth time, "and this is the first time anyone has ever made it through the whole hour without falling down once."

"I have good balance," I explain. "I used to dance. Back in California. Ballet."

He stares at me with narrowed eyes, like he can't figure out why I'd want to lie about something like that, unless I'm trying to show off. Or maybe he's stumped at the idea that some California yuppie could be good at something other than shopping.

"Well, that's it," he says abruptly. "End of lesson."

He turns toward the lodge.

"What should I do now?" I call after him.

"Try a chairlift," he says, and then he skis away.

For a while I stand outside the line for the beginner's chairlift and watch people get on. They make it seem easy enough. It's all about timing. I wish that Tucker hadn't been such a jerk. It would be nice to get some instruction for this part.

I decide to go for it. I get in line. When I near the front, an employee punches a hole in my ticket.

"You alone?" he asks.

"Yeah."

"Single!" he shouts toward the back of the line. "We have a single here!"

So embarrassing. I suddenly wish I had goggles.

"Okay," says the ski lift guy, waving somebody forward. When the guy gestures at me I shuffle up to the line they've drawn in the snow, position my skis, look over my shoulder, and nervously watch the chair swing toward me. It hits the back of my legs hard. I sit, and the chair lifts me into the air. Then I'm rising quickly up the mountainside, swaying gently. I breathe a sigh of relief.

"That bad, huh?"

I turn to see who I'm sitting with. All my breath leaves me in a rush.

I'm riding the chairlift with Christian Prescott.

"Hi," I say.

"Hey, Clara," he replies.

He remembers my name. It was just a dream. Just a stupid, stupid dream.

"Nice day for the slopes, huh?" he says.

"Yeah." My heart's drumming a crazy rhythm in my ears. He seems perfectly at home on the chairlift. With his forest green ski jacket and black ski pants, a black hat with goggles pushed up onto his head, and some kind of fuzzy neck warmer, he looks like the poster boy for skiing. His eyes are gorgeous against the jacket, a deep emerald green. He's so close I can feel the heat coming off him.

"Didn't I see you at Pizza Hut the other day?" he asks.

He had to bring that up. Heat rushes to my face. He could be looking at my hair right now thinking Bozo, Bozo the clown. Why oh why didn't I wear a stupid hat over my stupid hair?

"Yeah, maybe," I stammer. "I mean, I was there, I—maybe you saw me. I guess you saw me, right? I mean, I saw you."

"You should have come over and said hello."

"I guess I should have." I glance down at the ground rushing by beneath us, hoping for a topic of conversation. He's wearing fancy black skis with a kind of curve to them, which seem a lot different than mine.

"You don't snowboard?" I ask.

"I can board," he says. "But I ski more. I'm on the race team. You want a Jolly Rancher?"

"What?"

He sticks his poles under his thigh and takes off his gloves. Then he unzips his jacket pocket, reaches in, and takes out a handful of hard candies.

"I always keep these in my pockets for skiing," he says.

My mouth is suddenly incredibly dry. "Sure, I'll have one."

"Red hot or cherry?"

"Red hot," I say.

He unwraps a candy and pops it in his mouth. Then he holds another out to me. I can't even pick it up with my heavy glove.

118

"I'll get it." He unwraps the candy and leans toward me. I try to swipe my hair out of my face.

"Open up," he says, holding up the candy.

I open my mouth. Very carefully, he lays the candy on my tongue. Our eyes meet for a moment. When I close my mouth, he leans back against the chair.

"Thanks," I say around the candy. I cough. The candy is surprisingly hot. I wish I'd asked for cherry.

"You're welcome." He puts his gloves back on.

"So do you have to practice skiing every weekend if you're on the race team?" I ask.

"I come up here on the weekends to ski for fun, mostly, and races, when they hold them here. During the week, I practice nights up at Snow King."

"Wow, you can ski at night?"

He laughs.

"Sure. They have lights set up along the runs. I love it at night, actually. It's not so crowded. It's quiet. You can see the lights from town. It's beautiful."

"Sounds beautiful."

Neither of us says anything for a while. He knocks his skis together gently, sending a shower of snow down onto the hill below us. It's surreal, dangling in midair with him on the side of a mountain, seeing him up close, hearing his voice.

"Snow King's that ski area right inside Jackson Hole?" I ask.

"Yeah. It has only five runs, but it's a good hill to practice on. And when we race for the State Championships the kids from school can watch us from the parking lot."

I'm about to say something about wanting to see him race, but that's when I notice that the chair is approaching a little hut on the side of the mountain, and the skiers are getting off.

"Oh crap."

"What?" asks Christian.

"I don't know how to get off this thing."

"You don't—"

"This is my first day skiing," I say, panic rising in my throat. The little hut is getting closer and closer. "What do I do?"

"Keep the tips of your skis up," he says quickly. "We'll come up onto the mound. When it flattens out, stand up and get over to the side. You have to do it pretty fast, to get out of the way of the people coming behind you."

"Oh man. I don't know if this was such a great idea."

"Relax," he says. "I'll help you."

The chair is seconds away from the little hut. Every muscle in my body feels tense.

"Put your poles on," he instructs.

You can do this, I tell myself, sticking my fingers through the slots in the ski poles and gripping them tightly. *You're an angel-blood. Stronger, faster, smarter. Use it, for once.*

"Tips up," says Christian.

I lift my skis. We skim up a short embankment and then, just like he said, we slide onto level ground.

"Stand up!" orders Christian.

I struggle to my feet. The chair hits me in the calves, nudging me forward.

"Now push yourself over to the side," he says, already skiing away to the left. I try to follow him, planting my poles in the snow and pushing with all my strength. Too late I realize that he meant for me to go to the right while he went left. He turns to check how I'm doing just as I shoot toward him, already off balance. My skis slip on top of his. I flail, and one of my arms catches his shoulder.

"Whoa!" he yells, trying to steady himself, but there's no way. We slide for a ways and then go down in a heap.

"I am so sorry," I say. I'm facedown on top of him. My red-hot Jolly Rancher is lying next to his head in the snow. His hat and goggles are missing. My skis have come off and my poles are gone. I struggle to get off him, but I can't seem to get my feet under me.

"Hold still," he says firmly.

I stop moving. He puts his arms around me and rolls us gently to one side. Then he reaches down, pops off the ski that's still under my leg, and rolls away from me. I lie on my back in the snow, wanting to dig myself a hole and crawl into it for the rest of the school year. Possibly forever. I close my eyes.

"You okay?" he says.

I open my eyes. He's leaning over me, his face close to mine. I can smell the cherry candy on his breath. Behind him a cloud shifts from in front of the sun, the sky brightening in that way it has of opening up. I suddenly feel aware of everything: my heart pumping blood through my veins, the snow slowly beginning to melt under my body, the needles on the trees shifting in the breeze, the mixed smell of pine and Christian's cologne and something that could be ski wax, the rattling of the chairs as they pass over the poles of the ski lift.

And Christian, with hat hair, laughing at me with his eyes, a breath away.

I don't think of the fire then, or that he's my purpose. I don't think about saving him. I think, What would it be like to kiss him?

"I'm fine."

"Here." He brushes a strand of my hair out of my face, his bare hand skimming my cheek. "That was fun," he says. "Haven't done that in a while."

At first I think he means the thing with my hair, but then I realize he means falling.

"I guess I'm going to have to practice the chairlift thing," I say.

He helps me sit up.

"Maybe a little," he says. "You did great for a first timer,

122

though. If I hadn't gotten in your way you totally would have made it."

"Right. So you're the problem."

"Totally." He glances up at the guy sitting in the little hut, who's talking into a phone, probably calling the ski police to come drag me off the mountain.

"She's okay, Jim," Christian calls to the man. Then he locates my skis and poles, which luckily haven't gone very far.

"Were you wearing a hat?" he asks, finding his own and tugging it back onto his head. He readjusts his goggles on top of it. I shake my head, then reach up and gingerly touch my hair, which has once again rejected the ponytail elastic and hangs down in long strands around my shoulders, clumped with snow.

"No," I answer. "I, no, I didn't have a hat."

"They say ninety percent of your body heat escapes through your head," he says.

"I'll try to remember that."

He lines up my skis in front of me and kneels to help me step into them. I hold on to his shoulder for balance.

"Thanks," I murmur, looking down at him.

Once again, my hero. And here I'm supposed to be the one saving him.

"No problem," he says, looking up. His eyes narrow, like he's studying my face. A snowflake lands on his cheek and melts. His expression changes, as if he suddenly remembered something. He gets up and snaps into his own skis quickly.

"Over that direction there's a beginner's run, something not too steep," he says, pointing behind me. "It's called Pooh Bear."

"Oh, great." My sign is a green circle.

"I'd stay to help but I'm already late for running the race course farther up the mountain," he says. "Do you think you'll be okay getting down?"

"Sure," I say quickly. "I was doing fine on the bunny hill. I didn't fall once today. Until now, that is. How do you go farther up the mountain?"

"There's another chair, down there." He gestures to where, sure enough, another bigger chairlift is humming away, taking people up the side of an impossibly steep-looking rise. "And another one, after that."

"Crazy," I say. "We could go all the way to the top."

"I could. But it's not for beginners."

The moment is definitely over.

"Right. Well, thanks again," I say awkwardly. "For everything."

"Don't mention it." He's already moving away, skiing his way toward the other chairlift. "See you around, Clara," he calls over his shoulder.

I watch him ski down to the other chairlift and recline gracefully into the seat when it comes. The chair sways back and forth as it rises through the snowy air up the side of the mountain. I watch until his green jacket disappears.

"Yes, you will," I whisper.

It's a big step, our first real conversation. At the thought my chest swells with an emotion so powerful I feel tears prick my eyes. It's embarrassing.

It's something like hope.

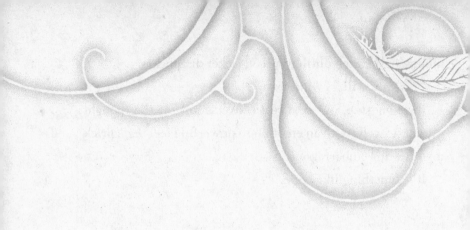

7

FLOCK TOGETHER

Monday around seven thirtyish, I drive to the Pink Garter to meet Angela Zerbino. The theater is completely dark. I knock but no one comes to the door. I get out my cell and then realize that I never got Angela's phone number. I knock again, harder. The door opens so fast that I jump. A short, wiry-thin woman with long, black hair peers up at me. She looks irritated.

"We're closed," she says.

"I'm here to see Angela."

Her eyebrows shoot up.

"You're a friend of Angela's?"

"Uh—"

"Come in," says the woman, holding the door open.

It's uncomfortably quiet inside, and it smells like popcorn and sawdust. I look around. An ancient-looking cash register sits on top of a glass snack counter with rows of candy lined up inside. The walls are decorated with framed posters of the theater's past productions, which are mostly cowboy themed.

"Nice place," I say, and then I bump into a pole with a velvet rope and nearly send the whole line of them crashing to the floor. I manage to right the pole before it starts a chain reaction. I cringe and look at the woman, who's watching me with a strange, unreadable expression. She looks like Angela except for the eyes, which are dark brown instead of Angela's amber color, and she has deep wrinkles around her mouth that make her look older than her body suggests. She reminds me of a Gypsy in one of those old movies.

"I'm Clara Gardner," I say nervously. "I'm doing a project with Angela for school."

She nods. I notice that she's wearing a large gold cross around her neck, the kind that has the body of Jesus draped across it.

"You can wait back here," she says. "She won't be long."

I follow her through an archway into the theater itself. It's pitch-black. I hear her moving off to one side; then a pool of light appears on the stage.

"Have a seat anywhere," she says.

Once my eyes adjust, I see that the theater is filled with round tables covered in white tablecloths. I wander over to the nearest one and sit down.

"When do you think Angela might get here?" I ask, but the woman is gone.

I've been waiting for maybe five minutes, completely creeped out by this point, when Angela comes bursting through a side door.

"Wow, sorry," she says. "Orchestra went late."

"What do you play?"

"Violin."

It's easy to imagine her with a violin tucked under her chin, sawing away on some mournful Romanian tune.

"Do you live here?" I ask.

"Yep. In an apartment upstairs."

"Just your mom and you?"

She studies her hands. "Yes."

"I don't live with my dad either," I say. "Just my mom and brother."

She kind of examines me for a couple seconds. "Why did you move here?" she asks. She sits down in the chair across from mine and stares at me with solemn honey-colored eyes. "I assume that you didn't actually burn your old school to the ground."

"Excuse me?" I say.

She looks at me sympathetically. "That's the rumor going around today. You mean you didn't know that your family had to flee California because of your delinquent behavior?"

I'd laugh if I wasn't so horrified.

"Don't worry," she says. "It will blow over. Kay's rumors

always do. I'm impressed by how quickly you were able to get on her bad side."

"Uh, thanks," I say, smirking. "And, my obvious delinquency aside, we moved because of my mom. She was getting sick of California. She loves the mountains, and she decided she wanted to raise us somewhere where we couldn't always see the air we breathed, you know?"

She smiles at my joke, but it's just to be polite. A pity smile.

Another long silence.

"Okay, so enough with the chitchat," I say restlessly. "Let's talk about our project. I was thinking about the reign of Queen Elizabeth. We could talk about what it was like to be a woman, even a woman with a lot of power, back in the day. A female empowerment kind of project." For some reason I think this will be right up Angela's alley.

"Actually," she says. "I had another idea."

"Okay. Shoot."

"I thought we could do a presentation on the Angels of Mons."

I almost choke. If I'd been drinking water I would have sprayed it all over the table.

"What are the Angels of Mons?" I ask.

"It's a story from World War I. There was this big battle between the Germans and the British, who were badly outnumbered but won. After it was over there was a rumor going around about these phantom men who appeared to help the

British. The mysterious men shot at the Germans with bows and arrows. One version said that the men were standing between the two armies, shining with a kind of unearthly light."

"Interesting," I manage.

"It was a hoax, of course. Some writer made it up and it got out of hand. It's like an early version of UFOs, a crazy story that kept getting told again and again."

"Okay," I say, taking a breath. "Sounds like you have it covered."

I can just picture the look on Mom's face when I tell her that I'm going to do a project on angels for British History.

"I thought it would be interesting for the class," says Angela. "A specific moment in time, like Mr. Erikson suggested. I also think we can relate it to today."

My mind races, trying to think up a tactful way to turn down her idea.

"Yeah, well . . . I did really like the Elizabeth thing, but—" I'm floundering.

She grins.

"What?"

"You should see your face," she says. "You're really freaking out."

"What? No, I'm not."

She leans forward across the table.

"I want to research angels," she says. "But it has to be

British, because it's British History after all. And this is the best British angel story there is. And wouldn't it be crazy if it were true?"

My heart feels like it's fallen into my stomach.

"I thought you said it was a hoax."

"Well, yes. That's what they would have wanted everyone to think, wouldn't they?"

"Who's they?"

"The angel-bloods," she says.

I stand up.

"Clara, sit down. Relax." Then she adds, "I know."

"You know wh—"

"*Sit down*," she says. In Angelic.

My jaw literally drops.

"How did you—?"

"What, you thought you were the only one?" she says wryly, looking at her nails.

I sink into the chair. I think this classifies as a real, honest-to-goodness revelation. Never in a million years would I have expected to stumble upon another angel-blood at Jackson Hole High School. I'm floored. Angela, on the other hand, is so energized that she's practically shooting out sparks. She scrutinizes me for a minute, then jumps up.

"Come on." She bounces onto the stage, still smiling that cat-ate-the-canary kind of grin. She waves at me impatiently to join her. I get up and slowly climb the stairs onto the stage, looking out into the empty theater.

"What?"

She takes off her coat and tosses it into the dark. Then she takes a few steps back so that she's about arm's length away from me. She turns to face me.

"All right," she says.

I'm starting to get pretty alarmed.

"What are you doing?"

"*Show thyself,*" she says in Angelic.

There's a flash of light, like a camera's. I blink and stumble with the sudden weight of my wings on my shoulder blades. Angela is standing with her own wings fully extended behind her, beaming at me.

"So it's true!" she says excitedly. Tears gleam in her eyes. She furrows her brows a little and her wings disappear with a snap. "Say the words," she says.

"*Show yourself!*" I shout.

The flash comes again, and then she's standing with her wings out. She claps her hands together delightedly.

I'm still stunned.

"How did you know?" I ask.

"The birds tipped me off," she says. "What you said in class about them."

So much for laying low. Mom's going to kill me.

"Birds drive me crazy, too. But I didn't know if that was a freak coincidence or what. And then I heard you were a whiz

132

in French class," she says. "I take Spanish, myself. I'm so good at it because I speak fluent Italian, on account of my mom's family, all those summers in Italy. It's similar, a Romance language and whatnot. That's my story, anyway."

I can't stop staring at her wings. It's such a shock for me to see them on someone I don't know, a crazy juxtaposition: Angela with her glossy black hair sweeping over one side of her face, black tank top, gray jeans with holes in the knees, dark eyeliner and lips, purple fingernails, and then these blindingly white wings stretched out behind her, reflecting the stage lights so she's lit with a radiance that is positively celestial.

"I didn't really know for sure, though, until your brother beat the wrestling team," she says.

"The *entire* wrestling team?" That's so not the version I heard from Jeffrey.

"Didn't you hear about it? He went to the coach and asked to be on the team, the coach said no, tryouts were in November, better luck next year, so Jeffrey said, 'I'll wrestle the best guys on the team for each weight class. If they beat me, fine, I'll try again next year. If I beat them, I'm on the team.' That's how the story circulated. I have gym first period, so I was right there, but I didn't pay much attention until he was halfway through the middleweight. Practically the whole school turned out to watch him beat the champion heavyweight. Toby Jameson. That guy's a monster. It was an amazing thing to watch. Jeffrey just took him down, didn't even look winded, and when I saw him like that I knew that he couldn't be entirely human. And then later I wore the angel shirt to Brit History and watched your face get all tense and broody when you looked at it. So I was pretty sure I was right."

"It was that obvious?"

"To me it was," she says. "But I'm glad. I've never known anybody else like me."

She laughs and before I can totally process what she's saying, she bends her knees and swoops up off the stage, gliding effortlessly over the darkened theater and up into the rafters.

"Come on," she says.

I stare after her, thinking of the huge amount of damage I will probably do if I try.

"I don't think you have enough insurance on this place for me to try to fly here."

She drops lightly back down to the stage.

"I can't fly," I admit.

"It's hard at first," she says. "I spent all last year climbing up into the mountains at night so I could jump off ledges and catch some air. It took months before I was really able to get the hang of it."

That's the first thing anybody has said that makes me feel better about flying.

"Didn't your mom teach you?" I ask.

She shakes her head wildly, as if she finds the idea hilarious.

"My mom's about as human as they come. I mean, what angel-blood would name their kid Angela?"

I stifle a smile.

"She lacks imagination, I guess," she says. "But she's always been there for me."

"So it's your dad then."

Her expression becomes instantly sober. "He was an angel."

"An angel? So that means you're a half blood, a Dimidius."

She nods. Which means she's twice as powerful as me. And she can fly. And her hair is a normal color. I'm a pot of envy.

"So your mom's not human," she says. "That means you're—"

"I'm only a Quartarius. My mom is a Dimidius and my dad's just a normal guy."

I suddenly feel a little exposed standing there on the stage with my wings out, so I fold them in and will them to disappear. Angela does the same. For a minute we stand contemplating each other again.

"You said in class you'd never met your father," I say.

Her face is carefully blank.

"Of course not," she says matter-of-factly. "He's a Black Wing."

I nod like I completely understand what she's talking about, but I don't. Angela turns away and wanders out of the pool of light on the stage into one of the darkened corners.

"My mother was married once, but her husband died of cancer right before she turned thirty. He was an actor, and she was this shy costume designer. This was his theater. They never had any kids. After he died, she went on a pilgrimage to Rome. She's Catholic, so Rome's a pretty important place for her, plus she has family there. One night she walked home from evening mass, and a man followed her. She tried to ignore it at first, but she had a bad feeling about him. He started to walk faster, so she ran. She didn't stop until she was at the family's house."

Angela sits down at the edge of the stage, her legs dangling over into the orchestra pit. She keeps her eyes downcast while she tells the story, her face turned slightly away, but her voice is steady.

"She thought she was safe," she says. "But that night she dreamed of the man standing at the foot of her bed. His face was like a statue, she said. Like Michelangelo's *David*, impassive, sad in the eyes. She started to scream, but then he said something in a language she couldn't understand. His words paralyzed her; she couldn't move or make a sound. She couldn't wake up."

I sit down beside her.

"And then he raped her," she murmurs. "And she realized it wasn't a dream."

She glances up, embarrassed. One corner of her mouth lifts.

"So the downside is that I wasn't exactly conceived in

love," she says. "But the upside is that I have all of these amazing powers."

"Right," I say, nodding. I've never heard of such a thing happening. An angel raping a human? I can't imagine it. The night is starting to take on a weird sort of *Twilight Zone* feel. I came to work on a history project, and now I'm sitting on the edge of a stage with another angel-blood as she spills her entire life story to me. It's surreal.

"I'm sorry, Angela," I say. "That . . . sucks."

She closes her eyes for a moment, as if she can see it all in her mind.

"So if your mom is human and you've never seen your dad, how did you even know you were an angel-blood?" I ask.

"My mom told me. She said that one night, a few days before I was born, another angel appeared to her and told her about the angel-bloods. She thought it was a crazy dream for a while. But she told me as soon as she saw that there was something different about me. I was ten."

It's not really the kind of story you want to hear from your mom. I think about the way Mom told me about the angel-bloods, only two years ago, and how hard it was to accept. It blows my mind to think about what I would have done if she'd sprung that kind of information on me when I was a kid. Or if she'd been raped.

"It took me a long time to find out anything else," Angela says. "My mom didn't know anything about angels besides what it says in the Bible. She said I was a Nephilim like in Genesis, and I would grow up to be a hero like in the days of Samson."

"No haircuts for you, then."

She laughs and drags her fingers through her long black hair.

"But you knew about the Dimidius and Quartarius and all of that," I say.

"I've picked up the facts here and there. I consider myself a bit of an angel historian."

It's quiet for a minute.

"Wow," I say.

"I know."

"I still think we should do our history project on Queen Elizabeth."

She laughs. She turns toward me and pulls her legs up and sits Indian-style, so close her knees brush mine.

"We're going to be best friends," she says.

I believe her.

I have to be home by ten, which gives us hardly any time to talk. I don't even know where to begin, the questions come so fast. One thing is clear right away: Angela knows tons about the angels, so much of the history, the powers they're rumored to have, the names and ranks of different angels who appear in literature and religious texts. But in other areas, things about angels and angel-bloods that you can only get from the inside, she doesn't know much at all. She and I could learn a lot from each other, I realize, being that my mom only tells me what she thinks is absolutely necessary, if that.

"You did all your research in Rome?" I ask.

"Most of it," Angela says. "Rome's a good place to find out about angels. Lots of history there. Although I met an Intangere in Milan last year, and I learned more from him than any other source."

"Hold up. What's an Intangere?"

"Silly," she says like I should have guessed. "That's the Latin for the full-blooded. It literally means whole, untouched, complete in itself. So there's the Intangere, Dimidius, Quartarius, you know."

"Oh right," I say like it had just slipped my mind. "So you met a real angel?"

"Yep. I saw him and I don't think I was supposed to. We were in this little out-of-the-way church, and I saw him standing there kind of glowing, so I said hello in Angelic. He looked at me and then grabbed me by the arm and suddenly we were someplace else, but like we were still in the church, too, at the same time."

"Sounds like heaven."

She frowns and leans closer like she hadn't heard me correctly.

"What?"

"Sounds like he took you to heaven."

Her eyes widen with sudden comprehension. "What do you know about heaven?" she asks.

I flush.

"Well, not a whole lot. I know that it's dimensional, that it exists right on top of Earth. Like a curtain, my mom says, a veil. She went there once—I mean, an angel brought her there."

"You're so lucky to have your mom," Angela says with envy in her eyes. "I have to work so hard to get all my information, and all you have to do is ask."

"Well, I can ask," I say a bit uncomfortably, "but that doesn't mean she has to answer my questions."

Angela looks at me closely.

"Why wouldn't she?"

"I don't know. She says I have to find out these things on my own, by experience, or some baloney like that. Like earlier, you said your father was a Black Wing. I have no idea what that is. I assume it's something like a bad angel, but my mom's certainly never mentioned it."

Angela thinks for a minute.

"A Black Wing is a fallen angel," she says finally. "I guess they fell a long time ago, closer to the beginning."

"Beginning of what?"

"Time."

"Oh. Right. Are their wings really black?"

"I think so," she answers. "That's how you know them. White wings equal good angel, black wings equal bad."

Crazy, all that I don't know. It makes me feel foolish. And uncomfortably curious. And scared. "You just go up and ask them to please show their wings?"

"You command them, in Angelic, to show themselves."

"And they have to?" I ask.

"Did it feel like you had a choice when I commanded you?"

"No, it just happened."

"That's how it is for them too, a kind of tool for imme-diate identification that's programmed into them," she says. "Useful, right?"

"How do you know all this?"

"Phen told me. He's the angel I met in the church. He warned me about the Black Wings."

She stops abruptly, dropping her eyes.

"What?" I prompt gently. "What did he say?"

She closes her eyes briefly and then opens them. "He said that they might try to find me, someday."

"But why would they want to find you?"

She looks up.

"Because my father was one. And because they want us," she says. Her gold eyes are suddenly fierce. "They're building an army."

"Mom!" I scream the minute the door of the house closes behind me. She comes running out of her office, alarm all over her face.

"What? What is it? Are you hurt?"

"Why didn't you tell me there's a war between the angels?"

She stops. "What?"

"Angela Zerbino's an angel-blood," I say, still spazzing out. "And she told me that there's this war that's going on between the good and bad angels."

"Angela Zerbino's an angel-blood?"

"Dimidius. Now answer my question."

"Well, honey," she says, still looking confused. "I assumed you knew."

"How would I know if you didn't tell me? You never tell me anything!"

"There's both good and evil in this world," she says after a long pause. "I told you that."

I can see how carefully she's choosing her words, even now. It's infuriating.

"Yeah, but you never told me about Black Wings," I exclaim. "You never told me that they go around recruiting or killing all the angel-bloods they come across."

She flinches.

"So it's true."

"Yes," she says. "Although I think they are more interested in the Dimidius."

"Right, because Quartarius don't have much power," I say sarcastically. "I guess I should be relieved, then."

Mom's still processing. "So Angela Zerbino told you she was an angel-blood. She just told you?"

"Yep. She showed me her wings and everything."

"What color were they?"

"Her wings? White."

"How white?" she asks intently.

"They were a perfect, eye-piercing white, Mom. Why does it matter?"

"The shade of our wings reflects our standing in the light," she says. "White Wings have white wings, of course, and Black Wings have black. For most of us in the middle, the offspring, our wings are varying shades of gray."

"Your wings have always looked pretty white to me," I say. I'm instantly struck with the urge to summon my wings, to see what shade they are, to discover what my spiritual state really is. I sure as heck don't know.

"My wings are fairly light," Mom admits, "but not as the new-fallen snow."

"Well, Angela's were white," I say. "I guess that means she's a pure soul."

Mom goes to the cupboard and gets a glass. She fills it with water at the sink, then stands drinking it slowly. Calmly.

"A Black Wing raped her mom." I look at her to see if there's any reaction to that. None. "She's worried that someday they'll show up to collect her. You should have seen her face when she talked about it. Scared. Like, really, really scared."

Mom puts the glass down and looks at me. She doesn't seem at all rattled by anything I've told her. Which rattles me even more. And then I realize.

"You already knew about Angela," I say. "How?"

"I have my sources. She hasn't exactly tried to hide her abilities. For someone who's worried about Black Wings, she's not being very careful. And to reveal herself to you like that. It's reckless."

I stare at her. At that moment it fully dawns on me how much my mother hasn't told me.

"You've been lying to me," I say. "I tell you everything, and you've been lying to me."

She meets my eyes, startled by my accusation. "No, I haven't. There are just some things that——"

"Are there a lot of angel-bloods in Jackson Hole?"

She seems hurt by my sudden question. She doesn't answer.

I pick up my backpack from where I tossed it onto the kitchen floor and head for my room.

"Hey," says Mom. "I'm still talking to you."

"No, apparently you're not."

"Clara," she calls after me in an exasperated voice. "If I don't tell you everything, it's for your own protection."

"That doesn't make sense. How does being clueless protect me?"

"What else did Angela tell you?"

"Nothing."

I go into my room and slam the door, take off my coat, and throw it on the bed, fighting the urge to scream, or cry, or both. Then I go to the mirror and summon my wings, gathering them around in front of me so I can see the feathers more closely. They're fairly white, I think, running my hand over them. Not as the new-fallen snow, as my mother said, but still white.

Not as white as Angela's, though.

I hear Mom come down the hall. She stops in front of my door. I wait for her to knock or come in and tell me that she doesn't want me hanging out with Angela anymore, for my own protection. But she doesn't. She just stands there for a minute. Then I hear her walk away.

I wait for a while, until I'm sure that Mom is safely downstairs again, and then I sneak down the hall to Jeffrey's room. He's sitting at his desk with his laptop, typing away, chatting with someone by the looks of it. When he sees me he types something really fast, then jumps up to face me. I turn the music down a notch so I can hear myself think.

"Did you tell her you'd b-r-b?" I say with a smirk. "What's her name, anyway? No point denying it. It will be more embarrassing for you if I have to ask around at school."

"Kimber," he concedes immediately. "Her name's Kimber." His expression stays neutral, but I can see a hint of red creeping into his ears.

"Pretty name. The blond girl, I assume?"

"You didn't come in here just to mock me, right?"

"Well, that's pretty fun, but no. I wanted to tell you something." I move a pile of dirty laundry off his beanbag chair and sit on it. My breath catches for a second, like I'm breaking a rule, Mom's all-important "don't tell your kids anything" rule, as a matter of fact. But I'm sick of living in the dark. And I'm ticked off, ticked off at everything, at my whole crappy life and all the people in it. I need to vent.

"Angela Zerbino's an angel-blood," I say.

He blinks.

"Who?"

"She's a junior, tall, long black hair, kind of Emo, gold eyes. Loner."

He looks at the ceiling thoughtfully like he's calling up Angela's face in his mind. "How do you know she's an angel-blood?"

"She told me. But that's not the right question, Jeffrey."

"What do you mean?"

"What you should be asking is *why* Angela Zerbino told me that she was an angel-blood. And if you asked me that, I would answer that she told me because she knew that *I* was an angel-blood."

"Huh? How did she know you were an angel-blood?"

"See, now that's the right question," I say. I lean forward. "She knew because she saw you take on the wrestling team last month. She watched you wrestle Toby Jameson, who probably weighs two hundred pounds, without even working up a sweat. And she said to herself, wow, that guy's a good wrestler, he must be an *angel*."

His face actually pales. It's mildly satisfying. Of course I'm leaving out some of the other troublesome details, my stupid thing about the birds and French class and the way I ogled her angel shirt, falling so neatly into her trap. But Jeffrey was the linchpin: She was only certain that we were something more than human after she observed him on the wrestling mat that day.

"Did you tell Mom?" He looks a little green at the thought. Because if I told Mom, that'd be it for Jeffrey. No more wrestling, or baseball in the spring, or football in the fall or whatever he was dreaming up. He'd probably be grounded until college.

"No," I say. "Although she's bound to ask the right question herself, sooner or later." It's kind of odd, come to think of it, that she hasn't asked me yet. Maybe her sources already told her that, too.

"Are you going to tell her?" he asks, so softly I can hardly hear him over the music. His expression is truly pathetic, and where a few moments before anger surged through me, now I feel drained and sad.

"No. I just wanted to tell you. I don't know why. I wanted you to know."

"Thanks," he says. He gives a short, humorless laugh. "I think."

"Don't mention it. I mean ever. Really." I get up to leave.

"I feel like a cheater," he says then. "All the ribbons and

medals and trophies I won in California, they don't mean anything. It's like I was taking steroids, only I didn't know it."

I know exactly what he means. It's why I dropped out of ballet, even though I loved it, and why I never picked it up again in Jackson. It felt dishonest, doing so easily, so naturally, what the other girls had to work so hard to accomplish. It was unfair, I thought, to take the attention away from them when I had such a huge advantage. So I quit.

"But if I hold myself back, I feel like a fake," says Jeffrey. "And that's worse."

"I know."

"I won't do it," he says. I look into his dead-serious gray eyes. He swallows, but holds my gaze. "I won't hold myself back. I won't pretend to be less than I am."

"Even if it puts us in danger?" I ask, glancing away.

"What danger? Angela Zerbino's dangerous?"

That's when I'm supposed to tell him about the Black Wings. There are bad angels now, angels that hunt us and sometimes kill us. There are shades of gray we didn't know about before, and it's something that I should tell him, something that he needs to know, but his eyes are pleading with me not to take any more away from him.

Mom told us that we're special, but what kind of "gift" comes with a war between angels as the strings attached? Maybe I don't want any more taken from me either. Maybe I don't want to be remarkable, don't want to fly or speak some bizarre angel language or save the world one hot guy at a time. I just want to be human.

"Watch yourself, okay?" I tell Jeffrey.

"I will." Then he adds, "Thanks. . . . You're all right some-times, you know."

"Remember that next time you're dragging me out of bed at five in the morning," I say wearily. "Tell Kimber I said hi, by the way."

Then I escape to my room and lay in the dark turning the words *Black Wing* over and over in my head.

8

BLUE SQUARE GIRL

This morning the sun's so bright it feels like I'm standing on a frozen cloud. I'm at the top of a run called Wide Open. It's a double blue square—more difficult than green circle, but not black diamond level. I'm getting there. The valley below is so white and serene it's hard to believe it's the first week of March.

I readjust my goggles, slip my hands into my poles, and flex forward in my boots to test the bindings. All set. I launch myself down the mountain. The cold air whips the exposed part of my face, but I'm grinning like an idiot. It feels so good, the closest I can come to flying. I almost feel the presence of my wings in moments like these, even though they're not there. There's a section of moguls on one side of the run, and I try them out, lifting and dropping in and out of them. It makes me aware of the strength of my knees, my legs. I'm getting good at moguls. And powder, which is literally like pushing through cloud, sinking up to your knees in fluffy white snow that flies out behind you as you go. I like to hit the runs first thing in the morning after a new snow, so I can carve my own path through the fresh powder.

I've got it bad for skiing. Too bad the season's almost over.

Wide Open deposits me at South Pass Traverse, a trail that cuts almost horizontally across the mountain. I straighten my skis and push off to gain momentum, cutting through the trees. There's a bird singing back there somewhere, and when I pass by it stops. The trail opens up onto another groomed slope, Werner, one of my faves, and I stop at the edge. People are setting up giant slalom gates on the hill. Race today.

Which means that Christian will be here.

"What time's the race?" I call to one of the guys setting up.

"High noon," he calls back.

I check my watch. It's a few minutes before eleven. I should go eat, then take the big quad chair up to the top of Werner and watch the race.

At the lodge I spot Tucker Avery having lunch with a girl. This is a new development. I've spent almost every weekend this winter at Teton Village (yay Mom for not scoffing at the ridiculously expensive season pass) and almost every weekend I see Tucker sometime in the afternoon, after he's done with his morning teaching on the bunny hill. But it's not like I'm bumping into him all over the mountain. He's more of a backcountry skier, off the groomed trails. I haven't tried that kind of thing yet—apparently it requires a partner so if something terrible happens to one of you the other can go for help. I'm not into the extreme stuff—my goal is to become a black diamond girl, nothing fancy. Teton Village is funny, with its signs always reminding you that THIS MOUNTAIN IS NOTHING YOU'VE EVER EXPERIENCED BEFORE and if you don't know what you're doing, YOU JUST MAY DIE. The backcountry signs say stuff like BEYOND THIS POINT IS A HIGH RISK AREA, WHICH HAS MANY HAZARDS INCLUDING, BUT NOT LIMITED TO, AVALANCHES, CLIFFS, AND HIDDEN OBSTACLES. YOU MAY BE RESPONSIBLE FOR THE COST OF YOUR RESCUE and I think, um, no thanks. I choose life.

Is this girl talking to Tucker now his backcountry partner? I take a few discreet steps to the side so I can see her face. It's Ava Peters. She's in my chemistry class, definitely one of the pretty people, a little busty with that superlight blond hair that almost looks white. Her dad owns a white-water rafting company. It doesn't surprise me to see Tucker with a popular girl, even though he's definitely a Have-Not. At school I've noticed that he's one of those guys who seems to get along with everybody. Everybody but me, that is.

Ava's wearing too much eye makeup. I wonder if he likes that kind of thing.

He glances over at me and smirks before I have a chance to look away. I smirk back, then try to saunter over to the deli counter, but I can't pull it off. It's impossible to saunter in ski boots.

I stand with a few spectators on the side of Werner run and watch Christian hurl himself at the gates, sometimes grazing them with his shoulders as he passes through. It's graceful, the way his body bends toward the gate, his skis coming up onto their edges and his knees nearly brushing the snow. His movements so careful, so purposeful. His lips pursed in concentration.

After he blasts through the finish line I penguin-walk over to where he's watching the other racers run the course and say hello.

"Did you win?" I ask.

"I always win. Except when I don't. This was one of the don'ts." He shrugs like he doesn't care, but I can tell by his face that he's unhappy with his performance

"You looked good to me. Fast, I mean."

"Thanks," he says. He fiddles with the number that's strapped to his chest: 9. It makes me think of 99CX, his license plate.

"Are you trying for the Olympics?"

He shakes his head. "Nope. I'm on the ski team, not the ski club."

I must look confused, because he smiles and says, "The ski team's the high school's official team, which only competes against other teams from Wyoming. The ski club's where all the hard-core people go, the skiers who get sponsors and national recognition and all that."

"Don't you want to win gold medals?"

"I was in club, for a while. But it's a little too intense for me. Too much pressure. I don't want to be a professional skier. I just like skiing. I like racing." He grins suddenly. "The speed is very addictive."

Yes it is. I smile. "I'm still trying to make it down the hill in one piece."

"How's that going? Getting the hang of it?"

"Better every day."

"Pretty soon you'll be ready for the racecourse, too."

"Yep, and then you'd better watch out."

He laughs. "I'm sure you'll crush me."

"Right."

He looks around like he's expecting someone to join us. It makes me nervous, like any moment Kay will materialize out of thin air and tell me to step away from her boyfriend.

"Does Kay ski, too?" I ask.

He gives a short laugh. "No, she's a lodge bunny. If she comes at all. She knows how to ski, but she says she gets too cold. She hates ski season, because I can't really do stuff with her on the weekends."

"That sucks."

He looks around again.

"Yeah," he says.

"Kay's in my English class. She never says much. I always wonder if she's even read the books."

Okay, so my mouth is completely disconnected from my brain. I look at his face to see if I've offended him. But he only laughs again, a longer, warmer laugh this time.

"She takes honors classes to look good on the college apps, but books aren't really her thing," he says.

I don't want to think about what her thing might be. I don't want to think about Kay at all, but now that we're talking about her, I'm curious.

"When did you and Kay start going out?"

"Fall, sophomore year," he answers. "She's a cheerleader, and back then I played football, and at the homecoming game she got hurt doing a liberty twist. I think that's what it's called—Kay usually tells the story. But she fell and hurt her ankle."

"Let me guess. You carried her off the field. And then it was happily ever after?"

He looks away, embarrassed. "Something like that," he says.

And there's the awkward silence, right on cue.

"Kay seems . . ." I want to say "nice," but I don't think I can pull that off. "She seems like she's really into you."

He doesn't say anything for a minute, just stares up the course where somebody is coming down now on a snowboard.

"She is," he says thoughtfully, like he's talking to himself more than to me. "She's a good person."

"Great," I manage. I don't particularly want Kay to be a good person. I'm perfectly comfortable thinking about her as the wicked witch.

He coughs uncomfortably, and I realize that I'm staring at him with my big owl eyes. I flush and look up the hill where the snowboarder is crossing the finish line.

"Nice run!" Christian shouts. "Smoking!"

"Thanks, dude," the snowboarder calls back. He pulls off his goggles. It's Shawn Davidson, snowboarder Shawn, the guy from the Pizza Hut who called me Bozo. He looks from me to Christian and back again. I feel his gaze on me like a spotlight.

"I better go," says Christian. "The race is over. Coach will want to break it down for us in the ski shack, watch the videos and all that."

"Okay," I say. "Nice to—"

But he's already gone, tearing his way down the hill, leaving me once again to make it the rest of the way down the mountain by myself.

In late March we hit a warm spell, and the snow in the valley melts in the space of about two days. Our woods fill up with clusters of red and purple wildflowers. Bright green leaves pop up on the aspens. The land, which has been so quietly pristine all winter, fills with color and noise. I like to stand on our back porch and listen as the breeze stirs the trees into a rhythmic whispering, the creek that cuts across the corner of our land gurgling happily, birds singing (and occasionally dive-bombing me), chipmunks chattering. The air smells like flowers and sun-warmed pine. The mountains behind the house are still white with snow, but spring has definitely sprung.

With it comes the vision, in full force. All winter that particular tingling in my head has been quiet; in fact, it only came to me twice since the first day of school when I saw Christian in the hallway. I thought I was being given a little heavenly break, but apparently that's over. I'm halfway to school one morning when out of the blue (poof!) I'm back in that familiar forest, walking through the trees toward Christian.

I call his name. He turns toward me, his eyes a green-gold in the slanted afternoon light.

"It's you," he says hoarsely.

"It's me," I answer. "I'm here."

"Clara!"

I blink. The first thing I see is Jeffrey's hand on the steering wheel of the Prius. My foot is still resting lightly on the gas. The car moves very slowly to the side of the road.

"I'm sorry," I gasp. I pull over immediately and park.

"Jeffrey, I'm so sorry."

"It's okay," he murmurs. "It's the vision, right?"

"Yes."

"Then it's not like you can control when it happens."

"Yeah, but you'd think that it wouldn't happen during a time when it might actually kill me. What if I'd crashed? So much for the vision then, right?"

"But you didn't crash," he says. "I was here."

"Thank God."

He smiles mischievously. "So does this mean I can drive us the rest of the way?"

When I tell Mom about the return of the vision she starts talking about teaching me to fly again, using the word *training* so often that our house feels like it's been converted to some kind of boot camp. She's been in a funky mood all winter, spending most of her time in her office with the door shut, drinking tea and hunched in a crocheted blanket. Whenever I knock or stick my head in she always gets this strained look, like she doesn't want to be bothered. And, truthfully, I've been quasi-avoiding her since that first day with Angela, when it became so clear that Mom's intentionally keeping me in the dark. I spend a lot of afternoons over at the Pink Garter with Angela, which Mom doesn't like, but as it's technically school related (we're working on our Queen Eliz project after all) she can't formally object. And weekends, I've been on the ski slopes. Which is, I argue, Christian related and, therefore, purpose related. So it's technically training, right?

Only now the snow on the mountain's getting awfully thin.

Wendy takes the warm weather as an opportunity to convince me to ride a horse. So that's how I find myself at the Lazy Dog Ranch sitting on the back of a black-and-white mare named Sassy. Wendy says Sassy's a good horse to learn on because she's about thirty years old and doesn't have much fight left in her. That's fine by me, although I instantly feel comfortable in the saddle, like I've been riding all my life.

"You're doing really well," says Wendy, watching me from the fence as I ride the horse slowly around the edge of the pasture. "You're a natural horsewoman."

Sassy's ears perk up. In the distance I see two men on horseback, galloping toward the big red barn at the end of the pasture. The sound of them laughing floats toward us across the field.

"That's Dad and Tucker," says Wendy. "Dinner will be ready soon. Better bring Sassy in."

I give Sassy a gentle kick and she starts toward the barn.

"Hey there!" greets Mr. Avery as we approach. "Looking good."

"Thanks. I'm Clara."

"I know," says Mr. Avery. He looks so much like Tucker. "Wendy's been talking about you nonstop for months now." He grins, which makes him look even more like Tucker.

"Dad," mutters Wendy. She walks up to her dad's horse and rubs it under the chin.

"Oh lord," laughs Tucker. "She's got you on old Sassy."

I promised myself that I was going to cool it around Tucker today for Wendy's sake, no matter what he throws at me. No rude remarks. No comebacks. I'm going to be on my best behavior.

"I like her." I lean forward and stroke Sassy's neck.

"She's the horse we put little kids on."

"Tucker, shut up," says Wendy.

"But it's true. That horse hasn't moved faster than a snail in about five years, I think. Sitting on her is practically like sitting in a chair."

Well, we'll show him.

"Good girl," I say to Sassy, very softly in Angelic. Her ears whip around to listen to my voice. "Let's run," I whisper.

I'm surprised by how quickly she obeys. In seconds we're in a full gallop, whipping across the far side of the pasture. For a moment the world slows down. The mountains in the background glow a peachy gold, lit by the setting sun. I savor the cool spring air caressing my skin, the strong, dusty feel of the horse under me, her legs stretching out like she's pulling the earth underneath us as she runs, the in-and-out huff of her hay-scented breath. It's wonderful.

Then a gust of wind blows my hair across my face and for one panicky moment I can't see, and everything is going much too fast. I picture myself being thrown off and landing face-first in a pile of manure, Tucker falling all over himself laughing. I toss my head wildly, and my hair is suddenly out of my eyes. My breath catches. The fence is rushing toward us, and Sassy shows no sign of slowing down.

"Can you jump it?" I ask, still whispering. She is, after all, a pretty old horse.

I feel her gather under me. I say a little prayer and lean over her neck. Then we're in the air, barely clearing the fence. We come down so hard my teeth clatter together. I turn the horse toward the barn, pulling back on the reins a bit to slow her. We trot up to Tucker, Wendy, and Mr. Avery, who are all staring at me with their mouths hanging open.

So much for being on my best behavior.

"Whoa," I say, and pull up the reins until Sassy stops.

"Holy smokes!" Wendy gasps. "What was *that*?"

"I don't know." I force a laugh. "I think it was mostly the horse's idea."

"That was amazing!"

"I guess she still has a bit of sass in her after all." I glance triumphantly at Tucker. For once he's speechless.

"That was sure something," says Mr. Avery. "I didn't know the old girl had it in her."

"How long have you been riding?" asks Tucker.

"This is her first time, isn't that amazing?" says Wendy. "She's a natural."

"Right," Tucker said, meeting my gaze steadily. "A natural."

"So, have you asked Jason Lovett to prom yet?" I ask Wendy as we're brushing down Sassy in the barn a few minutes later.

She's immediately the color of a beet. "It's prom," she says with forced lightness. "He's supposed to ask me, right?"

"Everyone knows he's the shy type. He's probably intimidated by your stunning beauty. So you should ask him."

"But maybe he has a girlfriend back in California."

"Long-distance relationship. Doomed. Anyway, you don't know that for sure. Ask him. Then you'll find out."

"I don't know—"

"Wen, come on. He likes you. He stares at you all through English. And I know you've got the hots for him, too. What is it with you and Californians, anyway?"

It's quiet for a minute, the only sound the steady breathing of the horse.

"So what's going on with you and my brother?" asks Wendy. Completely out of the blue.

"Your brother? What do you mean, 'going on'?"

"It seems like there's something going on there."

"You're joking, right? We just like to mess with each other, you know that."

"But you like him, don't you?"

My mouth falls open. "No, I—" I stop myself.

"You like Christian Prescott," she finishes for me, arching an eyebrow. "Yeah, I could tell. But he's like a god. You worship the gods but you don't go out with them. You only like guys like that from a distance."

I don't know what to say. "Wendy——"

"Look, I'm not pushing you on my brother. It kind of gives me the creeps, truthfully, my best friend dating my brother. But I wanted to tell you, in case you *were* interested, that it'd be okay. I could get over it. If you wanted to go out with him——"

"But Tucker doesn't even like me," I sputter.

"He likes you."

"Could have fooled me."

"In grade school, didn't you ever have a boy punch you on the arm?"

"Tucker's a junior in high school."

"He's still in grade school, trust me," she says.

I stare at her. "So you're saying Tucker's such a jackass because he *likes* me?"

"Pretty much."

"No way." I shake my head in disbelief.

"The thought never crossed your mind?"

"No!"

"Huh," she says. "I won't stand in the way or anything. It's okay."

My heart's beating fast. I swallow. "Wendy, I don't like your brother. Not that way. Not in any way, really. No offense."

"None taken," she says with a casual shrug. "I just wanted you to know I'm okay with it, the you-and-Tucker thing, if there's ever a you-and-Tucker thing."

"There's no me-and-Tucker thing, okay? So can we talk about something else?"

"Sure," she says, but I can tell by the pensive look on her face that she has more she wants to say.

9

LONG LIVE THE QUEEN

"Can I get into this thing by myself?" I ask.

"Put on as much as you can," Angela calls back, "and I'll help you with the rest."

I contemplate the gown and all of its many parts, which are hanging from a hook in the backstage dressing room at the Pink Garter. It looks complicated. Maybe we should have gone with the Angels of Mons idea.

"How long am I going to have to wear this tomorrow?" I call, pulling on the silk stockings and tying them with ribbon under the knee.

"Not long," answers Angela. "I'll help you put it on right before class and then you'll wear it during the entire presentation."

"Just so you know, this may kill me. I may have to sacrifice my life for us to get a good grade on this project."

"So noble of you," she says.

I struggle into the corset and the long crazy hoops of the petticoat. Then I grab the hanger with the dress on it and march out onto the stage.

"I think I need you to tie up the corset before I put the rest on," I say.

She jumps up to help me. That's one thing about Angela: She never does anything halfway. She yanks the laces.

"Not so tight! I still have to breathe, remember?"

"Quit whining. You're lucky we couldn't find any real whalebone for this thing."

By the time she slides the dress over my head I feel like I have on every item of clothing at the Garter. Angela walks around me pulling on the pieces underneath to make sure they look right. She steps back.

"Wow, that is good. With the makeup and the hair right, you'll look exactly like Queen Elizabeth."

"Great," I say without enthusiasm. "I'll look like a pasty-faced tart."

"Oh, I forgot the ruffs!"

She hops down from the stage and runs over to a cardboard box on the floor. She pulls out a stiff round collar that looks like the things you put on dogs to keep them from licking themselves. There are two more for the wrists.

"No one said anything about ruffs," I say, backing away.

She jumps toward me. Her wings come out with a flash and beat a couple of times, carrying her easily to the stage, then disappear.

"Show-off."

"Hold still." She puts the final ruff on the end of my sleeve. "My mom's a genius."

As if on cue, Anna Zerbino comes in from the lobby with a stack of table linens. She stops in the aisle when she sees me.

"So it fits," she says, her humorless dark eyes looking me up and down.

"It's great," I say. "Thank you for all your hard work."

She nods.

"Dinner's ready upstairs. Lasagna."

"Okay, so we're done with the fitting," I say to Angela. "Get me out of this thing."

"Not so fast," whispers Angela, glancing at her mom over her shoulder. "We haven't done much of our *other* research."

She's so predictable. Always with the angel research.

"Come on," I whisper back. "Lasagna."

"We'll be right up, Mom," says Angela. She pretends to fiddle with my collar until her mother leaves the theater. As soon as we're alone again, she says, "I figured out something good, though."

"What is it?"

"Angels—full-blooded angels, I mean—are all male."

"All male?"

"There are no female Intangere."

167

"Interesting. Now help me get out of this dress."

"But I think that angels could appear female if they wanted to. I believe they can change form, like shape-shifters," she says, her golden eyes dancing with excitement.

"So they can become cats and birds and stuff."

"Right, but more than that," she says. "I have another theory."

"Oh, here we go," I groan.

"I think that all the stories about supernatural creatures, like vampires, werewolves, ghosts, mermaids, aliens, you name it, could all be angel related. Humans don't know what they're seeing, but it could all be angels taking on other forms."

Angela has some wild theories, but they're always cool to consider.

"Awesome," I say. "Now let's eat."

"Wait," she says. "I also found something about your hair."

"My hair?"

"The blaze thing you told me about." She walks over to the table and grabs her notebook, flips through it. "It's called *comae caelestis*. The Romans used the phrase to describe 'dazzling rays of light emanating from the hairs of the head, a sign of a heavenly being.'"

"What, you find that on the internet?" I ask with a stunned laugh. She nods. As usual, Angela has taken the nugget of information I've given her and turned it into a gold mine.

"I wish it would happen to me," she says, twisting a strand of her shiny black hair around her finger wistfully. "I bet it's awesome."

"It's overwhelming, okay? And you'd have to dye your hair."

She shrugs like that doesn't sound so bad to her.

"So what do you have for me this week?" she asks.

"What about the concept of purpose?" This is a big one, something I probably should have gotten into a lot earlier, only I didn't especially want to talk about purpose, because then I'd have to talk about mine. But now I've literally told her everything else I know. I even broke out the angel diary and showed her my old notes. Secretly I hope that she, in her infinite wisdom, already knows all about purpose.

"Define purpose," she says.

No such luck.

"First get me out of this thing." I gesture to the dress.

She moves around me quickly, loosening and unfastening all the laces and ties. I go into the dressing room and change back into my normal clothes. When I come out, she's sitting at one of the tables drumming her pencil on her notebook.

"Okay," she says. "Tell me."

I take a seat across from her.

"Every angel-blood has a purpose on Earth. Usually it comes in the form of a vision."

She scribbles furiously into her notebook.

"When do you see this vision?" she asks.

"Everybody's different, but sometime between thirteen and twenty, usually. It happens after your powers start to manifest. I only got mine last year."

"And you only receive one purpose?"

"As far as I know. Mom always says it's the one thing I was put on this Earth to do."

"So what happens if you don't do it?"

"I don't know," I say.

"And what happens after you complete it? You go on to live a normal, happy life?"

"I don't know," I say again. Some expert I'm turning out to be. "Mom won't tell me any of that."

"What's yours?" she asks, still writing.

She looks up when I don't say anything. "Oh, is it supposed to be a secret?"

"I don't know. It's just personal."

"It's okay," she says. "You don't have to tell me."

But I *want* to tell her. I want to talk about it with someone other than my mom.

"It's about Christian Prescott."

She puts her pencil down, her face so surprised I almost laugh.

"Christian Prescott?" she repeats like I'm about to hit her with the punch line to a very silly joke.

"I see a forest fire, and then I see Christian standing in the trees. I think I'm supposed to save him."

"Wow."

"I know."

She's quiet for a minute.

"That's why you moved here?" she asks finally.

"Yep. I saw Christian's truck in my vision, and I read the license plate, so that's how we knew to come here."

"Wow."

"You can stop saying that."

"When is it supposed to happen?"

"I wish I knew. Sometime during fire season is all I know."

"No wonder you're so obsessed with him."

"Ange!"

"Oh, come on. You eye-hump him all through British History. I thought you were just enraptured, the way everyone else at school seems to be. I'm happy to find out that you have a good reason."

"Okay, enough angel talk," I say, getting up and heading for the door. I'm sure I'm beet red by this point. "Our lasagna's getting cold."

"But you didn't ask me about my purpose," she says.

I stop.

"You know your purpose?"

"Well, I didn't know until now that it was my purpose. But I've been having the same daydream thing, over and over again, for like three years."

"What is it? If you don't mind me asking."

She looks serious all of a sudden.

"No, it's fine," she says. "There's a big courtyard, and I'm walking through it fast, almost running, like I'm late. There are lots of people around, people with backpacks and cups of coffee, so I think it's like a college campus or something. It's midmorning. I run up a set of stone steps, and at the top is a man in a gray suit. I put my hand on his shoulder, and he turns."

She stops talking, staring off into the darkened theater like right now she's seeing it play out in her mind.

"And?" I prompt.

She glances over at me uncomfortably.

"I don't know. I think I'm supposed to deliver a message to him. There are words, there are things I am supposed to say, but I never can remember them."

"They'll come to you, when the time is right," I say.

I sound just like my mom.

What's comforting about Angela, I think as I get ready for bed that night, is that she reminds me that I'm not alone. Maybe I shouldn't feel alone, anyway, since I have Mom and Jeffrey, but I do, like I'm the only person in the world who has to face this divine purpose. Now I'm not. And Angela, in spite of her know-it-all nature, doesn't know what her purpose means any more than I do, and no amount of research or theorizing can help her. She simply has to wait for the answers. It makes me feel better, knowing that. Like I suck a smidge less.

"Hey, you," says Mom, poking her head in my room. "Did you have a good time with Angela?" Her face is carefully neutral, the way it always is whenever the topic of Angela comes up.

"Yeah, we finished our project. We're doing it tomorrow. So I guess we won't be hanging out as much now."

"Good, we'll have some time for flying lessons."

"Awesome," I deadpan.

She frowns. "I'm glad about Angela." She comes into my room and sits next to me on the bed. "I think it's great that you can have an angel-blood friend."

"You do?"

"Absolutely. You need to be careful, that's all."

"Right, because everyone knows what a hooligan Angela is."

"You feel like you can be yourself around Angela," she says. "I get that. But angel-bloods are different. They're not like your normal friends. You never know what their real intentions might be."

"Paranoid much?"

"Just be careful," she says.

She doesn't even know Angela. Or her purpose. She doesn't know how fun and smart Angela is, all the cool things that I've learned from her.

"Mom," I say hesitantly. "How long did it take you to get all the pieces for your purpose? When did you know—for absolute certain—what it was that you had to do?"

"I didn't." Her eyes are mournful for a few seconds, and then her expression becomes guarded, her body going stiff all the way up to her face. She thinks she's already said too much. She's not going to give me anything else.

I sigh.

"Mom, why can't you just tell me?"

"I meant," she continues like she didn't even hear my question, "that I didn't *ever* know for absolute certain. Not absolute. The whole process is usually very intuitive."

We hear a blast of music as Jeffrey comes out of his room and tromps his huge feet down the hall and into the bathroom. When I look at Mom again she's her usual sunny self.

"Some of it you have to take on faith," she says.

"Yeah, I know," I say resignedly. A lump rises in my throat. I want to ask so many questions. But she never wants to answer them. She never lets me into her secret angel world, and I don't understand why.

"I should sleep," I say. "Big British History presentation tomorrow."

"All right," she says.

She looks exhausted. Purple shadows under her eyes. I even notice a few fine lines in the corners I've never seen before. She might pass for mid-forties now, which is still good considering that she's a hundred and eighteen years old. But I've never seen her look so worn out.

"Are you okay?" I ask. I put my hand over hers. Her skin is cool and damp, which startles me.

"I'm fine." She pulls her hand out from under mine. "It's been a long week."

She gets up and goes to the door.

"You ready?" She reaches for the light switch.

"Yeah."

"Good night," she says, and turns off the light.

For a moment she stands in the doorway, silhouetted in the light from the hall.

"I love you, Clara," she says. "Don't forget that, okay?"

I want to cry. How did we get so much space between us in such a short time?

"I love you too, Mom."

Then she goes out and closes the door, and I'm alone in the dark.

"One more coat," says Angela. "Your hair is so . . . aggravating!"

"I told you," I say.

She sprays another toxic cloud of hair spray at my head. I cough. When my eyes stop watering I look into the mirror. Queen Elizabeth stares back. She does not look amused.

"I think we might actually land an A."

"Was there ever any doubt?" says Angela, pushing her glasses up on her nose. "I'm doing most of the talking, remember? You just have to stand there and look pretty."

"That's easy for you to say," I grumble. "This getup must weigh a hundred pounds."

She rolls her eyes.

"Wait a sec," I say. "When did you get glasses? You have perfect vision."

"It's *my* costume. You play the queen. I play the studious straight-A student who knows everything there is to know about the Elizabethan age."

"Wow. You're sick, you know that?"

"Come on," she says. "The bell's about to ring."

The other students part to let me pass as I follow Angela down the hall. I try to smile as they point and whisper. We stop right outside the door to British History. Angela turns and starts to fiddle with my dress.

"Nice ruffs," she teases.

"You so owe me."

"Wait here." She looks the tiniest bit nervous. "I'll announce you."

After she slips into the classroom, I stand in the hall listening, waiting, my heart suddenly beating fast. I hear Angela speaking, and Mr. Erikson answering. The class laughs at something he says. I peer through the tiny rectangular window in the classroom door. Angela is standing at the front of the class, pointing to the poster we whipped up with a timeline of the life of Queen Elizabeth. She's going to announce me after the death of Queen Mary. Any minute now. I take a deep breath and stand up as straight as I can under the crushing weight of the gown.

Christian is in there. I can see him through the window, sitting in the front row, resting his head on his hand.

Christian has the nicest profile.

"So without further ado," says Angela at last, loudly, "I give you Her Royal Highness, Queen Elizabeth the first of the house of Tudor, Queen of England and Ireland . . . Tucker, get the door."

The door swings open, and I step inside the classroom with as much poise as I can manage. Careful not to trip on the massive dress, I sweep to the front of the room to stand beside Angela. The class seems to take a collective breath.

Of course we weren't able to completely replicate any of the actual gowns from the portraits of Elizabeth we printed off Wikipedia, the ones encrusted with emeralds and rubies and made from yards and yards of expensive fabrics, but Angela's mom did a bang-up imitation. The gown is a deep gold color with a silver brocade pattern and a white silk undershirt that pokes through at the sleeves. We hot-glued fake pearls and glass jewels all around the edges. The corset cinches me into a little triangle in front; then the skirt flares out and down to the floor. The ruffs at my neck and wrists are made of stiff white lace, also decorated with faux pearls. To top it off, my face is painted nearly white, something that's supposed to represent Elizabeth's purity, with red lips. Angela parted my hair down the middle and rolled it into an elaborate braided bun in the back, then pinned on a small crownlike headpiece made out of wire and pearls, with a tiny pearl that dangles right in the middle of my forehead. A long piece of white velvet hangs off the back like a bride's veil.

The class stares at me like I am the real Queen Elizabeth, transported through time. I suddenly feel beautiful and powerful, like the blood of kings is truly pumping through my veins. I'm not Bozo anymore.

"Queen Mary is dead," Angela says. "Long live Queen Elizabeth."

Now it's my turn. I close my eyes, take in as much air as I can, given the corset, then lift my head and look out at the class like they are now my loyal subjects.

"My lords, the law of nature moves me to sorrow for my sister," I say in my best British accent. "The burden that is fallen upon me makes me amazed, and yet, considering I am God's creature, ordained to obey His appointment, I will thereto yield, desiring from the bottom of my heart that I may have assistance of His grace to be the minister of His heavenly will in this office now committed to me."

The class is quiet. I glance at Christian, who's looking

right at me like he's never seen me before. Our eyes meet. He smiles.

I suddenly catch a whiff of smoke in the air.

Not now, I think, as if the vision is a person I can command. The next line of my speech flies out of my head. I begin to see the outlines of trees.

Please, I think at the vision desperately. *Go away.*

No use. I'm with Christian in the forest. I look into his gold-flecked eyes. He's so close this time, so close that I can smell his wonderful mix of soap and boy. I could reach out and touch him. I want to. I don't think I've ever wanted anything so much in my life. But I feel the sorrow building in me, that grief so powerful and painful that my eyes instantly flood with tears. I'd almost forgotten that grief. I lower my head, and that's when I see that he's holding my hand, Christian's long fingers wrapped around mine. His thumb drags over my knuckles. I suck in a shocked breath.

What does it mean?

I look up. I'm in the classroom again, staring at Christian. Somebody snickers. Everybody's looking at me expectantly. I can feel Angela's tension rising up off her in waves. She's freaking out. She wanted to give me note cards. Maybe that wasn't such a bad idea.

"Your Majesty?" prompts Mr. Erikson.

I suddenly remember my next line.

"Take heart," I say quickly, unable to tear my gaze away

from Christian's. He smiles again, like we're having our own private conversation.

"I know I have the body but of a weak and feeble woman," I say. "But I have the heart and stomach of a king."

"Here, here!" says Angela, her golden eyes wide behind her glasses. "Long live the queen!"

"Long live the queen," repeats Mr. Erikson, and then the whole class is saying it.

I can't help but smile. Angela, looking relieved that my part is done, starts going into the details of Elizabeth's reign. Now I only have to stand there and look pretty, like she said. And try to calm my racing heart.

"Of course for a long time all anybody in England seemed to be interested in was finding the right husband for Elizabeth," Angela says, glancing over at Mr. Erikson like she's proving a point. "Everyone doubted that she'd be able to rule by herself. But she turned out to be one of the best and most revered monarchs in history. She ushered in a golden age for England."

"Yeah, but didn't she die a virgin?" asks Tucker from the back of the class.

Angela doesn't waver. She immediately launches into her stuff about the Virgin Queen, the way Elizabeth used the image of the virgin to make her unmarried status more attractive.

Tucker is leaning against the back wall, smirking.

"Sir Tucker," I say suddenly, interrupting Angela.

"Yeah?"

"I believe the correct response is, 'yes, *Your Majesty*,'" I say in my haughtiest tone. I can't just let him mock me in front of the entire class, can I?

"Yes, Your Majesty," he says sarcastically.

"Have a care, Sir Tucker, lest you find yourself in the stockades."

He scoffs and looks at Mr. Erikson. "She can't do that, can she? She's not the ruler of this class. Brady is."

"She's queen today," says Mr. Erikson, leaning back in his chair. "I'd shut up if I were you."

"You could strip him of his title," suggests Brady, apparently not minding at all that I have usurped his throne. "Make him a serf."

"Yeah," says Christian. "Make him a serf. Being a serf blows."

As a serf, poor Christian has already been killed several times in our class. Aside from dying of the Black Plague on the first day, he's starved to death, had his hands cut off for stealing a loaf of bread, and been run down by his master's horse just for kicks. He's like Christian the fifth now.

"Or you could get rid of him altogether. Throw him in the Tower of London. Have him drawn and quartered. Maybe the rack. Or a red-hot enema," says Mr. Erikson, laughing. You have to admire a teacher who'd suggest death via red-hot enema.

"Perhaps we should put it to a vote," I say, looking coolly

at Tucker, remembering how he almost got me burned as a witch. Sweet revenge.

"All in favor of death to Sir Tucker the heretic, raise your hand," says Angela quickly.

I look around the classroom at the raised hands. It's unanimous. Except for Tucker, who stands in the back with his arms crossed.

"Red-hot enema it is," I say.

"I'll mark it down," says Mr. Erikson gleefully.

"Now that that's settled," says Angela, looking at me sharply, "let me tell you about the defeat of the Spanish Armada."

I cast a triumphant glance at Tucker. The corner of his mouth lifts in a half smile. He nods at me, as if to say, *Touché*.

Point: Clara.

Go me.

"What was *that*?" hisses Angela as we beeline it for the restroom after class.

"The thing with Tucker? I know! I can't figure him out."

"No, the thing where you spaced out in the middle of your speech and left me hanging in front of the entire class."

"Sorry," I say. "I had the vision. How long was I out?"

"Only like ten seconds. But it was the longest ten seconds ever. I thought I was going to have to slap you."

"Sorry," I say again. "It's not something I can control."

"I know. It's fine." We burst into the girls' bathroom and stand in the handicap stall while Angela disassembles the dress and I step out of it. She unties the corset and I gasp in relief, finally able to take a full breath.

"You saw the forest fire?" she asks, peeking out to make sure we're alone.

"No, not this time."

She grins wickedly as she hands me my sweatshirt. "You saw Christian."

I feel a blush creeping up my cheeks.

"Yes." I carefully remove the headpiece and hand it to Angela, then pull the shirt over my head.

"So you were like, looking at Christian in class and then you were looking at him in the future. That's wild, C."

"Tell me about it." I pull on my jeans and walk over to the mirror to survey the damage to my hair. "Ugh. I need a shower."

"And in the future, what happened?"

"Nothing," I say quickly. "It was only ten seconds, remember? There wasn't time for anything to happen."

I turn on the sink and lower my head to splash my face, watching the white makeup dissolve into my hand and swirl down the drain. The cool water feels good against my flushed skin. Angela hands me a paper towel and I dry off, then wipe at the bright red lipstick. She gets a brush out of her backpack and starts to pull the pins out of my hair.

"Nothing new, huh?" she says, her eyes meeting mine in the mirror. "No new part of the vision?"

I sigh. I might as well tell her. Angela has a way of ferreting out the truth one way or another. She's nothing if not perceptive *and* persistent.

"He was—" I begin softly. "We were . . . holding hands."

"Shut up!" exclaims Angela. "So you two are like lovers!"

"No!" I protest. "I mean, maybe. I don't know what we are. We're holding hands, so what? It doesn't necessarily mean anything."

"Oh, *right*." Angela looks at me incredulously as she tugs the brush through my hair-spray-saturated hair. "Save it. You know you're totally in love with him."

"I don't even know him that well. Ouch! Take it easy!"

"Well, I've known him since kindergarten," says Angela, ignoring my protests as she works the tangles out of my hair. "And trust me when I say that Christian Prescott is all that he's cracked up to be. He's smart, funny, nice, and oh yeah, hotter than hell in July."

"Sounds like maybe *you're* in love with him," I point out.

"Eighth grade," Angela says. "Ava Peters's birthday party. We play spin the bottle. My bottle points to Christian, so we sneak out to the back porch to kiss."

"And?" I say.

"And it was fine. But no sparks. No chemistry. Nothing. It was like kissing my brother. Don't worry, he's all yours, C."

"Hey, this vision is a job, remember," I say. "Not a date. And I believe he's all Kay's, so enough with the crazy talk."

She scoffs. "Kay's pretty. And she's clever enough to keep his attention. But Kay's a normal high school girl. You're an angelic being. You're smarter and more attractive than she is in every way. You're genetically superior. Okay, so there's the hair thing. It's a bad color, distracts people, whatever. But you're totally hot. You've got a whole Scarlett Johansson thing going on, minus the boobs. Every guy at Jackson Hole High knows who you are, trust me." Then she adds, "Besides, Christian and Kay are almost over."

"What do you mean? What have you heard?"

"Nothing," she says flippantly. "It's just the timeline, you know? This kind of relationship has a definite shelf life."

"What kind of relationship is that, exactly?"

She looks at me levelly. "The physical kind. What, you think Christian's attracted to Kay's dazzling wit?

"Their expiration date is almost up. Trust me," she says when I don't answer, the corner of her mouth twisting up into her evil smile. It's unbelievable that her wings are whiter than mine.

"You're a weird one, you know that?" I say, shaking my head. "Weird."

"Just wait," she says. "You'll see. Soon he'll be all yours. He's your destiny, after all." She flutters her eyelashes.

"Oh really, you think my purpose is about me getting a boyfriend? That would be awfully nice and all, because clearly I could use some help on the romantic front, but don't you think the world is a little bigger than me and Christian and our love lives?"

"Maybe," she says, and it's impossible to tell whether or not she's serious. "You never know."

After school, I wait in the parking lot for Wendy. We're going back to my house to study for a Jane Austen exam in Phibbs's class. I can't help but locate Christian's Avalanche, parked in the back like always.

Wendy walks up and playfully punches me on the arm. "Tucker told me you were a queen today," she says.

I drag my gaze away from Christian's truck. "Yeah, I ruled. Literally."

"I wish I'd seen you in your costume," she says. "You should have come and gotten me at lunch. I could have helped you get ready."

"Oh, you didn't need to help me with the history class stuff," I reply as if I hadn't wanted to impose on her. But the truth is, I don't know how to handle Angela and Wendy in the same space. How weird would it be to talk about normal things like school and boys now when I'm so used to talking about angel stuff with Angela? The last couple weeks I've mostly seen Wendy in class and at lunch, where I still sit at the Invisibles table. I've been busy with Angela working on our project most days after school.

"Ready for Jane Austen?" I ask.

"You know I'm crushing on Mr. Darcy, big-time," she says.

"Oh, right," I say distractedly, because I've spotted Christian and Kay.

They're standing next to the silver truck, talking. Kay is smiling up at him. She leans into him as she talks, practically draping herself over him. He doesn't seem to mind. They kiss, not a little peck, but a long, lingering kiss where she twines her arms around his neck and he curls his arms around her waist and pulls her close and lifts her up. Then he steps back and brushes his hand across her cheek, tucking a strand of her hair behind her ear. He says something. She nods. He opens the driver's side door of the truck, and she climbs in. He hops in after her and closes the door. I don't have a good view of what happens next, but the Avalanche doesn't move. They aren't driving anywhere.

They don't look like a couple whose expiration date is almost up. They look happy.

"You're not listening to me, are you?" says Wendy then, loudly.

I jump, startled, and look over at her. She has her head cocked slightly to one side, her blue eyes narrowed.

"Sorry," I say quickly. I smile. "Did Tucker tell you that I had him executed today? It's good to be queen."

I expect her to lighten up, make some smart-aleck remark, but she just shakes her head.

"What?"

"Christian has a girlfriend, as you might have noticed," she says. "I suggest you get over it."

My mouth opens, then closes, then opens again.

"Hello, rude!" I finally sputter.

"It's true."

"You don't know anything about it," I shoot back.

"Well, maybe I would, if you ever bothered to talk to me anymore," she says, crossing her arms over her chest.

"Oh, I see, you're jealous now. Hence the rudeness."

She looks away quickly in a way that confirms it—she's jealous of Angela and all the time we've been spending together. "I'm sick of watching you drool over Christian Prescott like he's a piece of meat, is all."

It's been a long day. And so I lose my temper.

"What's it to you, Wen? It's my life. Why don't you stop being invisible for once and get your own?"

She stares at me for a long moment, her face slowly reddening, her eyes shining with the beginnings of tears that she's too stubborn to let fall. She turns away. I can see her shoulders starting to shake.

"Wen—"

"Forget it," she says. She picks up her backpack and slings it over her shoulder. "I thought I was your friend, for real, not

188

just until you found somebody better. My mistake."

"Whoa, Wendy, you are my friend," I say, taking a step back. "I—"

"No offense, Clara, but sometimes it's not all about *you*."

I stare at her.

"I'm going to catch the bus home," she says, pushing past me.

10

FLYING LESSON

I wish I could have had a fun spring break, some wild trip to Miami or even a simple road trip with my friends. But Wendy was still not talking to me (boy, can that girl ever hold a grudge!) and Angela was busy helping her mom with spring cleaning at the Pink Garter. So spring break consisted of seven fun-filled days cooped up in the house with Jeffrey, who was grounded because he'd won the Regional Wrestling Championships. Two weeks with no TV, no phone, no internet. I thought this was a bit excessive. Jeffrey was furious, Mom was cranky, and no amount of standing on the porch soaking in the sun could take away the chill inside the house.

It's a relief to be back at school. At lunch I sit waiting for

Angela to show up. I'm using a napkin to sop up the extra grease on a slice of pepperoni pizza when Wendy practically skips into the cafeteria. She gets in line for the fish and waves at the girls at the Invisibles table a little spastically. She's wearing her I-can't-wait-to-tell-you face. I'm guessing it involves prom.

I take a bite of soggy pizza and remind myself that I don't want to go to prom. I'd so much rather stay home with Ben and Jerry and watch chick flicks with Mom, who needs some major R & R.

Why does this plan depress me so much?

"You'll never guess what happened," I pick up from Wendy as she flops down into the chair at the Invisibles table a few feet away. For a moment she meets my eyes, and I know that we both wish that we could get over our stupid fight and make up and then she'd be telling me all her exciting news.

"You got a date for prom?" asks Emma.

Wendy's blue eyes sparkle. I wonder if a BFF victory squeal is going to be required in this situation.

"No," she says. "Well, yes. I'm going with Jason Lovett. But that's not my big news. I got the internship!"

"The internship," Lindsey repeats blankly.

Of course! The internship in Montana that she's been talking about nonstop since she found out about it! The one where all the vets graduated from Washington State. Come on, people! And you call yourselves her friends?

"At the All West Veterinary Hospital," she explains.

"Oh, right," says Lindsey vaguely. "The one in Bozeman?"

"Yes," she says, sounding a bit out of breath. "I would have killed to get that internship. Practically all of the vets graduated from Washington State, which is my dream school, as you know."

She glances at me again. I smile faintly. She looks away.

"Congrats!" the girls at the table are all saying practically in unison.

"Thanks." She looks genuinely happy and proud and excited for the future, even without the victory squeal.

"Wait, does this mean you're going to be gone all summer?" Audrey asks, frowning.

"June through August."

"That's great," says Emma. "Now tell us about how Jason Lovett asked you."

I can almost hear Wendy blush.

"Actually, I asked him."

I lean forward and rest my chin in my hands, like I'm really bored and not listening in to everything that's going on. I'm glad for Wendy. Jason seems like a good guy, a bit on the short side, big, hopeful brown eyes, a soft tenor voice that I hope for his sake deepens as he gets older. But nice. Somebody who will treat Wendy right.

Angela finally shows up. She tosses her brown paper lunch sack down on the table in front of me and slides into a chair. Intuitively her eyes flicker over to the Invisibles table, where

Wendy and her friends are still going on about how she asked Jason.

"You should make up with her," says Angela. "She's over it, whatever it was. What was it, anyway, that got her panties in a bunch?"

"Mostly I think it was because she was jealous of all the time I was spending with you," I say pointedly.

"Oh well, I can't exactly help you there. I am amazing, you know."

I grin. "I know."

"Oh! Speaking of me being amazing, have I got news for you." She leans forward, her eyes still bright with mischief. "I heard that Christian and Kay were having major problems during spring break," she whispers theatrically.

I quickly survey the cafeteria. It takes me a second, but I find Christian sitting by himself in the very back of the room. No Kay in sight. No friends. Interesting.

"What kind of problems?"

"A big screaming match in front of like a hundred people at a party kind of problems. There's this nasty rumor going around about Christian hooking up with a girl on the Cheyenne ski team at the State Championships."

"And who'd start a rumor like that?"

She smiles with that annoying, knowing look in her eyes. "I told you, didn't I? Rumor or not, it was only a matter of time. . . ."

That's when Kay Patterson enters the room.

Kay is wearing a skirt that I'm pretty sure violates the school dress code, and more makeup than usual, almost raccoonlike around the eyes, her lips a deep, brazen red. Her gaze immediately seeks out Christian. He appears to be completely absorbed by his Tater Tots, not looking up, but I can tell by his posture that he knows she's there. And she knows he knows it. For a moment I think she's going to burst into tears. Then she starts walking, and sways right up to a group of freshman/sophomore jocks in the corner. The whole cafeteria pivots to watch her. She chooses one of the guys seemingly at random and says something in a low, phone-sex-operator voice. She runs her fingers through his hair.

Then she turns and sits in Jeffrey's lap.

I think everybody's jaw hits the floor at approximately the same time.

This is way beyond Christian and Kay having problems. This is Kay leaning forward against Jeffrey's chest and saying something into his ear so close that she could have licked him. His eyes widen slightly but he's obviously trying to keep his cool. He doesn't move.

I stand up.

"Excuse me for a minute," I say politely to Angela, like I'm just going to powder my nose. But I'm seeing red. I fully intend to walk over there and use my angelic superstrength to punch Kay Patterson in her dainty turned-up nose, for a number of reasons, really, the least of which being that she's

194

chosen my baby brother for her twisted game and nobody better mess with my baby brother.

"Wait." Angela grabs my arm in a steely grip. "Calm down, C. Jeffrey's a big boy. He can take care of himself."

Jeffrey looks like he's going to swallow his Adam's apple.

"Where's Christian?" he croaks.

"I don't know where Christian is," Kay purrs as if she couldn't care less. "Do you?"

I tear my gaze away from the new slutty version of Kay. Christian has stopped eating and is gathering up his stuff onto his tray. He stands up and walks over to the tray drop-off, turns and points a look of general disdain in Kay's direction, then heads for the door.

Good for him, I think as he yanks the door open. It bangs shut behind him. I watch him through the window as he strides down the hall toward the main exit, his fury streaming out behind him as clearly as a trail of smoke in the air. Then he's gone.

"Now's your chance," whispers Angela. "Go after him."

I could say something to him. But what?

"He wants to be alone right now," I say to Angela. "Wouldn't you?"

"Coward," she says.

I glare at her. "Don't," I say, suddenly so furious that it's tough to get the words past my clenched teeth. "Call. Me. A coward."

I shake Angela off and stalk across the cafeteria to Kay.

I tap her on the shoulder.

"Excuse me," I say. "What do you think you're doing?"

Kay glances up, something calculating in her eyes. She smiles.

"Do you have a problem, Pippi?"

Pippi. As in Longstocking. Laughter circulates around the lunchroom. But Mom was right. It doesn't faze me. I've heard it before.

"Wow. Original. Now get off my brother, please."

Someone grabs my arm and squeezes very gently. I glance over to see Wendy standing next to me.

"This isn't you, Kay," Wendy says.

Which is true. As much as I want to believe Kay is evil incarnate, as much as part of me wants to see this little display as her true colors peeking through, Kay is not that girl. This is such an obvious, pathetic front. It has that wounded animal quality of lashing out. Seeing that so clearly lessens my desire to punch her lights out.

"I know you're upset, Kay, but—" I begin.

"You don't know anything." She loosens her octopus grip on Jeffrey and glowers at me with infuriated chocolate eyes. Jeffrey's eyes say something different altogether: Don't. You're embarrassing me. Go away.

"Christian's gone," I continue. "He left. So what's the point in drooling all over someone else's boyfriend? You trying to ruin our appetites or what?"

If Kay looks embarrassed or uncertain, it's only for a millisecond. She turns to Jeffrey.

"Do you have a girlfriend?" she asks in a sugary tone.

He looks at Kay with her dangerous black-ringed eyes and then his gaze darts to Kimber, who was standing in the pizza line when this all went down. She reminds me of a Keebler elf, her white-blond hair braided and wrapped around her head like the girl on the Swiss Miss hot chocolate. But she looks royally ticked off. Her face is pale, two hot splashes of red on her cheeks, her eyes throwing sparks.

Maybe I'm not going to be the one beating up Kay after all.

"Yeah," says Jeffrey, his mouth turning up in the hint of a smile. "Kimber Lane. She's my girlfriend."

The look that passes between Jeffrey and Kimber right then feels like it requires a swell of cheesy music in the background. Aw, I think. Baby brother's in love. I also find this kind of gross.

"All right, then," says Kay with forced lightness. She stands up and straightens her skirt, then lifts her head and gives this forced laugh like it was all a game, and it was amusing, but now she's bored.

"See you later," she says to Jeffrey, and then she saunters off, orbited by her little posse the minute she's away from us. They leave the cafeteria, and then there's an explosion of noise as the other students all start talking at once.

Wendy lets go of my arm.

"Hey," I say, turning to her. "I'm sorry about all that stupid stuff I said before."

"Me too."

"Do you want to hang out after school?"

She smiles.

"Sure," she says. "I'd love to."

Wendy and I hole up in my room and do our homework together, bent over our books without talking much, only looking up occasionally to smile or ask a question. I, of course, am not thinking about my aerodynamics class and the three theories of physics that are supposed to explain lift. The class is all numbers and angles, nothing that resembles what it would be like to fly in real life, but ironically I'm good at it.

I can't stop thinking about Christian. He was a no-show in British History.

"So, I heard you're going to prom with Jason Lovett," I say to Wendy, closing my book. I can't stand being trapped inside my own head a moment longer. "Is that a big woo-hoo or what?"

"Yeah," she says with a happy smile.

"What are you going to wear?"

She bites her lip. There is clearly a snag in the wardrobe department.

"You don't have a dress yet?" I ask.

"I have something," she says, trying to sound cheerful. "I wear it to church, but I think I can fancy it up a bit."

"Oh no. No church dress." I jump up and run to the back of my closet, where I grab two formal gowns that I wore for dances in California, then march back to Wendy. I hold the dresses out to either side of me. "Just pick the one you like."

Wendy suddenly has trouble meeting my eyes.

"But what about you?" she stammers.

"I'm not going."

"I can't believe somebody hasn't asked you yet."

I shrug.

"Well, why don't you ask someone? I mean, what good is women's lib if we can't use it to ask guys to dances? I asked Jason."

"There's no one I want to go with."

"Uh-huh."

"What?"

"I'm going to let that one slide."

"Anyway, Jason Lovett's going to be your Prince Charming on prom night, and you're totally going to need a Cinderella dress. So pick one."

She's already eyeing the pale pink gown in my left hand with hungry eyes.

"I think it would rock on you," I say, waving it at her.

"Really? You don't think I'd look ridiculous?"

"Try it on."

She snatches it out of my hand and runs into the closet to try it.

"You're too tall," she whines through the door.

"That's what heels are for."

"You have bigger boobs than I do."

"Impossible."

The door swings open. She stands there uncertainly, her long golden brown hair tumbling around her neck and shoulders. The gown sags around her feet, but it's nothing a hem won't fix.

"You look amazing." I rummage around in my jewelry box for the matching sparkly necklace. "We should go into Jackson tomorrow and find you some earrings. Too bad the nearest mall is all the way in Idaho Falls. Claire's has the best prom stuff. What is that, like two hours away?"

"Two and a half," she answers. "But I don't have pierced ears."

"I think I can find a potato and a sharp needle."

She gasps and puts her hands up to cover her earlobes.

"What did you ever do for fun before I came along?" I ask.

"Cow tipping."

There's a sharp knock on my door and my mom sticks her head in. Wendy instantly flushes to the roots of her hair and starts backing toward the closet door, but Mom charges right in to look at her.

"What? Dress up! How come I wasn't invited?" she exclaims.

"Prom. Saturday after next. I told you, remember?"

"Oh yes," she says. "And you're not going." She sounds disappointed.

"Did you want something, Mom?"

200

"Yes, I wanted to remind you that you and I have a date to practice our yoga tonight."

It takes me a second to catch up. And freak out a little.

"Couldn't we do it some other time? I'm kind of busy at the—"

"I know you girls are having such fun, but I have to steal you for some mother-daughter time."

"I need to go, anyway," mumbles Wendy. "I've got to finish this homework."

"You look lovely, Wendy," says Mom, beaming at her. "What about shoes?"

"I think my black pumps will work."

Mom shakes her head. "No black pumps with that dress."

"We're going to look for earrings in Jackson tomorrow," I offer. "We could look for shoes too."

Wendy starts to squirm unhappily at the suggestion. There aren't any shoe stores in Jackson that aren't priced for tourists.

"Or," Mom says, "we could skip Jackson and bring out the big guns. Road trip to Idaho Falls this weekend?"

I can't tell if she's been eavesdropping or if she and I just think on the same wavelength. "Sometimes," I tell her with a grin, "it's like you can read my mind."

"Wendy doesn't have a lot of money, you know," I say to Mom when Wendy is safely off the property. The sun's setting behind the mountains. I'm standing in a tank top and sweatpants in the backyard, shivering, trying to wrap a wool scarf around my neck. "So this thing in Idaho Falls for shoes, don't go dragging us into some fancy department store. It will embarrass her."

"I was thinking Payless," Mom says primly. "I thought it might be nice to have some girl time. You really haven't had much of that since we moved here."

"Okay."

"I also thought you could bring Angela along. Does she have a date for prom?"

I stop fiddling with the scarf and stare at her. "Yeah. She does."

"So she can come too."

"Why?"

"I want to know your friends, Clara. You bring Wendy to the house all the time, but you never bring Angela. So I want to meet her. I think it's time."

"Yeah, but—"

"I know you're nervous about it, but you shouldn't be," she says. "I'll behave."

It's not really Mom I'm worried about. Or maybe it is. "Okay, I'll ask her."

"Wonderful. Lose the scarf," says Mom.

"It's freezing!"

"It could snag."

She has a point. I dump the scarf.

"Do we have to do this now? I'm taking a class in aerody-namics at school, you know. I'm acing it, by the way."

"That's about flying a plane. This is about you. You need to train, Clara. I've let you have all winter to get adjusted. Now you need to focus on your purpose so you'll be ready when fire season starts. It's only a few months away."

"I know," I say glumly.

"Now, please."

"Okay, fine."

I unfold my wings behind me. It's been a while since I've had them out. At least it's gotten easier to summon them; I don't have to say the words in Angelic anymore. I still think my wings are beautiful—soft and white and perfect as an owl's. But at the moment they seem huge and silly, like a cheesy prop in a bad movie.

"Good, stretch them out," says Mom.

I extend them as far as I can, until their weight begins to strain my shoulders.

"To get off the ground you must lighten yourself." She keeps saying this and I have no clue how to do it.

"Next you're going to sprinkle me with pixie dust and tell me to think happy thoughts," I grumble.

"Clear your mind."

"Done."

"Starting with the attitude."

I sigh.

"Try to relax."

I stare at her helplessly.

"Try closing your eyes," she says. "Take deep breaths in your nose and out through your mouth. Imagine yourself becoming lighter, your bones weighing less."

I close my eyes.

"This really is like yoga," I say.

"You've got to empty yourself out, let go of all the things that mentally weigh you down."

I try to clear my mind. Instead I see Christian's face. Not from the vision, surrounded by fire and smoke, but a breath away like when he leaned over me on the ski slope. His dark, thick eyelashes. His eyes with their spatters of gold. Full of warmth. The way the corners crinkle when he smiles.

My wings don't feel as heavy then.

"That's good, Clara," says Mom. "Now try to lift off."

"How?"

"Flap your wings."

I imagine my wings catching the air the way hers did that time at Buzzards Roost. I think about shooting up into the sky like a rocket, streaking past clouds, brushing the treetops. It'd be wonderful, wouldn't it, to soar like that? To answer the call of the sky?

Nothing so much as twitches.

"It might help if you open your eyes now," Mom says with a laugh.

I open my eyes. *Flap,* I order my wings silently.

"I can't," I pant after a minute. I'm sweating, in spite of the chilly air.

"You're overthinking it. Remember, your wings are like your arms. You don't have to think at your arms to move them, you just move them."

I glare at her. My teeth clench in frustration. Then my wings slowly flex back and forth.

"That's it," says Mom. "You're doing it!"

Only I'm not doing it. My feet are still firmly planted on the ground. My wings are moving, fanning the air, blowing my hair all over my face, but I'm not lifting off.

"I'm too heavy."

"You need to make yourself light."

"I know!"

I try to think of Christian again, his eyes, his smile, anything tangible, but suddenly I can only picture him from the vision now, standing with his back to me. The fire coming.

What if I can't do this? I think. What if the whole thing depends on my ability to fly? What if he dies?

"Come on!" I scream, straining with everything I have. "Fly!"

I bend my knees, jump, and make it a few feet off the ground. For all of five seconds I think I might have done it. Then I come down hard, at an angle, twisting my ankle. Off balance, I crash onto the lawn, a tangle of limbs and wings.

For a minute I lie there in the soggy grass, gasping for breath.

"Clara," says Mom.

"Don't."

"Are you hurt?"

Yes, I'm hurt. I will my wings to vanish.

"Keep trying. You'll get it," Mom says.

"No, I won't. Not today." I get to my feet carefully and brush dirt and grass off my pants, refusing to meet her eyes.

"You're used to everything coming easy for you. You're going to have to work at this."

I wish she'd stop saying that. Every time, her face gets this look like I've let her down, like she expected more. It makes me feel like a big fat failure, both as a human, where I'm supposed to be remarkable—beautiful, fast, strong, sure on my feet, able to do anything that's asked of me—and as an angel. As a regular girl, I'm not proving to be anything magnificent. And as an angel, I am simply abysmal.

"Clara." Mom moves toward me, opening her arms like we're going to hug now and everything will be okay. "You have to try again. You can do this."

"Stop being so soccer mom about it, okay? Just leave me alone."

"Honey—"

"Leave me alone!" I screech. I look into her startled eyes.

"All right," she says. She turns and walks swiftly back

toward the house. The door slams. I hear Jeffrey's voice in the kitchen, and her voice, low and patient, answering him. I rub my burning eyes. I want to run away but there's nowhere to go. So I stand there, my neck and shoulders and ankle aching, feeling sorry for myself until the yard is dark and there's nothing left to do but limp inside.

11

IDAHO FALLS

Angela shows up at our house a whole hour early on Saturday morning, and the minute I see her standing on the porch I know this girls-day-out idea is a big mistake. She looks like a kid on Christmas morning. She's totally freaked-excited to meet my mom.

"Just play it cool, all right?" I tell her before I let her come in. "Remember what we talked about. Casual. No angel talk."

"Fine."

"I mean it. No angel-related questions at all."

"You told me like a hundred times already."

"Ask her about Pearl Harbor or something. She'd probably like that."

Angela rolls her eyes.

She doesn't seem to grasp the fact that our friendship largely depends on how clueless she appears to my mom. That if Mom knew what Angela and I've been talking about all these afternoons after school, the angel research and questions and Angela's wacky theories, I'd probably never be allowed to go to the Pink Garter again.

"Maybe it'd be best if you don't talk at all," I say. She puts her hand on her hip and glares at me. "Okay, okay. Come with me."

In the kitchen Mom is setting a huge plate of pancakes on the table. She smiles.

"Hello, Angela."

"Hi, Mrs. Gardner," Angela says in this completely reverential tone.

"Call me Maggie," Mom says. "It's good to finally meet you face-to-face."

"Clara's told me so much about you I feel like I already know you."

"All good, I hope."

I glance at Mom. We've hardly said three sentences to each other since the botched flying lesson. She smiles without showing her teeth, her company smile. "Clara hasn't really told me that much about you," she says.

"Oh," says Angela, "well there's not that much to tell."

"Okay, so pancakes," I say. "I bet Angela's starved."

Mom turns to get a plate out of the cupboard, and I shoot Angela a warning look.

"What?" she whispers.

She's completely starstruck by my mom. She stares at her all through breakfast. Which would have been okay—weird, but okay—except that after about two bites into pancakes she blurts out, "How high can an angel-blood fly? Do you think we could fly in space?"

Mom just laughs and says that sounds cool but she's pretty sure we still need oxygen. "No Superman trips to the moon," she says.

They smile at each other, which bugs me. If I asked that question, Mom would say she didn't know, or it wasn't important, or she'd change the subject. I know what she's doing: She's trying to figure Angela out. She wants to know what Angela knows. Which I definitely do not want to happen.

But there's no stopping Angela. "What about the light thing?" she asks.

"The light thing?"

"You know, when the angels shine with the heavenly light? What's that about?"

"We call that glory," Mom answers.

"So what's the point of it?" Angela asks.

Mom sets down her glass of milk and acts like this is a deep question that requires some serious thought. "It has many uses," she says finally.

"I'll bet the light comes in handy," says Angela. "Like your own personal flashlight. And it makes you look angelic, of course. No one would doubt you if you show the wings and the glory. But you're not supposed to do that, right?"

"We're never to reveal ourselves," Mom says, looking at me for an instant, "although there are exceptions. Glory has a strange effect on humans."

"Like what?"

"It terrifies them."

I sit up a little. I didn't know that, and neither did Angela.

"Oh, I see," says Angela, really cooking with gas now. "But what *is* glory? It has to be more than just light, to have that kind of effect, right?"

Mom clears her throat. She's in uncomfortable territory now, stuff she's never told me.

"You're always saying how much easier flying would be if I could tap into glory," I pipe up, not about to let her off the hook. "You make it sound like an energy source."

She gives a barely perceivable sigh. "It's how we connect with God."

Angela and I mull that over.

"Like how?" asks Angela. "Like when people pray?"

"When you're in glory, you're connected with everything. You can feel the trees breathing. You could count the feathers on a bird's wing. You know if it's going to rain. You're part of it, that force which binds all life."

"Will you teach us how to do it?" asks Angela. This whole conversation is clearly blowing her mind. She's itching to whip out her notebook and take some major notes.

"It can't be taught. You have to learn to still yourself, to strip away everything but the core of what makes you, you. It's not your thoughts or your feelings. It's the self under all of that."

"Okay, so that sounds hard."

"I was forty before I was able to do it well," Mom says. "Some angel-bloods never get to that state at all. Although it can be triggered by powerful events or feelings."

"Like Clara's hair thing, right? You told her that gets triggered by emotions," Angela says.

Mom gets up from the table and crosses to the window.

"Oh. My. God. Shut up," I whisper to Angela.

"There's a blue truck in the driveway," Mom says after a moment. "Wendy's here."

I abandon Mom and Angela and run to meet Wendy, who, unbeknownst to her, will save me from this angel conversation.

Tucker drove her over. He's leaning against Bluebell in the driveway, staring out at the woods, and somehow it feels like he shouldn't be allowed to be here, shouldn't be allowed to peer into my woods or listen to my stream or enjoy my birds singing.

"Hey, Carrots," he says when he spots me. I look around for Wendy, who I find rummaging around in the truck for something. "Beautiful day for shopping," he adds.

He's mocking me, I think. I don't have a comeback.

"Yep," I say.

Wendy slams the door of the truck and steps up onto the porch right as Angela exits the house. "Hey, Angela," she says brightly. She's apparently determined to be friendly with this other best friend of mine. "How's it going?"

"Great," says Angela.

"I'm so excited to go to Idaho Falls. I haven't been there in forever."

"Me neither."

Tucker's not leaving. He's looking at my woods again. Against my better judgment, I step down off the porch and walk over to him.

"Shopping for prom dresses, huh?" he asks as I come up beside him.

"Um, kind of. Wendy needs shoes. Angela's after accessories, since her mom's making her dress. And I'm along for the ride, I guess."

"You're not going to prom?"

"No." I glance away uncomfortably, back toward the house, where suddenly Wendy seems very into her awkward conversation with Angela.

"Why not?"

I give him a "why do you think?" glare.

"No one's asked you?" He looks at me.

I shake my head. "Shocking, right?"

"Yeah, actually, it is."

He rubs the back of his neck, then gazes at the woods. He clears his throat. For a second I get the crazy idea that he might be about to ask me to prom, and my heart does all kinds of stupid erratic leaps in my chest from sheer terror at the idea. Because I'd have to reject him right in front of Wendy and Angela, who are acting like they're talking but I can tell they're paying attention, and then he'd be humiliated. I have no real desire to see Tucker humiliated.

"Go stag," he says instead. "That's what I would do."

I almost laugh with relief. "I guess."

He turns and calls to Wendy. "I gotta take off. Come here a sec."

"Clara's going to take me home, so I won't be needing your services anymore today, Jeeves," says Wendy like he's her chauffeur. He nods and takes her arm and draws her over to the side of the truck where he speaks in a low voice.

"I don't know what prom shoes cost, but this might help," he says.

"Tucker Avery," Wendy says. "You know I can't take that."

"I don't know anything."

She snorts. "You're sweet. But that's rodeo money. I can't take it."

"I'll get more."

He must keep holding the money out to her, because then

she says no more emphatically.

"Okay, fine," he grumbles. He gives her a quick hug and gets in his truck, pulls around the circle, and stops, then rolls down the window to lean out.

"Have fun in Idaho. Don't provoke any potato farmers," he says.

"Right. Because that would be bad."

"Oh, and, Carrots . . ."

"Yes?"

"If you end up going to prom, save me a dance, okay?"

Before I have time to process this request, he drives away.

"Men," Angela says from beside me.

"I thought that was nice," says Wendy.

I sigh, flustered. "Let's just go."

Suddenly Wendy gasps. She pulls a fifty-dollar bill out of her sweatshirt pocket.

"That little stink," she says, smiling.

The second I lay eyes on the dress, I'm in love with it. If I were going to prom, this would be it. The one. Sometimes you just know with dresses. They call to you. This one's Greek inspired, strapless with an empire waist and a swath of fabric that comes up the front and over one shoulder. It's a deep blue, a little brighter than navy.

"Okay," says Angela after I've been staring at it on the rack for five minutes. "You have to try it on."

"What? No. I'm not going to prom."

"Who cares? Hey, Maggie, Wendy!" Angela calls across the department store to Wendy, who's in the shoe department with my mom looking through the clearance heels. "Come see this dress for Clara."

They drop everything and come to see the dress. And gasp when they see it. And insist I try it on.

"But I'm not going to prom," I protest from the dressing room as I pull my shirt over my head.

"You don't need a date," says Angela from the other side of the door. "You *could* go stag, you know."

"Right. Stag to prom. So I can stand around and watch everybody else dance. Sounds fantastic."

"Well, we know one person who will dance with you," says Wendy faintly.

"He did just break up with his girlfriend, you know," Mom says.

"Tucker?" Wendy asks, confused.

"Christian," Mom answers.

My heart misses a beat, and when Wendy and Angela don't respond, I open the dressing room door and stick my head out. "How'd you hear about Christian breaking up with Kay?"

She and Angela exchange a look. I only left them alone together for like five minutes this morning and Angela had obviously already presented her "Christian and Clara are soul mates" hypothesis. I wonder what Mom thinks of that.

"If I were Christian you wouldn't catch me anywhere near the dance," says Wendy. "It'd be like a snake pit for him."

That's true. This last week at school Christian seemed off—nothing too noticeable, but I watch him a lot, so I noticed. He didn't crack any of his usual jokes in Brit History. He didn't take notes during class. And then he was absent two days in a row, which never happens. Late, yes, but Christian's never absent. I guess he must be pretty upset about Kay.

I slip the dress over my head. It fits. Like it was made for me. So unfair.

"Come on, let's see it," orders Angela. I go out and stand in front of the big mirror.

"I wish my hair wasn't orange," I say, brushing an unruly strand out of my face.

"You should buy it," says Angela.

"But I'm not going to prom," I repeat.

"You should go to prom just so you can wear that dress," says Wendy.

"Totally," agrees Angela.

"You are so beautiful," Mom says, and then to my total shock she digs around in her purse for a tissue and blots at her eyes. Then she says, "I'm buying it. If you don't go to prom this year, you can wear it next year. It really is perfect, Clara. It makes your eyes this stunning cornflower blue."

There's no reasoning with them. So fifteen minutes later

we're walking out of the department store with the dress hanging over my arm. That's when we split up, divide and conquer, Mom calls it. Angela and I check out the bling stores, and Mom and Wendy head toward shoes, since there's nothing on heaven and earth my mother loves so much as new shoes. We agree to meet back at the mall entrance in an hour.

I'm in a weird mood. I find it ironic that Angela and Wendy are both going to prom and the only thing we've bought so far on this trip is a dress for me. And I'm not going. I'm also irritated because I can't wear real earrings because piercing my ears doesn't work—they heal too fast. I don't like any of the non-pierced earrings I see. I want something dangly and dramatic for this dance I'm not going to.

I'm feeling queasy and light-headed all of a sudden, so Angela and I stop at Pretzel Time and each get a cinnamon pretzel, hoping some food in my stomach will help. The mall's crowded and there's nowhere to sit, so we lean against the wall and eat our pretzels, watching the people stream in and out of Barnes & Noble.

"Are you mad at me?" Angela asks.

"What? No."

"You haven't said two words to me since breakfast."

"Well, you weren't supposed to talk angel stuff, remember? You promised."

"Sorry," she says.

"Just tone it down a notch or four with my mom, okay?

What with the staring and the questions and everything."

"Am I staring?" She blushes.

"You look like a Kewpie doll."

"Sorry," she says again. "She's the only Dimidius I've ever met. I want to know what she's like."

"I told you. She's like one part hip thirty-something, one part tranquil angelic being, and one part crotchety old lady."

"I don't see the old lady part."

"Trust me, it's there. And you're like one part crazy teenager, one part angelic being, and one part private detective."

She smiles. "I'll try to behave."

That's when I see him. A man, watching me from the doorway of the GNC. He's tall, with dark hair pulled back into a ponytail. He's wearing faded jeans and a brown suede coat that hangs off his body loosely. Out of all the people passing by in that swarming mall, I might not have noticed him except for how intensely he's staring at us.

"Angela," I say weakly, my pretzel dropping to the floor. A wave of terrible sadness crashes over me. I have to fight not to double over with the sudden intensity of the emotion. My hands clench into fists, my nails biting painfully into my palms. I start to cry.

"Whoa, what's the matter, C?" says Angela. "I swear, I'll behave."

I try to answer. I try to press through the sorrow to form the words. Tears pour down my face.

"That man," I whisper.

She follows my gaze. Then she sucks in a jagged breath and looks away.

"Come on," she says. "Let's find your mom."

She puts her arm around my shoulder and steers me quickly down the hall. We bump into people, push our way through families and groups of teenagers. She looks back again.

"Is he following us?" I can't manage anything louder than a whisper. I feel like I'm struggling to keep my head up in a pool of dark, icy water, chilled to the bone, wearier with every step I take, and it's too much. I want to sink down and let this blackness take me.

"I don't see him," says Angela.

Then, like an answered prayer, we find my mom. She and Wendy are coming out of Payless, both carrying shopping bags.

"Hey, you two," Mom says. Then she notices our faces. "What happened?"

"Can we talk to you for a minute?" Angela grabs Mom's arm and pulls her away from Wendy, who looks confused and somewhat offended as we walk away. "There's a man," she whispers. "He was staring at us, and Clara just . . . she just . . ."

"He's so sad," I manage.

"Where?" Mom demands.

"Behind us," says Angela. "I lost track of him, but he's definitely back there somewhere."

Mom zips her hoodie and pulls the hood up to cover her head. She walks back to Wendy and tries to smile.

"Everything okay?" asks Wendy.

"Clara's feeling sick," Mom says. "We should go."

It's not a lie. I'm hardly able to put one foot in front of the other as we make our way quickly toward the department store.

"Don't look back," Mom whispers close to my ear. "Walk, Clara. Move your feet."

We hurry through the cosmetics department and the lingerie, past the formal wear section where we started out the day. Within moments we're in the parking lot. When she sees our car, Mom breaks into a full run, towing me after her.

"What's going on?" asks Wendy as we run.

"Get in the car," Mom orders, and we all scramble in.

We gun it out of the parking lot. It's not until we're a few miles away from Idaho Falls that the sadness starts to dissipate, like a curtain lifting. I take a deep shuddering breath.

"Are you okay?" asks Wendy, still looking wildly confused.

"I just need to get home."

"She has medicine at home," chimes in Angela. "It's a medical condition she has."

"A medical condition?" repeats Wendy. "What kind of medical condition?"

"Uh—"

Mom shoots Angela an exasperated look.

"It's a rare form of anemia," Angela continues smoothly.

"Sometimes it makes her feel sick and wobbly."

Wendy nods like she understands. "Like that day when she passed out at school."

"Exactly. She needs to take her pills."

"Why didn't you tell me?" says Wendy. She glances at Angela and then back at me, as if she's really saying, "How come you told Angela about this and didn't tell me?" She looks hurt.

"It's not usually a big deal," I say. "I'm feeling much better now."

Angela and I share a glance. Especially given the way my mom reacted, we both know that it's a very, very big deal.

When we pull up to the house three hours later, after first dropping Wendy at the Lazy Dog, Mom says to us, "All right. Go up to your room. Wait for me there. I'll be a little while."

Angela and I go into the house. It's not dark yet but I have the urge to turn on all the lights as we retreat to my room. We sit down together on my bed.

We hear Mom knock on Jeffrey's door.

"Hey," she says when he answers. "I thought I'd drop you off at a movie in Jackson, since I've spoiled your sister all day. It's only fair."

After they're gone, Angela puts her arms around me and pulls my quilt around us both, because I can't stop shivering. And we wait. Mom's car crackles up the driveway about an hour later. The door slams. We listen to the careful creak of her feet on the stairs. Then she knocks, very lightly.

"Come in," I croak.

She smiles when she sees us huddled together.

"You shouldn't have taken Jeffrey away," I say. "What if that guy's out there?"

"I don't want you two to be scared, okay?" she says. "We're safe here."

"Who was he?" Angela asks.

Mom sighs, a resigned, tired exhalation. "He was a Black Wing. Chances are he was only passing through."

"A fallen angel hanging out in the mall in Idaho Falls?" says Angela.

"When I saw him, I . . ." I start to choke up, remembering.

"You felt his sorrow."

"His sorrow?" repeats Angela.

"Angels don't have the kind of free will that you or I do. When they go against their design, it causes them an enormous amount of physical and psychological pain. All Black Wings feel this."

"Why didn't you or Angela feel it?" I ask.

"Some of us are more sensitive than others to their presence," she says. "It's actually an advantage. You can feel them coming."

"And what should we do, if we see them?"

"You do what we did today. You run."

"We can't fight them?" asks Angela, her voice higher-pitched than normal. Mom shakes her head. "Not even you?"

"No. Angels are almost infinitely powerful. The best you can do is escape. If you're lucky—and today we were lucky—the angel won't consider you worth his time."

We're all quiet for a minute.

"The surest defense is to stay undetected," Mom says.

"So why didn't you want me to know about them?" I can't keep the accusation out of my voice. "Why don't you want Jeffrey to know?"

"Because your consciousness draws them, Clara. If you're aware of their existence, you're more likely to be discovered."

She looks steadily at Angela, who meets her gaze for a few seconds before she turns away, her fingers tightening on the edge of my quilt. Angela was the one who told me about the Black Wings.

"I'm sorry," whispers Angela.

"It's all right," says Mom. "You didn't know."

Later I crawl into bed with Mom. I want to feel safe next to her radiating heat, but she's cold. Her face is pale and pinched, like she's worn out trying to be the brave and knowing one, trying to protect us. Her feet are like blocks of ice. I put my feet against them, hoping to warm her.

"Mom," I say into the dark. "I was thinking."

"Uh-oh."

"In my vision, when I suddenly feel so sad, is that a Black Wing?"

Silence. Then another sigh.

"When you talked about the sorrow you felt, the way you described it, it seemed like a possibility." Mom grabs my waist and pulls me closer. "Don't worry, Clara. You won't help it by worrying. You don't know your purpose yet. You're still working with a few very small pieces. I don't want to fill your head with preconceptions before you see everything for yourself."

Another shiver passes through me.

12

SHUT UP AND DANCE

By Monday, everything starts to get back to normal. I walk the halls of Jackson High with the same students, and I attend the same boring classes (except for Brit History, of course, where I watch Christian and Brady do a presentation on William Wallace and entertain a brief fantasy of Christian in a kilt) and soon enough, the Black Wing seems like a bad dream, and I feel safe again.

Still, I decide I need to take the whole purpose thing more seriously. No more playing at being a normal girl. I'm not. I'm an angel-blood. I have a job to do. I need to quit whining, quit stalling, quit questioning everything. I need to do it.

So Wednesday after school I catch up with Christian at his locker. I go right over to him and touch him on the shoulder.

A small zing passes through me like a static shock. He turns and fixes me with those green eyes. He doesn't look like he's in any mood to talk.

"Hey, Clara," he says. "Can I help you with something?"

"I thought I could help *you*. I noticed you were out of class last week."

"My uncle took me camping."

"Do you want to borrow my notes for British History?"

"Sure, notes would be great," he says like he couldn't care less about British History but he's humoring me. He's not acting like himself at all, no jokes, no confidence, no subtle swagger in his step. There are shadows under his eyes.

I hand him my notebook. Right as he takes it, a group of girls pass by, popular girls, Kay's friends. They whisper and shoot him dirty looks. His shoulders stiffen.

"They'll forget," I tell him. "You're front-page news today, but give it another week. It will all settle down."

"Yeah? How do you know so much?"

"Oh, you know. I'm queen of the rumor mill. It seems like there's been a new rumor about me every week since I got here. Comes with being the new girl, I guess. Have you heard the one where I seduced the basketball coach? That's a personal favorite."

"The rumors about me aren't true," says Christian heatedly. "I broke up with Kay, not the other way around."

"Oh. In my experience, rumors aren't usually—"

"I was trying to do the right thing. I couldn't be what she

needed, and I was trying to do the right thing," he says, a fierceness in his eyes that reminds me of how he looks in the vision, this combination of intensity and vulnerability, which only makes him impossibly hotter.

"It's really none of my business," I say.

"I didn't know it was going to be like this."

We stand in the hallway as the other students stream by. On the ceiling, practically dangling over Christian's head, hangs a banner for prom. MYTHIC LOVE, it reads in bright blue letters. Saturday, seven to midnight. Mythic Love.

My mind is suddenly spinning a million miles an hour, like the wheel on *Wheel of Fortune*. Then it stops.

"Do you want to go to prom with me?" I blurt out.

"What?"

"I don't have a date, and you don't have a date, so maybe we should go together."

He stares at me. If my heart beats any harder I will pass out. I try to keep cool, act casual like if he says no it's no big deal.

"No one's asked you?" he asks.

Why does everyone keep saying that? "No."

A light comes on in his eyes. "Sure, why not? A date with Queen Elizabeth." He smiles.

I can't help but smile back. "Apparently it's Saturday, seven to midnight." I gesture at the banner. He turns and looks up at it.

"I don't even know where to pick you up," he says. I quickly rattle off my address and start to explain how to get there. He stops me by doing this thing where he laughs by exhaling. He shakes his head and reaches into his locker to pull out a pen. Then he grabs my wrist, and instantly the back of my neck prickles with electric heat.

"Email me your address," he says. He uncurls my fingers and writes his email address across my palm in green ink.

"Okay," I say, my voice suddenly ridiculously high and quivery. A strand of hair falls across my face, and I swipe it behind my ear.

He clicks the pen closed and swings his backpack over his shoulder. "Seven o'clock?"

"Okay," I say again. It seems that I've been reduced to single syllables by a touch. Maybe Angela's right. Maybe the swoony hand-holding in my vision means that part of my purpose is getting this really hot guy as my boyfriend. That wouldn't suck.

"Okay, I've got to bail," he says, startling me out of my reverie.

His mouth lifts into that lopsided half smile he pins on all the girls. He seems himself all of a sudden, the thing about Kay forgotten for the moment.

"See you Saturday," he says.

"See you then."

As he walks away I close my hand into a fist around his email address. I'm a genius, I think. This is a genius idea.

I'm going to prom with Christian Prescott.

Mom's crying again. I'm standing in front of the full-length mirror in her bedroom a few minutes shy of seven o'clock on prom night, and she's crying, not sobbing or anything because that would be too undignified for her, but tears spilling down her cheeks. It's alarming. One minute she's helping me pull two silver ribbons through my hair, something Greekish, she said, and the next she's sitting on the edge of her bed silently weeping.

"Mom," I say helplessly.

"I'm just so happy for you," she sniffles, embarrassed.

"Right. Happy." I can't help the disconcerting feeling that she's unraveling lately. "Get it together, okay? He's going to be here any minute."

She smiles.

"Silver Avalanche coming up the driveway," calls Jeffrey from downstairs. Mom stands up.

"You stay up here," she says, wiping at her eyes. "It's always better for him to have to wait."

I go to the window and covertly watch Christian pull up to the house and park. He straightens his tie and sweeps a hand through his tousled dark hair before he comes to the door. I give myself a last once-over in the mirror. The theme Mythic Love is supposed to bring to mind the myths of gods and goddesses, Hercules, that kind of thing, so my Greek-inspired dress is perfect. I've let my hair hang in waves down my back so I won't have to wrestle it into a style. I'll have to dye it again soon. My gold roots are starting to show.

"Here she comes," says Mom when I appear at the top of the stairs. She and Christian look up at me. I smile and carefully descend the steps.

"Wow," says Christian when I stop in front of him. His gaze sweeps me from head to foot. "Beautiful."

I'm not sure if he's talking about me or the dress. Either way, I'll take it.

He's wearing a sleek black tux with a silver vest and tie, white shirt with cuff links and everything. He is, in a word, mouthwatering. Even Mom can't take her eyes off him.

"You look great," I say.

"Christian was telling me that he lives close by," says Mom, her eyes sparkling, no trace of the earlier tears on her face. "Three miles directly east of here, did you say?"

"Give or take," he says, still looking at me. "As the crow flies."

"Do you have brothers and sisters?" she asks.

"No, it's just me."

"We should be going," I say, because I sense that she's trying to figure out how my vision will finally come together, and I'm afraid she'll scare him off.

"You look so wonderful together," says Mom. "Can I take a picture?"

"Sure," says Christian.

She runs to the office for her camera. Christian and I wait for her in silence. He smells amazing, that wonderful mix of soap and cologne and something all his own. Pheromones, I guess, but it seems like more than simple chemistry.

I smile at him. "Thanks for being so patient. You know how moms can get."

He doesn't respond, and for a moment I wonder if he and I will ever have a chance at a breakthrough tonight. Then my mom's back and she has us stand against the door while she takes our picture. Christian puts his arm behind me, his hand lightly touching the middle of my back. A tiny tremor ripples through me. There's something that happens between us when we touch, something I can't explain, but it makes me feel weak and strong at the same time, aware of my blood moving through my veins and the air moving in and out of my lungs. It's like my body recognizes his. I don't know what it means, but I kind of like it.

"Oh, I forgot," I say after the flash goes off. "I got you a boutonniere."

I dash off to the kitchen to get it out of the refrigerator. "Here," I say, walking back to him. I step up to him to pin the boutonniere—a single white rose and a bit of greenery—to his lapel and immediately stab myself in the finger with the pin.

"Ow," he says, flinching as if the pin has pierced his finger instead of mine. I hold my finger up and a single drop of blood forms on it.

232

Christian takes my hand and inspects it. My breath catches. I could get used to this.

"Think you'll survive?" he asks, gazing into my eyes, and I need to close them to keep my breath from shaking.

"I think so. It's not even bleeding anymore." I take a tissue from Mom and hold it on the spot of blood on my finger, careful not to touch my dress.

"Let's try this again," I say, and this time I lean close, our breath mingling as I carefully fasten the boutonniere. It's the same feeling I had when we were lying in the snow on the ski hill, a breath apart. Like I could lean in and kiss him, in front of my mother and everything. I take a quick step back, thinking things are either about to go very right tonight, or very wrong.

"Thanks," he says, looking down at my handiwork. "I got you a corsage, too, but it's in the truck." He turns to Mom. "Nice to meet you, Mrs. Gardner."

"Please, call me Maggie."

He nods cordially.

"Be home before midnight," she adds. I stare at her. She can't possibly mean that. The dance doesn't even end until midnight.

"Shall we?" asks Christian before I can think of a reasonable argument. He extends his arm, and I tuck my hand into the crook.

"We shall," I reply, and then we get the heck out of there.

233

At the door to the art museum in Jackson where prom's being held, they give the girls delicate laurels made from silver spray-painted leaves and the boys long sashes of white fabric that they're supposed to wear over one shoulder of their tuxedos, toga style. Now that we officially look like ancient Greeks, we're allowed to enter the lobby, where prom is in full swing.

"Pictures first?" says Christian. "The line doesn't look too long."

"Sure."

A slow song begins to play as we make our way over to the picture area. I watch Jason Lovett ask Wendy to dance. She looks like a bona fide princess in my pink dress. She nods and then they put their arms around each other and start to sway awkwardly to the music. It's adorable. I also spot Tucker in a corner dancing with a redhead I don't know. He sees me, almost starts to wave, but then he sees Christian. His eyes flick back and forth between us, like he's trying to figure out what happened since last Saturday when I said I didn't have a date.

"All right, you two, you're up," says the photographer. Christian and I shuffle onto the platform they've set up. Christian stands behind me and puts his arms loosely around me like it's the most natural thing in the world. I smile. The camera flashes.

"Come on, let's dance," says Christian.

Suddenly happy, I follow him onto the dance floor, which is covered in fog and strewn with white roses. He takes my hand and twirls me, then catches me in his arms, still holding my hands lightly in his. I'm swamped with that electric awareness, which buzzes through me like I've had a shot of espresso.

"So you can dance," I say as he moves us deftly through the crowd.

"A bit." He grins. He really knows how to lead, and I relax and let him take me where he wants me to go, making an effort to look at his face instead of at our feet sweeping through the fog and roses or the people I can feel watching us.

I step on his foot. Twice. And here I call myself a dancer.

I'm trying not to stare at him. Sometimes it's still a shock to see him from the front. It reminds me of a story my mom used to tell of a sculptor whose statue suddenly came to life. That's how I feel about Christian now. He's alive in a way that seems impossible, as if I've created him from the sketches I drew when I first had the vision. From my dreams.

But this isn't a fairy tale, I remind myself. I'm here for a purpose. I need to try to understand what will bring us together in the forest.

"So, you said your uncle took you camping? Was your campsite close to here?" I ask.

He looks confused. "Uh, it was in Teton. An out-of-the-way kind of place."

"So you didn't drive there?"

"No, we hiked." He's still thrown by my choice in topic.

"I just ask because I want to get into camping this summer. I want to try hiking, too. Sleeping under the stars. We never did that in California."

"You've moved to the right place then," he says. "There are entire books written about the awesome places to camp here."

I wonder if we'll be together at one of these campsites when the forest fire starts.

We dance closely through the final chorus, then the song ends, and we step back from each other a little awkwardly.

"You know what I'm suddenly craving?" I say to break the silence. "Punch."

We make our way over to the refreshments table and pile a few Greek olives, crackers, and a little bit of Feta cheese on tiny plastic plates. I don't get a lot because I'm not sure what it would do to my breath. We find an empty table and sit. I spot Angela gyrating around in a dance with a tall, blond boy I've seen in the hall a few times. Tyler something, I think she said his name was. The bloodred dress that her mother sewed for her looks fantastic. She's lined her golden eyes with heavy black that tips up in the corners like an ancient Egyptian's. If this dance is about Mythic Love, then she's a goddess, all right. Only she's the kind of goddess who demands blood sacrifices. She catches my eye and gives me a quick thumbs-up, then dances suggestively around the boy while he simply stands there bobbing in time to the music.

"You're friends with Angela?" asks Christian.

"Yeah."

"She's kind of intense."

"You're not the first person to tell me that," I say, laughing because he has no idea how crazy intense Angela can be. He hasn't heard her discussing the mind-reading abilities of the Intangere. "I think people get intimidated by how smart she is. Like people get intimidated by you—" I stop myself.

"What? You think people are intimidated by me? Why?"

"Because you're so . . . perfect and popular and good at everything you try."

"Perfect," he scoffs, and he has the grace to look genuinely embarrassed.

"It's annoying, actually."

He laughs. Then he reaches across the table and grabs my hand, making all my nerves light up.

"Believe me, I'm not perfect," he says.

From that point on things go really well. Christian's a model date. He's charming, attentive, thoughtful. Not to mention hotness personified. For a while I forget all about my purpose. I just dance. I let that magnetic feeling of being near him fill me up until everything else falls away. I'm literally having the time of my life.

Until Kay shows up. Of course she's gorgeous in this lavender lace gown that hugs her shoulders and accentuates her tiny waist. Her dark hair is pinned up, curls cascading down to brush the back of her neck. Something in her hair catches the light and sparkles. She has one elbow-length-white-satin-glove-covered arm curled around her date's waist as she walks in, laughing up into his face like she's having a marvelous time. She doesn't even look in our direction. She pulls her date onto the dance floor as the next slow song begins to play.

Christian draws me closer. Our bodies come together. My head fits perfectly against the curve of his shoulder. I can't help but close my eyes and breathe him in. And suddenly I'm having the vision again, the strongest I've ever had it.

I walk down a dirt road through the forest. Christian's truck is parked at the road's edge. I smell smoke; my head feels clouded with it. I start to move away from the road, deeper into the trees. I'm not worried. I know exactly where to find him. My feet take me there without me even having to direct them. When I see him, standing there with his back to me in his black fleece jacket, his hands in his pockets, I'm filled with that familiar grief. The intensity of the sadness makes it hard to breathe. I'm so fragile in that moment, like

I could be shattered into a million pieces.

"Christian," I call.

He turns. He looks at me with a mix of sorrow and relief.

"It's you," he says. He starts to walk toward me. Behind him, the fire crests the hill. It's raging toward us, but I don't feel afraid. Christian and I walk toward each other until we're standing face-to-face.

"It's me," I answer. "I'm here." I reach out and take his hand, which feels easy, like I've been with him all my life. He lifts his other hand to touch my cheek. His skin's so hot it's like a burn, but I don't pull away. For a moment we stay like that, standing still as if time has stopped, as if the fire isn't coming for us. And then we're suddenly in each other's arms, holding each other tightly, our bodies pressing together like we're becoming one person, and the ground is falling away beneath us.

I'm back at the dance, gasping for breath. I look up into Christian's wide green eyes. We've stopped dancing and are standing in the middle of the dance floor staring at each other. My heart feels about to beat out of my chest. A wave of dizziness crashes over me, and I sway, my knees suddenly wobbly. Christian's arms steady me.

"You okay?" He glances around quickly to see if people are watching us. They are. Over his shoulder I see Kay, who looks at me with open hatred in her eyes.

"I need some air." I break free and run toward the door onto the balcony, bursting out into the cool night. Leaning against the wall, I close my eyes and try to calm my racing heart.

"Clara?"

I open my eyes. Christian's standing in front of me, looking as shaken as I am, his face pale in the lamplight.

"I'm okay," I say, smiling to prove it. "It just got a little stuffy in there."

"I should get you something to drink," he says, but he doesn't go anywhere.

"I'm okay." I feel stupid. Then a flash of anger. I didn't ask for any of this. So I will fly away with Christian in my arms. And then what? Gorgeous Christian Prescott will go off to save the world, and my part will be done. I'll have completed—and served—my purpose.

It's like I'm a prop in someone else's life.

"I'll go get that punch," says Christian.

I shake my head. "This was a bad idea."

"What?"

"You don't want to be here with me," I say, meeting his eyes. "It's still all about Kay."

He doesn't answer.

"I thought I felt this connection between us but . . . I wanted you to like me, that's all, really like me. What you and Kay had—have—whatever, I've never had that." To my

240

horror there are tears in my eyes.

"I'm sorry," he says finally, moving to lean against the wall next to me. He looks over at me earnestly. "I do like you, Clara."

I'm starting to get whiplash from the emotional roller coaster I've been on all night. I'm also getting a headache.

"You don't even know me," I say.

"I'd like to."

If only he knew how important this is. But before I have a chance to reply, the door opens. Brady Hunt steps out.

"They're announcing the prom king," he says, looking at Christian expectantly.

Christian hesitates.

"You should go," I tell him. Brady looks at me curiously before going back inside. Christian goes to the door and holds it open for me, but I shake my head.

"I just need another minute, okay?" I close my eyes until I hear the door close. The air is suddenly cold. One by one Mr. Erikson announces the king's court, who are nearly all from the athletic crowd.

"And the prom king is . . . ," says Mr. Erikson. The room is absolutely silent. ". . . Christian Prescott."

I step back inside in time to see Miss Colbert, my French teacher, hand Christian a gold scepter. Christian smiles graciously. He handles attention so well, like a movie star or a politician. Maybe he *will* be president someday. Miss Colbert takes a bit too much pleasure in making him kneel down so she can put the crown of gold leaves on his head. He thanks her and stands up to wave at the crowd, who cheer wildly.

Then he stands to one side while Mr. Erikson reads off the court for prom queen, and that's when I start to get nervous. Of course I'm not named. I wasn't even nominated. I'm Bozo the Clown. But every single one of the girls in the queen's court is Kay's friend. Which can only mean . . .

"And now the prom queen," says Mr. Erikson. "Kay Patterson."

The room reverberates with the thunderous applause of the students who voted for her. Kay approaches the stage with infinite grace and poise. She takes the bouquet of white roses under her arm and leans down as Mr. Erikson replaces her little silver laurel with a big gold one.

"Now, as is customary, the king and queen will share a dance," says Mr. Erikson.

A string of very un-angelic curse words come to mind.

Kay looks at Christian expectantly. He glances down as if deciding something, then looks up and smiles again. As the music starts to play he walks over to Kay and takes her hand. She puts her other arm around his shoulder. They start to dance. Everybody around me begins to chatter excitedly, watching them move so beautifully together to the music. Christian and Kay, together again.

I feel like I've slipped into the hell dimension.

"Hey, Carrots," says a voice.

I cringe. "Not now, Tucker. I can't deal with you right now."

"Dance with me," he says.

"No."

"C'mon, you look pathetic standing here watching your date dance with someone else."

I turn and glower at him. But one thing I will say for him: He cleans up nice. The white shirt against his neck sets off his tan. In the tux his shoulders look broad and strong. His short tawny hair is combed and styled. His blue eyes blaze under the lights. I even smell cologne.

"Fine," I say.

He holds out his hand, and I take it, then stalk over to the edge of the dance floor with him and put my arms around his neck. He doesn't say anything, just moves his feet from side to side, looking at my face. All the anger drains out of me. He's doing me a favor, or so it seems. I scan the ceiling for the telltale bucket of pig's blood he's about to douse me with.

"Where's your date?" I ask.

"Well, that's a complicated question. Depends on what you mean."

"Who did you come with tonight?"

"Her," says Tucker, gesturing with his head to the red-headed girl standing over by the punch table.

"And her," he says, looking over toward the DJ, where a brunette I don't know, a senior I presume, is putting in a request.

"And her," he says finally, and points to a blonde who's dancing very close to the second runner-up for prom king.

"You came with three girls?"

"They're on the rodeo team," he says as if that explains it. "None of them had dates, and I figured I was the only one man enough to handle the three of them."

"You're unbelievable."

"And you came with Christian Prescott," he says. "Your dream come true."

At the moment it seems like more of a nightmare. I cast a look at Christian and Kay over my shoulder. Predictably, Kay is crying. She's clinging to Christian's shoulders and sobbing.

Tucker turns to follow my gaze.

Christian leans closer to Kay and whispers something. Whatever it is, she does not take it well. She starts crying even harder.

"Man, you couldn't pay me to be in his shoes right now," says Tucker.

I glare at him.

"Sorry," he says. "I'll shut up."

"You do that."

He stifles a smile, and we finish out the song wordlessly.

"Thanks for the dance," he says.

"Thanks for asking," I say, still looking at Christian. He has his arms around Kay. Her face is buried in his chest. I don't know what to do. I just stand there watching him. He pulls back from Kay and says something to her gently, then leads her over to a table and pulls a chair out for her to sit down. He even goes to get her some punch, but she waves it away. Lines of mascara are drying on her face. She looks exhausted. At first I thought this might be a ploy, an act like her slutty rogue routine, but seeing her slumped in that chair it's impossible not to believe that she is genuinely devastated.

Christian walks over to me, clearly flustered.

"I am so sorry," he says. "I didn't know this would happen."

"I know," I say quietly. "It's all right. Where's Kay's date?"

Let *him* comfort her, I think.

"He left," says Christian.

"He left," I repeat incredulously.

"So I was thinking," says Christian, red in the face now, "that I should take Kay home."

I stare at him, stunned.

"I'll come right back and get you," he says quickly. "I thought I'd get her home safe and then I'd take you home."

"I'll take Clara home," says Tucker, who's been standing next to me the whole time.

"No, it'll only take a minute," protests Christian, standing up straighter.

"The dance will be over in ten minutes," says Tucker. "You expect her to wait for you in the parking lot?"

I feel like Cinderella sitting in the middle of the road with a pumpkin and a couple of mice, while Prince Charming charges off to rescue some other chick.

Christian looks sick with guilt.

"Go ahead and take Kay home," I say, practically choking on the words. "I'll ride home with Tucker."

"That's all right with you?"

"Sure. I have to be home by midnight, remember?"

"I'll make it up to you," he says.

I swear I see Tucker roll his eyes.

"Okay." I look at Tucker. "Can we go now?"

"You bet."

After I find Wendy and Angela and say good-bye, I wait at the door as Tucker rounds up his other dates. They look at me with something like pity, and for a moment I actually hate Christian Prescott. We ride crammed together in Tucker's rusty pickup, four girls in formal wear, squeezed into the cab. He drops off the blonde first, because she lives in Jackson. Then the redhead. Then the brunette.

"Bye, Fry," she says as she gets out of the truck.

Now it's just him and me in the cab. It's quiet as he drives out to Spring Creek Road.

"So . . . Fry, huh?" I tease after a while, unable to stand the silence. "What's that about?"

"Yeah," he says, shaking his head as if he still can't understand it. "In junior high they called me Friar Tuck. Now it's just Fry. But my good friends call me Tuck."

When we pull into my driveway, I'm already fifteen

minutes past my curfew. I open the door, then stop and look at him. "Can you . . . not mention this whole fiasco to anybody else at school?"

"They already know," he says. "One thing about Jackson Hole High, everybody is in everybody's business."

I sigh.

"Don't worry about it," he says.

"Yeah, they'll forget by Monday, right?"

"Right," he says. I can't tell if he's mocking me or not.

"Thanks for the ride," I say. "Fry."

He groans, then grins. "My pleasure."

He's such a strange guy. Stranger by the minute.

"See you." I jump down from the truck, slam the door shut, and make for the house.

"Hey, Carrots," he calls suddenly.

I turn back to him. "You and I will probably get along better if you stop calling me that."

"You like it."

"I don't."

"What do you see in a guy like Christian Prescott?" he asks.

"I don't know," I say wearily. "Anything else you want?"

His dimple appears. "Nope," he says.

"Good night, then."

"Night," he says, and drives off into the dark.

The porch light comes on as I creep up the steps. Mom stands in the doorway.

"That wasn't Christian," she says.

"Brilliant observation, Mother."

"What happened?"

"He's in love with another girl," I say, and pull the silver laurel out of my hair.

Later, in the darkest time of night, my vision turns into a nightmare. I'm in the forest. I'm being watched. I feel the amber eyes of the Black Wing. Then he's holding me down, pressing me into the cold ground beneath, his body blotting out the light. Pine needles stab into my back. I scream and flail. One hand strikes his wing and I pull out a fistful of black feathers. In my fingers they evaporate. I keep pulling at the angel's wings, each feather a piece of his evil, until he suddenly dissolves into a heavy cloud of smoke, leaving me coughing and panting in the dirt.

I jolt awake, tangled in my blankets. Someone's standing over my bed. I suck in a breath to start screaming again, but his hand comes over my mouth.

"Clara, it's me," Jeffrey says. He removes his hand and sits down at the edge of the bed. "I heard you screaming. Bad dream, huh?"

My heart's pounding so hard I hear it like a war drum. I nod.

"Want me to get Mom?"

"No. I'm fine."

"What was it about?"

He still doesn't know about Black Wings. If I tell him, he'll be more vulnerable to them, Mom said. I swallow.

"Prom didn't exactly go as planned."

His eyebrows bunch together and he frowns. "You had a nightmare about prom?"

"Yeah, well, it was that kind of night."

He looks over at me like he doesn't believe me, but I'm too tired to explain how my life seems to be coming apart at the seams.

13

GOTH TINKER BELL

My cell phone chirps. I take it out of my pocket, look at it, click IGNORE, and then put it back into my pocket. Across the dining room table, Mom raises her eyebrows at me.

"Christian again?"

I cut a bite of French toast and put it in my mouth. I can hardly taste it, I'm that mad. Which makes me madder still. Normally I love French toast.

"Maybe you should talk to him. Give him a chance to make it right," she says.

I put my fork down.

"The only possible way for him to make it right is if he builds a time machine, goes back to last night, and . . ."

My voice fades. And what? And turns his back on Kay while she's falling apart? And takes me home instead? And kisses me on the doorstep? "I just need to be mad for a little while, okay? I know it might not be the most mature thing, but there it is."

The phone in the kitchen starts to ring. We look at each other.

"I'll get it," she says, and slides out of her chair to grab the phone off the wall.

"Hello?" she says. "I'm afraid she doesn't want to talk you."

I slump at the table. My French toast is cold. I pick up my plate and go into the kitchen, where Mom leans against the counter, nodding as she listens to whatever he's saying. Like she's totally taking his side.

She puts her hand over the receiver. "I really think you should talk to him."

I slide my French toast into the trash, then casually rinse my plate in the sink, put it in the dishwasher, and dry my hands on a kitchen towel. I hold out a hand for the phone. Surprised, she gives it to me. I put it to my ear.

"Clara?" Christian says hopefully.

"Take the hint," I say into the phone, then hang up.

I hand the phone back to Mom. She's smart enough not to say anything as I stalk past her and up the stairs toward my bedroom. I shut the door behind me and throw myself onto my bed. I want to scream into my pillow.

I won't be that girl who lets the guy treat her like crap and still fawns all over him. I went to prom with Christian Prescott. It wasn't supposed to be magical, I tell myself. It wasn't supposed to be romantic. It's my job, pretty much. But it wasn't supposed to end with me being dumped out of Tucker's truck at the end of the night.

So that's it, I decide. From now on, this Christian thing is strictly business. You go to the forest, fly him out of there, apparently, drop him wherever he needs to go, and that's that. No need to be his friend, or anything else. No hand-holding. No staring rapturously into his eyes. At the memory of the vision, the vividness of it, my chest gets tight. His hot hand against my cheek. I close my eyes. I curse the warmth that floods my belly. I curse the vision for, I don't know, lead-ing me on.

My cell phone rings. It's Angela. I answer it.

"Don't say anything," I say.

There's silence on the other end.

"Are you there?"

"You told me not to say anything."

"I meant about last night."

"Okay. Let's see. My mom has decided to run *Oklahoma!* this fall at the Garter. I am trying to talk her out of it. Whoever heard of *Oklahoma!* in Wyoming?"

"Was everybody talking about it?" I ask. "After we left?"

She pauses for a minute, then dutifully changes the subject.

"Nice weather we're having today. Almost like summer."

"Angela."

She sighs.

"Yes," she admits.

I groan. "Do they think I'm a total dork?"

"Well, I can only speak for myself." I can actually hear her grinning. I start to smile in spite of myself. "Come over for dinner," she says. "My mom's making fettuccine Alfredo. I'll find something for you to punch."

I literally go limp with relief. God bless Angela. I'd never be able to make it through the day in the house with the constant ringing of the phone, and Mom breathing down my neck. "When can I come over?"

"How soon can you get here?" she says.

Angela and I see a double feature at the Teton Theatre, a horror movie and an action movie, sheer mindless fun, just what the doctor ordered. Afterward we hang out on the empty stage at the Garter. I'm beginning to love this place. It feels like it's Angela's and mine, a secret hideout where nobody else can find us. And Angela's good at distraction.

"Here's something that will cheer you up," she says as we sit on the edge of the stage with our feet dangling into the orchestra pit. She stands up and summons her wings. She closes her eyes. A fly falls onto my shoulder. I quickly shake it off. The flies in the theater creep me out. They're always flying up into the lights and getting their wings singed, and then they drop out of the air and buzz around on the stage, alive. I look back at Angela. Nothing's different.

"Am I supposed to see something?" I ask after a minute.

She frowns. "Wait for it."

For a minute nothing happens. Then her wings begin to shimmer, the way the air does over concrete on a hot summer day. Slowly, they start to change form, smoothing out, curving into a different shape. Angela opens her eyes. Her wings look like a huge moth's, still pristinely white but smoother, segmented, dotted with small white scales like what you would see on a butterfly's if you looked real close.

My mouth drops open. "How did you do that?"

She smiles. "I can't change the color," she says. "I thought it would be so cool to have purple wings, but it didn't work. But I can make them look like pretty much anything if I try hard enough."

"What do they feel like when they're like that?" I ask, watching the gigantic butterfly wings open and close behind her, back and forth, such a different movement from our feathered wings. She looks like a Goth Tinker Bell.

"More fragile. And I don't think they would fly the same way. I don't even know if I could fly like this. But that's a limitation of my brain. I think our wings can be whatever we want. We see feathered wings because they are iconic of angels. But really they're only a tool. We choose the form."

I stare at her. It would never have occurred to me in a million years to try to change the form of my wings.

"Wow," I say, pretty much speechless.

"I know, right?"

"What do you mean, they're only a tool? They feel real to me," I say, thinking about the heaviness of my wings on my shoulder blades, the mass of muscle and feather and bone.

"Have you ever wondered where our wings go when we don't have them out?"

I blink at her.

"No."

"I think they might exist between dimensions." She brushes sawdust off her pants. "Watch this."

She closes her eyes again. The butterfly wings dissolve, becoming a misty cloud that hovers around her head and shoulders.

"Do you think I could do that?" I stand up and summon my wings awkwardly. I can't help my sudden flash of jealousy. She's so much stronger than I am. So much smarter about everything. She has twice the angel blood.

"I don't know," she muses. "I guess I could have inherited the shape-shifting thing. But it makes more sense if we all could do it."

I close my eyes.

"Butterfly," I whisper.

I open my eyes again. Still feathers.

"You have to free your mind," says Angela.

"You sound like Yoda."

"Free your mind, you must," she says in her best Yoda voice.

She raises her arms over her head and stretches. Her wings disappear.

"That was unbelievably cool," I tell her.

"I know."

At that moment another fly drops right down the front of my shirt, and between the shrieking and digging around to get it out, and the hysterical laughing afterward, I'm so grateful that I have a friend like Angela, who always reminds me of how cool it is to be angel-blood when I'm feeling like a freak of nature. Who can make me forget about Christian Prescott, even for a minute.

Christian's sitting on the front step when I get home. The porch light casts a halo of soft glow around him, like a spotlight. He has a mug of what I can only guess is my mom's raspberry tea in his hand, which he instantly puts down on the porch. He jumps to his feet. I fervently wish I could fly away.

"I'm sorry," he says earnestly. "I was dumb. I was stupid. I was an idiot."

I have to admit, he does look adorable standing there all moony-eyed telling me how stupid he is. Not fair.

I sigh.

"How long have you been sitting here?" I ask.

"Not long," he says. "Like three hours." He points to the mug. "The free refills made it only seem like two."

I refuse to smile at his joke and push past him into the house, where my mom suddenly jumps up from the couch and heads for her office without a word. For that I'm grateful.

"Come in," I call to him, as it's clear he's not going to go away any time soon.

He follows me into the kitchen.

"Okay," I say. "Here's the deal. We will not discuss prom, ever, ever again."

His eyes flash with relief. I grab his mug and put it next to the sink. I take a moment to steady myself against the counter.

"Let's start over," I say, my back to him.

That'd be nice, I think, to start over. No visions, no expectations, no humiliation. Just boy meets girl. Him and me.

"Okay."

"I'm Clara." I turn to face him and hold out my hand.

The corner of his mouth lifts in a suppressed smile. "I'm Christian," he murmurs, taking my hand in his and squeezing it gently.

"Nice to meet you, Christian," I say like he's a normal guy. Like when I close my eyes I don't see him standing in the middle of a forest fire. Like him touching me right now doesn't send a pang of yearning and recognition rippling through me.

"Totally."

We go back out to the front porch. I make more tea and get a blanket for him and a blanket for me and we sit on the front step, looking at the diamond-studded sky.

"Stars were never this bright in California," he says.

I was thinking the same thing.

By the time my mom comes out of her office and politely (and ecstatically, I think) informs us that it's late and it's a school night and Christian had better get himself home, I know so much more about him. I know that he lives with his uncle, who owns the Bank of Jackson Hole and a couple of real estate offices in town. Where his parents are, he doesn't really go into, although I get the distinct impression that they're dead, and have been for a long time. He's super attached to their housekeeper, Marta, who's been around since he was ten years old. He loves Mexican food, and skiing of course, and playing the guitar.

"Enough about me," he says after a while. "Let's talk about you. Why did you come here?" he asks.

"Oh, uh——" I search my brain for my rehearsed answer. "My mom. She wanted to get out of California, move somewhere that's not so crowded, get some fresh air. She thought it'd be good for us."

"And was it? Good for you, I mean?"

"Sort of. I mean, school hasn't exactly been easy, trying to make friends and all that." I blush and glance away, wondering if he's thinking about the nickname Hot Bozo that's so popular among his buddies. "But I like it. . . .

I feel like I belong here."

"I know what that's like," he says.

"What?"

Now it's his turn to look embarrassed. "I just mean, when I moved here, it was hard for a while. I didn't fit in."

"Weren't you, like, five?"

"Yeah, I was five, but even then. This is a weird place to move to, on a lot of levels, especially from California. I remember that first snowstorm—I thought the sky was falling down."

I laugh and shift slightly, and our shoulders touch. Zap. Even through our clothes. I move away. *Business, Clara, business*, I tell myself. *Don't lose it over this guy now.* I clear my throat lightly.

"But you feel like you belong now, right?"

He nods. "Yeah, of course. There's no doubt in my mind that this is where I belong."

Then he tells me that he's thinking about going to New York for the summer, on some kind of business school internship for high school students.

"I'm not stoked at the idea of the internship, but summer in New York City sounds like an adventure," he says. "I'll probably go."

"All summer?" I ask, a little stricken. *But the fire,* I want to say. *You can't go.*

"My uncle," he says, and then he's quiet for a moment. "He

wants me to get a business degree and take over at the bank someday. He's got expectations, you know, things he thinks I should do to prepare myself and all that mumbo jumbo. I don't know what I want to do."

"I get that," I say, thinking he doesn't know the half of it. "My mom's like that, always expecting so much out of me. She's always saying that I have a purpose in life, something I was born to do, and that I just need to figure out what it is. No pressure there, right? I'm afraid of letting her down."

"Well," he says, turning to me and smiling in a way that makes my heart speed up. "Sounds like we're both in trouble."

The remaining weeks of school fly past in a blur. Christian calls me every few days, and we make small talk. He sits next to me in class and cracks jokes all period. A couple of times he even eats lunch at my table, which totally wigs out the Invisibles. In the space of a week the entire school is speculating over whether or not we're a red-hot item.

I'm wondering that myself.

"Told you," says Angela when I talk to her about it. "I'm never wrong, C."

"That's comforting. Can you focus, please? I still don't know anything about the fire. I don't know why he would be there that day. I don't know where it happens. I thought if I got to know him better, I'd find out, but—"

"You've got time. Just enjoy the company," she says.

Wendy, on the other hand, is barely masking her disapproval over the whole Christian thing. But then she never liked the idea.

"I told you," she says primly. "Christian's like a god. And gods don't make good boyfriends."

"If you're about to try to sell me on Tucker again, save it. Although it was nice of him to drive me home from prom."

"Hey, I'm on your side. I'll cheer for you and Christian if that's what you want me to do."

"Thanks," I say.

"Even if I think it's a big mistake."

Great friends I have.

I'm confused by Christian suddenly coming on so strong. Just when I decide to keep it strictly professional between us, angel business only, he seems totally into me in a way that makes my head spin. But he doesn't ask me out. He doesn't touch me. I tell myself that I shouldn't care whether or not he does.

"Silver Avalanche coming up the driveway," calls Jeffrey from upstairs.

"What are you, security?" I call back.

"Something like that."

"Thanks for the heads-up."

I'm standing on the porch when Christian pulls up to the

house. "Hey, stranger," I say.

He smiles. "Hey."

"Fancy meeting you here."

"I wanted to say good-bye," he says. "I'm being shipped off to New York tomorrow." He makes his trip to New York sound like boarding school.

"Ah, come on, you get to have adventure in the Big Apple. My dad lives in New York, you know, but I've only been there once. He had to work the whole time, so I sat on the couch and watched TV for a week."

"Your dad? You've never mentioned him before."

"Yeah, well, there's not much to mention."

He shrugs. "Same thing with my dad."

A touchy subject, I can tell. I wonder if my face gets like that too when I talk about my dad, like I'm totally fine, I couldn't care less that my parent doesn't really give a crap about me.

I pretend to pout. "This sucks. School's only been out for two days, and everybody's bailing," I whine. "You, Wendy, Angela, even my mom. She's going back to California for business next week. I feel like the only rat dumb enough to stay on this sinking ship."

"Sorry," Christian says. "I'll text you, okay?"

"Okay."

His cell phone rings in his pocket. He sighs. He doesn't answer. Instead he takes a step toward me, closing the distance between us. It feels like the vision. It feels like he's going to take my hand.

"Clara," he says, my name sounding different somehow when it passes through his lips. "I'll miss you."

You will? I think.

"Bluebell coming up the driveway!" comes Jeffrey's voice from an upstairs window.

"Thank you!" I shout back.

"Who's that? Your brother?" asks Christian.

"Yeah. He's apparently a watchdog."

"Who's Bluebell?"

"Uh——" Tucker's rusty blue truck pulls up behind Christian's Avalanche. Wendy gets out. Her expression is clouded, like she's confused to find me here with Christian. Still, she tries to smile.

"Hi, Christian," she says.

"Hey," he says.

"I wanted to stop by," she says. "Tucker's driving me up to the airport."

"Today? I thought it wasn't until tomorrow," I say in dismay. "I haven't wrapped your send-off present. Wait here." I run into the house and return with the iPod Shuffle I got her. I hand it over. "I couldn't really figure out what you'd need on a veterinary internship, unless it's extra socks. But they'll let you listen to music while you work, right?"

She looks more shocked than I was going for, her smile

still a little forced. "Clara," she says. "This is too . . ."

"I already put some songs on it that you'll like. And I found the score for *The Horse Whisperer*. I know you have that movie practically memorized."

She stares at the iPod for a minute, then folds her fingers around it. "Thank you."

"You're welcome."

Tucker taps the horn. She turns to me apologetically. "I don't have any time, sorry. I've got to go."

We hug. "I am going to miss you so much," I whisper.

"There's a pay phone at the general store. I'll call you," she says.

"You'd better. I'm feeling majorly abandoned here."

Tucker sticks his head out the window. "Sorry, sis, but we have to take off now. Can't miss your plane."

"All right, all right." Wendy hugs me one last time, then dashes for the truck.

"Hey, Chris," Tucker says out the window to Christian.

Christian smiles. "How's it going, Friar Tuck?"

Tucker doesn't look particularly amused. "You're blocking me," he says. "I could go around, but I don't want to mess up their grass."

"Yeah, no problem." Christian looks at me. "I should get going too."

"Oh, well, you can stay for a minute, can't you?" I ask, trying not to sound like I'm pleading.

"No, I really have to go," he says.

He hugs me, and for the first few seconds it's awkward, like we don't know where to put our hands, but then the familiar magnetic force takes over and our bodies fit together perfectly. I rest my head on his shoulder and close my eyes, which keeps the business part of my brain temporarily disabled.

Tucker revs the engine. I pull back abruptly. "Okay, so call me."

"I'll be back the first week of August," he tells me. "And then we'll hang out more, okay?"

"Sounds like a plan." I hope there aren't any, oh I don't know, *forest fires* before he gets back. But there can't be, can there? The fire can't take place unless he's there, right? Is it possible to miss my purpose because my subject won't cooperate?

"Bye, Clara," says Christian. He nods at Tucker and walks back to the Avalanche, which roars to life and makes Bluebell look even rustier and shabbier. I wave as both trucks pull out and disappear into the woods, leaving me in a literal cloud of dust. I sigh. I think about how Christian's good-bye seemed so final.

A few days later I help Angela pack for Italy, where she spends every summer with her mom's family.

"Think of it as a time-out," Angela says as I mope around her bedroom.

"A time-out? I'm not two, you know."

"A time to reflect. A time to *learn how to fly*, for crap's sake, and try for glory and find out all the other cool stuff you can do."

I sigh and throw a pair of socks into her suitcase.

"I'm not like you, Ange. I can't do what you can do."

"You don't know what you can do," she says matter-of-factly. "You won't know until you try."

I change the subject by lifting up a black silk nightdress that she's laid out with her other clothes.

"What's this for?" I ask, gawking at her.

She snatches the fabric from my hand and stuffs it at the bottom of her suitcase, her face expressionless.

"Is there a sexy Italian boy you never told me about?" I ask.

She doesn't answer, but her pale cheeks take on a rosy glow.

I gasp. "There *is* a sexy Italian boy I don't know about!"

"I have to get to bed early tonight. Long flight tomorrow."

"Giovanni. Alberto. Marcello," I say, trying out all the Italian names I can think of, watching her face for a reaction.

"Shut it."

"Does your mom know?"

"No." She grabs my hand and pulls me down to sit on the bed. "And you can't tell her, all right? She would freak."

"Why would I say anything to your mom? It's not like we hang out."

This is big. Angela is usually all talk when it comes to boys, nothing serious. I picture her with a dark-haired Italian boy, darting hand in hand down a narrow street in Rome, kissing under archways. I'm instantly wildly jealous.

"Just don't, okay?" She squeezes my hand hard. "Promise me, you won't tell anybody."

"I promise," I say. I think she's being a tad melodramatic.

She refuses to say anything more about it, closes up tighter than a clam. I help her pack the rest of her things. She's leaving really early in the morning, driving to Idaho Falls to catch her first flight at some ungodly hour, so I'll have to say goodbye tonight. At the doorway to the theater, we hug tightly.

"I'm going to miss you most of all," I tell her.

"Don't worry," she says. "I'll be back before you know it. And I'll have tons of new information for us to chew on."

"Okay."

"Keep sharp." She mock punches me in the arm. "Learn to fly, already."

"I will," I sniffle.

It's going to be a very lonely summer.

The next night I drive to Teton National Park after dinner. I park the car at Jenny Lake. It's a small, quiet lake, surrounded by trees, the mountains towering over it. For a while I stand on the shore as the setting sun glimmers on the water before it drops beneath the horizon. I watch a white pelican glide over the lake. It dives into the water and comes up with a fish. It's beautiful.

When it's dark, I start to hike.

The quiet is unbelievable. It's like there's no one else on earth. I try to relax and breathe in the cold, pine-scented air deeply, letting it fill me. I want everything in my life to fall away and simply enjoy the strength of my muscles as I climb. I go up and up, out of the tree line, closer to that big, open sky. I climb until I'm warm, and then I look for a good place to stop. I find a perch on the side of the mountain where the earth drops away. The map calls this spot Inspiration Point. It sounds like a good place for my experiment.

I climb out onto the perch and look down. It's a long drop. I see the lake reflecting the moon.

"Let's do this," I whisper. I stretch my arms. I summon and stretch my wings. I look down again. Big mistake.

But I'm going to fly if it kills me. I have to fly. I've seen it in the vision.

"Gotta be light," I say, rubbing my hands together. "No big deal. Light."

I take another deep breath. I think of the pelican I saw over the lake. The way the air just seemed to carry it. I spread my wings.

And I jump.

I drop like a rock. The air rushes my face, sucks the breath out of my lungs so that I can't even scream. The trees reach up for me. I try to brace for impact, although I have no idea how exactly one is supposed to brace for impact. I haven't really thought the whole thing through, I realize a tad too late. Even if the fall miraculously doesn't kill me, I could land on the rocks below and break my legs, and nobody knows I'm out here, nobody will find me.

Just jump off the mountain, I scold myself. *What a great idea, Clara!*

But then my wings catch and open. My body wrenches down like a skydiver's when the parachute finally deploys. I wobble awkwardly in the air, trying to get my balance. My wings strain to bear my weight, but they hold me. I sweep out and away from Inspiration Point, carried by the wind.

"I'm flying," I whisper. I suddenly feel so incredibly light, relieved that I'm not going to die, high on adrenaline and the pure thrill of feeling the cold air holding me, lifting me. It's the best feeling of my life, bar none. "I'm flying!"

Of course, I'm not flying so much as coasting over the treetops like a hang glider or a freakishly large flying squirrel. I think the birds in the area are dying laughing watching me try not to crash. So I'm not a natural, not some beautiful angelic being winging my way heavenward. But I haven't died yet, which I consider a plus.

I push down with my wings once, trying to go higher. Instead I swoop farther downward over the trees until my feet nearly brush the top branches. I try to remember a single thing I've learned in all those hours in aerodynamics class, but I can't translate any of that stuff about planes—lift, thrust, drag—to what my wings are doing in this moment. Flying in real life isn't a mathematical equation. Anytime I try to change direction I overdo it and careen around wildly in the air and my life flashes before my eyes before I get it all under control again. The best I can do for now is to flap every now and then and angle my wings to keep me in the air.

I come to the lake. As I pass over it, my reflection is a blur of shining white on the dark moon-touched surface. For a moment I see myself as the pelican skimming the water. I sweep down and feel the lake's coolness ripple through my fingers. I'm dancing with the sparkles of the moon. I laugh.

I'm going to do this, I tell myself. *I'm going to save him.*

14

THE JUMPING TREE

My seventeenth birthday is June 20. That morning I wake up to a completely empty house. Mom's back in California for the week, working. Jeffrey's been pretty much AWOL the entire week. He just passed Driver's Ed and got his day license (when he learned that in Wyoming, fifteen-year-olds can legally drive during the day, he was even more over California), and I haven't seen much of him since—he's too busy cruising around Jackson in his new truck, compliments of dear old Dad. My only clue that he's still alive is the growing pile of dishes accumulating in the sink.

For the first time that I can remember there won't be a party on my birthday. No cake. No presents. Mom gave me a gift before she went off to California, a sunshine yellow sundress that rustles against my calves when I walk. I love the dress, but standing in my bedroom looking at it on the hanger, such a sweet, perfect dress for a birthday party or a date or a night out, I'm instantly depressed. I go downstairs and sit at the kitchen counter munching Cheerios, feeling even sadder that there's no banana to slice up into my cereal, and turn on our small kitchen television to watch the news.

The reporter's talking about what a dry season it's been in Jackson Hole this year. We only got two-thirds the normal amount of snowfall, she says, and the spring runoff has been pretty low. The reservoir is way down. She stands in front of the lake and motions to the low water level. You can clearly see where the water usually comes to, the color of the rocks lighter once it hits the regular waterline.

"This year's drought may not affect us much now," she says, staring with solemn eyes into the camera, "but as the summer progresses, the land will get drier and drier. Fires are likely to start earlier in the year, and the fires are likely to be more destructive."

Last night I tried to fly again, this time carrying a duffel bag. I couldn't find a better equivalent of a human being. I filled it with a bunch of cans of soup and a couple of gallons of water, along with some blankets and padding, lugged it into the backyard, and tried to take off with it. No such luck. It probably weighed half of what Christian does, if that. And I could not for the life of me get off the ground with it. All the focus that goes into making myself light so that my wings can lift me is worthless when I try to pick up something heavy. I'm too weak.

Now, as I stare at the television, which is running footage of the Jackson area's previous forest fires, my skin prickles like the reporter is speaking directly to me. I get the message. Try harder. The fire's coming soon. I have to be ready.

I spend the morning painting my toenails and watching daytime TV. I should get out, I tell myself, but I can't think of anywhere to go that won't make me feel even more pathetically lonely.

Around noon there's a knock on the door. I don't expect to see Tucker Avery standing on my doorstep. But here he is, holding a shoe box under his arm. The sun's falling directly across him.

I open the door. "Hi."

"Hi." He presses his lips together to keep from smiling. "Just get up?"

I realize I'm wearing a very dopey pair of pink plaid pajamas with the word PRINCESS embroidered across the left breast. Not my idea, these pj's, but they're warm and comfy. I take a step back, into the frame of the door.

"Can I help you?" I ask.

He holds out the box. "Wendy wanted me to give this to you," he says. "Today."

I gingerly take the shoe box out of his hand. "There's not a snake in here, is there?"

He grins. "I guess you'll find out."

I start to turn back into the house. Tucker doesn't move. I glance at him anxiously. He's waiting for something.

"What, you want a tip?" I ask.

"Sure."

"I don't have any cash. Do you want to come in?"

"Thought you'd never ask."

I motion for him to follow me inside. "Wait here." I set the shoe box on the kitchen counter and sprint upstairs to put on jeans and a yellow-and-blue flannel shirt. I catch a glimpse of myself in the mirror, and it stops me cold. My orange hair is a rat's nest. I duck into the bathroom and try to comb the snarls out, then braid it in one long plait down my back. I dust on a little blush. A coat of lip gloss and I'm presentable again.

When I come back down the stairs, I find Tucker in the living room sitting on the couch, his booted feet on the coffee table. He's looking out the window where the wind stirs the big aspen outside, the tree a flurry of motion, each leaf trembling with life. I love that tree. Seeing him there, admiring it, unnerves me. I want to put Tucker in a safe little box where I can predict what he wants, but he refuses to stay in it.

"Nice tree," he says.

The boy has unexpected depth.

"Open it," he says, without turning to look at me or the shoe box on the counter. I pick up the box and lift the lid. Inside, wrapped in white tissue paper, is a pair of Vasque hiking boots. They're noticeably used, with some wear on the edges and soles, although clean and well cared for. These are expensive boots. I wonder if Wendy and I have the same size feet, even though I'm so much taller than she is. I wonder how she could have afforded such great boots, and why on earth she would give them up now.

"There's a note," says Tucker.

Inside one of the boots is a three-by-five card with Wendy's slanted scrawl on the front and back. I start reading.

Dear Clara, I am so sorry I can't be with you on your birthday. While you're reading this I'm probably shoveling horse puckey or worse, so don't feel too sorry for yourself! The boots are not your birthday present. They are a loaner, so take care of them. Tucker is your birthday present. Now before you get that mad face, hear me out. Last time we talked, you sounded lonely and like you weren't getting out much. I refuse to allow you to mope around your house when you're surrounded by the most beautiful land ever. No one on earth knows this part of the country better than Tucker. He is the finest tour guide to the area that you are ever likely to meet. So suck it up, Clara, put on the boots, and let him show you around for a few days. That is really the best possible present I can give you. Big hug! Love, Wendy.

I look up. Tucker's still looking at the tree. I don't know what to say.

"She wanted me to sing you a little jingle, too, like I'm a singing delivery guy." He glances at me over his shoulder, a corner of his mouth lifting. "I told her where she could stick it."

"She says . . ."

"I know."

He lets out a sigh like he's facing a particularly unpleasant chore, and gets up. He looks at me from top to bottom, as if he's unsure that I'm up to whatever he has planned.

"What?" I say hotly.

"That's pretty good. But you'll have to go back upstairs and put on a suit."

"A suit?" Somehow that doesn't seem plausible.

"A swimming suit," he clarifies.

"We're going swimming?" I ask, instantly unsure about this whole Tucker thing, no matter what Wendy's intentions were. I glance over at him. A lot of girls would be thrilled to receive Tucker Avery as a present, I know, what with the stormy blue eyes and the golden tawny skin and hair, the dimple carved into his left cheek. I have a mortifying flash of Tucker standing in front of me wearing a big red bow and nothing else.

Happy Birthday, Clara.

My cheeks are suddenly unpleasantly warm.

Tucker doesn't answer my swimming question. I guess the surprise is supposed to be part of the experience. He gestures back to the stairs. I smile and run upstairs to agonize over which of my California beach bikinis would be the least humiliating in this situation. I settle on a deep sapphire-colored two-piece, only because it covers the most skin. Then I hurriedly throw on my jeans and the flannel shirt, grab a towel from the linen closet, and go down to meet Tucker. He tells me to put on the boots.

After I'm outfitted to Tucker's liking he walks me to his truck and opens the door for me before crossing around to climb in himself. We bump along the dirt road away from my house in silence. I'm hot in my flannel shirt. It's a full-blown summer day, the sky a perfect cloudless blue, and while it isn't as hot as California, it's shorts weather. I wonder if we're going to have a long hike.

"Does this thing have air-conditioning?" My shirt is already starting to stick to my back.

Tucker shifts to a higher gear. Then he reaches across me and rolls down the window.

"I could have done that," I say, sure he did that just so he could jostle me. He smiles, an easy, relaxed smile that somehow puts me at ease.

"That window can be tricky" is all he says.

I put my arm out the window and let the cool mountain air pass through my fingers. Tucker starts to whistle softly, a song I eventually recognize as "Danny Boy," which Wendy sang at the Spring Choir Concert. His whistle has a nice, full quality to it, perfectly in tune.

We turn on the highway toward the school.

"Where are we going?" I ask him.

"Hoback." I've heard the word mentioned at school, and seen it on the road signs along the highway. There's a Hoback Canyon, a Hoback pass, if I remember it right, and a Hoback Junction. Which one we're going to, I can't tell. We drive past the school, down the highway for about a half hour where the buildings disappear and it's mountain and forest again. Suddenly we come into a tiny, one-stop-sign town, Hoback. The road splits into a Y right after the Hoback General Store. Tucker takes the road on the left, and then we're cruising back up toward the mountains, and on our right is a fast-flowing green river.

"Is that the Snake River?" I ask. With the window still down, the air rushes at me as the truck picks up speed. I pull my arm in.

"Nope," he replies. "That's the Hoback."

I smell the river, the smaller pine trees crouched on the hillside, and the sagebrush that stretches on either side of the road.

"I love the smell of sage," I say, breathing in deep.

Tucker snorts. "Sage is a fighter. It spreads over the land like wildfire, sucking up all the water, the nutrients in the earth, until everything else dies. It's a hearty little plant, that I'll give it. But it's gray and ugly and ticks love to hide in it. You ever seen a tick?" He glances over at me. The look on my face must be pretty appalled because he suddenly gives an uncomfortable cough and says quietly, "Sage does have a nice smell."

Then he swerves off the road into a small grassy turnout.

"We're here," he says, turning to me.

We park along a weather-beaten log fence right next to a big orange sign that reads, PRIVATE PROPERTY. TRESPASSERS WILL BE SHOT. Tucker lifts his eyebrows at me like he's double-dog-daring me. He swings himself through a gap in the fence and holds out his hand. I take it. Tucker threads me through the fence. Once we're on the other side, the hill drops down to the river at a steep angle. Beer cans litter the sagebrush. Tucker keeps hold of my hand and starts on a path winding over to a huge tree right at the water's edge. I'm suddenly grateful for the sturdiness of the boots.

At the bottom Tucker sticks his towel at the base of the big tree and starts shucking off his clothes. I turn away, then start to slowly unbutton my flannel shirt. It's a cute swimsuit, I reassure myself. I'm no prude. I take a deep breath and slide the shirt off my shoulders, then make quick work of the jeans and boots. I turn back toward Tucker. To my relief, he's watching the river, although he could be raking my body over with his peripheral vision for all I know. His red-and-black swim trunks come to his knees. He's golden brown all over. I quickly look away from his body and put my clothes and towel in a pile next to his.

"What now?" I ask.

"Now we climb the tree."

I gaze up into the branches, which sway slightly in the wind. A series of boards have been nailed to the trunk as a kind of ladder. On one of the biggest branches, which leans way out over the water, someone has fastened a long black cord.

We're going to jump off that cord, into the river.

I look at the river again, which seems impossibly high and fast.

"I think maybe you're trying to get me killed on my birthday," I say teasingly, hoping he doesn't see the flash of fear in my eyes. Angel-bloods can drown. We need oxygen as much as regular humans, although we can probably hold our breath longer.

His dimple appears.

"Why don't I go first?" Without another word he's climbing the tree, his hands and feet finding the places they're supposed to go like he's done this a thousand times before, which is mildly reassuring. When he reaches the higher branches I can hardly see him anymore, just a flash of his tanned legs now and then or a glimpse of his hair against the leaves and the sun. Then I can't see him at all, but suddenly the rope jerks.

"Come on up here," he directs. "There's room for two."

I start awkwardly up the tree. I manage to skin my knee in the process and get a deep sliver in the palm of my hand, but I don't complain. The last thing I want is for Tucker Avery to think I'm a baby. Tucker's hand appears in front of my face and I grab it and he hauls me up to the highest branches.

We can see a long way down the river. I look for a place where it flattens out or slows, but there isn't any. Beside me, Tucker grasps the rope, which looks stretchy like a bungee cord. He turns his face up toward the sun and closes his eyes for a minute.

"They call this the Solarium," he says.

"This, like where we're standing? The top of the tree?"

"Yeah." He opens his eyes. I'm close enough that I see his pupils contract in the light. "Kids from school have been coming here for generations," he says.

"Hence the private property sign," I say, turning away to look toward the road.

"I think the owner lives in California," says Tucker wryly.

"Yay for us. I won't actually get shot on my seventeenth birthday."

"Nope." Tucker readjusts his hold of the rope. His knees bend. "You'll just get wet," he says, and leaps out of the tree.

The rope swoops over the water at an angle. Tucker lets

go and hollers as he drops straight into the water. The rope springs back and I reach out and catch it, staring down at where Tucker's head bobs in the water. He turns toward me and waves as he's swept downriver.

"Come on!" he yells. "You'll love it."

I take a deep breath, grip the rope more firmly between my hands, and jump.

Amazing, the difference between falling and flying, and I've experienced a lot of both. The rope lurches out over the river and stretches under my weight. I grit my teeth to keep my wings back, the desire to fly is so strong. Then I scream and let go, because I know if I don't let go the rope will bring me crashing back into the tree.

The water's so cold all my breath leaves me in a rush. I pop up to the surface, coughing. For a minute I don't know what to do. I'm a competent swimmer, but not a great one. Most of my swimming has taken place in swimming pools and along the beaches of the Pacific Ocean. Nothing could have prepared me for the way the river grabs me and pulls me along. I get another mouthful of river water. It tastes like dirt and ice and something else I can't identify, something mineral. I come up sputtering, then start to swim for the side in earnest before I'm swept completely down the river, never to be seen again. I can't see Tucker. Panic rises in my throat. I can just see the news report now, Mom's sorry face, Angela's, Wendy's when she realizes that this whole thing is her fault.

An arm snakes around my waist. I turn and almost knock heads with Tucker. He tightens his hold on me and pushes hard toward the shore. He's a strong swimmer. All that beefy arm muscle definitely helps. I can do little better than hang on to his shoulders and kick with my legs in the right direction. In no time we're gasping on the sandy riverbank. I flop onto my back and watch a fluffy white cloud pass over.

"Well," says Tucker simply. "You're brave."

I glare at him. Water drips off his hair, down his neck, and then I jerk my gaze up to his eyes again, which are impossibly blue and filled with laughter. I want to punch him.

"That was dumb. We both could have drowned."

"Nah," he says. "The river's not so fast right now. I've seen it worse."

I sit up and look upriver toward the tree, which looks like it's a good half mile away now.

"I guess the next step is to hike back to the tree."

Tucker chuckles at the irritation in my voice. "Yep."

"Barefoot."

"It's pretty sandy, not too bad. Are you cold?" he asks, and I see in a flash that if I am he'll gladly put his arms around me. But I'm not really cold, not now that the sun is out and the water has mostly evaporated from my skin. Just a little damp and chilly. I try not to think of Tucker so close with his bare chest, heat pouring off him, and me in this itsy-bitsy two-piece with goose bumps rising across my belly.

I scramble to my feet and start walking up the bank. Tucker jumps up to walk alongside me.

"Sorry," he says. "Maybe I should have warned you about how fast the river is."

"Maybe," I agree, but I'm sick of being mad at Tucker, when, after all, he did come to my rescue at prom. I haven't forgotten that. And he's here now. "It's okay."

"Want to try it again?" he asks, his dimple showing as he smiles at me. "It's lots easier the second time."

"You really are trying to get me killed." I shake my head at him incredulously. "You're crazy."

"I work for the Crazy River Rafting Company during the summers. I'm in the river five days a week, sometimes more."

So he was pretty confident that he'd be able to pull me out, no matter how crappy a swimmer I was. But what if I'd gone straight to the bottom?

"Tucker!" someone yells from upriver. "How's the water?"

At the tree there are at least four or five people watching us make our way toward them up the shore. Tucker waves.

"It's good!" Tucker calls back. "Nice and smooth."

By the time we reach the tree, two other people have climbed up and jumped into the river. Neither of them seems to have the least bit of trouble getting to shore. Seeing that is what has me up in the tree again. This time I make an effort to whoop as I fall, the way Tucker did, and strike out for the shore as soon as I'm in the water. By the fourth time I jump, I'm not scared anymore. I feel invincible. And that, I now understand, is the draw of places like this.

"You're Clara Gardner, right?" asks a girl waiting to climb the tree. I nod. She introduces herself as Ava Peters, even though we were in chemistry together. She's the girl I saw with Tucker that one day at the ski lodge.

"There's a party Saturday at my house if you want to come," she tells me. Like I've suddenly been allowed in her club.

"Oh," I say, stunned. "I will. Thanks."

I flash a grateful smile at Tucker, who nods like he's tipping his hat. For the first time it feels like we might, just maybe, be friends.

Tucker takes me to dinner at Bubba's that night. Even in that casual barbecue joint, it feels enough like a real date that I'm a bit antsy. But after the food arrives it's so delicious that I relax and wolf it down. I haven't eaten since my bowl of Cheerios this morning, and I don't remember ever being so hungry. Tucker watches me as I gnaw on a barbecued chicken wing like it's the best thing I've ever tasted. The sauce is insanely good. After I've cleared a quarter of a chicken, barbecued beans, and a big helping of potato salad off my plate, I dare to look up at him. I half expect him to say something snide about the way I pigged out. I'm already formulating a comeback, something to call attention to the fact that I need some extra meat on my bones.

"Get the vanilla custard pie," he says without a trace of judgment. He's even looking at me with a hint of admiration in his eyes. "They bring it with a slice of lemon and when you bite the lemon and then eat a piece, it tastes exactly like lemon meringue."

"Why not just get the lemon meringue?"

"Trust me," he says, and I find that I do trust him.

"Okay." I wave at the waiter to order the vanilla custard pie. Which is divine, and I ought to know.

"Wow, I am so full," I say. "You're going to have to roll me home."

For a minute neither of us says anything, the words hanging in the air between us.

"Thank you for today," I say finally, finding it hard to meet his eyes.

"A good birthday?"

"Yes. Thank you, also, for not blabbing to the restaurant so they would come over here and sing to me."

"Wendy said you would hate that."

I wonder how much of this day was orchestrated by Wendy.

"What are you doing tomorrow?" he asks.

"Huh?"

"I have tomorrow off, and if you want I could take you to Yellowstone, show you around."

"I've never been to Yellowstone."

"I know."

He's just the gift that keeps on giving. Yellowstone sounds loads better than sitting at home channel surfing, worrying about Jeffrey, and trying to lug a big Christian-sized duffel bag into the air.

"I'd love to see Old Faithful," I admit.

"Okay." He looks suspiciously pleased with himself. "We'll start there."

15

TUCKER ME OUT

Our trip to Yellowstone is marred only by me accidentally speaking Korean to a tourist who'd lost track of her five-year-old son. I help her talk to the ranger, and they locate the kid. Happy story, right? Except for the part where Tucker stares at me like I'm a mutant until I lamely explain that I have a Korean friend back in California and I'm good with languages. I don't expect to see him after that, assuming that my birthday gift from Wendy is all used up. But Saturday there's a knock on my door and there he is again, and an hour later I find myself in a large inflated raft with a group of out-of-state tourists, feeling enormous and bloated in the bright orange life jacket we all have to wear. Tucker perches on the end of the boat and rows in the direction of the rapids, while the other guide sits at the front and shouts orders. I watch Tucker's strong brown arms flex as he tugs the oars through the water. We hit the first set of rapids. The boat lurches, water sprays everywhere, and the people in the raft scream like we're on a roller coaster. Tucker grins at me. I grin back.

That night he takes me to the party at Ava Peters's house and stays by me through the entire thing, introducing me to people who don't know me past my name. I'm amazed at how being with him changes everything for me, socially speaking. When I walked the halls of Jackson Hole High, the other students looked at me with careful disinterest, not entirely hostile, but definitely like I was an intruder on their turf. Even Christian's attention in those final weeks hadn't made much of a difference in getting people to talk *to* me instead of *about* me. Now with Tucker by my side the other students actually converse with me. Their smiles are suddenly real. It's easy to see that they all, regardless of what clique they belong to or how much money their parents rake in, genuinely like Tucker. The boys yell, "Fry!" and bump fists with him or do their shoulder bump thing. The girls hug him and murmur their hellos and look me over with curious but friendly expressions.

While Tucker goes to the kitchen to get me a drink, Ava Peters grabs my arm.

"How long have you and Tucker been together?" she asks with a sly smile.

"We're just friends," I stammer.

"Oh." She frowns slightly. "Sorry, I thought . . ."

"You thought what?" asks Tucker, suddenly standing beside me with a red plastic cup in each hand.

"I thought you two were an item," says Ava.

"We're just friends," he says. He meets my eyes briefly, then hands me one of the cups.

"What is this?"

"Rum and Coke. I hope you like coconut rum."

I've never had rum. Or tequila or vodka or whiskey or anything but the tiniest bit of wine at a fancy dinner now and then. My mom lived during Prohibition. But right now she's a thousand miles away probably sound asleep in her hotel room in Mountain View, completely unaware that her daughter is at an unsupervised teen party about to guzzle down her first hard liquor.

What she doesn't know can't hurt her. Cheers.

I take a sip of the drink. I don't detect even the slightest hint of coconut, or alcohol. It tastes exactly like regular old Coca-Cola.

"It's good, thank you," I say.

"Nice party, Ava," Tucker says. "You really pulled out all the stops."

"Thanks," she says serenely. "I'm glad you made it. You

too, Clara. Good to finally get to know you."

"Yeah," I say. "It's good to be known."

Tucker's so different from Christian, I muse on the way home from the party. He's popular in a completely different way, not because he's rich (which he's definitely not, in spite of his many jobs—he doesn't even have a cell phone) or because he's good-looking (which he definitely is, although his appeal is this kind of sexy-rugged whereas Christian's is sexy-broody). Christian's popular because, like Wendy always says, he's kind of like a god. Beautiful and perfect and a little removed. Made to be worshipped. Tucker's popular because he has this way of putting people at ease.

"What are you thinking about?" he asks because I haven't said anything in a while.

"You're different than I thought you were."

He keeps his eyes on the road but the dimple appears in his lean cheek. "What did you think I was?"

"A rude hick."

"Geez, blunt much?" he says, laughing.

"It's not like you didn't know. You wanted me to think that."

He doesn't reply. I wonder if I've said too much. I can never seem to hold my tongue around him.

"You're different than I thought you were too," he says.

"You thought I was this spoiled California chick."

"I still think you're a spoiled California chick." I punch

him hard on the shoulder. "Ow. See?"

"How am I different?" I ask, trying to mask my nervousness. It's amazing how much I suddenly care about what he thinks of me. I look out the window, dangling my arm out as we drive through the trees toward my house. The summer night air is warm and silky on my face. The full moon overhead spills a dreamy silver light onto the forest. Crickets chirp. A cool, pine-scented breeze rustles the leaves. A perfect night.

"Come on, how am I different?" I ask Tucker again.

"It's hard to explain." He rubs the back of his neck. "There's just so much to you that's under the surface."

"Hmm. How mysterious," I say, trying hard to keep my voice light.

"Yep, you're like an iceberg."

"Gee, thanks. I think the problem is that you always underestimate me."

We pull up to my house, which seems dark and empty, and I want to stay in the truck. I'm not ready for the night to be over.

"Nope," he says. He puts the truck in park and turns to look at me with somber eyes. "I wouldn't be surprised if you could fly to the moon."

I suck in a breath.

"You want to pick huckleberries with me tomorrow?" he asks.

"Huckleberries?"

"They sell in town for fifty bucks a gallon. I know this spot where there are like a hundred bushes. I go out there a few times a summer. It's early in the season, but there should be some berries because it's been so hot lately. It's good money."

"Okay," I say, surprising myself. "I'll go."

He jumps out and circles around to open the door for me. He holds out his hand and helps me climb down from the truck.

"Thanks," I murmur.

"Night, Carrots."

"Night, Tuck."

He leans against the truck and waits as I go inside. I flip on the porch light and observe him from a corner of the living room window until the back of the rusty truck disappears in the trees. Then I run upstairs to my bedroom and watch the taillights as they move smoothly down our long driveway to the main road.

I look at myself in the full-length mirror on my closet door. The girl who stares back was tossed around by a wild river and her tangerine-colored hair dried in loose waves all around her face. She's starting to tan, even though angel-bloods don't burn or tan easily. And tomorrow she'll be on the side of some mountain, hunting for huckleberries with a real-live rodeo cowboy.

"What are you doing?" I ask the girl in the mirror. She doesn't answer. She gazes at me with bright eyes like she knows something I don't.

∽∾

I'm not totally cut off from the world. Angela emails me every now and then, tells me about Rome and says, in her own version of code, that she's finding out amazing stuff about angels. She'll write things like, *It's dark outside right now. I'm turning on the light*, which I take to mean she's getting a lot of good info on Black Wings. When she writes, *It's so hot I have to change my clothes all the time*, I think she's telling me she's practicing changing the form of her wings. She doesn't say much more. Nothing about the mysterious Italian lover, but she sounds happy. Like she's having a suspiciously good time.

I also hear from Wendy occasionally, whenever she can make it to a pay phone. She sounds tired but content, spending her days with horses, learning from the best. She doesn't mention Tucker, or the time I've been spending with him lately, but I suspect that she knows all about it.

When I get a text from Christian I realize it's been a while since I've thought about him. I've been so busy running around with Tucker. I haven't even had the vision lately. This week I almost forgot I was an angel-blood and simply let myself be a regular girl having a perfectly normal summer. Which is nice. And makes me feel guilty, because I'm supposed to be focusing on my purpose.

His text says:

Have you ever been to a place you're supposed to love, but all you can think about is home?

Cryptic. And as usual when it comes to Christian, I don't know how to respond.

I hear a car pulling into the driveway, and then the sound of the garage door. Mom's home. I do a quick sweep around the house to make sure everything is in order, dishes washed, laundry folded, Jeffrey still in a food coma upstairs. All is right in the Gardner house. When she comes in, towing her huge suitcase, I'm sitting at the kitchen counter with two tall glasses of iced tea.

"Welcome home," I say brightly.

She puts her suitcase down and holds out her arms. I jump off my stool and step sheepishly into her hug. She squeezes me tight, and it makes me feel like a kid again. Safe. Right. Like nothing was normal when she was gone.

She pulls back and looks me up and down. "You look older," she says. "Seventeen suits you."

"I feel older. And stronger lately, for whatever reason."

"I know. You should be feeling stronger every day now, the closer we get to your purpose. Your power is growing."

There's an uncomfortable silence. What are my powers, exactly?

"I can fly now," I blurt out suddenly. It's been two weeks since Inspiration Point, a hundred crashes and scrapes, but I've finally gotten the hang of it. It feels like something she should know. I lift my pant leg to show her a scratch on my shin from the top of a pine tree I passed over too closely.

"Clara!" she exclaims, and she tries to act pleased but I can tell she's disappointed that she hadn't been there, like I'm a baby taking my first steps and she missed it.

"It's easier for me when you're not watching," I explain. "Less pressure or something."

"Well, I knew you'd get it."

"I totally love the dress you gave me," I say in an attempt to change the subject. "Maybe we could go out to dinner tonight and I'll wear it."

"Sounds like a plan." She releases me, grabs her suitcase, and lugs it down the hall toward her bedroom. I follow.

"How was work?" I ask as she lays her suitcase on her bed, opens her top dresser drawer, and begins to stack her underwear and socks neatly inside. I have to shake my head at what a neat freak she is, all her panties folded, arranged by color in perfect little rows. It seems impossible that we're related, she and I. "Did you get it all straightened out?"

"Yes. It's better, anyway. I really needed to go out there." She moves on to the next drawer. "But I'm sorry I missed your birthday."

"It's okay."

"What did you do?"

For some reason I've been dreading telling her about Tucker, the Jumping Tree, and the time I've been spending with him all week, hiking, picking huckleberries, white-water rafting, speaking Korean to random people in front of him. Maybe I'm afraid that she'll call Tucker what I know deep down that he is: a distraction. She'll tell me to get back to work on the Saving Christian mission. Then I'll have to tell her that, even though I'm feeling stronger lately, finally flying, I still can't get that heavy duffel bag off the ground. And then she'll give me that look, that speech about lightness and strength and how much I am capable of if only I put my mind to it. I just don't want to go there. Not yet, anyway. But I have to give her something.

"Wendy loaned me her brother and a pair of hiking boots, and he took me out to this place where all the kids go to jump into the Hoback River," I say all in one breath.

Mom looks at me suspiciously.

"Wendy *loaned* you her brother?"

"Tucker. You met him that time our car slid off the road, remember?"

"The boy who brought you home from prom," she says thoughtfully.

"Yep, that's him. And thanks so much for bringing *that* up."

For a minute neither of us says anything else.

"I brought you something," she says finally. "A present."

She unzips a compartment of her suitcase and pulls out something made of dark purple fabric. It's a jacket, a gorgeous corduroy jacket the exact color of Mom's African violet on the kitchen windowsill. It will play down the orange of my hair and play up the blue in my eyes. It's perfect.

"I know you have your parka," Mom says, "but I thought you could use something lighter. And besides, you can never have too many jackets in Wyoming."

"Thanks. I love it."

I reach to take it from her. And the moment my fingers touch the soft, velvety fabric, I'm in the vision, walking through the trees.

I trip and fall, scraping the palm of my right hand. I haven't had the vision in weeks, since prom when I saw myself fly away from the fire with Christian in my arms. It doesn't feel as familiar to me now, as I make my way up the hillside toward him. But he's still there waiting for me, and when I see him I call his name, and he turns, and I run to him. I missed him, I realize, although I don't know if it's what I'm feeling now or in the future. He makes me feel complete. The way he always looks at me like he needs me. Me, and no one else.

I take his hand. The sorrow's there, too, mixed with everything else: elation and fear and determination and even a serving of good old-fashioned lust. I feel it all, but overshadowing every other emotion is the grief, the sense that I've lost the most important thing in the world, even as I seem to be gaining it. I bend my head and look at where our hands join, Christian's hand so finely constructed, like a surgeon's hand. The nails are neatly clipped, his skin smooth and almost hot to the touch. His thumb strokes over my knuckles, sending a shiver through me. Then I realize.

I'm wearing the purple jacket.

I come back to myself to find Mom sitting next to me on her bed, her arm around my shoulders. She smiles sympathetically, her eyes worried.

"Sorry," I say.

"Don't be, silly," she says. "I know what it's like."

Sometimes I forget that Mom had a purpose once upon a time. It was probably a hundred years ago if she was my age at the time. Which (I do the math quickly in my head) would put her at sometime between 1907 and 1914, approximately. Which means ladies in long, white dresses and men with top hats and big, bristly mustaches, horse-drawn carriages, corsets, Leo DiCaprio about to win his ticket on the *Titanic*. I try to picture my mother in that time, reeling with the force of her visions and lying awake in the dark trying to put the pieces together, trying to understand what it was she was meant to do.

"Are you all right?" she asks.

"I'm going to wear that jacket," I say shakily. It's lying on the floor near the bed. It must have slipped out of my hands when the vision struck me.

"Good," says Mom. "I thought it would look good on you."

"No. In the vision. I'm *wearing* that jacket."

Her eyes widen slightly.

"It's happening." She calmly smoothes a strand of my hair

behind my ear. "Everything's aligning for you. It's going to happen this year, this fire season, I'm sure of it."

That's weeks away. Just weeks.

"What if I'm not ready?"

She smiles knowingly. Her eyes are twinkling again with that strange inner light. She lifts her arms and stretches them over her head, yawning. She looks a lot better. Not so tired. Not so worn down and frustrated about everything. She looks like her old self, like she's ready to jump up and get started on my training again, like she's excited about my purpose and determined to help me succeed at it.

"You'll be ready," she says.

"How do you know?"

"I just know," she says firmly.

The next morning I sneak quietly down the stairs and get myself a quick bowl of granola cereal, stand in the middle of the kitchen eating it, and wait for the familiar rattle of Tucker's truck in the driveway. Mom startles me by appearing as I'm pouring a glass of orange juice.

"You're up early." She examines the new woodsy version of me in the hiking boots, water resistant shorts, sports polo, the backpack hanging off one shoulder. I'm sure I look like I walked out of an Eddie Bauer ad. "Where are you off to?"

"Fishing," I say, swallowing my juice quickly.

Her eyebrows lift. I've never been fishing in my life. The

closest I've come is marinating salmon steaks for dinner.

"With who?"

"Some kids from school," I say, inwardly wincing. *Not quite a lie,* I tell myself. Tucker is a kid from school.

She cocks her head to one side.

"What's that smell?" she asks, wrinkling up her nose.

"Bug spray." Mosquitoes never bother me, but apparently they eat Tucker alive if he forgets bug spray. So I wear it for solidarity. "All the kids wear it," I explain to Mom. "They say the mosquito is the Wyoming state bird."

"You're really fitting in now."

"Well, I wasn't exactly friendless before," I say a little too sharply.

"Of course not. But something's new, I think. Something's different."

"Nah."

She laughs.

"Nah?"

I blush.

"Okay, so I talk more like the kids at school," I say. "You hear it so much, you pick it up. Jeffrey does it too. They tell me I still talk too fast to be from Wyoming."

"That's good," she says. "Fitting in."

"It's better than sticking out," I say nervously. I just caught sight of the rusty blue truck snaking its way through the trees in front of the house.

"Gotta run, Mom." I give her a quick hug. Then I'm out the door, down the driveway, jumping into Tucker's truck while it's still moving. He yelps in surprise and slams on the brake.

"Let's go." I flash him an innocent smile. His eyes narrow.

"What's with you?"

"Nothing."

He frowns. He can always tell when I lie. It's annoying when there's so much I have to hide from him. I sigh.

"My mom's back," I confess.

"And you don't want her to see you with me?" he asks, offended. I glance over my shoulder, out the window of the truck where I clearly see Mom's face in the front window. I wave at her, then look back at Tucker.

"No, silly," I say. "I'm stoked to learn fly-fishing, that's all."

He still doesn't believe me, but he lets it slide. He tips his Stetson at Mom through the windshield. Her head vanishes from the window. I relax. It's not that I don't want Mom to see me with Tucker. I just don't want to give her the chance to question him. Or question me about what I think I'm doing with him. Because I have no idea what I'm doing with Tucker Avery.

"Fly-fishing is easy," Tucker says about two hours later, after he's shown me all the elements of fishing from the relative safety of the grass along the Snake River. "You just have to think like a fish."

"Right. Think like a fish."

"Don't mock," he warns. "Look at the river. What do you see?"

"Water. Stones and sticks and mud."

"Look closer. The river's its own world of fast and slow, deep and shallow, bright and shadowed. If you look at it like that, like a landscape where the fish live, it'll be easier to catch one."

"Nicely said. Are you some kind of cowboy poet?"

He blushes, which I find completely charming.

"Just look," he mumbles.

I gaze upriver. It does seem like its own little corner of paradise. There are golden motes of sunlight cutting through the air, deep pockets of shade along the bank, aspen and cottonwoods rustling in the breeze. And above everything else is the sparkling river. It's alive, rushing and bubbling, its green depths full of mysteries. And supposedly full of wonderful, tasty fish.

"Let's do it." I lift the fly rod. "I promise, I'm thinking like a fish."

He snorts and rolls his eyes.

"All right, *fish*." He gestures to the river. "Right there's a sandbar you can stand on."

"Let me be sure I've got this right. You want me to stand in the middle of the river?"

"Yep," he says. "It'll be a bit chilly, but I think you can

handle it. I don't have any waders your size."

"This isn't another one of your ploys to have to rescue me, is it?" I tilt my head and squint at him in the sun. "Because don't think I've forgotten the Jumping Tree."

"Nah," he says with a grin.

"Okay." I take a step into the river, gasping at the cold, then another and another until I'm standing up to just above my knee. I stop on the edge of the narrow sandbar that Tucker pointed out, trying to get a firm footing on the smooth river rocks under my feet. The water is cool and strong against my bare legs. I straighten my shoulders and adjust my hands on the rod the way he showed me earlier, pull the line through the guides and wait as he wades out next to me and starts to tie on the fly.

"This is one of my favorites," he says. His hands move quickly, gracefully, to fasten on the bit of fluff and hook meant to look like an insect on the water. "Pale Morning Dun."

"Nice," I say, although I have no clue what he's talking about. It looks kind of like a moth to me. To a fish it's supposed to look like prime rib, apparently.

"All set." He releases the line. "Now try it like we practiced on the grass. Two beats back to two o'clock, one beat forward to ten. Pull out a little line, and back again. Once you cast the line forward, relax it to about nine o'clock."

"Ten and two," I repeat. I raise the rod and cast the line backward, to what I hope is about two o'clock, then whip it forward.

"Gently," coaches Tucker. "Try to hit along that log over there, so the fish thinks it's a nice juicy bug."

"Right, think like a fish," I say with an embarrassing giggle. I try it. Ten and two, ten and two, over and over, the line looping around and around. I think I'm getting it, but after about ten minutes no fish has even looked at my Pale Morning Dun.

"I don't think I'm fooling them."

"Your line is too tight—your fly is dragging. Try not to cast like windshield wipers," says Tucker. "You have to pause on the back cast. You're forgetting to pause."

"Sorry."

I can feel him watching me, and frankly it's wrecking my concentration.

I suck at fly-fishing, I realize. I don't suck because I'm holding back; I just plain suck.

"This is fun," I say. "Thanks for bringing me."

"Yeah, it's kind of my favorite thing. You wouldn't believe some of the fish I've caught in this river: brook trout, rainbow trout, cutthroat trout, some brown trout. The native cutthroat are getting rarer, though; the introduced rainbows breed them out."

"Do you throw them back?" I ask.

"Mostly. That way they grow to be bigger, smarter fish. Better to catch next time. I always release the cutthroat. But if I catch the rainbows I'll take them home. Mom makes a fierce fish dinner, just fries them up in butter with some salt and pepper, a bit of cayenne sometimes, and it almost melts in your mouth."

"Sounds heavenly."

"Well, maybe you'll catch one today."

"Maybe."

"I have tomorrow off," he says. "You want to meet me at the butt crack of dawn and hike up to watch the sun rise from the best place in Teton? It's kind of a special day for me."

"Sure." I have to admit that as distractions go, Tucker is top-notch. He just keeps asking me to do things and I just keep saying yes. "I can't believe summer's going by so fast. And I thought it would drag on forever. Ooh, I think I see a fish!"

"Hold on," groans Tucker. "You're just waving it around now."

He steps toward me at the exact moment that I cast the line back. The fly catches his cowboy hat and jerks it off his head. He swears under his breath, lunges to grab it, and misses.

"Whoops! I'm so sorry." I draw the line in and manage to snag the hat and free it from the hook. I hold it out to him, trying not to giggle. He looks at me with a little mock scowl and snatches it out of my hands. We both laugh.

"I guess I'm lucky it was my hat and not my ear," he says. "Stay still for a minute, all right?"

He wades into the river and sloshes over to stand behind

me in his hip waders, suddenly so close that I can smell him: sunscreen, Oreo cookies for some mysterious reason, a mix of bug spray and river water, and a hint of musky cologne. I smile, suddenly nervous. He reaches over and takes a strand of my hair between his fingers.

"Your hair isn't really red, is it?" he asks, and my breath freezes in my lungs.

"What do you mean?" I choke out. When in doubt, I've learned from Mom, answer a question with a question.

He shakes his head. "Your eyebrows. They're, like, dark gold."

"You're staring at my eyebrows now?"

"I'm looking at you. Why are you always trying to hide how pretty you are?"

He seems to gaze right into me, like he's seeing me for who I truly am. And in that moment, I want to tell him the truth. Crazy, I know. Stupid. Wrong. I try to take a step back, but my foot slips and I almost go headfirst into the river but he catches me.

"Whoa," he says, snaking both hands around my waist to steady me. He pulls me closer to him, bracing against the current. The water parts around us, icy and relentless, tugging and pulling at us as we stand there for a few slow-passing seconds trying to regain our balance.

"You got your legs under you?" he asks, his mouth close to my ear. Goose bumps jump up all along my arm. I turn slightly and get a really close look at his dimple. His pulse is going strong in his neck. His body's warm against my back. His hand closes over mine on the fishing rod.

"Yeah," I rasp. "I'm fine."

What am I doing here? I think dazedly. This is beyond distraction. I don't know what this is. I should—

I don't know what I should do. My brain has suddenly checked out.

He clears his throat. "Watch the hat this time."

We lift the rod together and swing it back, then forward, Tucker's arm guiding mine.

"Like a hammer," he says. "Slow back, pause on the back cast, and then"——he casts the rod forward so that the line whirs by our heads and unrolls gently on the water—"fast hammer forward. Like a baseball pitch." The dun lights delicately on the surface and hesitates a moment before the current swirls and carries it on. Now that it's riding on the water, it does resemble an insect, and I marvel at its play on the water. Quickly, though, the line pulls it unnaturally and it's time to cast again.

We try it a few times, back and forth, Tucker setting the rhythm. It's mesmerizing, *slow back, pause, forward*, over and over again. I relax against Tucker, resting almost totally against him as we cast and wait for the fish to rise to take the fly.

"Ready to try it on your own again?" he asks after a while. I'm tempted to say no, but I can't think of any good reason.

I nod. He lets go of my hand and moves away from me, back toward the bank where he picks up his own rod.

"You think I'm pretty?" I ask.

"We need to stop talking," he says a little gruffly. "We're scaring the fish off."

"Okay, okay." I bite my lip, then smile.

We fish for a while in silence, the only noise the burbling of the river and the rustling of trees. Tucker catches and releases three fish. He takes a moment to show me the cutthroat, with their scarlet slash of color beneath the gills. I, on the other hand, don't get so much as a nibble before I have to retreat from the cold water. I sit on the bank and attempt to rub the feeling back into my legs. I have to face the ugly truth: I'm a terrible fisherwoman.

I know it sounds weird to say this, but that's a good thing. I enjoy not excelling at everything, for once. I like watching Tucker fish, the way his eyes scan the shadows and riffles, the way he throws the line over the water in perfect, graceful loops. It's like he's talking with the river. It's peaceful.

And Tucker thinks I'm pretty.

Later I drag the good old duffel bag into the backyard and try it one more time. Back to reality, I remind myself. Back to duty. Mom's in the office on the computer, drinking a cup of tea the way she does when she's trying to de-stress. She's been home all of one day and already she seems tired again.

I stretch my arms and wings. I close my eyes. *Light,* I coach myself. *Be light. Be part of the night, the trees, the wind.* I try to picture Christian's face, but suddenly it's not so clear to me. I try to conjure up his eyes, the flash of green and gold, but I can't hang on to that either.

Instead I get images of Tucker. His mouth smeared with red as we crouch on the side of the mountain filling empty ice-cream tubs with huckleberries. His husky laugh. His hands on my waist in the river, keeping me steady, holding me close. His eyes so warm and blue, reeling me in.

"Crap," I whisper.

I open my eyes. I'm so light the tips of my toes are the only thing on the ground. I'm floating.

No, I think. This isn't right. It's supposed to be Christian who makes you feel this way. I am here for Christian Prescott. Crap!

The thought weighs me down and I sink back to the earth. But I can't get Tucker out of my head. I keep replaying the moments between us over and over in my head.

"What do you see in a guy like Christian Prescott?" he asked me that night when he dropped me off from prom. And what he was really saying then, what would have come through loud and clear if I hadn't been so blind was, *Why don't you see me?*

I know the feeling.

Get a grip, I tell myself. *Just fly already.*

I tighten my hold on the duffel bag. I lift my wings and

stretch them skyward. I push with all the muscle in them, all the strength I've gained over months and months of practice. My body shoots up a few feet, and I manage to hold on to the duffel bag.

I pull myself higher, almost to the top of the tree line. I can barely make out the sliver of the new moon. I move toward it, but the duffel bag unbalances me. I lurch to one side, flapping wildly and dropping the bag. My arms feel like they're going to tear out of my sockets. And then I fall, crashing into the pine tree at the edge of our yard, cussing all the way down.

Jeffrey's standing at the kitchen sink when I drag myself through the back door, scratched and bruised and close to tears.

"Nice," he says, smirking.

"Shut it."

He laughs. "I can't do it either."

"You can't what?"

"I can't carry stuff when I fly. It gets me off balance."

I don't know whether to feel better because Jeffrey can't do it either, or to feel worse because he's evidently been watching me.

"You've tried?" I ask.

"Lots of times." He reaches over and pulls a pinecone out of my hair. His eyes are friendly, sympathetic. Out of everybody I know, Jeffrey's the one person who can really understand what I'm going through. He's going through it, too. Or at least he will, when his purpose comes.

"Do you—" I hesitate. I look behind him to the hallway toward Mom's office. He glances over his shoulder, then back at me curiously.

"What?"

"Do you want to try it together?"

He stares at me for a minute. "Sure," he says finally. "Let's do it."

It's so dark in the backyard that I can't see much past the edge of the lawn.

"This would be so much easier during the day," I say. "I'm starting to hate practicing at night."

"Why not practice during the day?"

"Um—because people could see us?"

He smiles mischievously. "Who cares?" he says.

"What do you mean?"

"People don't really see you. It's not like they're looking up."

"What? That's crazy," I say, shaking my head.

"It's true. If they notice you at all, they'll think you're a big bird or something. A pelican."

"No way." But I immediately flashed back to when I flew over Jenny Lake and my reflection was a streak of pure white, like a bird's.

"It's no big deal. Mom does it all the time."

"She does?"

"She flies almost every morning. Just as the sun's coming up."

"How have I not noticed this?"

He shrugs. "I get up earlier."

"I can't believe I didn't know that!"

"So we can fly during the day. Problem solved. But now let's get on with it, okay? I've got things to do."

"Of *course* you do. All right, then. Watch this. *Show yourself!*" I yell.

His wings flash out.

"What was that?" he gasps.

"A trick I learned from Angela."

His wings are a light gray color, several shades darker than mine. Probably nothing to worry about, though. Mom said we're all varying shades of gray. And his don't look dark so much as they look . . . dirty.

"Well, warn me next time, okay?" Jeffrey folds his wings slightly, makes them smaller, and turns his back to me as he walks over to the edge of the lawn where I left the duffel bag. He lifts it easily and jogs over to me. All those muscles from the wrestling team are a big advantage.

"Okay, let's do this thing." He holds the bag out, and I grab one of the handles. "On the count of three."

I suddenly picture the two of us bashing our heads together as we lift off. I take a step back, putting as much space between us as I can while still holding the duffel bag. With him sharing half the weight, it isn't too heavy at all.

"One," he says.

"Wait, which direction should we go?"

"That way." He tilts his head toward the northern end of our property, where the trees are thinner.

"Good plan."

"Two."

"How high?"

"We'll figure that out," he says in an exasperated tone.

"You know, your voice is starting to sound just like Dad's. I don't think I like it."

"Three!" he exclaims, and then he bends his knees and flexes his wings and heaves upward while I do my best to do the same.

There's no room for hesitation. We go up and up and up, timing the beats of our wings together, holding the duffel bag between us a bit shakily but in a way that we're able to handle it. In about ten seconds we're over the tree line. Then we start to move north. I look over at Jeffrey, and he shoots me a smug, self-satisfied smile, like he knew all along that this would be easy. I'm kind of shocked by how easy it is. We could have lifted twice as much. My mind races with all that this could mean. If I can't lift Christian myself, am I meant to have help? Is it against the rules?

"Jeffrey, maybe this is it."

"This is what?" he says a bit distractedly, trying to pull the duffel bag up to get a better grip on it.

"Your purpose. Maybe we do it together."

He lets go. The bag jerks me down instantly, and then I let

go, too. We watch it crash into the brush on the forest floor.

"It's not my purpose," he says in a flat voice. His gray eyes grow cold and distant.

"What's the matter?"

"Nothing. Everything's not about *you*, Clara."

The same thing that Wendy said to me. Like a punch to the gut.

"Sorry," I mumble. "I guess I got excited at the idea of getting some help. I'm having a hard time doing this on my own."

"We have to do it alone." He turns away in the air, heading back toward the yard. "That's just the way it is."

I stare after him for a long time, then drop down to the ground to pick up the duffel bag. One of the gallons of water I put inside is broken, and the water leaks out in a slow trickle onto the dry earth.

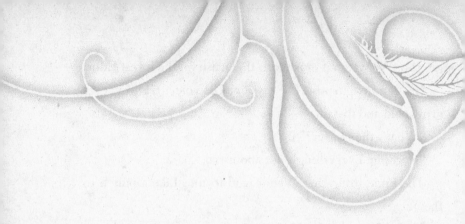

16

BEAR REPELLENT

The next morning my cell phone rings at some ungodly hour. Under the covers, I groan and grope around for it on the nightstand, find it, pull it in with me, and answer cheerfully.

"What?"

"Oh good. You're up." Tucker.

"What time is it?"

"Five."

"I'm going to kill you."

"I'm on my way over," he says. "I'll be there in about a half hour. I thought I'd call so you had time to brush your hair and put on your face."

"You think I'm going to wear makeup to go hiking with you?"

"See, that's what I like about you, Carrots. You're not fussy."

I hang up on him. I throw the blankets off and lie for a minute gazing up at the ceiling. Outside it's pitch-dark. I was dreaming about him, I realize, although I can't remember the details. Something about the big red barn on the Lazy Dog Ranch. I yawn. Then I force myself to get up and get dressed.

I don't shower, because the noise would wake Mom. I splash cold water on my face and put on some moisturizer. I don't need makeup. My skin lately is starting to have its own natural glow, another sign that things are starting to change, starting to intensify the way Mom said they would. I put on mascara and apply some lip gloss, then turn my attention to the wild waves of hair cascading down my back. There's a clump of tree sap clinging to a strand, evidence of last night's flying practice. I spend the next fifteen minutes trying to get rid of the sap, and when I finally remove it, along with a fat chunk of my hair, I hear tires on the gravel road outside.

I slip quietly downstairs. Jeffrey's right. Mom's not in her room. On the kitchen counter I write her a note: *Mom, going out to see the sunrise with friends. Be back later. I have my cell. C.* Then I'm out the door.

This time I'm nervous, but Tucker acts like nothing's changed, so completely normal that I wonder if maybe I imagined all the tension between us yesterday. I relax into our familiar banter. His smile's infectious. His dimple's out the whole drive, and he drives fast enough to have me clutching that handle above the door as we round corners. He takes a secret side road to get into Grand Teton, bypassing the main gate, and then we're zooming down the empty highway.

"So what day is it?" I ask.

"Huh?"

"You said it was a special day."

"Oh. I'll get to that."

We drive to Jackson Lake. He parks and hops out of the truck. I wait for him to come around and open my door. I'm getting used to his "yes, ma'am" manners, so much that I'm starting to find his gentlemanly ways sweet.

He checks his watch.

"We've got to hike fast," he says. "Sunrise is in twenty-six minutes."

I lean down to tighten the laces on my boots. And we're off. I follow him up and out of the parking lot and into the woods.

"So what classes are you taking next year?" he asks over his shoulder as we make our way up the hill on the other side of the lake.

"The usual," I say. "AP Calculus, College English, government, French, physics, you know."

"Physics, huh?"

"Well, my dad *is* a physics professor."

"No kidding? Where?"

"NYU."

He whistles. "That's a long way from here. When did your folks split up?"

"Why are you suddenly so chatty?" I ask a tad sharply. Something about the idea of telling him about my personal history makes me uncomfortable. Like I'll start telling him and won't be able to stop. I'll blab the whole story: Mom's half-angel, I'm a quarter, my vision, my powers, my purpose, Christian, and then what? He'll tell me about the rodeo circuit?

He stops and turns around to look at me. His eyes are dancing with mischief.

"We've got to talk because of the bears," he says in a low tone, hamming it up.

"The bears."

"Got to make some noise. Don't want to surprise a grizzly."

"No, I guess we don't want to do that."

He starts up the trail again.

"So, tell me about this thing that happened with your grandpa, where your family lost the ranch," I say quickly before he has a chance to get back to the subject of my family.

He doesn't break his stride but I can almost feel him tense up. The tables are turned. "Wendy says it's why you hate Californians. What happened there?"

"I don't hate Californians. Clearly."

"Whew, that's a relief."

"It's a long story," he says, "and we don't have that long to hike."

"Okay. Sorry. I didn't mean to——"

"It's fine, Carrots. I'll tell you about it someday. But not now."

Then he starts to whistle and we stop talking. Which seems to suit us both fine, bears or not.

After a few more minutes of hard climbing, we come out on a clearing at the top of a small rise. The sky's bathed in a mix of gray and pale yellow, with a tangle of bright pink clouds hanging right above where the Tetons jut into the sky, pure purple mountain majesty, standing like kings on the edge of the horizon. Below them is Jackson Lake, so clear it looks like two sets of mountains and two skies, perfectly replicated.

Tucker checks his watch. "Sixty seconds. We're right on time."

I can't look away from the mountains. I've never seen anything so formidably beautiful. I feel connected to them in a way I've never felt anywhere else. It's like I can feel their presence. Just looking at the jagged peaks against the sky makes peace wash over me like the waves lapping on the shore of the lake below us. Angela has a theory that angel-kind are attracted to mountains, that somehow the separation between heaven and earth is thinner here, just as the air is thinner. I don't know. I only know that looking at them fills me with the yearning to fly, to see the earth from above.

"This way." Tucker turns me to face the opposite direction, where across the valley the sun's coming up over a distant, less familiar set of mountains. We're completely alone. The sun is rising only for us. Once it clears the mountaintops, Tucker takes me gently by the shoulders and turns me again, back toward the Tetons, where now there are a million golden sparkles on the lake.

"Oh," I gasp.

"Makes you believe in God, doesn't it?"

I glance over at him, startled. I've never heard him talk about God before, even though I know from Wendy that the Averys attend church nearly every Sunday. I would have never pegged him as the religious type.

"Yes," I agree.

"Their name means 'breasts,' you know." The side of his mouth hitches up in his mischievous smile. "Grand Teton means 'big breast.'"

"Nice, Tucker," I scoff. "I know that. Third-year French, remember? I guess the French explorers hadn't seen a woman in a really long time."

"I think they just wanted a good laugh."

For a long while we stand side by side and watch the light stretch and dance with the mountains in complete silence. A light breeze picks up, blows my hair to the side where it catches against Tucker's shoulder. He looks over at me. He swallows. He seems like he's about to say something important. My heart jumps to my throat.

"I think you're—" he begins.

We both hear the noise in the brush behind us at the same moment. We turn.

A bear has just come onto the trail. I know immediately that it's a grizzly. Its massive shoulders glow in the rays of the rising sun as it stops to look at us. Behind it two cubs tumble out of the bushes.

This is bad.

"Don't run," warns Tucker. Not a possibility. My feet are frozen to the ground. In my peripheral vision I see him slide his backpack from his shoulder. The bear lowers her head and makes a snuffling sound.

"Don't run," says Tucker again, loudly this time. I hear him fumbling with something. Maybe he's going to hit her with an object of some kind. The bear looks right at him. Her shoulders tense as she prepares to charge.

"No," I murmur in Angelic, holding up my hand as if I could hold her back by the force of my will alone. "No."

The bear pauses. Her gaze swings to my face, her eyes a

light brown, absolutely empty of any feeling or understanding. Sheer animal. She looks intently at my hand, then rises to stand on her hind legs, huffing.

"We won't harm you," I say in Angelic, trying to keep my voice low. I don't know how it will sound to Tucker. I don't know if the bear will understand. I don't have time to think. But I have to try.

The bear makes a noise that's half roar, half bark. I stand my ground. I look into her eyes.

"Leave this place," I say firmly. I feel a strange power moving through me, making me light-headed. When I look at my outstretched hand I see a faint glow rising under my skin.

The bear drops to all fours. She lowers her head again, woofs at her cubs.

"Go," I whisper.

She does. She turns and crashes back into the brush, her cubs falling in behind her. She's gone as suddenly as she appeared.

My knees give out. Tucker's arms come around me. For a minute he crushes me to him, one hand on the small of my back, supporting me, the other on the back of my neck. He pulls my head to his chest. His heart is pounding, his breath coming in panicked shudders.

"Oh my God," he breathes.

He has something in one of his hands. I pull away to investigate. It's a long, silver canister that looks vaguely like a fire extinguisher, only smaller and lighter.

"Bear repellent," says Tucker. His face is pale, his blue eyes wild with alarm.

"Oh. So you could have handled it."

"I was trying to read the directions on how to spray the thing," he says with a grim laugh. "I don't know if I would have figured it out in time."

"Our fault." I sink down so I sit on the rocky ground near his feet. "We stopped talking."

"Right."

I don't know what he heard, what he thought.

"I'm thirsty," I say, trying to buy myself some time to come up with an explanation.

He slips the canister back into his backpack and retrieves a bottle of water, opens it, and kneels beside me. He holds the bottle to my lips, his expression still tight with fear, his movements so jerky that water spills down my chin.

"You did warn me about the bears," I stammer after I try to drink a few swallows. "We were lucky."

"Yeah." He turns and gazes down the trail in the direction that the bear went, then back at me. There's a question in his eyes that I can't answer. "We were pretty lucky, all right."

We don't talk about it. We hike back down and drive into Jackson for breakfast. We go back to Tucker's house later in the morning for Tucker's boat and spend the afternoon on the Snake fishing. Tucker hooks a few and throws them back.

He catches a big rainbow trout, and that one we decide to eat for dinner along with fish he caught the day before. It's not until we're standing in the kitchen of the Avery farmhouse, Tucker teaching me how to gut the fish, that he brings the bear up again.

"What did you do today, with the bear?" he asks as I stand with the fish at the kitchen sink, trying to make a clean incision up the belly the way he showed me.

"This is so gross," I complain.

He turns to look at me, his expression hard the way it always gets whenever I try to get something past him. I don't know what to say. What are my options? Tell the truth, which is against the only absolute rule Mom has really given me about being an angel-blood: *Don't tell humans—they won't believe you and if even they did, they couldn't handle it.* And then there's option two: Come up with some sort of ridiculous-sounding lie.

"I sang to the bear," I try.

"You talked to it."

"I sort of hummed at it," I say slowly. "That's all."

"I'm not stupid, you know," he says.

"I know. Tuck—"

The knife slips. I feel it slide into the fleshy part of my hand below my thumb, slicing through skin and muscle. There's a sudden rush of blood. Instinctively I close my fingers around the gash.

"Okay, whose brilliant idea was it to give me a knife?"

325

"That's a bad cut. Here." Tucker curls back my fingers to press a dish towel over the wound. "Put pressure on it," he directs, letting go. He dashes out of the room. I press for a moment, like he said, but the bleeding's already stopped. I feel suddenly strange, light-headed again. I lean against the counter dizzily. My hand starts to throb and then a flare of heat like a tiny lick of flame shoots from my elbow to the tip of my pinkie finger. I gasp. I can actually feel the gash closing itself, the tissue knitting together deep inside my hand.

Mom was right. My powers are growing.

After a moment, the sensation fades. I peel back the dish towel and examine my hand. By now it's only a shallow cut, little more than a scratch. It seems to have stopped healing itself. I flex my fingers back and forth gingerly.

Tucker appears with a tube of antibiotic ointment and enough bandages to fix up a small army. He dumps it all on the counter and crosses quickly over to me. I pull the dish towel tight across my palm and tuck my hand into my chest protectively.

"I'm okay," I say quickly.

"Let me see," he orders. He holds out his hand.

"No, it's fine. It's only a scratch."

"It's a deep cut. We need to close it."

I slowly lower my hand to his. He takes it and gently turns it so my injured palm faces up. He tugs back the dish towel.

"See?" I say. "Only a minor flesh wound."

He stares at it intently. I'm holding my breath, I realize. I tell myself to relax. Just act normally, like Mom says. I can explain this. I have to explain this.

"Are you going to read my future?" I say with a weak laugh.

His mouth twists. "I thought you were going to need stitches for sure."

"Nope. False alarm."

He sets right to fixing me up. He cleans the cut with water, smears on a bit of ointment, then smoothes a bandage over it carefully. I'm relieved when the cut's covered by the bandage and he finally has to stop staring at it.

"Thanks," I tell him.

"What's going on with you, Clara?" His eyes when he looks up at me are fierce, full of so much hurt and accusation that it takes my breath away.

"What—what do you mean?" I stammer.

"I mean," he starts. "I don't know what I mean. I just . . . You're just . . ."

And then he doesn't say anything else.

Insert the biggest, most awkward silence in the history of big awkward silences. I stare at him. I'm suddenly exhausted by all the lies I've told him. He's my friend, and I lie to him every day. He deserves better. I wish I could tell him then, more than anything I've ever wanted. I wish I could stand in front of him and truly be myself and tell him everything. But it's against the rules. And these aren't rules you break lightly. I don't know what the consequences would be if I told.

"I'm just me," I say softly.

He scoffs. He picks up the dish towel and holds it up, a bit of white terry with my incredibly bright red blood soaked into the middle of it. "At least now I know you can bleed," he says. "That's something, I guess. You're not completely invincible, are you?"

"Oh right," I retort as sarcastically as I can manage. "What, did you think I was Supergirl? Vulnerable only to Kryptonite?"

"I don't know what I think." He's managed to tear his gaze away from the dish towel and is now looking at me again. "You're not . . . normal, Clara. You try to pretend you are. But you're not. You talked to a grizzly bear, and it obeyed you. Birds follow you like a Disney cartoon, or haven't you noticed? And for a while after you came back from Idaho Falls, Wendy thought you were on the run from someone or something. You're good at everything you try. You ride a horse like you were born in the saddle, you ski perfect parallel turns your first time on the hill, you apparently speak fluent French and Korean and who knows what else. Yesterday I noticed that your eyebrows kind of glitter in the sun. And there's something about the way you move, something that's beyond graceful, something that's beyond human, even. It's like you're . . . something else."

A violent shiver passes through me from head to foot. He

really has put it all together. He just doesn't know what it adds up to.

"And there couldn't possibly be any rational explanation for all of that," I say.

"Considering your brother, the best I've been able to come up with is that maybe your family's part of some kind of secret government experiment, some kind of genetically altered animal-friendly superhumans," he says. "And you're in hiding."

I snort. It would be funny if the truth wasn't so much weirder. "You sound crazy, you know that?"

Another silence for the record books. Then he sighs.

"I know. It's crazy. I feel like——" He stops himself. He suddenly looks so miserable that my heart aches for him.

I hate my life.

"It's okay, Tuck," I say gently. "We've had kind of a crazy day."

I reach to touch his shoulder but he shakes his head. He's about to say something else when the screen door opens and Mr. and Mrs. Avery enter the house, talking loudly because they know they're interrupting us. Mrs. Avery spots the pile of bandages and ointment on the counter.

"Uh-oh. Someone have an accident?"

"I cut myself," I say quickly, avoiding Tucker's eyes. "Tucker was teaching me how to clean out the fish, and I got careless. I'm okay, though."

"Good," says Mrs. Avery.

"That's a nice fish," Mr. Avery says, peering down in the sink where I dropped the big rainbow trout. "You catch that today?"

"Tucker did, yesterday. Today he caught the one over there." I gesture to the open cooler. Mr. Avery looks at it and gives a low whistle of appreciation.

"Good eating tonight."

"You sure that's what you want for your birthday dinner?" asks Mrs. Avery. "I can make anything you like."

"It's your birthday!" I gasp.

"Didn't he tell you?" laughs Mr. Avery. "Seventeen years old today. He's almost a man."

"Thanks, Pop," mutters Tucker.

"Don't mention it, son."

"I would have gotten you something," I say softly.

"You did. You gave me my life today. Guess what?" he says to his parents, louder than his usual gruff speech. "Today we ran into a mama grizzly with two cubs up at the ridge off Colter Bay, and Clara sang to it to make it go away."

Mr. and Mrs. Avery stare at me, aghast.

"You sang to it?" Mrs. Avery repeats.

"Her singing is that bad," said Tucker, and they all laugh. They think he's joking. I smile weakly.

"Yep," I agree. "My singing is that bad."

After Mrs. Avery fries up the fish for dinner, there's cake and ice cream and a few presents. Most of the gifts are for

Tucker's prize rodeo horse, Midas, which I think is a funny name for a horse. Mr. Avery brags about the way Tucker and Midas can pick a single cow out of a herd.

"Most horses that compete are trained by professionals and cost well over forty grand," he says. "But not Midas. Tucker raised and trained him from a colt."

"I'm impressed."

Tucker looks restless. He rubs the back of his neck, a gesture I know means he's wildly uncomfortable with the way the conversation's going.

"I wish I could have seen you compete," I say. "I bet that's something to behold."

"You'll have to catch him this year," says Mr. Avery.

"I know!" I exclaim. I drop my chin into my hand as I lean on the kitchen table and grin at Tucker. I know I'm making it worse, teasing him. But maybe if I just act normal everything will go back to the way it was.

"Let's go out to the barn and show Midas the new bridle," Tucker says.

With that he whisks me out of the house to the safety of the barn. The horse comes to the front of his stall the moment we go in, ears cocked forward expectantly. He's a beautiful, shiny chestnut color with large, knowing brown eyes. Tucker strokes under his chin. Then he puts on the new bridle his parents gave him.

"You should have told me it was your birthday," I say.

"I was going to. But then we were almost eaten by a grizzly."

"Oh, right. What about Wendy?" I ask.

"What about her?"

"It's her birthday, too. I'm the worst friend ever. I should have sent her something. Did you exchange gifts?"

"Not yet." He turns toward me. "But she gave me the perfect gift."

The way he's looking at me sends butterflies into my stomach. "What?"

"You."

I don't know what to say. This summer hasn't turned out at all the way I'd planned. I'm not supposed to be standing in the middle of a barn with a blue-eyed cowboy who's looking at me like he's about to kiss me. I shouldn't be wanting him to kiss me.

"What are we doing?" I ask.

"Carrots . . ."

"Don't call me that," I say shakily. "That's not me."

"What do you mean?"

"An hour ago you thought I was some kind of freak."

He tugs a hand through his hair in agitation and then looks directly into my eyes.

"I didn't ever think you were a freak. I think . . . I thought you were magic or something. I thought that you were too perfect to be real."

I so want to show him, to fly to the top of the hayloft and smile down on him, to tell him everything. I want him to know the real me.

"I know I said some stupid things today. But I like you, Clara," he says. "I really like you."

It might be the first time he's actually said my name.

He sees the hesitation in my eyes. "It's okay. You don't have to say anything. I just wanted you to know."

"No," I say. He's a distraction. I have a purpose, a duty. I'm not here for him. "Tuck, I can't. I have to—"

His expression clouds.

"Tell me this isn't about Christian Prescott," he says. "Tell me you're over that guy."

I feel a flash of anger at how condescending he sounds, like I'm some silly girl with a crush.

"You don't know everything about me," I say, trying to rein in my temper.

"Come here." His voice is so warm and rough-edged that it sends a shiver down my spine.

"No."

"I don't think you really want to be with Christian Prescott," he says.

"Like you know what I want."

"I do. I know you. He's not your type."

I stare helplessly down at my hands, afraid to look at him. "Oh, and I suppose you're my type, right?"

"I suppose I am," he says, and he's crossing the distance between us and taking my face in his hands before I can even think to stop him.

"Tuck, please," I manage in a quivery voice.

"You like me, Clara," he says. "I know you do."

If only I could laugh at him. If only I could laugh and pull away and tell him how stupid and wrong he is.

"Try to tell me you don't," he murmurs, so close his breath is on my face. I look up into his eyes and see the beckoning heat in them. I can't think. His lips are too close to mine and his hands are drawing me closer.

"Tuck," I breathe, and then he kisses me.

I've been kissed before. But nothing like this. He kisses me with surprising tenderness, for all of his gutsy talk. Still cupping my face, he gently brushes his lips against mine, slowly, like he's memorizing what I feel like. My eyes close. My head swims with his smell, grass and sunshine and musky cologne. He kisses me again, a little more firmly, and then he pulls back to look down into my face.

I so don't want it to be over. All other thoughts vanish from my brain. I open my eyes.

"Again," I whisper.

The corner of his mouth lifts, and then I kiss him. Not so gently this time. His hands drop from my face and grab at my waist and pull me to him. A small soft groan escapes him, and that noise makes me feel absolutely crazy. I lose it. I wind my hands around his neck and kiss him without holding anything back. I can feel his heart thundering like mine, his

334

breath coming faster, his arms tightening around me.

And then I can feel what he feels. He's waited such a long time for this moment. He loves how I feel in his arms. He loves the smell of my hair. He loves the way I looked at him just now, flushed and wanting more from him. He loves the color of my lips and now the taste of my mouth is making his knees feel weak and he doesn't want to seem weak in front of me. So he draws back, and his breath comes out in a rush. His arms drop away from me.

I open my eyes.

"What's wrong?" I ask.

He can't speak. His face has gone pale beneath his golden skin. And then I realize that it's too bright in there, too bright for the shady dark of the barn, and the light's coming from me, radiating off me in waves.

I'm in glory. Tucker stares at me in shock. I can *feel* his shock. He can see everything now in all this light, glowing out through my clothes so I might as well be standing naked in front of him. I inhale sharply. Part of me twists painfully at the look of terror in his eyes, and just like that, the light goes out. His presence in my mind fades away as the barn darkens.

"I'm sorry," I say. I watch the color slowly come back into his face.

"I don't know what . . . ," he tries, and then stops himself.

"I'm sorry. I didn't mean to—"

"What *are* you?"

I flinch.

"I'm Clara." My name, at least, has not changed. I take a step toward him, put my hand out to touch his face. He shies away. Then he grabs my hand, the one with the cut. I gasp as he jerks the bandage away.

The wound is completely healed. There isn't even a scar. We both peer down at my palm. Then Tucker's hand falls away.

"I knew it," he says.

I'm flooded with a strange mix of panic and relief. There's no explaining this away. I'll have to tell him. "Tuck—"

"What are you?" he demands again. He staggers back a few steps.

"It's complicated."

"No." He shakes his head suddenly. His face is still so pale, greenish like he's about to throw up. He keeps backing away from me, and then he's at the door of the barn and he turns and runs toward the house.

All I can do is watch him go. I feel disconnected from myself, shaky with the shock of what's happened. I don't have a ride home. And Tucker could be in the house getting a shotgun for all I know. So I run. I stumble toward the woods at the back of the ranch, grateful for the cover of the trees. It's starting to get dark. Once I'm a little ways in, my wings snap out without me even having to summon them. I fly carelessly, getting completely lost before I can sense the way home, instantly soaked by clouds and so cold I'm shivering hard enough to make my teeth chatter, tear-blinded and half panicked.

I cry as I wing my way home. I cry and cry. It feels like the tears will never stop.

Mom discovers me in my room sobbing into my pillow a few hours later. I'm scratched and scraped and tear-streaked, but what she says when she sees me is "What happened to your hair?"

"What?" I'm desperately trying to get it together so I can decide how much I'll tell her about the whole Tucker thing.

"It's back to its natural color. The red is completely gone."

"Oh. I brought the glory. It must have zapped the color right out."

"You attained glory?" she says, her blue eyes wide.

"Yeah."

"Oh, my darling. No wonder you're upset. It's such an overwhelming experience."

She doesn't know the half of it.

"Rest now." She presses a kiss to my temple. "You can tell me more about it in the morning."

When she's gone I send a frantic email to Angela: *Emergency*, I write, hardly able to make my fingers and brain work well enough together to get out a simple message. *Call me ASAP.*

There's no one to talk to. No one to tell. And already I miss him.

I give in to the need to hear his voice and call Tucker on my cell. He answers on the first ring. For a minute neither of us speaks.

"Leave me alone," he says, and then he hangs up.

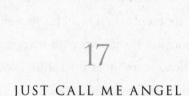

17

JUST CALL ME ANGEL

Three days pass, three agonizing days where I don't call him again or try to see him, reliving the kiss until I think I'll go bonkers and tear all my feathers out by the handful. I keep telling myself this is all for the best. Okay, so not the *best*, since I've essentially revealed myself to a human and I don't even know what the punishment for that will be, if anybody ever finds out. But maybe it's for the best that Tucker rejected me. So he knows there's something weird about me, sure. Can he prove it? No. Will anybody believe him? Probably not. It doesn't seem likely that he'd even tell anyone. If he did, I could deny it all. We could go back to the way things were before, him accusing me of stuff and me pretending like

I don't have a clue what he's talking about.

Right.

I'm not that good a liar, even when I'm lying to myself. I wish Angela would call me back and I could ask her what to do.

As if the daytime wasn't bad enough, I dream about him. Every night for three nights in a row. I can't get out of that moment when I was in his head, feeling what he felt, hearing his thoughts as he kissed me. I can feel him loving me. And it kills me, that moment when I feel his love shift into fear.

The third morning I wake up with tears streaming down my face, and when I stare up at the ceiling, wallowing in my misery, a thought occurs to me.

He *loves* me. Inside his head, his every thought and reaction was born of love, love inside and out, crazy, irrational (and sure, a bit lustful) love. He loves me, and that's also what terrified him when he saw me all lit up like a Christmas tree. He doesn't know what I am, but he loves me.

I sit up. Maybe I should have figured this out a long time ago. I shouldn't have needed to read his heart in order to see it. But when I felt all that love rising up in him, I didn't know I *was* inside his head. I didn't notice that the feelings weren't mine. And why is that?

Easy.

It's all me, the human part, the angel part. I love Tucker Avery.

Talk about revelation.

So that's why I'm waiting now outside the Crazy River

Rafting Company, sitting on the sidewalk outside of his workplace like some creepy stalker ex-girlfriend, waiting for him to come out so I can ambush him with love. Only he doesn't come out of the building. I wait for more than an hour past when he usually gets off, and nobody comes out but a blond woman who I assume is the secretary.

"Can I help you?" she asks.

"I don't think so."

She hesitates, not quite sure how to interpret my answer. "You waiting for someone?"

"Tucker."

She smiles. She likes Tucker. Everybody in their right mind likes Tucker.

"He's still on the river," she says. "His raft overturned, nothing serious, but they'll all be in a bit late. You want me to walkie him, tell him you're here?"

"No," I say quickly. "I'll wait."

Every few minutes I check my watch, and every time a truck drives by I hold my breath. A few times I decide that this is all a very bad idea and get up to leave. But I can never make myself get into my car. If anything, I just have to see him.

Finally a big red truck pulls into the parking lot towing an open trailer loaded with rafts. Tucker's sitting in the passenger seat, talking with the older guy I met before who led the rafting trips. Tucker called him Murphy, although I don't know if that's his first or last name. When they announced the rules of the raft that time he took me down the river with him, he'd called them Murphy's laws.

Tucker doesn't see me right away. He smiles the way he does when he delivers the punch line for a joke, a wry, knowing little flash of teeth and dimple. I melt seeing that smile, remembering the times when it's been aimed at me. Murphy laughs, then they both hop out of the truck and circle back to the trailer to start unloading the rafts. I stand up, my heart beating so fast I think it's going to shoot right out of my chest and hit him.

Murphy rolls open a huge garage door, then turns back toward the truck, which is when he sees me standing there. He stops in his tracks and looks at me. Tucker is busily unfastening the rafts from the trailer.

"Tuck," says Murphy slowly. "I think this girl's here for you."

Tucker goes completely still for a minute, like he's been hit with a freeze ray. The muscles in his back tighten and he straightens and turns to look at me. A succession of emotions flashes across his face: surprise, panic, anger, pain. Then he settles back on anger. His eyes go cold. A muscle ticks in his jaw.

I wilt under his glare.

"You need a minute?" Murphy asks.

"No," says Tucker in a low voice that would break my heart if it wasn't already in pieces around my feet. "Let's get this done."

I stand like I'm rooted to the spot as Tucker and Murphy

drag the rafts from the trailer and into a garage on the side of the office. Then they inspect each one, work through some kind of checklist with the life vests, and lock the garage up.

"See ya," says Murphy, then jumps into a Jeep and gets the heck out of here.

Tucker and I stand in the parking lot staring at each other. I still can't form words. All the things I planned to say flew out of my head the minute I laid eyes on him. He's so beautiful, standing there with his hands shoved in his pockets, his hair still damp from the river, his eyes so blue. I feel tears in my eyes and try to blink them away.

Tucker sighs.

"What do you want, Clara?"

The sound of my name is strange coming from him. I'm not Carrots anymore. My hair is back to blond. He can probably tell even now that I'm not quite what I appear to be.

"I'm sorry I lied to you," I say finally. "You don't know how much I wanted to tell you the truth."

"So why didn't you?"

"Because it's against the rules."

"What rules? What truth?"

"I'll tell you everything now, if you'll hear me out."

"Why?" he asks sharply. "Why would you tell me now, if it's against the rules?"

"Because I love you."

There. I said it. I can't believe I actually said it. People cast around those words so carelessly. I always cringe whenever I hear kids say it while making out in the hall at school. *I love you, babe. I love you, too.* Here they're all of sixteen years old and convinced that they've found true love. I always thought I'd have more sense than that, a little more perspective.

But here I am, saying it and meaning it.

Tucker swallows. The anger fades from his eyes but I still see shadows of fear.

"Can we go somewhere?" I ask. "Let's go somewhere off in the woods, and I'll show you."

He hesitates, of course. What if I'm an alien invader trying to lure him to a secluded place so I can suck his brains out? Or a vampire, ravenous for his blood?

"I won't hurt you." *Be not afraid.*

His eyes flash with anger like I've come right out and called him chicken.

"Okay." His jaw tightens. "But I drive."

"Of course."

Tucker drives for an hour, all the way out to Idaho, into the mountains above Palisades Reservoir. The silence between us is so thick it makes me want to cough. We're both trying to look at each other without getting caught looking at each other. At any other time I'd find us hilarious and lame.

He turns down a dirt road that's marked as private property and heads past the log cabins tucked back in the trees, up the mountainside until we come to a big wire fence. Tucker jumps out and fumbles with his keys. Then he unlocks the rusty metal padlock that holds the gate together, gets back in the truck, and drives through. When we reach a broad, empty clearing, he puts the truck in park and finally looks at me.

"Where are we?" I ask.

"My land."

"Yours?"

"My grandpa was going to build a cabin here but then he got cancer. He left the land to me. It's about eight acres. It's where I'd come if I ever had to bury a dead body or something."

I stare at him.

"So tell me," he says.

I take a deep breath and try not to focus on his eyes staring me down. I want to tell him. I've always wanted to tell him. I just don't exactly know how.

"I don't even know where to start."

"How about you start with the part about you being some kind of supernatural being made of light."

My breath catches.

"You think I'm made of light?"

"That's what I saw." I can see the fear in him again, in the way he averts his eyes and shifts slightly to put more space between us.

"I don't think I'm made of light. What you saw is called

glory. It's kind of hard to explain, but it's this way of communicating, being connected to each other."

"Communicating. You were trying to communicate with me?"

"Not intentionally," I say, blushing. "I didn't mean for it to happen. I'd never done it before, actually. Mom said that sometimes strong emotions can trigger it." I'm babbling. "I'm sorry. I didn't mean to freak you out. Glory tends to have that effect on humans."

"And you're not human," he says flatly.

"I'm mostly human."

Tucker leans back against the door of the truck and sighs in frustration. "Is this a joke, Clara? Is this some kind of a trick?"

"I'm a Nephilim," I say. "We don't usually use that term, because it means 'fallen' in Hebrew, and we don't like to think of ourselves as fallen, you know, but that's what we're called in the Bible. We prefer the term *angel-blood*."

"Angel-blood," he repeats.

"My mom is a half angel. Her father was an angel and her mother was human. And that makes me a quarter angel, since my dad's an average Joe."

The words tumble out of me fast, before I can change my mind. Tucker stares at me like I've grown an extra head.

"So you're part angel." He sounds exactly the way I did when Mom first broke the news to me, like he's making a list of mental institutions in the area.

"Yes. Let's get out of the truck."

His eyes widen slightly. "Why?"

"Because you won't believe me until I show you."

"What does that mean? You'll do that light thing again?"

"No. I won't do that again." I put my hand down lightly on his arm, trying to reassure him. My touch seems to have the opposite effect. He pulls away quickly, opens the door, and hops out of the truck to get away from me.

I get out, too. I walk to the middle of the clearing and face him.

"Now, don't be afraid," I tell him.

"Right. Because you're going to show me that you're an angel."

"Part angel."

I summon my wings and pivot slightly to show him. I don't extend them or fly, the way Mom did to prove it to me. I think seeing them, folded against my back, will be enough.

"Holy crap." He takes a step back.

"I know."

"This isn't a joke. This isn't some head game or magic trick. You really have wings."

"Yeah." I walk toward him slowly, not wanting to spook him, then turn my back to him again so that he can see them completely. He lifts a hand like he's going to touch the feathers. My heart feels like it will stop, waiting. No one else has

347

ever handled my wings, and I wonder what it will feel like, to have him touching me there. But then he pulls his hand back.

"Can you fly?" he asks in a strangled voice.

"Yes. But mostly I'm a normal girl." I know he won't believe that. I wonder if he'll ever treat me like a normal girl again. That's part of what I love about being with Tucker. He makes me feel normal, not in a plain Jane, nondescript way, but like I'm enough, just being me, without all the angel stuff. I almost start to cry thinking I'm going to lose that.

"And what else? What else can you do?"

"Not much, really. I'm only a quarter angel. I don't even know all that the half angels can do. I can speak any language. I guess that comes in handy for the angels when they're delivering messages."

"That's how you understood the Korean lady at Canyon. And how you talked to the grizzly bear?"

"Yes."

I glance down at my feet. I'm too afraid to see his face and know that it's all over. The kiss was three days ago, but it somehow feels like another person's life. Another girl, standing in the barn, kissing Tucker for the first time. Another girl he loves. Not me. Not little pathetic me humiliating myself by starting to cry.

"I'm sorry," I choke out.

He's quiet. Tears drip off my chin. He lets out a slow, shaky breath.

"Don't cry," he says. "That's not fair."

I laugh and sob at the same time.

"It's okay," he whispers. His fingers brush at the tears on my cheeks. "Don't cry."

Then he puts his arms around me, wings and all. I curl my arms around his neck and bury my face in his chest and breathe in the smell of the river on him. Somewhere in the woods a crow caws. A blackbird answers. And then we're kissing and everything goes away but Tucker.

"Okay, wait," he says after a minute, pulling back. I blink up at him in a daze. *Please, please,* I think, *don't let this be the part where you change your mind.*

"Is it okay to kiss you?" he asks.

"What?"

"I won't get struck by lightning?"

I laugh. Then I lean in and brush my lips lightly against his. His hands on my waist tighten.

"No lightning," I say.

He smiles. I run my finger along the length of his dimple. He lifts a strand of my hair (which has popped free from my ponytail) and inspects it in the sunlight.

"Not red," I say with a shrug.

"I always felt like there was something off about your hair."

"So you thought you'd torture me by calling me Carrots?"

"I still thought I'd never seen anyone as beautiful as you." He drops his head and rubs the back of his neck, embarrassed. He's blushing.

"You're a real Romeo," I say, blushing, too, trying to cover it by teasing him, but then he puts his arms around me again and runs his hands over my wings. His touch is light, careful, but it sends a wave of pleasure straight to the pit of my stomach so strong that my knees get weak and wobbly. I lean into him and press my cheek to his shoulder, working to keep the air going in and out of my lungs as he strokes slowly up and down the length of my wings.

"So you're an angel, that's all," he murmurs.

I kiss his shoulder. "Part angel."

"Say something in the angel language."

"What should I say?"

"Something simple," he says. "Something true."

"I love you," I whisper automatically, shocking myself yet again. The words in Angelic are like murmurs of wind and stars, a low, clear music. His arms tighten around me. I gaze up into his face.

"What did you say?" he asks, but his eyes tell me he heard me loud and clear.

"Oh, you know. I just kinda like you."

"Huh." He kisses the corner of my mouth and pushes a strand of hair away from my face. "I really, *really* like you, too."

So I'm in love. That crazy, forget to eat, float around in a daze, talk on the phone all night and bounce out of bed every morning hoping to see him kind of love. The days of summer fly past, and every day I find something else I love about him.

It feels like no one else knows him the way I do. I know that he doesn't really dig country music, but it's part of the whole Western scene so he tolerates it. He admits that he inwardly cringes every time he hears the twang of a steel guitar. I think it's hilarious whenever we hear it, knowing that. He loves Cheetos. He believes one of the greatest tragedies in this world is the way the land keeps getting eaten up, all the wild spaces filled with condos and dude ranches. He both loves and hates the Lazy Dog, for that reason. His recurring fantasy is to go back in time and ride the range in those days before fences, out in the heat with the little dogies, driving them across the land like a real cowboy.

He's good to people, respectful. He doesn't cuss. He's kind. Thoughtful. He likes to pick me wildflowers, which I weave into garlands for my hair so I can smell them all day long. He doesn't make a big deal about me being different. In fact, he hardly ever brings up the whole angel-blood thing, although sometimes I see him looking at me with a kind of curiosity in his eyes.

I love how he sometimes gets embarrassed by the mushy stuff between us and then his voice gets all gruff and he tickles me or kisses me to shut us both up. Boy, do we ever kiss. We make out like champions.

Tucker never takes it too far, though I sometimes want him to. He'll kiss me, kiss me, kiss me until my head swims and my body goes light and heavy at the same time, kiss me until I start tugging at our clothes, wanting as much contact as I can get. Then he groans, grabs my wrists, and moves away from me, closing his eyes and taking deep breaths for a minute.

I think he seriously believes that deflowering an angel could mean an eternity in fiery hell.

"What about church?" he asks me one night after he pulls away, gasping for breath. It's the first week of August. We're lying on a blanket in the bed of his pickup truck, a riot of bright stars over our heads. He kisses the back of my hand and then twines my fingers with his. For a second I forget the question.

"What?"

He laughs. "Church. Why doesn't your family go to church?"

Another thing I usually love about Tucker: He's unflinchingly honest, forthright to a fault. I gaze up at the stars.

"I don't know. My mom took us every Sunday when we were kids, but not since we got older."

He rolls over to look at me.

"But you know that there's a God. I mean, you're part angel. You have proof, right?"

What proof do I really have? Wings. The speech thing. Glory. All powered by God, or so I've been told. God seems like the most likely explanation.

"Well, there's the glory thing," I say. "How we connect

with God. But I don't know a lot about that. I've only felt it that one time."

"What was it like?"

"It was good. I can't really describe it. It was like I could feel everything you felt, your heart beating, your blood moving through your veins, your breath, like we were the same person, and we felt this incredible . . . joy. Didn't you feel it, too?"

"I don't think so," he admits, glancing away. "I was just so crazy happy to be kissing you. And then you were glowing. And then you were shining so bright I couldn't look at you."

"Sorry."

"I'm not," he says. "I'm glad it happened. Because then I got to know who you really are."

"Oh yeah? Who am I?"

"A really, really *spiritual*, spoiled California chick."

"Shut up."

"It's cool, though. My girlfriend is an angel."

"I'm not an angel. I don't live in heaven or play a golden harp or have heart-to-heart conversations with the Almighty."

"You don't? You don't have a big Christmas dinner with God?"

"No," I say, giggling. "We have our own traditions, but we don't actually get to hang out with God. My mom says that every angel-blood meets God eventually, though, after our purpose on earth is fulfilled. Face-to-face. I can't really imagine it, but that's what she says."

"Yeah, but that's the same for everybody, isn't it? Humans too?"

"What?"

"We all supposedly get to meet God. When we die."

I stare at him. I've never thought of it like that before. I assumed the meeting was like a kind of debriefing about our purpose. The idea has always terrified me.

"Right," I say slowly. "We all get to meet God someday."

"So maybe I should keep going to church."

"Church couldn't hurt."

I stroke his cheek, totally loving the hint of stubble under my hand. I want to say something profound, something about how grateful I am that he can accept me for who I am, wings and everything, but I know that would sound cheesy beyond words. Then I'm thinking about church. Mom and Jeffrey and me in church when I was little, sitting in the pews, singing and praying with everybody else. Falling under the colored light of the stained-glass angels.

We're bumping along a dirt road in Bluebell and I'm trying to behave myself, keep a Bible's worth of space between us so that we will actually end up fishing, unlike last time. But then he reaches over to shift, and when he's done he puts his hand on my knee and I instantly get all quivery.

"Ruffian." I grab the offending hand and trap it in mine.

His thumb strokes over the top of my knuckles, sending my heart into overdrive.

"Sometimes you say the weirdest things, I swear," he says.

"It's from having a mom who's over a hundred years old. And the language thing," I explain. "I understand every word I hear. Gives me an awesome vocabulary."

"Awesome," he teases.

"Exemplary, as a matter of fact. Hey, have you talked to your sister lately?"

"Yeah, a couple nights ago," he says.

"Did you tell her about us?"

He frowns. "Am I not supposed to?"

I smile. "You can tell her. But I think she already knows. I talked to her yesterday and she was acting all funny."

"So *you* didn't tell her."

"No, I thought that might be weird like, guess what, I'm dating your brother. I thought it'd be better coming from you."

"I told her," he admits. "I can't really keep secrets from Wendy. I've tried. Doesn't work."

"But—" I hesitate. "You didn't tell her about—y'know."

He gives me a fake clueless look and says, "What? Is there something about you I should know?"

"Just call me angel of the morning," I sing.

He laughs. "Of course I didn't tell her. I wouldn't know how to tell her something like that." Then he adds quietly,

"But it will be hard, when she gets back."

I look out the window. The truck whizzes past lodgepole pines on both sides of the road, aspens here and there that are beginning to turn colors. It's hot, even by Wyoming standards. The air smells dry and dusty.

Then everything starts to look very familiar. Like the worst case of déjà vu ever.

My hand tightens in Tucker's.

"Stop the truck," I gasp.

"What?"

"Just stop!"

Tucker hits the brakes, sending a cloud of dust around us. Before the truck has even stopped moving I scramble out. When the dust settles I'm standing in the middle of the road turning in a slow circle.

Then I walk in a daze toward the side of the road, brushing past the shadow of a big silver pickup in my mind's eye. I turn, one foot leading the other, and move off into the forest. I faintly hear Tucker calling me, but I keep walking. I don't know if I could stop even if I tried. I push on through the trees. Once I stumble, slipping to one knee on the needle-strewn ground, but even then I keep going, deeper into the forest, not even bothering to brush myself off.

And then I stop.

It's all here. The little clearing. The ridge.

The air's full of smoke. The sky a golden orange. Christian wearing his black fleece jacket, his hands tucked up into his pockets, hips slightly shifted to the side. He's standing very still, looking up at the top of the ridge.

Oh God, I think. I can see the flames. I step toward him. Everything's so dry. I lick my lips, glance down at my hands, which are shaking. It's like I'm leaving my whole life behind in this moment. I'm so sad I could cry.

"Christian," I croak out.

He turns. I don't know how to read his expression.

"It's you," he says.

"It's me . . . I'm . . ."

He crosses toward me. I keep walking to him. In another minute we both stop, arm's length away from each other, and stare. I feel like I'm on drugs or something. I want to touch him so badly it feels like pain not to. I reach out. His hand wraps around mine. His skin's so hot, feverish. I close my eyes for a second against the wave of sensation. Recognition blasts through me.

We belong together.

I open my eyes. He steps closer. His gaze brushes across my face like a touch. He looks at my lips, then my eyes, then my lips again. He lifts a hand to touch my cheek. I'm crying, I realize, tears slipping down my cheeks.

"It's really you," he whispers. Then his arms are around me and the fire rushes at us, moving swiftly over the ground like a monster stalking us, clouds of thick, white smoke curling from its nostrils, crackling and roaring its warning. I press my body into Christian's and summon my wings, grab at the air with all my strength, and push us skyward.

Only I don't fly. I sink to the ground on the forest floor, my hands clutching at empty air, because Christian isn't there. And then everything goes black.

I become vaguely aware of being carried. I know without even having to open my eyes that it's Tucker carrying me. I'd be able to identify his sun-and-man smell anywhere. My head's lolling back across his arm, my arms dangling.

I've had the vision. Again. If vision is even the right word for it now. I've done so much more than see it. I've been there.

And apparently I fainted. Again.

I try to sit up a little, regain the use of my arms and legs, but the minute I move I start coughing. As if I inhaled some smoke. Tucker immediately stops walking.

"Oh thank God," he says. "You're okay."

I don't know if I'd go that far. Okay seems like the last thing that I am. I cough and cough and my lungs finally clear and I look up into Tucker's crazy worried eyes and try to smile. And promptly cough some more.

"I'm fine," I say. Hack, hack, hack.

"Hold on. We're almost there."

He starts walking again and in a couple minutes we're back at the truck. He opens the back, grabs that big familiar blanket, and spreads it out, all with one hand as he holds me with the other. He lays me gently down into the bed of his truck. Then he climbs in beside me.

"Thanks," I rasp. "You're my hero." Understatement. The coughing, at least, has stopped.

"What happened?"

I stare up at the sky, the big, fluffy clouds slowly lumbering over us. A tiny shiver passes through me. Tucker notices.

"You can tell me."

"I know."

I look at him. His sweet blue eyes are filled with so much love and concern it makes a lump rise in my throat.

"Are you all right? Do you need a doctor?"

"No, I just passed out."

He waits. I take a deep breath.

"I had a vision," I tell him.

Then the story comes tumbling out.

"Where are we?" I ask when I'm done. We're both sitting up now, Tucker leaning back against the cab trying to process it all. I can't tell if he's mad about the Christian aspect of the whole thing or relieved that my obsession with Christian Prescott was for a good reason. He hasn't said anything for an entire ten minutes.

"What are you thinking?" I ask when I can't stand it anymore.

"I think it's amazing."

That word again.

"It's like a sacred duty you have to do."

"Right."

Of course the version I told Tucker doesn't include those pesky little details about the hand-holding and the cheek touching, the way we both, Christian and I, were totally into each other in all kinds of ways at that moment. I don't know what to think about that stuff myself.

"So where are we?" I ask again.

"We're good, I think. Don't you?"

"No, I mean, where are we? Literally?"

"Oh. We're out on Fox Creek Road."

Fox Creek Road. Such a simple, unassuming name for this place where destiny's going to go down. Now I know the where. And the who, and the what.

All I have to figure out is the when.

And the why.

18

MY PURPOSE-DRIVEN LIFE

I'm sitting in a boat with Tucker, smack in the middle of Jackson Lake, when Angela finally calls me back.

"Okay, what's up?" she asks. I hear bells ringing in the background. "Has the fire happened yet?"

"No."

"Did you finally get some action with Christian?"

"No!" I stammer, completely flustered. "He's—I'm not— He's not in town." I glance at Tucker. He raises his eyebrows and mouths, "Who's that?" I shake my head slightly.

"So what's the big emergency?" she asks impatiently.

"I sent that email weeks ago. You only now got it?"

"I haven't had an internet connection for a while," she says a bit defensively. "I've been kind of off the beaten path. So everything's okay now? Crisis averted?"

"Yes," I say, still looking at Tucker. He smiles. "Everything's fine."

"So what happened?"

"Do you want me to take us in?" Tucker asks. I shake my head again and smile to show him that everything is, like I said, completely fine.

"Can I call you back later?" I ask Angela.

"No, you can't call me back later! Who was that?"

"Tucker," I answer with forced lightness. He moves across the boat and slides into the seat next to me, grinning wickedly the whole time in a way that makes my breath catch and my heart accelerate.

"Tucker Avery," she says.

"Yes."

"And Wendy's there, too?"

"No, Wendy's still in Montana."

Tucker lifts my free hand in his and starts to kiss my knuckles one by one. I shiver and try to pull my hand away, but he doesn't let go.

"So just Tucker," Angela says.

"Right." I stifle a laugh as Tucker nips one of my fingers.

"What are you doing with Tucker Avery?"

"Fishing." We've spent the afternoon turning in slow circles on the lake, kissing, splashing each other, eating grapes and pretzels and turkey sandwiches, kissing some more, snuggling, tickling, laughing, oh yeah, some kissing, but in there somewhere was definitely fishing. I distinctly remember a fishing pole in my hands at some point during the day.

"No," says Angela in a low voice.

"What?"

"What are you doing with Tucker Avery?" she asks again, pointedly.

Sometimes she's too smart for her own good.

I sit up and pull away from Tucker. "This really isn't a good time. I'll call you back."

She refuses to be sidetracked.

"You're screwing it up, aren't you?" she says. "You're losing your focus at the time when you should be sharpening it, preparing yourself. I can't believe you're messing around with Tucker Avery now. What about Christian? What about destiny, Clara?"

"I'm not screwing up." I stand up and walk carefully to the other end of the boat. "I can still do what I'm supposed to do."

"Oh, right. Sounds like you've got it all under control."

"Leave me alone. You don't know anything."

"Does your mom know?"

When I don't answer, she gives a short, bitter little laugh.

"This is perfect," she says. "Wow."

"It's my life."

"Yes, it is. And you are totally screwing it up."

I hang up on her. Then I turn and face Tucker's questioning eyes.

"What was that all about?" he asks softly.

He doesn't know about Angela's angel-blood status, and it's not my secret to tell.

"Nothing. Just somebody who's supposed to be my friend."

He frowns. "I think we should go in. We've been out here long enough."

"Not yet," I plead.

Overhead there are storm clouds darkening. Tucker gazes up at them.

"We really should get off the lake. We're starting into storm season, when the thunderstorms pop up out of nowhere. They only last for like twenty minutes but they can be brutal. We should go."

"No." I grab him by the hand and tug him to the end of the boat, where I pull him down and sit curled against him, arranging his arms around me and retreating safely into his heat, his familiar, comforting smell. I press a kiss against the pulse that beats in his neck.

"Clara—"

I put a finger to his lips. "Not yet," I whisper. "Let's just stay here a little longer."

The next time the phone chirps at me I'm eating pork tenderloin with apples and fennel, one of Mom's more impressive recipes. It's delicious, of course, but I'm not thinking about the food. I'm not thinking about Angela either. It's been two days since the phone call on the lake and I'm doing my best to forget about it. Instead, I'm all wrapped up in some Tucker daydream. He's been out on the river for the last couple days, working so he'll have the money to buy his girlfriend a steak dinner for our monthiversary, he said. We've been together one entire month, which is crazy. Every time he calls me his girlfriend I still get a thrill. He's going to take me dancing, teach me how to two-step and line dance and everything.

"Aren't you going to get that?" Mom asks, arching an eyebrow across the dinner table. Jeffrey stares at me, too. I try to collect my jumbled thoughts. I pull the cell out of my pocket and look at it.

It's an unknown number. Curiosity gets the better of me, and I hit the TALK button.

"Hello," I say.

"Hey there, stranger," says a familiar voice.

Christian.

I almost drop the phone.

"Oh, hi. I didn't recognize your number. Wow, so how are you? How's your summer? How's New York?" I'm asking too many questions.

"It was boring. But I'm back now."

"Already?"

"Well, it's August. We've got to go back to school soon,

365

you know. I actually plan to show up this year. Graduate and stuff."

"Right," I say, and try to laugh.

"So, like I said, I'm back, and I've been thinking about you all summer and I'm asking you to have dinner with me tomorrow night. An actual date, in case that wasn't clear," he says in a voice that's deliberately light but has so many serious undertones that it feels like the air suddenly got sucked out of the room. I look up to see Mom and Jeffrey staring at me.

He waits for me to say *yes, yes I'd love to have dinner with you, when can you pick me up, I can't wait,* but I'm not saying anything. What can I say? *Sorry, I know it seemed like I was crazy about you before, but that was before. I have a boyfriend now? You snooze you lose?*

"You still there?" he asks.

"Yeah, sure. I'm sorry."

"Okay . . ."

"I can't tomorrow night," I say quickly, quietly, but I know Mom heard me. She has very good ears.

"Oh." Christian sounds surprised. "That's okay. How about Saturday?"

"I don't know. I'll have to get back to you," I say, totally chickening out.

"Sure," Christian says, trying to act like it's no big deal, but we all know, him and Mom and Jeffrey and me, that it's a very big deal. "You have my number." Then he quickly mumbles a good-bye and hangs up.

I close the phone. There's a minute of uncomfortable silence. Mom and Jeffrey have nearly the same expression: like I've completely lost my mind.

"Why did you say no?" asks Mom. The million-dollar question, the one I so do not want to answer.

"I didn't say no. I just can't do it tomorrow."

"Why not?"

"I have plans. I have a life, you know."

She looks angry. "Yes, and what could possibly be more important to your life right now than Christian?"

"I'm going out with Tucker." All this time, I've been telling her that I was going out with people from school, and she believed me. She's never had a reason not to. And she's been too stressed out and preoccupied with work to pay attention.

"So cancel," she says.

I shake my head and say, "No," to indicate that she's misunderstood me. I look at her. "I'm going out with Tucker."

"You've got to be kidding," chokes Jeffrey, and I know it's not because he doesn't like Tucker, but because it's simply so unbelievable to anybody in my family that I'd be interested in anyone but Christian. He's why we came here, after all.

"No. Tucker's my boyfriend." *I love him,* I want to say, but I know that would be over the top.

Mom sets down her fork.

367

"Sorry I didn't tell you before," I say awkwardly. "I thought—I don't know what I thought. I mean, I'll still save Christian, just like in the vision."

Only not like in the vision, I think, with the hand-holding and cheek touching and mushy stuff. But I *will* save him. That much I've decided. "I've been practicing my flying. I'm getting stronger, like you said. I think I can carry him."

"How do you know your purpose is about *saving* Christian?"

"Because in the vision I fly him out of the fire. That's called saving, right?"

"And that's all?"

I look away from her knowing eyes. *We belong together.* That thought's been like a piece of glass in my brain ever since I had the latest version of the vision. I've been going over and over it, trying to find a way that I might have misinterpreted what it meant. I don't want to be in love with Christian Prescott. Not anymore.

"I don't know," I say. "But I'll be there. I'll save him."

"This isn't some random errand you have to do, Clara," says Mom quietly. "This is your purpose on Earth. And it's time. Teton County went on high fire alert yesterday. The fire could happen any minute. You have to focus. You can't allow yourself to be distracted now. This is your life we're talking about."

"Yeah," I say, my chin lifting a notch. "It's *my* life."

I've been saying that a lot lately.

Her face is pale, her eyes stony, lusterless. One morning when we were kids, Jeffrey found a rattlesnake curled up on the patio in our backyard, lethargic with cold. Mom went to the garage and returned with a garden hoe. She ordered us to stay back. And then she lifted the hoe and chopped the head off the snake in one clean blow.

She has the same expression on her face now, stoic and resolved. It scares me.

"Mom, it's okay," I try.

"It is not okay," she says very slowly. "You're grounded."

That night's the first time I ever sneak out of the house. It's such an easy thing, really, sliding the window open, stepping out, balancing on the edge of the roof for a minute before I summon my wings and escape. But I've been a good girl all my life. I've obeyed my mother. My feet have never slipped off the path she placed before me. This simple act of rebellion makes my heart so heavy that it's tough to get airborne.

I land outside Tucker's window. He's reclined on his bed, reading a comic book, X-Men, and this makes me smile. His hair's shorter than it was yesterday. He must have gotten it cut for our monthiversary. I tap lightly on the glass. He looks up, grins because he's happy to see me, and my heart twists inside me. I'm glad I didn't turn out to be a messenger angel-blood. I hate to be the bringer of bad news.

He stashes the comic book under his pillow and crosses to

the window. He has to force it open, which takes some muscle because the air's hot and heavy and the window sticks. His eyes dart briefly to my wings, and I see him trying to contain the instinctive fear he has every time he's confronted with proof that things in this world aren't quite the way they seem. Then he leans out and reaches for my hand. I put away my wings. I try to smile.

He pulls me into his bedroom. "Hi. What's up? You look . . . upset."

He leads me over to his bed and I sit down. Then he grabs his desk chair and sits across from me, his eyes worried but steady, like he thinks he can take anything I have to dish out. He's with me; that's what his eyes say.

"Are you okay?" he asks.

"Yes. Kind of."

There's nothing left to do but tell him. "I'm not supposed to be here. I'm grounded."

He looks confused. "For how long?"

"I don't know," I say miserably. "Mom wasn't very specific. Indefinitely, I think."

"But why? What did you do?"

"Uh—" How can I explain that it's all because I turned Christian Prescott down for a date? That my mom is punishing me because I didn't tell her about being Tucker's girlfriend. Not that I hid it from her, exactly. I simply didn't tell her, because I expected her to frown on the idea. Just not this much.

My face must betray something because Tucker says, "It's me, isn't it? Your mom doesn't approve of me?"

I hate the hurt I detect in his voice. I hate looking at him and spotting the Avery brave face in his expression. This is so unfair. Tucker's the type of guy most mothers would love their daughters to date. He's respectful, polite, even down-right chivalrous. Plus he doesn't smoke, drink, or have any crazy piercings or tattoos. He's golden.

But my mother doesn't care about any of that. After she grounded me she told me that if I was a normal girl, she would have no problem with me dating Tucker Avery. But I'm not a normal girl. I have a purpose. And it doesn't involve Tucker.

"Is this about Christian?" he asks.

"Sort of." I sigh.

"What about him?"

"I'm supposed to be concentrating on Christian. My mom thinks you're distracting me from that. Hence the grounding." He deserves a better explanation, I know, but I don't want to talk about it anymore. I didn't want to feel like I'm cheating on him, when none of this is my choice, and that's the way he's looking at me now.

He's quiet for another long moment.

"What do *you* think?" he asks then.

I hesitate. I don't know any stories of angel-bloods who didn't fulfill their purpose. I hardly know any stories about angel-bloods, period. For all I know they shriveled up and died if they failed. Mom certainly never presented me with another option. She always made it sound inevitable. What I was made for.

"I don't know what to think," I admit.

It's the wrong answer. Tucker blows out a long breath.

"Sounds like we have to see other people. At least you do."

"What?"

He turns away.

"You're breaking up with me?" I stare at him, shock waves moving through me like an earthquake. He exhales, runs his fingers over his short-cropped hair, then looks back into my eyes.

"I think so."

I stand up. "Tuck, no. I'll figure it out. I'll make it work, somehow."

"Your mom doesn't know, right?"

"What do you mean?"

"She doesn't know that I know about you. That I know about the angel-bloods and all of that."

I sigh and shake my head.

"And you'd get in even more trouble if she knew."

"It doesn't matter—"

"It *does* matter." He starts to pace back and forth. "I'm not going to be the one who messes you up, Clara. I'm not going to stand in the way of you and your destiny."

"Please. Don't."

"It's going to be okay," he says, I think more to himself than to me. "Maybe when this is all over, after the fire happens and you save him and all that, everything can go back to the way it was before."

"Yeah," I agree weakly. It will only be a few weeks, a month or two at the most until fire season's over, and then the whole Christian thing will be done and I can go back to Tucker with nothing to stand between us ever again. Only I don't believe that. I can't. Something inside of me knows that if I go with Christian in the forest I'll never be able to find my way back to Tucker. That it will be over, for good.

He's not meeting my eyes anymore. "We're young," he says. "We've got lots of time to fall in love."

I stay in bed for two days, the world without color, food without taste. It seems dumb, I know. Tucker's only a boy. People get dumped; it's a fact of life. It should have made me feel better that he hadn't really *wanted* to dump me. He was trying to do the right thing. Wasn't that what Christian said when he dumped Kay? *I'm just trying to do the right thing. I can't be what she needs.* But I need Tucker. I miss him.

On the morning of the third day the doorbell rings, which almost never happens, and the first thing that passes through my mind is that it must be Tucker, that he changed his mind, that we'll make it work after all. Mom's off getting groceries. I hear Jeffrey jog downstairs to answer the door. I leap out of bed and run to the bathroom to untangle my hair and wash the tear streaks off my face. I throw on some clothes, look at myself in the mirror, and change into a different top, the flannel shirt Tucker loves most on me, the one he says brings out the deep ocean in my eyes. The one I was wearing that day at the Jumping Tree. But even as my hand touches the doorknob to my room, even as I step out into the hallway, I know it won't be Tucker at the door. Deep down I know that Tucker isn't the type to change his mind.

It's Angela. She's talking to Jeffrey about Italy, smiling. She looks tired, but happy. They both turn as I come down the stairs, one slow step at a time. Considering our last conversation, I can't decide if I'm happy to see her.

Her smile fades as she looks at me.

"Wow," she breathes like she's shocked at how bad a person can look.

"I forgot you were coming home this week," I say from the bottom step.

"Yeah, well, it's good to see you, too." A corner of her mouth quirks up. She crosses over to me and pulls me off the steps. Then she picks up a fistful of my hair and holds it up in the light that's pouring in through the window.

"Wow," she says again. She laughs. "This is so much better than orange, C. You've changed. Your skin's all glowy." She presses her hand to my forehead like I'm a sick kid. "And warm. What happened to you?"

I don't know how to answer her. I didn't see what she's

apparently seeing when I looked in the mirror upstairs. All I really saw was my broken heart.

"My purpose is coming, I guess. Mom says I'm getting stronger."

"Crazy." I don't understand the naked envy in her golden eyes. I'm not used to her envying me; it's usually the other way around. "You're beautiful," she says.

"She's right," Jeffrey says suddenly. "You do kind of look like an angel."

But it doesn't matter that I'm beautiful now. I'm terrible. Tears spill onto my cheeks.

"Oh, C . . ." Angela puts her arms around me and squeezes.

"Just don't say I told you so, okay?"

"How long has she been like this?" she asks Jeffrey.

"A couple days. Mom made her break up with Tucker."

Not quite the truth, but I don't bother to correct him.

"It's going to be fine," Angela says to me. "Let's get you cleaned up—because even with the glowy skin and every-thing, you're a little rank, C—and let's get some food in you, spend some girl time, and it'll be fine, you'll see." She pulls back and gives me her excited-angel-blood-historian face. "I have amazing stuff to tell you."

I decide I'm glad, after all, that she's here.

When Mom gets home from town she discovers Angela and me in the living room, Angela painting my toenails a shade of deep rose, me fresh out of the shower. They exchange this look where my mom says, without words, how happy she is that I'm finally out of my room, and Angela says that she's got everything under control. I do feel better, I'll admit, not because Angela's a particularly comforting person, but because I hate to look weak in front of her. She's always so strong, so sharp, so focused. Whenever we hang out it's like we're continually playing a game of truth or dare, and right now we're on dare, and she has dared me to stop moping around and be a freaking angel-blood for once. My time to be a heartbroken teenager is officially over and done. Time to move on.

"It's a beautiful day outside," Mom says. "You girls want to go out for a picnic? I'll whip you up some sandwiches."

"Can't. I'm grounded."

I'm still mad at Mom. Because of her I lost Tucker, and I still refuse to believe it had to be that way. In fact this whole mess, my purpose, my shipwrecked love life, my current state of misery, not to mention my utter cluelessness about how this is all going to work out, leads back to her. Her telling me about this divine obligation that I was supposed to fulfill. Her idea to move to Wyoming. Her insisting and her reassuring me that there are reasons for things and her stupid rules and her keeping me in the dark. All. Her. Fault. Because if it's not her fault, it's God's, and I'm not ready to be pissed at the Almighty.

Angela frowns at me, then turns to Mom and smiles. "A picnic would be awesome, Mrs. Gardner. We obviously need to get out of the house."

Angela wants to eat outside, find some picnic table in the mountains, maybe Jenny Lake, she says, but I can't handle it. It makes me think of Tucker. Just being outside makes me yearn for Tucker. I've resigned myself to the idea that I may never go outside again. So we go to the Garter. The stage is set for *Oklahoma!*, complete with rows of fake corn, a broken-down wagon, trees, bushes, and a yellow farmhouse, a blue sky in the background. Angela spreads out a blanket in the middle of the stage and we sit down on it and eat our lunch.

"I've been studying about Black Wings," she says, taking a big bite of a green apple.

"Is that safe? Considering what Mom said about the con-sciousness thing, and all that?"

She shrugs. "I don't think I'm more conscious of them than I was before. I just know more." She pulls out a new notebook, one of those plain, black-and-white composition books, the pages covered front and back with all that she'd gleaned about angels. Angela typically writes in a tight, loopy cursive, but the writing in her notebook is always hastily scrawled and smeared, like she can't get the words down fast enough. She flips through the pages. I think about my own journal, which I started with such passion and determination the first week I got my vision. I haven't touched it in months. She puts me to shame, really.

"Here," she says. "They're called the *Moestifere*, the Sorrowful Ones. I found this old book in a library in Florence that mentioned them. Sad demons, it translated."

"Demons? But they're supposed to be angels."

"Demons are angels," explains Angela. "It's more of an artistic distinction, really. Painters would always depict angels with beautiful, white, bird wings, and so the fallen angels had to have wings, too, but it wasn't enough to simply give them black feathers. They made them bat wings, and then it evolved to the whole horns and tail and pitchfork image that people think of now."

"But that guy we saw in the mall, he looked like a regular man."

"Like I said before, I think they can look however they choose to. I guess it's how they make you feel that's important, right? Suddenly bawling your eyes out, for example, would be a bad sign."

"The sorrow in my vision, my mom said it could be a Black Wing."

Angela's expression is sympathetic. "Have you been having the vision more now?"

I nod. I've been having it about once a day, every day, for the past week. It only lasts a few minutes, a flash really, nothing substantial. Nothing more than what I already know: the

Avalanche, the forest, walking, the fire, Christian, the words we say to each other, the touching, the hug, the flying away. I've been trying to ignore it.

"Mom keeps saying I need to train, but how? I can fly fine. I can carry stuff; I'm getting stronger, but it's not my muscles that need to get stronger, right? So how can I train? What am I supposed to do?"

She chews on my questions for a minute, then says, "It's your mind you have to train, like your mom said that one time, you have to separate yourself from all the crap, get down to the core, focus. We can do it together." She smiles. "I'll help you. It's time, C. I know this thing with Tucker sucks, but you can't really turn your back on this. You know that, right?"

"Yeah."

"So let's do it," she says, clapping her hands together and jumping up like we're going to start right this minute. "No time to lose. Let's train."

She's right, as usual. It's time.

19

CORDUROY JACKET

So we train. Every morning I rise with the sun, and I try not to think about Tucker. I shower, comb my hair, brush my teeth, and try not to think about Tucker. I go downstairs and make myself a smoothie—Angela has us on a raw food diet; she says it's purer, better for the mind. I go along with it. I even add the seaweed, which, oddly, makes me think about Tucker. And fishing. And kissing. I gag it down. After breakfast there's meditation on the front porch, which is pretty much a vain attempt not to think about Tucker. Then I go inside and spend some time on the internet. I look up the weather report, the direction and speed of the wind, and, most important, the level of the current fire danger. In these last days of August, it's always on yellow or red alert. Always imminent.

On yellow days I pass the afternoons flapping around the back woods with the duffel bag, exercising my wings, adding more and more weight each time, trying not to think of Tucker in my arms. Sometimes Angela comes with me and we fly side by side, weaving patterns into the air. If I work hard enough, push myself long enough, I'm able to banish Tucker from my mind for a few hours. And sometimes I have the vision and don't think of him at all for a while.

Angela's got me documenting the vision. She has a spreadsheet. On the days that she isn't hanging out, helping me, she usually calls around dinnertime, and I can hear the music from *Oklahoma!* in the background, and she grills me about the vision. She gave me a little notebook that I keep in the back pocket of my jeans, and if I have the vision I'm supposed to drop everything (and when I have the vision, I usually drop everything, anyway) and write it down. Time. Place. Duration. Every facet of the vision I can remember. Every detail.

It's because of this that I begin to notice the variations. At first I assume the vision's exactly the same every time, over and over again, but when I have to write it down I realize that there are small differences from day to day. The gist is still the same: I'm in the forest, the fire approaches, I find Christian, and we fly away. Every single time I wear the purple jacket. Every time Christian wears his black fleece. These things seem constant, unchangeable. But sometimes I climb the hill from a different angle, or I find Christian standing a few steps to the right or left from the day before, or we recite our lines: "It's you," "Yes, it's me," in a different way or a different order. And the sorrow, I notice, changes. Sometimes I feel the ache of it from the first moment. Other times, I won't feel it until I see Christian, and then it crashes over me like a breaking wave. Sometimes I cry, and sometimes my attraction to Christian, the magnetism between us, overwhelms the grief. One day we fly away in one direction, and the next day we fly away in the other.

I don't know how to explain it. Angela thinks the variations could be tiny alternate versions of the future, each based on a series of choices I will make on that day. This makes me wonder: How much of this is choice? Am I a player in this scenario or a puppet? I guess, in the end, it doesn't matter. It is what it is: my destiny.

On red alert days I fly around the mountains near Fox Creek, scouting, searching for signs of smoke. Given the direction that it comes from in my vision, Angela and I figured out that the fire will most likely start in the mountains and sweep down Death Canyon (chillingly appropriate, I think) until it ends up at Fox Creek Road. So I patrol in a twenty-mile radius of the area. I fly without worrying about whether people will see me. Even in my depressed, self-pitying state, that's pretty cool. I quickly learn to love flying in the daylight, when I can see the earth below me, so quiet and pristine. I'm truly like a bird, casting my long shadow over the ground. I want to be a bird.

I don't want to think about Tucker.

"I'm sorry you're so unhappy right now," Mom says to me one night as I numbly flip through the channels. My shoulders are sore. My head aches. I haven't eaten a satisfying meal in over a week. This morning Angela thought it'd be an awesome experiment to try to burn my finger with a match, to see if I'm flammable. Turns out, I am. And in spite of the fact that I'm doing what she wants me to do now, a good little trouper, which is, ironically, thanks to Angela, God bless her, Mom and I are still on rocky soil. I can't forgive her. I'm not exactly sure what part I can't forgive her for, but there it is.

"Do you see this thing? It's like a tiny blender. You can chop garlic and puree baby food and make a margarita, all for the low-low price of forty-nine ninety-nine," I say, not looking at her.

"It's partially my fault."

That gets my attention. I turn the TV down. "How?"

"I've neglected you this summer. I let you run wild."

"Oh, so it's your fault because if you'd been paying better attention you would have stopped me from dating Tucker in the first place. Nipped those pesky emotions in the bud."

"Yes," she says, willfully missing my sarcasm.

"Good night, Mom," I say, turning the volume back up. I flip to the news. Weather report. Hot and dry. Some high winds. Fire weather. Storms likely later in the week, where a single lightning strike could set the entire area ablaze. Fun times ahead.

"Clara," says Mom slowly, obviously not finished with her confession.

"I get it," I snap. "You feel bad. Now I should get some sleep, in case I have to fulfill my destiny tomorrow."

I shut off the television and chuck the remote down on the couch, then get up and push past her to the stairs.

"I'm sorry, baby," she says, so low I don't know if she means for me to hear her. "You have no idea how sorry I am."

I stop in the middle of the stairs and turn back.

"Then tell me," I say. "If you're sorry, tell me."

"Tell you what?"

"Everything. Everything you know. Starting with your purpose. That'd be nice, don't you think, if the two of us could sit down over a cup of tea and discuss our purpose?"

"I can't," she says. Her eyes darken, the pupils dilating like my words are causing her physical pain. Then it's like she closes a door between us, her expression emptying out. My chest gets tight, partly because it makes me so furious that she can do that, that she's so effectively shutting me out, but also because it just occurred to me that the only reason she'd work so hard to keep me in the dark is if she doesn't believe I can handle the truth.

And that must mean the truth is pretty bad.

Either that, or, in spite of all her supportive motherly talk, she really doesn't have any faith in me at all.

The next day's a red alert day. That morning I stand in the front hallway, trying to decide whether or not to wear the purple jacket. If I don't wear it, will the fire still happen? Could it be as simple as that? My entire fate resting on a simple fashion decision?

I decide not to test it. Anyway, at this point, I'm not trying to avoid the fire. I want it over with. And it gets cold up there in the clouds. I put the jacket on and head out.

I'm halfway through my patrol when the wave of sadness hits me.

It's not the usual sadness. It isn't about Tucker or Christian or my parents. It's not pity or teenage malaise. This is pure, unfiltered grief, like everyone I've ever loved has suddenly died. It rages through my head until my vision blurs. It chokes me. I can't breathe. My lightness disappears. I start to fall, grabbing at the air. I'm so heavy I drop like a stone.

Thankfully I hit a tree and don't splat right against the rocks and die. Instead I strike the top branches at an angle. My right arm and wing catch a branch. There's a snapping sound, followed by the worst pain I've ever felt, high in my shoulder. I scream as the ground rushes up at me. I put my working arm in front of my face, getting whipped and stung and scratched all the way down. Then I come to rest about twenty feet off the ground, my wings tangled in the branches, my body hanging.

I know there's a Black Wing. In my panic and pain I've still been able to make that small deduction. It's the only thing that makes sense. Which means that I have to get out of here, fast. So I bite my lip and try to free myself from the tree. My wings are really stuck, and I'm pretty sure the right one's broken. It takes me a minute to remember that I can retract them, and then I tumble out of the tree the rest of the way.

I hit the ground hard. I scream again, wildly. The pain from my shoulder is so intense from the jolt against the ground that I come close to passing out. I can't get air into my lungs. I can't think clearly. My head's so clouded with the sadness. If anything, it's getting worse, more intense by the second, until I think my heart will explode with the pain of it.

That means he's getting closer.

I struggle to sit up and find that I can't move my arm. It hangs off my shoulder at a weird angle. I've never been this hurt before. Where's my amazing healing power when I need it? I pull myself gingerly to my feet. The side of my face feels wet. I lift a hand to touch my cheek and come away with blood.

Never mind that, I think. *Walk. Now.*

Every move I make jolts my shoulder, sending a shock wave of pain all through my body. In that moment I feel like I could literally die. There's no hope, no light, no prayer on my lips. I'm so done. I'm tempted to just lie down and let him have me.

No, I tell myself. *That's the Black Wing you're feeling. Keep walking. Put one foot in front of the other. Get out of here.*

I stagger forward another few feet and lean against a tree, panting, trying to gather my strength. Then I hear a man's voice behind me, drifting toward me through the trees like it's carried on the wind. Definitely not human.

"Hello, little bird," he says.

I freeze.

"That was quite a fall. Are you all right?"

20

HURT LIKE HELL

Really, really slowly, I turn. The man's standing not ten feet away, regarding me with curious eyes.

He's insanely attractive. I can't believe I didn't notice that day at the mall. I guess all full-blooded angels are supposed to be drop-dead gorgeous, but I didn't understand that they are literally *drop-dead* gorgeous. If there is a mold for the perfect male form, this guy was cast from it.

He's so not what he seems. He's not young or old, his skin without even the smallest wrinkle or flaw, his hair coal-black and gleaming. But I know he's old as the rocks under my feet. He holds himself supernaturally still. The sadness I feel shooting through my every nerve doesn't show on his face. His lips are even slightly turned up in what's supposed to be a sympathetic smile. If I didn't know better I would think that his voice is kind and that he genuinely wants to help me. Like he isn't some big bad angel who could kill me with his pinkie finger. Like he's merely a concerned passerby.

I can't run. There's no way. I can't fly. The grief takes all my lightness away, like a shadow blocking the sun. I'm probably going to die. I want to cry out for my mother. I try to remind myself, through the Black Wing's despair, which lays on me heavy as a wet blanket, that on the other side of a thin veil there's heaven, and this man, this impostor of a man, can kill my body but he can't touch my soul.

I didn't know I truly believed that until now. The thought makes me momentarily brave. I try not to think about Tucker and Jeffrey and all the other people I'll be leaving behind if this guy kills me now. I struggle to stand up straight and look him in the eye.

"Who are you?" I demand.

He raises an eyebrow at me.

"You're a courageous little one," he says, taking a step closer. When he moves there's a kind of blurring in the air around him that settles when he stops. The more I look at him, the less human he appears, like the body standing in front of me is just a suit he put on this morning and there's some other creature underneath, pulsing with grief and fury, barely restraining itself from breaking free. He takes another step toward me.

I take a step back. He gives a tiny, soft laugh, a chuckle,

but the noise causes fear to shudder through me from head to toe.

"I am Sam," he says. He has a slight accent, but I can't place it. He speaks in a low, lilting voice, trying to soothe me.

I think this is a pretty ridiculous name for this creature with cold, dark power radiating off him in waves in some kind of anti-glory. I almost laugh. I don't know if it's the terrible pain from my shoulder or the weight of his emotional baggage, but I feel like I'm losing all sense of reality. I'm cracking already and the torture hasn't even started. I start to numb everything out, like my body can't handle it and is shutting down piece by piece. It's a huge relief.

"Who are *you*?" he asks pointedly.

"Clara."

"Clara," he repeats like he's tasting my name on his tongue and likes it. "Appropriate, I think. What level are you?"

For once my mother's practice of keeping me in the dark about everything pays off. I have no idea what he means. I guess I look about as clueless as I feel.

"Who are your parents?" he asks.

I bite my lip until I taste blood. I can feel a strange pressure in my head, like he's prodding my brain for the information he wants. It will be deadly for everybody I know if he finds out. I see a flash of Mom's face, then try desperately to think about something else. Anything else.

Go with polar bears, I say to myself. *Polar bears at the North Pole. Baby polar bears scooting along after their mothers in the* snow. *Polar bears drinking Coca-Cola.*

He's staring at me.

Polar bears pushing through the ice to get to baby seals. Long, sharp, polar bear teeth. Polar bears with pink muzzles and paws.

"I could make you tell me," says the angel. "It will be more pleasant if you volunteer."

Polar bears starving to death. Polar bears swimming and swimming, looking for dry land. Polar bears drowning, their bodies bobbing in the water. Their eyes glazed and dead. Poor, dead polar bears.

He takes another slow, deliberate step toward me. I watch helplessly. My body won't respond to my urgent order to run away.

"Who are your parents?" he asks patiently.

I'm out of polar bears. The pressure in my head intensifies. I close my eyes.

"My dad's human. My mom's Dimidius," I say quickly, hoping that will satisfy him.

My head lightens. I open my eyes.

"You're strong for having such weak blood," he says.

I shrug. I'm just relieved that he's not still trying to hijack my brain. Somewhere deep inside me, though, I know he'll try again. He'll get the names. Where we live. Everything. I wish there was some way to warn my mom.

Then I remember my phone.

"Yeah, I'm not worth much to you. Why not let me go?" As I say the words, I slide my hand into my jacket pocket. Good thing my cell is in the left pocket, because I can't seem to get my right arm to work. I feel for the number two and press it, inwardly cringing at the tiny beep it makes. It starts to ring. I pray that the Black Wing isn't close enough to hear it. I clamp my fingers around the speaker.

"I simply want to speak with you," he says gently. He talks like my mom, sounding completely normal and contemporary one moment, and the next, old-fashioned, like he's stepped straight out of the pages of a Victorian novel.

"Hello?" says my mother.

"Don't be afraid," he says. He moves closer. "I wouldn't dream of hurting you."

"Clara?" says my mother quietly. "Is that you?"

I have to get the message through to her. Not to come save me, because I know there isn't a way that she could fight an angel and win. But to save herself.

"I just want to get out of here," I say as loudly and clearly as I can without drawing the angel's suspicion. "Get out of here and never come back."

He takes another step toward me and suddenly I'm inside the radius of his dark glory. The numbness evaporates. I feel the full brunt of the sadness, an ache so deep and raw it hits me like a two-by-four in the chest.

What was it that Mom said? That angels were designed to please God and when they go against that, it causes them all this emotional and physical pain?

This guy's in some serious pain. He's up to no good.

"Your shoulder's dislocated," he says. "Hold still."

His cold, rock-hard fingers curl around my wrist before I have time to register anything else and then there's a loud pop and I scream and scream until my voice fails. A wall of gray pushes in on my vision. The angel's arms fold around me. He pulls me to his chest as I collapse.

"There now," he says, smoothing my hair.

I let the gray take me.

When I come to I slowly become aware of two things. First, the pain in my arm is almost completely gone. And second, I'm basically hugging a Black Wing. My face is pressed right against his chest. His body feels immovable and hard as a statue's. And he's touching me, feeling my skin, one hand moving against the back of my neck, stroking, the other resting at the small of my back. Under my shirt. His fingers are as cold as a corpse. My skin crawls.

The worst part is that I can feel his mind like I'm swimming in the icy pool of his consciousness. I feel his rising interest in me. He thinks I'm a lovely child, pity that I have such diluted blood. I remind him of someone. I smell pleasant to him, like lavender shampoo and blood and a hint of cloud. And goodness. He can smell the goodness on me, and he wants it. He wants me. He will take me. One more, he thinks, the rage bursting through the lust. How simple it is.

I stiffen in his arms.

"Don't be afraid," he says again.

"No." I put my hands on his brick wall of a chest and push with all my strength. I don't even budge him.

He responds by lowering me to the rocky ground.

I beat at him uselessly with my fists. I scream. My mind races. I'll pee on him. Puke, bite, scratch. Sure, I'll lose, but if he's going to mark me I am going to mark him too, if such a thing is possible.

"It's no use, little bird."

His lips brush my neck. I feel his thoughts. He is utterly alone. He's cut off. He can never go back.

I scream in his ear. He gives a regretful sigh and clamps one hand over my mouth, while the other gathers up my wrists and pulls my hands up over my head, pinning me. His fingers are like cold metal digging into my flesh.

He tastes like ash.

My brave thoughts of heaven fade in the reality of that moment.

"Stop," commands a voice.

The Black Wing takes his hand off my mouth. Then he stands up in a quick, fluid movement and lifts me in his arms like a rag doll. Someone's standing there. A woman with long red hair.

My mom.

"Hello, Meg," he says, like she's joining him for afternoon tea.

She stands under the trees about ten feet away, her feet

planted shoulder-width apart like she's bracing for impact. Her expression is so fierce she looks like a different person. I've never seen her eyes like that, blue like the hottest part of the fire, fixed on the face of the Black Wing.

"I was wondering what had become of you," he says. He looks younger, all of a sudden. Boyish, even. "I thought I saw you not long ago. At a mall, of all places."

"Hello, Samjeeza," she says.

"I suppose this one is yours." He glances down at me. I can still feel him in my head. His desire for me faded the moment he saw my mom. He thinks she's truly beautiful. It's her, he realizes, who I remind him of. Her sweet spirit. Her courage. So like her father.

"You surprise me, Meg," he says in a friendly tone. "I would never have taken you for the mothering kind. And so late in life, too."

"Take your hands off her now, Sam," she says wearily, like he's annoying the crap out of her.

His grip tightens. "Don't be disrespectful."

"She's only a quarter, not worth your time. She's little more than human."

Her eyes flicker to mine for a second. She has a plan.

"No," says Sam stiffly. "I want her. Unless you'd rather it was you?"

"Go to hell," she snaps.

His anger feels like a rising mushroom cloud to me,

although the expression on his face doesn't change.

"All right," he says.

He murmurs something in Angelic, a word that for once I don't understand, and suddenly the air around us shimmers and splits. There's a shrieking sound, a tearing. The ground under our feet jolts slightly, the way it feels when someone drops something heavy on the floor. Then the earth I know peels away into a gray world.

It's like the forest we were in but diminished to a bleak and hopeless wasteland. The shape of the land is the same as the place we left, the side of a mountain with trees, but here the trees have no leaves or needles. They're just bare, gray trunks and twisted branches against the grainy, rumbling sky. There's no color or smell or sound beyond occasional thunder. No birds. The light is fading like the sun is setting, and black storm clouds roll over what had been, on earth, a perfectly blue sky.

I've always envisioned hell as all hot fire and brimstone, lakes of sulfur, demons with horns and glowing eyes torturing the souls of the damned. But here the air's so cold I can see my breath. A slimy kind of mist passes over, chilling me to the bone. I'm shivering like crazy.

Mom is brighter than everything else, still in black and white but like the contrast on her has been turned way up. Her skin glows radiantly white. Her hair is inky black.

The Black Wing loosens his grip on my arm. We both

know I have nowhere to run now. He looks way more relaxed. In hell he's bigger, taller, and meatier, if that's possible. More powerful. His eyes gleam. He closes them for a moment, inhales deeply like he's enjoying the feel of the air, and then his wings appear behind him. They're huge—much larger than Mom's or mine—and an oily, absolute black, a dark hole opening up behind him, sucking all light into it.

He smiles, a sad smile. He's proud of himself. The transition to hell from where we were is no easy thing. He wants to impress my mother.

"You're a bigger fool than I thought," Mom says bluntly. She doesn't sound impressed. "You can't keep us here."

That's good news to me.

"You forget who I am, Margaret." He's completely unruffled by her sass, charmed by it even. He's being so patient. He prides himself on his patience. He knows she's afraid. He's waiting to see the cracks appear in her calm.

"No," answers my mother softly. "You forget who *I* am, Watcher."

I feel the fear stab through him, immediate and sharp. He's not frightened of my mom, exactly, but someone else. Two people. I can see them vaguely in his mind, standing in the distance. Two men with snowy white wings. One with bright red hair and blazing blue eyes. The other, blond and golden-skinned and fierce, even though I can't make out the particulars of his face.

397

But he's holding a flaming sword.

"Who are they?" I whisper before I can stop myself.

Sam glances down at me, frowning.

"What did you say?"

He probes my mind again, a momentary pressure, and suddenly it's as if a door slams between my thoughts and his. His hand drops away from me like I've burned him. The second he's not touching me anymore his thoughts disappear. The anger and sadness are cut in half. I feel like I can move again. I can breathe. I can run.

I don't think about it. I mash my foot down on his instep— not that that does any damage at all—and then dart forward, straight at my mother. She holds out her hand to me and I grab it. She tugs me behind her but doesn't let go of my hand.

The Black Wing makes a sound like a growl that has the hairs on the back of my arm standing on end. There's no mistaking the look on his face. He will destroy us.

He extends his wings. The clouds over us crackle with energy. Mom squeezes my hand.

Close your eyes, she orders without speaking. I don't know what shocks me more, that she can talk in my head or that she expects me to close my eyes at a moment like this. She doesn't wait for me to obey. A bright light explodes around us. Wherever its rays touch there's a hint of color and warmth.

Glory.

The Black Wing instantly retreats, shielding his eyes. His

face contorts in pain. For once his expression reflects the way he truly feels, like he's being eaten up from the inside out.

Don't look at him. Close your eyes, Mom orders again.

I shut my eyes.

Good girl, comes Mom's voice in my head again. *Now get out your wings.*

I can't. One of them's broken.

It won't matter.

I summon my wings. There's a flash of pain so intense that I gasp and almost open my eyes, but it only lasts a second. Heat sears along my wings, burning through muscle and sinew and bone, and then, like with the cut on my palm, the pain is gone. Not just my wings. The scratches on my arms and face, the bruises, the soreness in my shoulder. It's all gone. I'm completely healed. Still terrified, but healed. And warm again.

Are we still in hell? I ask Mom.

Yes. I can't get us back to earth by myself. I'm not that powerful. I need your help.

What do I do?

Think of earth. Think of green and growing things. Flowers, trees. Grass under your feet. Think of the parts you love.

I picture the aspen outside our front window at home, rustling in the breeze, quivering, a thousand little waves of green, translucent leaves moving together like a dance. I remember Dad. Cutting out old credit cards in the shape of razors for me and the two of us shaving on Sunday mornings, dragging the plastic across my face, mimicking him. Meeting his warm gray eyes in the steamy mirror. I think of our house now and the smell of cedar and pine that instantly hits you when you walk in the door. Mom's infamous coffeecake. Brown sugar melting on my tongue. And Tucker. Standing so close to him that we're breathing the same air. *Tucker.*

The ground beneath us trembles but Mom holds me fast.

Perfect. Now open your eyes, she says. *But do not let go of my hand.*

I blink in the bright light. We're on earth again, standing almost exactly where we were before, the glory enclosing us like a heavenly force field. I smile. It feels like we've been gone for hours, even though I know it's only been a few minutes. It's so good to see color. Like I just woke up from a nightmare and everything is back to the way it should be.

"You haven't won, you know," says that cold, familiar voice.

My smile fades. Sam is still there, standing back, out of range of the glory, but looking at us cool and composed.

"You can't hold that forever," he says.

"We can hold it long enough," Mom says.

That answer makes him nervous. His eyes scan the sky quickly.

"I don't have to touch you." He holds out his hand to us, palm facing up.

Get ready to fly, says Mom in my head.

Smoke drifts up from the Black Wing's hand. Then a small flame. He stares at Mom. Her grip on me tightens as he turns his hand over and fire drips off of his fingers and onto the forest floor. It catches quickly in the dry brush, moving from the bushes up the trunk of the nearest tree. Sam stands in the middle of the fire completely untouched as great plumes of smoke billow up around him. I know we won't be so lucky. Then he steps forward out of the sudden wall of smoke and looks at my mother.

"I always thought you were the most beautiful of all the Nephilim," he says.

"That's ironic, because I always thought you were the ugliest of all the angels."

It's a good line. That I'll give her.

Black Wings don't have the best sense of humor, I guess.

Neither of us expect the stream of flame shooting from his hand. The fire strikes Mom in the chest and instantly catches her hair. The glory radiating off us blinks out. The second the glory's gone, the angel is on us, his hand wrapped around Mom's throat. He lifts her into the air. Her legs kick helplessly. Her wings flail. I try to pull my hand away from hers so I can fight him but she holds on to me tight. I shriek and beat at him with my free hand, yanking at his arm, but it's no use.

"No more happy thoughts," he says. He stares into her eyes sadly. Again I'm filled with his sorrow. He's sorry to kill her.

I see her through his eyes, a memory of her with cropped brown hair, smoking a cigarette, smirking up at him. He has held that image of her in his mind for almost a hundred years. He genuinely believes that he loves her. He loves her but he's going to strangle her.

Her lips are turning blue. I scream and scream.

Be quiet, comes her voice in my head again, sternly, surprisingly strong for someone who looks like she's dying right in front of me. The scream fades in my throat. My ears ring with the echoes of it. I swallow painfully.

Mom, I love you.

I want you to think of Tucker now.

Mom, I'm so sorry.

Now! she insists. Her kicks are getting weaker, her wings drooping against her back. *Close your eyes and think of Tucker* NOW*!*

I close my eyes and try to focus my mind on Tucker, but all I can think of is my mother's hand going limp in mine and nobody is going to save us now.

Think about a good memory, she whispers in my mind. *Remember a moment when you loved him.*

And just like that, I do.

"What did the fish say when it hit a concrete wall?" he asks me. We're sitting on the bank of a stream and he's tying a fly onto my fishing rod, wearing a cowboy hat and a red lumberjack-style flannel shirt over a gray tee. So adorable.

"What?" I say, wanting to laugh and he hasn't even told me the punch line.

He grins. Unbelievable how gorgeous he is. And that he's mine. He loves me and I love him and how rare and beautiful is that?

"Dam!" he says.

I laugh out loud, remembering that. I let myself fill with the delight I felt in that moment. The way I felt that day in the barn, kissing him, holding him close to me, being one with him and every living being on earth.

I suddenly know what my mother wants. She needs me to bring the glory. I have to strip away everything else but the core of me, that part that's connected with everything around me, that part which fuels my love. That's the key, I realize, the missing part of glory. Why I lit up that day with Tucker in the barn. There's nothing else but love. Love. *Love.*

There, Mom says in my head. *There it is.*

I open my eyes and it takes a minute for my eyes to adjust to the intense light, which is coming out of me now. Blaring off me. I'm lit up like a torch, the light rippling and sparkling off me like a sparkler on the Fourth of July.

The Black Wing flinches. I'm still holding on to his arm, and where I touch him his skin disintegrates, like I'm digging through that part of his body that's false, that human suit he wears, and grasping the creature underneath. Heat blazes from my fingertips.

"No," he whispers in disbelief.

He releases my mother and she crumples facedown to the ground. I let go of her hand and grab the angel by the ear, which he doesn't expect. He pulls back, but I hold on easily. His great strength is gone. I grip his ear tighter. He howls in pain. A misty smoke pours off him like what comes off dry ice. He's evaporating.

Then his ear comes off in my hand.

I'm so shocked I almost lose the glory. I drop the utterly gross ear, which explodes into tiny particles the moment it hits the ground. I reach for the angel again, thinking I might catch him in the neck this time, but he twists away. The skin on his arm where I'm clutching him is dissolving too, like ash in the rain. No. Like dust. Like dust scattering in the wind.

"Let go," he says.

"Go to hell." I push him away from us. He stumbles back.

There's a ripple in the air, a cold blast of wind, and he's gone.

Mom coughs. I drop to my knees and slowly turn her over. She opens her eyes and looks at me, opens her mouth but no sound comes out.

"Oh, Mom," I breathe, taking in the darkening bruises on her throat. I can even make out his handprint. The glory starts to fade away.

She reaches for my hand and I take it.

Don't let it go yet, she says in my mind. *Hold on to me.*

I lean over her, bathing her in my light. As I watch, the

wounds on her head and neck fade and disappear. The hair that had burned grows back. She takes a breath like a swimmer coming up for air.

"Oh, thank God." I feel limp with relief.

She sits up. She looks steadily over my shoulder at something behind me.

"We have to get out of here," she says.

I turn. The fire the Black Wing started has grown into a real, crackling, honest-to-goodness forest fire, wild and unstoppable, eating up everything in its path, including us if we stay here more than a moment longer.

I look back at Mom. She climbs slowly to her feet, moving carefully in a way that reminds me of an old person getting out of a wheelchair.

"Are you okay?"

"I'm weak. But I can fly. Let's go."

We spiral up together, holding hands. When we get up far enough I can see how big the fire has gotten. The wind picks up. It catches the fire and suddenly it's twice as big as it was a minute ago, a wall of flame moving steadily down the mountain into Death Canyon.

I know this fire. I would recognize it anywhere.

"Come on," says Mom.

We start toward home. As we fly I try to wrap my exhausted brain around the fact that this is *the* fire from my vision, and now, after all of this, I'm going to have to fly off to save Christian. Funny how the vision never specifically included a Black Wing. Or hell. Or any number of things that might have been useful.

"Honey, stop," Mom calls to me. "I have to stop."

We come down at the edge of a small lake.

Mom sits down on a fallen log. She's panting with the exertion of flying so far, so fast. She's pale. What if the Black Wing hurt her in some way that glory can't heal? I think. What if she is dying?

I suddenly remember my phone. I pull it out of my pocket and start to fumble for 9-1-1.

"Don't," Mom says. "I'll be fine. I just need to rest. You should go to Fox Creek Road."

"But you're hurt."

"I told you, I'll be fine. Go."

"I'll take you home first."

"There's no time for that." She shoves me away from her. "We've lost so much time already. Go to Christian."

"Mom—"

"Go to Christian," she says. "Go now."

21

SMOKE GETS IN YOUR EYES

I beeline it for Fox Creek Road. I'm so frazzled by all that's happened, but I just fly and my wings seem to know the way. I drop onto the road right in the spot where my vision usually begins.

I look around. There's no silver Avalanche parked along the road, no orange sky, no fire. Everything looks completely normal. Peaceful, even. The birds are singing, leaves are rustling gently on the aspens and all seems right with the world.

I'm early.

I know the fire is on the other side of the mountain, moving steadily toward this place. It will come here. All I have to do is wait.

I move off the road, sit down against a tree, and try to

focus. Impossible. Why would Christian even be here? I wonder. What could possibly bring him all the way out to Fox Creek Road? Somehow I have a hard time picturing him in hip waders, flicking a fishing line back and forth over the stream. It doesn't seem right.

None of this is right, I think. In my vision, I'm not sitting here waiting for him to show up. He gets here first. I come down when the truck is already parked, and walk up into the forest, and he's already there. He's watching the fire as it comes.

I glance at my watch. The hands aren't moving. It's stopped at eleven forty-two. I left the house at about nine in the morning, probably had my big crash around ten thirty, so at eleven forty-two . . .

At eleven forty-two I was in hell. And I have no idea what time it is now.

I should have stayed with Mom. I had time. I could have taken her home or to the hospital. Why did she insist that I leave her? Why would she want to be alone? My heart seizes with fear at the thought that she might be hurt much worse than she let on and she knew she wouldn't be able to hide it much longer, so she made me go. I picture her lying on the bank of the lake, the water lapping at her feet, dying. Dying all alone.

Don't, I scold myself. *You still have work to do.*

All these months of having the vision, over and over

and over again, all these months of trying to make sense of it, and now it's finally here and I still don't know what to do, or why I will do it. I can't get over the feeling that I'm already doing something wrong. That I was supposed to go on that date with Christian, maybe something important would've happened to lead him here today. *Maybe I've already failed.*

That's pretty bleak to consider. I lean my head back against the tree trunk just as my phone rings. It's from a number I don't recognize.

"Hello?"

"Clara?" says a familiar, worried voice.

"Wendy?"

I try to pull it together. I wipe at my face. It feels really strange to be having a normal conversation all of a sudden. "Are you home?"

"No," she says. "I'm supposed to fly in on Friday. But I'm calling about Tucker. Is he with you?"

A dart of pain shoots through me. Tucker.

"No," I say awkwardly. "We broke up. I haven't seen him in a week."

"That's what my mom said," says Wendy. "I guess I was hoping you'd gotten back together or something, and he was with you since he has the day off."

I look around. The air is getting heavier. I can distinctly smell the smoke. The fire's coming.

"My mom called me when she saw the news. My parents are in Cheyenne at an auction and they don't know where he is."

"What news?"

"Don't you know? The fires?"

So the fire is on the news. Of course.

"What are they saying? How big is it?"

"What?" she says, confused. "Which one?"

"What?"

"There are two fires. One pretty close, moving fast down Death Canyon. And a second one, over in Idaho near Palisades."

A cold, sick dread crashes over me.

"Two fires," I repeat, stunned.

"I called the house but Tucker wasn't there. I think he might be hiking. He loves the fishing out there at the end of Death Canyon. And Palisades, too. I was hoping you were with him with your phone."

"I'm sorry."

"I just have a bad feeling." She sounds close to tears.

I have a bad feeling, too. A very, very bad feeling. "You're sure he's not home?"

"He might be out in the barn," she says. "The phone doesn't ring out there. I've left him like a million messages. Could you go check?"

I don't have a choice now. I can't leave here, not with the

fire so close, not without knowing how long it will be until it comes.

"I can't," I say helplessly. "Not right now."

There's a minute of silence.

"I'm really sorry, Wendy. I'll try to find him as soon as I can, okay?"

"Okay," she says. "Thank you."

She hangs up. I stand for a minute staring at the phone. My mind races. Just to make sure, I call Tucker's house and agonize while the phone rings and rings. When the answering machine picks up I hang up.

How long would it take me to fly to the Lazy Dog Ranch from here? Ten minutes? Fifteen? It's not far. I start to pace. My gut says that something is wrong. Tucker is lost. He's in trouble. And I'm just standing here waiting for who knows what to happen.

I'll go. I'll fly as fast as I can, then come right back.

I summon my wings and stand for a minute in the middle of Fox Creek Road, still trying to decide.

No one said there wouldn't be sacrifices. You belong here, in this moment.

I can't think. I find myself in the air, shooting toward Tucker's house as fast as my wings will take me.

It's okay, I tell myself. *You have time. You'll just go find him and come right back.*

Then I tell myself to shut up and concentrate on moving

411

through the air quickly, trying not to think about what it all means, Tucker and Christian and the choice I'm making.

It only takes a few minutes to reach the Lazy Dog Ranch. I'm screaming Tucker's name before I even hit the ground. His truck isn't in the driveway. I stare at the spot where he usually parks, the smear of oil on dirt, the crushed weeds and little wildflowers, and I feel like the bottom has dropped out of my stomach.

He's not here.

I run into the barn. Everything looks normal, chores all done, stalls cleaned out, the riding tack shining on the pegs. But Midas isn't there either, I realize. Tucker's horse isn't there or the bridle he got for his birthday or the saddle that's usually propped along the far wall. Back outside in the yard, I see that the horse trailer is gone, too.

He's out there. On a horse. Away from phones or radios or news.

The sky is turning that familiar golden orange. The fire is coming. I have to get back to Fox Creek Road. I know that this is it, the moment of truth. I was meant to come here to check for Tucker, but that's all. When I go back to Fox Creek Road, the silver truck will be there. Christian will be standing there waiting for me. I will save him.

Suddenly I'm in the vision. I'm standing at the edge of the road, looking at Christian's silver Avalanche, about to go to him. My hands clench into fists at my sides, fists so tight that my nails cut into my palms, because I know. Tucker is trapped. I can see him so clearly in my mind, leaning against Midas's neck, looking around him for a way out of the inferno that has overtaken him, looking for me. He whispers my name. Then he swallows and bends his head. He turns to the horse and gently strokes its neck. I watch his face as he accepts his own death. In just a few heartbeats, the fire will reach him. And I'm miles away, taking my first steps toward Christian. I am so very far away.

I understand it now. The sorrow in the vision is not the grief of a Black Wing. This sorrow is all mine. It strikes me with such force it feels like someone has struck me in the chest with a baseball bat. My eyes flood with hot, bitter tears.

Tucker's going to die.

And this is my test.

I jerk back to Lazy Dog, sobbing. I look up into the sky, where storm clouds are gathering in the east, a bit of hell spilling over onto Earth.

You are not a normal girl, Clara.

"This isn't fair," I whisper furiously. "You're supposed to love me."

"What did the fish say when it hit the concrete wall?"

"What?"

"Dam!"

I love him. He's mine and I am his. He saved me today.

413

Loving him saved me. I can't leave him to die.

I won't.

"Damn it, Tuck." I throw myself into the air and streak toward Idaho. My instincts tell me that he'll be at Palisades, at his land. It's a starting point, anyway.

I fly straight to Palisades, and that's when I see the other fire.

It's huge. It has burned right up to the lake line and now it's eating its way up the mountainside, not moving along the forest floor but higher, in the trees. The flames shoot up at least a hundred feet into the sky, curling and crackling and tearing at the sky. It's a literal inferno.

I don't think. I fly right at it. Tucker's land is hidden somewhere back in those trees. The fire is making its own wind, somehow, a strong steady stream of wind that I have to fight against to go in the right direction. There's so much smoke that it's hard to keep my bearings. I fly lower, trying to get below the smoke to see the road. I can't see squat. I just fly, and hope that my angel sense will somehow guide me.

"Tucker!" I call.

My wing catches a stray branch and I lose my balance and spin toward the ground. I right myself in the nick of time, jolting down hard on the forest floor but managing to stay on my feet. I'm close, I think. I've been to Tucker's land maybe five times this summer, and I recognize the shape of the mountain. Then the smoke drifts for a moment and I can clearly see the road snaking its way up. It's too hard to try to fly, too many obstacles, so I sprint onto the road and hurry up it.

"Tucker!"

Maybe he's not here, I think. My lungs fill with smoke and I start coughing. My eyes water. Maybe you're wrong. Maybe you've done all this and he's over at Bubba's getting an early dinner.

It's my first moment of real doubt, but I quickly squash it. He's close, he just can't hear me. I don't know how, but I know this is where I'll find him, and when the road turns and I come up to the clearing at the edge of his land, I'm not surprised to see his truck parked there with the trailer attached.

"Tucker!" I call again hoarsely. "Tucker, where are you?"

No answer. I glance around wildly, looking for some clue to where he's gone. At the edge of the clearing is a trail, very faint, but definitely a trail. I can make out hoofprints stamped in the dust.

I look down the road. The fire has already swallowed up the road at the bottom of the ridge. I can hear it coming, branches crackling as they burn, this loud popping and snapping. Animals flee before it, rabbits and squirrels and snakes, even, all running away. Smoke moves toward me along the ground like an unrolling carpet.

I have to find him. Now.

I can see much better now that I'm ahead of the fire, but still not great. There's so much smoke. I glide above the trail yelling his name and peering ahead through the trees.

"Tuck!" I call again and again.

"Clara!"

Finally I see him, coming toward me on Midas as fast as the horse can go on such steep terrain. I drop down onto the trail at the same time that he slides off the horse's back. We run toward each other through the smoke. He stumbles but keeps running. Then we're in each other's arms. Tucker crushes me to him, wings and all, his mouth close to my ear.

"I love you," he says breathlessly. "I thought I wasn't going to get to tell you." He turns away and coughs hard.

"We have to go," I say, pulling away.

"I know. The fire's blocking the way out. I tried to find a way over the top but Midas couldn't do it."

"We'll have to fly."

He stares at me, his blue eyes uncomprehending.

"Wait," he says. "But Midas."

"Tuck, we have to leave him."

"No, I can't."

"We have to. We have to go. Now."

"I can't leave my horse." I know how this must be for him. His most prized possession in this world. All the rodeos, the rides, the times when this animal felt like his best friend in the whole world. But there's no choice.

"We will all die here," I say, looking into his eyes. "I can't carry him. But I can carry you."

Tucker suddenly turns away from me and runs to Midas.

For a minute I think he's going to run away and try to make it out with the horse. Then he unfastens the horse's bridle and throws it onto the side of the trail.

The wind shifts, like the mountain is taking a breath. The fire is moving quickly from branch to branch, and any minute the trees around us will catch.

"Tuck, come on!" I yell.

"Go!" he shouts at Midas. "Get out of here!"

He hits the horse on the rump and it makes a noise like a scream and darts away back up the mountain. I run to Tucker and grab him tight around the middle, under the arms.

Please, I pray even though I know I have no right to ask. *Give me strength.*

For a moment I strain with all the muscle in my body, arms, legs, wings, you name it. I reach toward the sky with everything I have. We push off in a burst of sheer will, rising up through the trees, through the smoke, the ground dropping away beneath us. He holds me tight and presses his face into my neck. My heart swells with love for him. My body tingles with a new kind of energy. I lift Tucker effortlessly, with more grace than I've ever had in the air before. It's easy. It's like being carried on the wind.

Tucker gasps. For a few seconds we see Midas running along the side of the mountain, and I feel Tucker's sorrow over losing his beautiful horse. When we get higher we can see the flames pushing steadily up. There's no way to tell if Midas will make it. It doesn't look good. Below us Tucker's land, the little clearing where I first showed him my wings, has already been engulfed. Bluebell is burning, sending out thick, black plumes of smoke.

I turn us in the air and then move away from the mountain, out into the open where I can fly more smoothly and the air is clearer. Three green fire trucks are tearing up the highway toward the fire, sirens blaring.

"Look out!" yells Tucker.

A helicopter shoots past us to the fire, so close we feel the force of its blades cutting the air. It pours a sheet of water onto the flames, then circles back toward the lake.

Tucker shudders in my arms. I tighten my grip on him and head for the closest place that I know will be safe.

When I come down in my backyard, I let go of Tucker and we both stumble and fall onto the lawn. Tucker rolls onto his back on the grass, covers his eyes with his hands, and lets out a low groan. I fill up with a relief so overwhelming that I want to laugh. All I care about in this moment is that he's safe. He's alive.

"Your wings," he says.

I look over my shoulder at my reflection in the front window of our house. The girl staring back ripples with power the way heat shimmers over a sidewalk. I can suddenly see part of that other creature in her, like the one behind the Black Wing. Her eyes are shadowed with sorrow. Her wings, half folded behind her, are a dark, sweet gray. It's clear even in the hazy reflection of the glass.

"What does it mean?" asks Tucker.

"I have to go."

At that exact moment my mom pulls up in the Prius.

"What happened?" she asks. "I heard on the radio that the fire just passed Fox Creek Road. Where's—"

Then she sees Tucker kneeling in the grass. The smile fades. She looks at me with wide, stricken eyes.

"Where's Christian?" she asks.

I can't meet her eyes. The fire has been at Fox Creek Road, she said. She crosses quickly over to me and grabs me by the wing, turning me so that she can get a good look at the dark feathers.

"Clara, what have you done?"

"I had to save Tucker. He would have died."

She looks so fragile in that moment, so drained and broken and lost. Her eyes so hopeless. They close for a moment, then open.

"You need to go find him now," she says then. "I'll look after Tucker. Go!"

Then she kisses my forehead like she's saying good-bye to me forever and turns toward the house.

22

DOWN CAME THE RAIN

I'm too late, but then I knew I would be.

The fire has already been here.

I land. The place where I usually start my vision is scorched and black. There's nothing alive. The trees are blackened poles. The silver Avalanche is parked on the side of the road, smoke still rolling off it, charred and gutted by fire.

I run up the hillside to the place where he always stands in my vision. He isn't there. The wind picks up and hurls hot ash into my face. The forest looks like the hell dimension, the land the same as I knew it, but burned. Empty of everything beautiful and good. No color or sound or hope.

He's not here.

The weight of it hits me. This is my purpose, and I have

failed. All this time I've only been thinking about Tucker. I saved him because I didn't want to live on earth without him. I didn't want that kind of pain. I'm that selfish. And now Christian is gone. He's supposed to be important, my mom said. There was a plan for him, something bigger than me or Tucker or anything else. Something he was meant for. And now he's gone.

"Christian!" I scream raggedly, the noise echoing off the blackened tree trunks.

There's no answer.

For a while I look for his body. I wonder if it could have been burned into ash, if the fire was that hot. I circle back to the truck. The keys are still in the ignition. That's the only sign of him. I wander the burned forest in a daze, searching. Then the sun is setting, a fiery red ball descending behind into the mountains. It's getting dark.

The storm clouds that have been moving in from the east open up and pour like a faucet being turned on. Within minutes I'm soaked to the skin. Shivering. Alone.

I can't go home. I don't think I can stand to see the disappointment on Mom's face. I don't think I can live with myself. I walk, cold and wet, strands of hair sticking to my face and neck. I hike to the top of the ridge and watch the fire burning in the distance, the flames licking at the orange sky. It's beautiful, in a way. The glow. The dance of the smoke. And then there's the storm, the black rumbling clouds, the little flashes of lightning here and there. The rain so cool on my face, washing away the soot. That's how it always is, I guess. Beauty and death.

Behind me, something moves in the bushes. I turn.

Christian steps out of the trees.

Time is a funny thing. Sometimes it crawls endlessly on. Like French class. Or waiting for a fish to bite. And other times it speeds up, the days zooming by. I remember this one time in first grade. I was standing in the middle of the elementary school playground near the monkey bars and a bunch of third graders ran by. They seemed huge to me. Someday, a long, long time from now, I thought at that moment, I will be in third grade. That was more than ten years ago, but it feels like ten minutes. I was just there. Time flies, isn't that what they say? My summer with Tucker. The first time I had the vision until now.

And sometimes time really does stop.

Christian and I stare at each other like we're both under a spell and if one of us moves, the other one will disappear.

"Oh, Clara," he whispers. "I thought you were dead."

"You thought I . . ."

He reaches to touch a strand of my wet hair. I'm suddenly dizzy. Exhausted. Wildly confused. I sway on my feet. He catches me by the shoulders and steadies me. I press my eyes closed. He's real. He's alive.

"You're soaked," he observes. He pulls off the black fleece jacket, which is only slightly less damp, and drapes it around my shoulders.

"Why are you here?" I whisper.

"I thought I was supposed to save you from the fire."

I stare at him so intently that he flushes.

"I'm sorry," he says. "That was a weird thing to say. I meant—"

"Christian—"

"I'm just glad you're safe. We should get you inside before you catch cold or something."

"Wait," I say, tugging at his arm. "Please."

"I know this doesn't make any sense. . . ."

"It makes sense," I insist, "except for the part where you're supposed to save me."

"What?"

"I'm supposed to save *you*."

"What? Now *I'm* confused," he says.

"Unless . . ." I take a few steps back. He starts to follow, but I hold up a trembling hand.

"Don't be afraid," he murmurs. "I won't hurt you. I would *never* hurt you."

"Show yourself," I whisper.

There's a brief flash of light. When my eyes adjust I see Christian standing under the burned trees. He coughs and looks at his feet almost like he's ashamed. Sprouting from his shoulder blades are large speckled wings, ivory with black flecks, like someone has splattered him with paint. He flexes them carefully and then folds them into his back.

"How did you . . . ?"

"In your vision, did we meet down there?" I ask, gesturing down toward Fox Creek Road. "You say, 'It's you,' and I say, 'Yes, it's me,' and then we fly away?"

"How do you know that?"

I summon my wings. I know the feathers are dark now, and what that will mean to him, but he deserves to know the truth.

His eyes widen. He lets out an incredulous breath, the way he does when he laughs sometimes. "You're an angel-blood."

"I've been having the vision since November," I say, the words tumbling out. "It's why we moved here. I was supposed to find you."

He stares at me, stunned.

"But it's my fault," he says after a moment. "I didn't get here on time. I didn't expect there to be two fires. I didn't know which one."

He glances up at me. "I didn't know it was you at first. It was the hair. I didn't recognize you with the red hair. Stupid, I know. I knew there was something different about you, I always felt—in my vision you always have blond hair. And for a while that's all I saw—I'd hear someone walk up behind me, but before I'd turn around completely, the vision would end. I never saw your face until I had the vision at prom."

"It's not your fault, Christian. It's mine. I wasn't here to meet you. I didn't save you."

My voice is loud and shrill in the emptiness of the burned forest. I put my hands over my eyes and will myself not to cry.

"But I didn't need to be saved," he says gently. "Maybe we were supposed to save each other."

From what, I wonder.

I drop my hands to see him walking toward me, reaching out. We aren't in the vision now, but I still find him beautiful, even wet with rain and smudged with ash. He takes my hands in his.

"You're alive," I choke out, shaking my head. He squeezes my hands, then pulls me in for a hug.

"Yeah, that's good news to me, too."

One hand strokes slowly down my wings, sending a tremor through me. Then he pulls back and lifts his hand in front of him, looking at it. His palm is black. I stare at it.

"Your wings are covered with soot," he says with a laugh.

I grab his hand, draw my finger across it, and sure enough, come away with a mix of soot and rain. He wipes his hand against the sides of his jeans.

"What do we do now?" I ask.

"Let's just play it by ear." He looks into my eyes again, then down at my lips. Another quake shakes me. He wets his lips, then looks back into my eyes. Asking me.

This could be my second chance. If neither one of us needed saving. What else is there, but this? It seems like we've been set up on some kind of heavenly ordained date. We don't need the fire. We could reenact the vision here and now.

"It was always you," he says, so close I could feel his breath on my face.

I'm drowning. I do want him to kiss me. I want to make everything right again. To make my mother proud. To do what I am supposed to do. To love Christian, if that's what I'm meant for.

Christian starts to lean in.

"No," I whisper, unable to get my voice any louder. I pull back. My heart doesn't belong to me anymore. It belongs to Tucker. I can't pretend that away. "I can't."

He steps back immediately.

"Okay," he says. He clears his throat.

I take a deep breath, try to clear my head. The rain's finally stopped. Night has fallen. We're both soaking wet, and cold, and confused. I'm still holding his hand. I tighten my fingers around his.

"I'm in love with Tucker Avery," I tell him simply.

He looks surprised, like the idea that I might be already taken never crossed his mind. "Oh. I'm sorry."

"It's okay. Please don't be sorry. Anyway, aren't you still in love with Kay?"

His Adam's apple jerks as he swallows. "I feel stupid. Like

this is all some big joke. I don't know what to think anymore."

"Me neither."

I drop his hand. I extend my wings and grab the air, rising from the top of the ridge and up over the burned forest. Christian stares up at me for a minute, then lifts off himself. Seeing him like that, riding the air with those beautiful speckled wings, sends a chill down my spine and a wave of confusion into my already shell-shocked brain.

You're in big trouble, Clara, says my heart.

"Come on," I say as we hover for one final moment over Fox Creek Road. "Come with me."

We stand outside the front door for a long time. It's dark now. The porch light's on. A moth is hurling itself against the glass again and again in a kind of rhythm. I fold my wings and will them gone. I turn to Christian. Our wings are no longer out, but he looks like he would rather fly away now and never come back. Pretend none of this ever happened. That the fire never happened. That we don't know what we know, and everything isn't impossibly screwed up.

"It's okay." I don't know if I'm talking to myself or to him.

This is my home, the beautiful, secluded log house I fell in love with eight months ago, but suddenly I'm a stranger here, darkening this doorstep for the very first time. So much has changed in the last few hours. My mind is clogged with all I've seen, what I've survived, battles with evil angels, forest fires, and the implications of what I've done. Christian is alive, standing there looking as jumpy as I am, smoke-streaked but beautiful and so much more than I ever expected him to be. But I've failed at my purpose. I don't know what will happen now. I only know I have to face it.

There's a noise behind us, and both Christian and I spin around to gaze out into the growing blackness. A figure flies toward us through the trees. I don't know if Christian's aware of the existence of Black Wings, but instinctively we reach for each other's hand, as if this could be it, our last moments on this earth.

It turns out to be Jeffrey. He lands at the edge of the lawn, wild-eyed like something's after him. He's carrying his backpack over one shoulder, curling his arm around it to keep it out of the way of his wings. He turns to look down our driveway. For a moment his back is to me, and all I see are his wings. The feathers are nearly black, the color of lead.

"Is that your brother?" asks Christian.

Jeffrey hears him and turns like he expects a fight. When he spots us on the porch he lifts his hand to shield his eyes from the glare of the porch light, squinting to identify us.

"Clara?" he calls. It reminds me of when he was a little kid. He used to be scared of the dark.

"It's me," I answer. "Are you okay?"

He takes a few steps forward into the circle of light from the porch. His face is a flash of white in the darkness. He smells like the burned forest.

"Christian?" he asks.

"In the flesh," Christian replies.

"You did it. You saved Christian," says Jeffrey. He sounds relieved.

I can't stop staring at his dark wings. "Jeffrey, where have you been?"

He flutters up to the roof, landing gingerly in front of his bedroom window, which is wide open.

"Looking for you," he says in an anxious hush before he ducks inside. "Don't tell Mom."

I look up at the starless sky.

"We should go in, before anything else happens," I say to Christian.

"Wait." He lifts his hand like he's going to touch my face. I flinch, and then he flinches. His hand stops inches from my cheek, an almost identical pose as what I've seen a hundred times in the vision. We both know it.

"Sorry," he says. "You have a smudge." He takes a breath like he's making a deliberate decision and his fingers graze my skin. His thumb strokes a place on my cheek, rubbing at a spot. "There. I got it."

"Thanks," I say, blushing.

Just then the door swings open and Tucker stands on the other side staring at us, first at me, his eyes sweeping over me from head to foot to make sure I'm all in one piece, and then

429

at Christian and his hand, which still hovers near my face. I watch his expression change from something worried and loving to something darker, a resigned determination that I've seen before, when he broke up with me.

I jerk away from Christian.

"Tucker," I say. "I'm glad you're still here."

I throw myself into his arms. He hugs me tightly.

"I couldn't leave," he says.

"I know."

"I mean, literally. I don't have a ride."

"Where's Mom?"

"She's asleep on the couch. She seems okay, but kind of thrashed. She didn't really want to talk to me."

Christian clears his throat uncomfortably.

"I should go," he says.

I hesitate. I intended to bring him home and sit him down with Mom, tell his side of the story, try to figure out what it all means. That doesn't seem possible now.

"We'll talk later," he says.

I nod.

He turns quickly and goes down the porch steps.

"How are you going to get home?" Tucker asks.

Christian's eyes meet mine for an instant.

"I'll call my uncle," he says slowly. "I'll walk out to the road to meet him. I don't live too far."

"Okay," says Tucker, clearly confused.

"See you later," he says, and turns his back on us both and jogs down the driveway into the dark.

I pull Tucker inside before he can see Christian fly away.

"So you flew him out of the fire too, huh?" he asks after I close the door.

"It's a long story, and I don't even understand a lot of it yet. And some of it's not mine to tell."

"But it's over? I mean, the fire's over now. You're all done with your purpose?"

The word still feels like a knife sticking me.

"Yes. It's over."

And that's true. The fire is over. My vision is done. So why do I get the feeling that I'm lying to him again?

"Thanks for saving my life today," Tucker says.

"I couldn't help it," I say, trying for funny, but neither of us smiles. Neither of us says I love you either, but we both want to. Instead I offer to take him home.

"Flying?" he asks hesitantly.

"I thought we'd take the car."

"Okay."

He leans in and tries to press a quick, gentlemanly kiss to my lips. But I don't let him pull away. I grab his T-shirt and hold on, crushing my lips to his, trying to pour everything out of me into this one kiss, all that I'm feeling, all that I'm still afraid of, all my love, so strong it borders on pain. He groans and tangles his hands in my hair and kisses me enthusiastically, walking me backward until my back hits the door. I'm shaking, but I don't know if it's because of him or because of me. I only know I never want to let him go again.

From behind him Mom clears her throat. Tucker steps back from me, breathing hard. I stare up into his eyes and smile.

"Hi, Mom," I say. "How are you doing?"

"I'm fine, Clara," she says. "How are you?"

"Good." I turn to look at her. "I was just going to take Tucker home."

"Okay," she says. "But then come straight back."

Afterward, after I drop Tucker off and come back, I take a shower. I stand under the water and turn it up as hot as I can bear. The water runs through my hair and down my face, and only then do the tears come, pouring out of me until some of the heaviness in my chest lifts. Then I summon my wings and carefully wash the soot from them. The water swirls gray around my feet. I scrub at the feathers and they come clean, although they aren't as white as they were before. I wonder if they will ever be bright and beautiful again.

When the hot water runs out, I towel off and take my time combing out my hair. I can't look at myself in the mirror. I lie in bed, exhausted, but I can't sleep. Finally I give up and go downstairs. I open the refrigerator and stare inside before deciding I'm not hungry. I try to watch TV, but nothing holds my attention, and the light from the flickering screen casts shadows on the wall that spook me even though I know there's nothing there.

I think I'm becoming scared of the dark.

I go to Mom's room. I thought she'd interrogate me when I got back from Tucker's, but she was already in bed, asleep again. I just look at her lying there, wanting to be close to her but not to disturb her. A shaft of light from the open door falls across her. She seems so frail, so small curled up on her side in the middle of the bed, one arm cast over her head. I move closer to the bed and touch her shoulder, and her skin is cool. She frowns.

Go away, she says. I step back from her, hurt. Is she mad over what happened today? That I chose Tucker?

Please, she says. I can't tell if she's speaking out loud or in my head. But she's not talking to me, I realize. She's dreaming. When I touch her again, I feel what she feels: anger, fear. I remember how she looked in the Black Wing's memory, that image of her he'd carried for so long: the short brown hair, bright lipstick, and dangling cigarette, the way she'd looked at him with this knowing little smirk. She wasn't afraid then, not of him, anyway. Not of anything. She's a stranger to me, that younger version of my mother. I wonder if I'll ever know her, if now that my purpose is over she'll be free to tell me her secrets.

Mom sighs. I pull the quilt up to cover her, smooth a strand of hair back from her face. Then I slip quietly from the room. I go back to the kitchen, but I can still feel her dream if I tune in to it. This is something new, I think, this ability to feel what others feel, like when I felt Tucker as he kissed me, like what I felt when I touched the Black Wing. I reach for Mom with my consciousness, and I can find her, feel her. It's amazing and terrifying at the same time. I cast myself upstairs to Jeffrey's room and I can feel him. Asleep and dreaming, and there's fear in his dreams too, and something like shame. Worry. It makes me worry *for* him. I don't know where he was during the fire, what he was doing that weighs on him now.

I go to the sink for a glass of water, then drink it slowly. I smell smoke, the scent of the fire still lingering in the air. This makes me think of Christian. Three miles due east, he said, as the crow flies. Three miles isn't so far. I imagine myself slipping across the earth, like I'm traveling along the roots of the trees and grass, stretching a line between me and Christian's house like a piece of string between two tin cans, my own makeshift telephone.

I want to feel what he feels.

And then I do. I find him. Somehow I know it's him and not anyone else. He's not asleep. He's thinking of me, too. He's thinking about the moment when he wiped the smudge of ash from my cheek, the way my skin felt under his fingers, the way I looked at him. He's confused, churning, frustrated. He doesn't know what's expected of him anymore.

I get that. We didn't ask for any of this; we were born into it. And yet we're supposed to serve blindly, to follow rules we don't understand, to let some larger force map out our lives and tell us who we should love and what, if anything, we should dare to dream.

In the end, when Christian and I flew away together, there were no flames below us. There was no fire chasing us. We weren't saving each other. We weren't in love with each other. Instead, we were changed. We were thrown for a cosmic loop. I don't know if I've fallen from grace, or if I'm on some sort of Heavenly Plan B. Maybe it doesn't matter.

One thing I do know is that we can never go back.

ACKNOWLEDGMENTS

It takes a village to raise a book. I want to thank:

The brilliant, hardworking team at HarperCollins, including Kate Jackson and Susan Katz, for their enthusiasm and support of Clara and her world; Sasha Illingworth, who turned my plain little pages into such a gorgeous, sparkly book; Catherine Wallace, for all her behind-the-scenes hard work; and so many others who made this book possible, most especially my editor, Farrin Jacobs. I was born under a lucky star indeed to end up with such a wise and thorough editor. I like every colored-pencil Farrin, even blue.

Katherine Fausset, the best agent a writer could wish for,

for guiding me so smoothly along the path to realizing my wildest dreams.

My mother, Carol Ware, for staying up late to hear the newest chapter and for (bless her) always loving it, and my father, Rodney Hand, for wholeheartedly supporting my decision to study writing even though he was pretty sure it meant I'd go hungry.

Joan Kremer, my writing partner, a big part of why writing this book was so much fun.

My best friend extraordinaire, Lindsey Terrell, for being a beacon of love and sanity in a crazy time.

My early readers: Kristin Naca, Cali Lovett, Robin Marushia, Amy Yowell, and Melissa Stockham, the most loyal cheerleaders and funniest peanut gallery ever.

My readers from Bishop Kelly High School, Victoria Agee and Katy Dalrymple in particular. You so totally rock.

The friendly and informative rangers at Teton National Park, and the students and staff at Jackson Hole High School, with a special shout-out to Gary Elliott, the now-retired principal, who welcomed me so warmly and answered my endless questions with gracious enthusiasm. Without you, Clara's world would have been so much more generic.

Shannon Fields (and Emily!) for taking such great care of my son so that I could work without worry.

My amazing and talented students at Pepperdine, who are always eager to hear the latest book news and who keep me honest as a writer, and glad to be one, day after day.

And last, but certainly not least, I want to thank John Struloeff, my husband, co-conspirator, editor, sounding board, and support system, who helped me in more ways than I can name. And my son, Will, who's the reason I started writing about angels in the first place.

Read on for a sneak peek at
HALLOWED,
the breathtaking sequel to UNEARTHLY

PROLOGUE

In the dream, there's sorrow. I feel it over everything else, a terrible grief that chokes me, blurs my sight, weighs down my feet as I move through the tall grass. I walk among pine trees up a gentle slope. It's not the hillside from my vision, not the forest fire, not anyplace I've seen before. This is something new. Overhead the sky is a pure, cloudless blue. Sun shining. Birds singing. A warm breeze stirring the trees.

A Black Wing must be nearby, *really* nearby, if the raging grief is any indication. I glance around. That's when I see my brother walking beside me. He's wearing a suit, black jacket and everything: dark gray button-down shirt, shiny shoes, a striped silver tie. He gazes straight ahead, his jaw set in determination or anger or something else I can't identify.

"Jeffrey," I murmur.

He doesn't look at me. He says, "Let's just get this over with."

I wish I knew what he meant.

Then someone takes my hand, and it's familiar, the heat of his skin, the slender yet masculine fingers enfolding mine. Like a surgeon's hand, I once thought. Christian's. My breath catches. I shouldn't let him hold my hand, not now, not after everything, but I don't pull away. I look up the sleeve of his suit to his face, his serious green gold-flecked eyes. And for an instant the sorrow eases.

You can do this, he whispers in my mind.

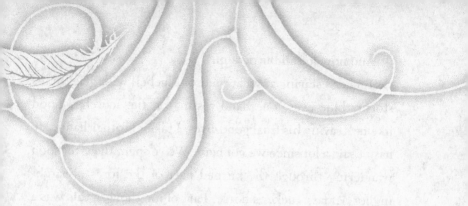

1

LOOKING FOR MIDAS

Bluebell's not blue anymore. The fire has transformed Tucker's 1978 Chevy LUV into a mix of black, gray, and rusty orange, the windows shattered by the heat, the tires missing, the interior a sickening blackened twist of metal and melted dashboard and upholstery. It's hard to believe, looking at it now, that a few weeks ago one of my favorite things in the world was riding around in this old truck with the windows rolled down, letting my fingers trail through the air, sneaking glances over at Tucker just because I liked looking at him. This is where everything happened, pressed against Bluebell's beat-up, musty seats. This is where I fell in love.

And now it's all burned up.

Tucker's staring at what's left of Bluebell with grief in his stormy blue eyes, one hand resting on the scorched hood like he's saying his final good-byes. I take his other hand. He hasn't said a lot since we got here. We've spent the afternoon wandering through the burned part of the forest, searching for Midas, Tucker's horse. Part of me thought this was a bad idea, coming out here again, looking, but when Tucker asked me to bring him here I said yes. I get it—he loved Midas, not only because he was a champion rodeo horse, but because Tucker had been there the night Midas was born, watched him take his first shaky steps, raised him and trained him and rode him on practically every horse trail in Teton County. He wants to know what happened to him. He wants closure.

I know the feeling.

At one point we came across the carcass of an elk, burned nearly to ash, which for an awful moment I thought was Midas until I saw the antlers, but that was all we found.

"I'm sorry, Tuck," I say now. I know I couldn't have saved Midas, no way I could have flown carrying Tucker and a full-grown horse out of the burning forest that day, but it still feels like my fault, somehow.

His hand tightens in mine. He turns and shows me a hint of dimple.

"Hey, don't be sorry," he says. I loop an arm around his

neck as he pulls me closer. "I'm the one who should be sorry for dragging you out here today. It's depressing. I feel like we should be celebrating or something. You saved my life, after all." He smiles, a real smile this time, full of warmth and love and everything I could ask for. I tug his face down, finding all kinds of solace in the way his lips move over mine, the thump of his heart against my palm, the sheer steadiness and strength of this boy who stole my heart. For a minute I let myself get lost in him.

I failed at my purpose.

I try to push the thought away, but it lingers. Something twists inside me. A sharp gust of wind hits us, and the rain, which was drizzling on us before, starts to come down harder. It's been raining for three solid days, ever since the fires. It's cold, that kind of chilly damp that passes right through my coat. Fog rolls between the blackened trees.

Reminds me of hell, actually.

I pull away from Tucker, shivering.

God, I need therapy, I think.

Right. As if I can picture telling my story to a shrink, stretched out on a sofa talking about how I'm part angel, how all angel-bloods have this purpose we're put on earth to fulfill, how on the day of my purpose I happened to bump into a fallen angel. Who literally took me to hell for about five minutes. Who tried to kill my mother. And how I fought him with a type of magical holy light. Then I had to fly off to save a boy from a forest fire, only I didn't save him. I saved my boyfriend instead, but it turns out that the original boy didn't need saving, anyway, because he's part angel, too.

Yeah, somehow I have the feeling that my first visit to a therapist would end with me in a straitjacket getting comfy in my new padded cell.

"You okay?" Tucker asks quietly.

I haven't told him about hell. Or the Black Wing. Because Mom says that when you know about Black Wings you're more likely to draw their attention, however that works.

I haven't told him about a lot of things.

"I'm fine. I'm just . . ." What? What am I? Hopelessly confused? Completely screwed up? Eternally doomed?

I go with: "Cold."

He hugs me, rubs his hands up and down my arms, trying to warm me. For a second I see that worried, slightly offended look he gets when he knows I'm not telling him the entire truth, but I stretch up and give him another kiss, a soft one, at the corner of his mouth.

"Let's never break up again, okay?" I tell him. "I don't think I could handle it."

His eyes soften. "It's a deal. No more breaking up. Come on," he says, taking my hand and leading me back to where my car is parked at the edge of the burned clearing. He opens my door for me, then runs around to the passenger side and gets in. He grins. "Let's get the heck out of here."

I love that he says heck.

I've totally had enough of hell.

It's a different girl this year, sitting in the silver Prius in the parking lot of Jackson Hole High School on her first day of class. First off, this girl's a blonde: long, wavy gold hair with subtle tints of red. She wears her hair in a tight ponytail at the base of her neck, and on top of that she's crammed a gray fedora, which she hopes will come off as cool and vintage and will take some of the attention away from her hair. She looks sun-kissed—not tan exactly, but with a very definite glow. But it's not the hair or the skin that I don't quite recognize as my own when I peer into the rearview mirror. It's the eyes. In those large blue-gray eyes is a brand-new knowledge of good and evil. I look older. Wiser. I hope that's true.

I get out of the car. Overhead the sky is gray. Still raining. Still cold. I can't help but scan the clouds, search around inside my own consciousness for any hint of sorrow that could mean there's a bad angel lurking, even though Mom said Samjeeza's unlikely to come after us right away. I injured him, and apparently it takes a while for Black Wings to heal, something to do with the way time works in hell. A day is a thousand years, a thousand years a day, something like that. I don't pretend to understand it. I'm just glad we don't have to hightail it out of Jackson and leave my entire life behind. At least for the time being.

No bad-angel vibes, so I look around the parking lot hoping to see Tucker, but he's not here yet. Nothing left to do but head inside. I straighten the fedora one last time and start for the door.

My senior year awaits.

"Clara!" calls a familiar voice before I even make it three steps. "Wait up."

I turn to see Christian Prescott climbing out of his brand-new pickup truck. This one is black, huge, glinting silver at the wheels, the words MAXIMUM DUTY stamped onto the back. The old truck, the silver Avalanche that used to be permanently parked on the edges of my visions, burned up in the forest too. That was not a good day to be a truck.

I wait as he jogs over to me. Just looking at him makes me feel weird, nervous, like I'm losing my balance. The last time I saw him was five nights ago when we were standing on my front porch, both of us drenched with rain and smeared with soot, trying to work up the nerve to go inside. We had so much craziness to figure out, but we never ended up doing it, which, I confess, is not Christian's fault. He did call. A lot, those first couple days. But whenever I saw his name light up on my phone, part of me always froze, the proverbial deer in the headlights, and I wouldn't pick up. By the time I finally did, we didn't seem to know what to say to each other. It all boiled down to: "So, you didn't need me to save you." "Nope. And you didn't need me to save you." And we laughed

8

awkwardly as if this whole purpose thing was some kind of a prank, and then we both fell silent, because really what is there to say? I'm sorry, I blew it, it looks like I messed up your divine purpose? My bad?

"Hi," he says now, sounding out of breath.

"Hi."

"Nice hat," he says, but his eyes go straight to my hair, like every time he sees me with the correct hair color it confirms that I'm the girl from his visions.

"Thanks," I manage. "I'm going for incognito here."

He frowns. "Incognito?"

"You know. The hair."

"Oh." His hand lifts like he's going to touch the obnoxious strand of hair that's already sprung loose from my ponytail, but instead closes into a fist, drops. "Why don't you just dye it again?"

"I've tried." I take a step back, tuck the runaway strand behind my ear. "The color won't take anymore. Don't ask me why."

"Mysterious," he says, and the corner of his mouth quirks up into a tiny smile that would have melted my heart to butter last year. He's hot. He knows he's hot. I'm taken. He knows I'm taken, and yet here he goes smiling and stuff. This irritates me. I try not to think about the dream I keep having this week, the way that Christian seems to be the only thing in the entire dream that keeps me from completely losing my mind. I try not to think about the words *we belong together*, those words that used to come to me over and over in my vision.

I don't want to belong to Christian Prescott.

The smile fades, his eyes going serious again. He looks like he wants to say something.

"So, see you around," I say, maybe a little too brightly, and start off toward the building.

"Clara——" He trots along after me. "Hey, wait. I was thinking that maybe we could sit together at lunch?"

I stop and stare at him.

"Or not," he says with that laugh/exhale thing he does. My heart kicks into high gear. I'm not interested in Christian anymore, but my heart doesn't seem to have gotten that message. Crap. Crap. Crap.

Some things change. Some things don't, I guess.

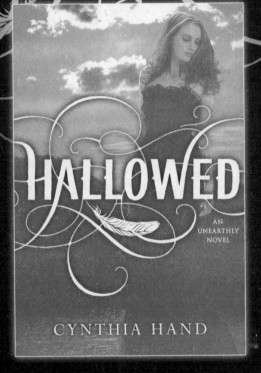